D1284309

To Kalex & Jaa

the

RUBIK MEMORANDUM

All my best

aka CLG

the

RUBIK MEMORANDUM

a novel by Jeremy Logan

Deeds Publishing | Atlanta

Copyright © 2016—Jeremy Logan

ALL RIGHTS RESERVED—No part of this book may be reproduced in any form or by any electronic or mechanical means, including information storage and retrieval systems, without permission in writing from the authors, except by a reviewer who may quote brief passages in a review.

Published by Deeds Publishing in Athens, GA
www.deedspublishing.com

Printed in The United States of America

Cover art by Mark Babcock & Matt King

Library of Congress Cataloging-in-Publications Data is available upon request.

ISBN 978-1-944193-07-2
EISBN 978-1-944193-08-9

Books are available in quantity for promotional or premium use. For information, email info@deedspublishing.com.

First Edition, 2016

10 9 8 7 6 5 4 3 2 1

THIS NOVEL IS DEDICATED TO THE EMERGENCY RESPONSE TEAM who served with me for twenty years at my old employer. It began with the late Jim Sorrow, Tom C., Dave P., Jim C., Bill B., Tommy G., Harry R., Buzz L., Hal M., Gary S, Ron M., Terry M., Jim M., and Gary G.

We started with what was called the Mother's and Father's Day incidents in the late 1970s and ended in Nashville in 1999. At first we were just a few specialists: an environmental engineer, a metallurgist, an area manager, and me. We grew as the events grew, as well as the regulations. Our job was to reduce the damage and scope of the incident, manage the teams of workers, and limit the exposure. We had so many events (thirty-four) that we became experts.

We made up the rules as we went along, and we made most of the decisions. Every now and then, an issue would arise for which we felt we needed executive authority, and on those occasions, we had to recommend an action plan among a list of alternatives. Everything was high stakes and high pressure—get it right, and get it done fast.

The hours were tough. Everyone outside the response would be mad at us, at least at the beginning. Before we left to go home, everyone was our friend—maybe with a few exceptions. I came to know the real Vic Majeski (not his real name) after a report I received while on the way to respond to a major disaster in Reston, Virginia. This employee, Majeski, saw that fuel oil was pouring out of the company's pipeline and into a nearby creek. He hopped onto a bulldozer parked nearby because the land was being contoured for a medical complex, and he built a makeshift dam to collect the oil and stop it from flowing into the creek. He risked his life to protect the lives of strangers and their environment. This book is dedicated to him and others like him, who exist for the greater good of all of us. And thanks to him for being a true cowboy and allowing me to base this book on his character. I also thank him for permission to use real photos of him in the body of the text.

In such circumstances, we were all brothers and sisters, comrades without egos. It was our job to repair the assets, the environment, and the relationships. Our focus rarely strayed. We hated it, and we loved it. It took us away from our families and our normal jobs, and it wore us out. But, on the other hand, we got the chance to take off our Clark Kent outfits and wear the ones with a company logo on our hard hats and sleeves. Those were the days of the adrenalin rush.

ACKNOWLEDGMENTS

THE BACKGROUND FOR THIS NOVEL IS PERSONAL EXPERIENCE. A significant portion of the author's career was in the energy industry. The actual backdrop, a response to an energy industry disaster, is an event the author knows too well. This story, however, is based upon a conspiracy that is unlike any cause he experienced. Included are the names of some companies that might appear to be companies that existed during the dates of the story; however, all companies, events, and characterizations mentioned herein are pure fiction. Some of the technical operations described have been intentionally fictionalized to withhold the facts from anyone with intentions to use my descriptions as a guide to do harm. The same goes for the references to the military and their response personnel, which I hold in the highest regard.

Much credit is given to the professionals in the emergency response arena, both governmental and corporate, who perform their jobs at a high level with little fanfare. Thanks is given to the countless unsung heroes in the US Coast Guard and the National Transportation Safety Board. The author has had the opportunity to work alongside them within the Unified Command structure, which has no equal outside of the United States.

I must also pay homage to the conspiracy novelists who shaped my youth. I hope I didn't borrow too much from their genius and originality. They made me make hard choices: Do I read tonight instead of being with friends/family? Do I stay up way past bedtime and finish it under the covers with a flashlight?

CAST OF CHARACTERS

Keith Adams. NOAA

David Alvarez. Attorney and Latin community dealmaker

William Bailey. U. S. President

Oliver Benatar. Latin America expert

Herbert Bennett. President of the United States

Matthew Berg. Reporter, NY Times

Skip Blackmon. Dana's father

Joanne Blackmon. Dana's mother

Charles Bobick. Lobbyist/Attorney representing PETGO

Evan Brockington. USCG, Investigator—Liquid Fuel

Ann Calloway. Lawyer, DOJ

Alvin Carpenter. Navy Admiral & member of the Joint Chiefs of Staff

Howard Chandler. CGCIS Ensign

Irene Cohen. Secretary to Gary French

Blake Cooper. Environmental engineer

Mariano Cota. Mercenary employed by the JanitorakaMr. Othello

Angela Cramer. Analyst, FBI, Violent Crimes Division

Madeline Crawford. Assistant Attorney General

Samuel Criss. NTSB

Felix Culbert. Big player in the U.S. oil business

Art Daniels. CEO—Purified

Forest Detwiler. General, U.S. Air Force at the Joints Chiefs of Staff—office in the Pentagon

Wingate Doss. Billionaire

Trammel Doss. Billionaire

Neil Driscoll. DOJ Attorney

Richard Dugan. IT programmer

Mark Durant. Firefighting School Instructor

Conrad Ellingson. Admiral, Commander Hughes's superior

Hank Fisher. Daneli Office Manager

Richard Fleming. DOJ Attorney

Simon Flores. Body guard to Dan Witherspoon

Aaron Foster. FERC

Gary French. GAO General Counsel

Frank Gilbert. Mid-Atlantic Bureau Chief—FBI

Adam Goodman. U. S. Attorney General

Alan Grasier. Friend of Matusak, Enron

Daniel Greenwood. Supervisor, FBI, Violent Crimes Division

Calvin Harper. Vice President of the United States

Roy Hayworth. General

Mike Hillendorf. Investigator and evidence expert

Dieter Hoff. Mercenary employed by the Janitor

Kent Houck. CIA Counter-terror Chief

Mitchell Hughes. Commander, U.S. Navy

Raymond Inge. Deputy Director of the FBI

Mack Joiner. Failure analysis expert

Eugene Kravitz. The name given to Crystal City Marriott by the Janitor

Sarah Jones. EPA—Mid Atlantic Division

Scott Lemay. NCIS Lieutenant

Maryanne Madison. Greater Washington Visitor's Bureau

Victor Majeski. Daneli Operations Chief Consultant

Brian Matusak. Auditor for the GAO

Dana Matusak. Brian's wife

Faith Miller. Public relations and media consultant

Louis Milton. Colonel, USAF—Pentagon

Emile Montag. Alias for Kravitz

Captain Jay. Nash Portsmouth Fire Department

Sam Nugent. Attorney working for BB&S law firm(Bennett, Bancroft and Sperling)

Patricia O'Galvin. Vic's squeeze Office Manager at GAO

Shelby O'Hare. Energy trader

Friedrich Olms. Expert on foreign oil shipping

Mel Owens. Chief Warrant Officer, U.S. Navy

Eric Parma. Harbitron IT man on the Navy Account

James Paulding. Chief petty officer, U.S. Navy

Ignacio Ramirez. Uncle to Horatio Ramirez

Fritz Reynolds. Fairfax County Cop

Clyde Richardson. Fire and air hazard expert

Mark Rogoff. IT systems consultant

Michael Ross. Virginia Dept. of Transportation

Oliver Rudd. DOJ Investigator

Lucious Sandifer. Seaman 1st Class, U.S. Navy

Norman Shearer. Deputy Attorney General

Eli Taylor. Consultant to the Energy Industry

Danielle Taylor. Eli's wife and trainer to the pro tennis circuit

Thomas Thatcher. FBI agent

Derek Trimble. Homeland Security Advisor

Ramon Veras. Head of Security—PETGO Oil

Robby Vickers. Safety Compliance Manager—NAPCO Houston Terminal

Ensign Volk. USN—under Mitchell Hughes

Dan Witherspoon. Purified security director

Stuart Yarborough. NSA Domestic Anti-terror Director

1. THE CALL

AT TEN O'CLOCK IN THE EVENING (2200 HOURS MILITARY TIME), the Navy's Craney Island Fuel Supply Depot in Chesapeake, Virginia, was manned by two individuals, a part-time delivery operator and a manual laborer classified as a "utility." The remainder of the tank farm operation was remotely controlled and monitored by computer. The Craney Island facility was one of the largest military owned and operated fuel depots in the Defense Department portfolio. The entire island was only some sixty acres, and the facility occupied all of it.

The petroleum products stored at Craney Island fueled the majority of the Navy's East Coast fleet and aircraft. It was a large facility by anyone's standard. The utility person, Seaman Lucious Sandifer, was pole gauging the jet fuel tanks lining the south boundary of the facility. Pole gauging is how one measures the amount of fuel in each tank. He climbed the fifty or so steps that coiled up the side of the tank, stood on the landing porch, and pulled up the pole that reached to the bottom. He read where the pole became wet with fuel and wrote down the number that was on the pole next to the wet line. He was new to this assignment. He had completed training just five weeks ago.

Seaman Sandifer had served in Iraq for two separate stints before being assigned to CIFSD. His wife and parents were grateful that he was able to land a noncombat position that would serve as a career for him in the future, in or out of the military. Sandifer's mother and father-in-law chose to relocate from North Carolina to Portsmouth, Virginia, so they could be close to their only child's family.

Sandifer was attending the evening program at Old Dominion College to pursue a technical degree. He had just arrived from classes to begin his night shift, which would take him to six in the morning. This allowed him time to have breakfast with his wife and children. After breakfast, he would study until it was sack time, usually about nine o'clock. He'd awaken in time for dinner with the family, and then he'd be off to evening classes. He was living the dream he and his wife envisioned when they wed seven years ago in La Grange, North Carolina, located in the middle of nowhere. For the first time in his life, he felt he was going somewhere. He could envision a career path that would build a solid future for him and his family.

As Seaman Sandifer climbed the stairway of tank twenty-eight, he couldn't help but think how every night seemed identical to the night before. The evening air was cool, misty, and breezy. The lights from the vessels and the tank farm sported a halo of fog. The salty smell of the Atlantic was mixed with the almost-sweet odor of diesel fuel, but after a month of working among the tanks, Seaman Sandifer noticed the odor only when someone mentioned it to him.

Not more than a half hour into his shift, his routine was shattered. An overflow alarm coming from the other end of the facility began blaring. Barely visible because of the mist, the red warning light atop one of the tanks was flashing. Seaman Sandifer attempted communication with the facility operator, Chief Petty Officer James Paulding, via two-way radio, but there was no response.

Fearful that something bad was happening, Seaman Sandifer took off his breathing apparatus, dismounted his perch on the rim of tank sixteen, and ran down the stairs that coiled around it. His Schwinn bicycle—the staff used them to get around more efficiently—was waiting at the bottom of the stairway. Seaman Sandifer hopped on it and headed for the control building and offices as fast as he could pedal.

As he approached the control building, the odor of No. 2 fuel oil grew stronger. Once he was inside the two-room building, it became obvious that operator James Paulding was not there. The control panel was making beeping noises and flashing red lights. That meant danger to Seaman Sandifer. He grabbed two breathing masks and put on a pair of high-topped rubber boots from the safety gear shelves and headed in the direction of the alarm. He placed one breathing mask on himself and the other in the saddle basket on his bicycle.

Each tank at the facility was numbered, and the fuel tank closest to the control building was tank one. As he pedaled past tank two, he could definitely sense the fumes growing stronger. As he approached tank five, he could see that the dike surrounding tank seven was overflowing. As he looked upward, the facility lights allowed him to observe the fuel oil cascading down the outside wall of the tank and into the dike that surrounded each tank like a moat around a castle. Seaman Sandifer determined his mission was to find his CPO, and if he was incapacitated, to revive him or carry him to the control building. To this end, he rode his bicycle as close to tank seven as safety permitted and called out the CPO's name. However, fuel oil rapidly evaporates.

The gas that is formed is heavier than air, so it seeks to the lowest level it can find. In this case, that level was the ground surrounding the tanks near where Seaman Sandifer was searching.

Even with his mask on, Seaman Sandifer could tell he had only minutes before he needed to find air free of fuel-oil fumes. Panic began to consume him. As he scanned the grounds, his eyes caught what appeared to be a shooting star or a Roman candle flare moving across the sky. That observation would be one of the last he would make. The sky around Craney Island Fuel Depot lit up like the surface of a small star.

Tank seven had a floating roof. When the fuel in it, on it, and at its base caught fire, the fifty-thousand-barrel tank blazed so hot that there was a danger that it would explode and threaten the remaining twenty or so tanks. If that happened, there might be no Craney Island to visit in the future.

The evaporated gas exploded, sending Seaman Sandifer and his bicycle through the air in the direction he had come from. He was badly burned and disoriented, but he instinctively recalled his training and rolled over and over on the ground to smother the flames on his clothing. He had only seconds to find a route that would take him away from the epicenter. Unfortunately, his injuries and state of disorientation were too much to overcome. He perished there, never knowing what had gone wrong.

At 2206 hours, the Navy's James River Fuel Movements Control Center alarms were also sounding. The controller on the ten-to-six shift was hastily verifying that the signals were not a malfunction. Attempts to reach the operator on duty, CPO James Paulding, via the dedicated telephone landlines were unsuccessful. What disturbed Chief Warrant Officer Mel Owens was the fast busy signal indicating trouble on the telephone line. Subsequent attempts to reach him and Utility Sandifer by telephone and radio were also unsuccessful.

Before CWO Owens could place a call to the emergency response team to investigate a potential incident at Craney Island Fuel Depot, the control center phones started to ring, and reports of explosions and a huge fire were being reported at Craney Island. CWO Owens immediately called his commander.

Commander Mitchell Hughes answered his telephone at his Norfolk home at 2209 hours. Commander Hughes was the chief operating manager for the Navy's Virginia fuel facilities. The call from CWO Mel Owens was to inform him of the emergency at Craney Island. Without delay, Commander Hughes chose to deploy the emergency response team. He told Owens that he would be heading toward Craney Island immediately and ordered him to activate the automated notification list. As he hung up with Owens, Hughes paused and took a deep breath. His wife, Donna, was lying next to him in bed reading a book. She didn't even ask.

The commander took one look at her, and after she looked back, he said, "It's Craney Island. It could be bad. I'll try to call you when things calm down."

Mitchell Hughes dreaded incident responses, even the drills. With the way the Navy moved personnel around the world, keeping an experienced emergency response staff that was well versed with the facilities and their territory was difficult. His blood pressure was rising, but he put on his game face as he found a freshly laundered uniform.

Commander Hughes's Jeep Cherokee was always loaded with emergency response gear. That was the burden of his command. His promotions were often based upon his readiness to respond quickly and effectively to breakdowns in the military's fuel-supply chain. He was available twenty-four-seven/three-sixty-five. By 2223 hours, he was on the road. On the passenger seat was his crisis response manual. As he traveled away from his home, he did what he always did in a crisis. His mind raced through the list of duties and items he should be considering. Under the notification tree on the first page of his manual, he noticed the scribbled name of Eli Taylor of Daneli Crisis Management Group. He recalled the visit he had had with Eli that past summer and how impressed he had been with him and his emergency response experience.

Taylor and his group were oil industry professionals with a real talent for crisis management and public relations—a rare combination in the oil industry's side of the emergency response business. An incident of this scale required such talent. Commander Hughes did not hesitate to dial Taylor's emergency number.

2. CALLING ALL EXPERTS

IT WAS 2226 HOURS WHEN ELI TAYLOR'S CELL PHONE RANG AT HIS home in Atlanta, Georgia. As usual, he was still awake. On the line was Commander Mitchell Hughes of the Navy.

"Hello, Commander, this is Eli Taylor."

"Mr. Taylor, I'm sorry to call at this time of night, but we have an incident. I'm in my vehicle now on the way to our Craney Island, Virginia, fuel depot. I should arrive in about fifteen minutes. Can you mobilize your major incident response unit this evening?"

"I can place our team on the ground at the Norfolk Airport by—uh—0200 hours tomorrow morning. That's about three and a half hours from now."

"Perfect! Please call my cell phone as soon as you deplane. From what I gather, we have an event of historical proportions."

"That's a roger. I'll arrive with my best. Take care."

The first minutes and hours of an emergency are critical. There is no time for cordialities on the telephone. It's all business.

Eli had been on his own in the crisis management business for less than a year. To the shock of the oil industry, and at the age

7

of thirty-eight, while holding the title of executive vice president and general counsel, he left one of the largest and most progressive independent oil companies in the world to start up his own firm.

Now that he was married and had a child, he wanted a job that wasn't so demanding of his time. In theory, it seemed logical to him and his wife, Danielle, that once he ran his own firm, he could control the demands on his time. In practice, however, it wasn't working out that way. Danielle, a tennis coach to world-class competitors, had to travel some. Her parents lived in the same town, and that helped. They were always happy to babysit when Eli and Danielle's schedules didn't mesh. Even with a live-in nanny, Danielle needed days off. They were making it work.

To activate his firm's response team, Eli called his vice president and chief crisis coordinator, Hank Fisher. Hank was an early-to-bed, early-to-rise guy, and Eli's call woke him up.

"Hank, we have a full-blown emergency. You're familiar with the Navy's Craney Island Fuel Depot, aren't you?"

"Sure am. I helped them redesign their pump motor configurations back in the 1980s. I visited the site several times."

"The notification from its commander suggests it's fully involved in fire."

"Oh my God! Eli, a disaster there could be catastrophic to defense security. I'll activate the team deployment notification plan and then head for the office. I assume you'll take care of the transportation."

"You got it. Keep me informed."

One of the firm's first major acquisitions had been a jet. It was hangared at PDK (Peachtree DeKalb) Airport, a general aviation strip twenty minutes from Eli's home. Its pilot was Daneli's chief crisis operations officer, Victor Majeski. Daneli did not yet have the resources to hire a pilot crew, so Vic, an ex-marine with training on small aircraft and helicopters, was trained to pilot the company's 1994 Citation CJ3. When the company jet was put to use, Vic would rent a copilot from Epps Aviation Services. As expected, Vic was still up when Eli called.

Vic answered the call with, "Hey, amigo, what's up?"

"We have an incident, and it's a big one."

"No shit! Where is it?"

"The Navy Fuel Supply Depot at Craney Island."

"I know those guys. They were part of my territory at West."

"I thought about that. They really have no idea how ready we'll be to hit the ground running. Anyway, get yourself ready, and I'll meet you at PDK."

"You got it, boss. I'm gonna call Anh Nguyen, the pilot we used when we flew to Boulder a couple of weeks ago."

"Sure. See you then."

In addition to Vic, the mobile crisis team was comprised of an environmental engineer, a failure analysis expert, a fire and air hazard expert, an ex-FBI investigator and evidence expert, and a public relations specialist and media consultant. Hank Fisher's job was to stay in Atlanta with Erica, the office manager, and coordinate all of Daneli's operations from there.

Eli walked into the bedroom, sat on the edge of the bed, and gently placed his hand on the his wife's shoulder, stirring her from a deep sleep to a low level of alertness. She had been curled up in the fetal position, oblivious to the conscious world.

Danielle's cobalt blue eyes flickered when she heard Eli speak.

"Hey, sweetheart. I just got a call from the US Navy. They want us to respond to a major disaster in Virginia."

"Are you leaving right away?" Danielle replied in a weak, raspy tone.

"Afraid so. Will you have any trouble making do without me for a week or so?"

Danielle seemed to gather herself and managed to adjust her position from fetal to sitting. She was awake now, and her mind was active. "I think Rachel and I can handle things. Call me in the morning if you get the chance."

She looked into his eyes, and Eli into hers. A wry smile grew on her angelic face. "Good luck, and try to resist hanging out with Vic. Last time you were so run down you got sick with the flu."

"I'll do my best. Love you," Eli said as they kissed goodbye.

Even awaking from a full sleep, Danielle was gorgeous. Eli paused for a moment just to marvel at her. On his way to his event storage closet, he walked into the nursery to take a peek at Samantha, his eighteen-month-old daughter. Eli bent down and kissed her on the forehead.

"Daddy's going to miss you so much," he whispered.

His next stop was the storage closet in the garage where he kept his response gear. The storage closet was Exhibit A of Eli's tendency toward obsessive-compulsive disorder. Two orange canvas duffel bags occupied the waist-high shelf. On the handles, two identical tags displayed the date Eli last inspected their contents. On the wall was a calendar with a circle around the date of his last response. If the bag tags postdated the calendar, that was his reassurance that everything in the bags was fresh and inventoried. A quick glance confirmed the bags postdated the last event. To make sure, he unzipped one duffel and saw folded clothes. Eli bent down to smell the clothes and confirmed the scent of laundry detergent and not asphalt. His last gig had been a fire at an asphalt refinery. He quickly peeked into the other duffel and confirmed his safety gear and response equipment was as it should be—hard hat, cameras, shock-resistant laptop, satellite phone and battery chargers, two-way radio, safety glasses, breather, coverall, moon-suit protective outerwear, and response regulations manuals.

They're good to go, he thought.

After loading the duffel bags in the back of his Ford SUV, Eli observed that the time was 2241 hours, and he noted it on the voice recorder that was tethered to one of the duffel straps. It also occurred to him that his public relations specialist and claims adjuster were the only members of the team who might not be familiar with Craney Island Depot or dealing with the military in a response setting. Eli connected his cell phone with his Bluetooth hands-free system and called his media expert first, Faith Miller.

"Hi, Faith. I take it Hank called you?"

"Yeah, we just got off the phone a minute ago."

"Since this is your first response with us and maybe your first with the military, I thought I would brief you while driving to PDK. Is that OK with you?"

"That's so kind of you. I have to admit that I am feeling a little inadequate at the moment."

"That's to be expected. Where are you?"

"I'm five minutes from pulling out of my driveway. Luckily, I live close to PDK. I should arrive before or about the same time as everyone else."

"No sweat. Here is what I know about the layout of Craney Island. Although it's technically an island, it doesn't appear to be one. The facility is strategically placed near a cluster of Navy bases, airfields, and shipyards. Two major pipeline companies, Provincial and Confederated, deliver fuel to it, and their delivery facilities are just outside the Navy's fence. If the Navy's facility is fully involved, then it makes sense that the pipeline assets are also involved. That leaves precious little real estate to stage a response. It's going to be crowded and highly emotional.

"The US Coast Guard is going to assert that it has jurisdiction to assume command of the response. The Navy will stubbornly resist giving away command over its operations. Hopefully, we can help them reach a joint command resolution. I don't have any facts yet on the event, but my experience suggests that we are probably dealing with one of the following scenarios: a tank failure, a tank that was being overloaded during a delivery, a pipeline rupture, or sabotage. And don't think sabotage is a low potential. These facilities are built to eliminate ignition sources. Spills are common. But spills that catch fire are very rare. Nowadays, you'd almost have to go out of your way to find an ignition source close to the fuel or its fumes.

"There is going to be competition among media specialists and spokespersons for face time with the news media. The media will recognize you and me. They will eventually find us for comment. We need to make sure that we have authority from the Navy to say anything, and we need to get approval from both the Navy and Coast Guard regarding the subjects we will cover and what should be our focus.

"It's going to be a madhouse in the command center. I want you to stay close to me, observing, listening, and taking notes. As events dictate, we will need to go our separate ways for short periods, but when you are through dealing with a matter, I need for you to check back with me. Situations change rapidly during this size of event, and we need to remain updated and in touch as often as practical.

"Hank and Erica will be ordering us rental vehicles to be picked up at Norfolk International Airport. If they can't find enough, we'll be sharing. In any event, we might not have the best of luck with our cell phones. That means that the radios we bring may be our best way to communicate.

"I think I need to call Mike and give him a similar briefing. Do you have any questions at this time?"

"Nothing that can't wait until we get on the plane."

"OK, see you at PDK."

Eli met Mike Hillendorf when he was a Crawford & Company investigator on a West Industries spill in the mid-1990s. They had worked on two other events since then. He was fortyish and African American, and he had a hell of a mustache. Mike had a top-notch sense of value, and he was a detail freak. Both qualities were just what Eli needed in a claims adjuster. Eli used to do his own claims work for West. Once he added Mike to Daneli, Eli found he could leave all of the adjusting matters on Mike's plate without worry that something might be overlooked. Eli called him at 2252 hours. He was ten minutes from PDK.

"Hey, Mike, I was wondering if you were familiar with Craney Island."

"It has been on my radar, but I never visited the facility. What can you tell me about it?"

"Not a whole lot. I just wanted to tell you that I expect there is going to be a strong motivation from the Navy to focus on the human error or mechanical failure as a cause. I want you to keep an open mind on all potentials and to remain curious about all events and circumstances. Since there is a fire, much of the evidence will be destroyed. If the fire is still raging when we arrive at the scene, I want you to see if you can approach the facility from the water. That means you will need to persuade the Coast Guard and the Navy's Criminal Investigation Service to join you in a shoreline investigation for, among other things, an ignition agent or evidence of sabotage or both. That means we will need the Coast Guard's assistance in securing the shoreline from anything that might disturb evidence of an intruder."

"So you think that's a real possibility."

"I've been there more than once. I've been impressed by their attention to safety. My instincts are raging right now, and they are telling me their people are too well trained to let an accident get out of hand. Also, it's hard for me to imagine that all safety systems and their backups coincidentally failed at the same time. Let's just say we are being careful not to ignore something and let the evidence and the facts get away from us."

They hung up as Eli was entering PDK. Daneli shared a hangar and a flight office with Atlanta Gas Light Company, and Eli could see by the office lights being on that he wasn't the first to arrive. Daneli's jet was just pulling out of the hangar and getting into position for loading baggage and boarding. Vic was at the controls, and he waved to Eli as he parked the aircraft.

As Eli turned off the car's ignition, he could feel the adrenalin rush running through his body. Emergency response was a drug so powerful it could keep him alert for thirty-six hours straight.

He thought, I've been told it's almost the same rush soldiers feel in battle. What's scary, it's addictive.

Eli picked up the fifty-pound duffel bags as if they were cotton candy and carried them toward the aircraft. As he scanned the scene, he admired the all-blue denim jeans outerwear Erica had picked out for the response team. We look good, he thought.

Vic Majeski was staring at Eli with that shit-eating grin that meant only one thing, and he said it before Eli could get the words out of his mouth.

"It's time to rock 'n roll!"

***

Later that evening, in a hotel room in Washington, DC, a man sat down on the standard hotel desk chair and opened up his laptop computer on the desk. The man's clothing had a faint odor of petroleum products, which came from being in close proximity to other clothing in his vehicle that reeked of it.

He was communicating with his benefactor and coconspirators. The method of communication was Facebook, using coded words and language. His fingers typed, "Good Day at the hospital—Operation Junior a success." In essence, the message told all of the success of the exploits of his team of saboteurs at the Craney Island Fuel Depot.

With that mission complete, the man at the hotel desk pondered how long it would be before his benefactor would need him to put in motion the succeeding missions of sabotage. Little did he realize that this week would be busy with tying up loose ends.

3. RUBIN'S RUBIK MEMO

BRIAN MATUSAK HAD BEEN AN AUDITOR FOR THE GOVERNMENT Accountability Office for sixteen years. He was in his late thirties, with a full brown beard and horn-rimmed glasses. Most of his audits were mundane and repetitive. Every now and then he would find something scandalous or in violation of government guidelines. That was what kept his fires burning. Had he not been credited with discovering several wasteful or corrupt practices over the years, he would have jumped ship a long time ago and entered the private sector. He was considered a very capable auditor and a reliable researcher.

His latest assignment had been in an area of government procurement that was new to him, the matching of fuel purchases to actual billings. It was a routine GAO responsibility to analyze the budget-making process. His assignment included verifying whether a department of government that had created a budget actually needed the items purchased and whether it received what it had ordered. Not only had he never worked on Department of Defense audits in the past, he had no experience in fuels. He was assigned this audit due to the random rotation practice used by his office.

On this day he became fascinated by a July 17, 2006, memo he found in a folder labeled "Tracking Fuel Shipments, Origin to USN CIFD (United States Navy, Craney Island Fuel Depot)." The memo was to the Department of Defense (DOD) Deputy Director of Acquisition—Fuels, from the Chief Auditor of the Defense Finance and Accounting Service (DFAS). The subject was the IDIQ or Indefinite Delivery–Indefinite Quantity contract for jet aviation fuel with North American Products Company (NAPCO).

The memo appeared to be an opportunity to learn more about the area he was about to audit. The deputy director was inquiring about the route fuels undertook to reach their final destination. Apparently, he was conducting a routine review of invoices for fuel shipments to verify that they were in compliance with current contracts and whether the DOD actually received what it ordered and paid for. The chief auditor was expressing exasperation because he was having difficulty following the orders in the chain of custody from the supplier to the Navy destination facility.

A part of his confusion was due to the type of pipelines that carried the fuel products along this route. Both were interstate common carrier lines. That meant the shipper didn't have custody of the fuel for the vast majority of its 1,100-mile route from the refinery near Houston, Texas, to the Navy's facility near Portsmouth, Virginia. The huge pipelines owned by Provincial and Confederated delivered about 99 percent of the refined fuel products along this route, letting streams of it out at major metropolitan areas such as Birmingham, Alabama; Atlanta, Georgia; and Washington, DC.

That memo was stapled to a July 21, 2006, reply memo from Ryan Rubin, a DOD procurement specialist. In the memo, Rubin explained that the fuel ordered—in this case, aviation kerosene to be shipped to the US Navy—was nominated by the supplier to be shipped on various pipeline systems. He provided an example of how an order made January 30 for twenty-five thousand barrels of jet aviation fuel from the supplier, NAPCO, in Houston, Texas, to arrive at the Navy's Craney Island Fuel Depot by June 15, was nearly impossible to trace.

What piqued Brian's interest was that most auditing assignment folders were nothing more than a set of orders, receipts, invoices, and accompanying payment vouchers. To find a separate folder full of memos, correspondence, and research about a set of transactions was unheard of. His curiosity was running high in anticipation of what he might find. It turned out he would not be disappointed.

According to the memo's first two paragraphs:

It's impossible to trace interstate pipeline shipments because neither NAPCO nor any other marketer of fuels selects and places a segregated, unaltered batch of aviation fuel in motion headed for Craney Island or any other Navy destination. In other words, no separate 25,000-barrel batch of fuel leaves a refinery by a pipeline or any other transportation mode and enters NAPCO's delivery chain and heads toward its DOD customer, where it arrives intact. Instead, a typical batch of fuel from a supplier departs a tanker or refinery in its custody and heads to an interstate pipeline common carrier, where it is deposited in the pipeline operator's tank farm and intermingled with identical products from other suppliers. Fuel grades such as aviation kerosene are called a fungible product because no matter the supplier, the fuel must achieve measured standards that make it no different from products of other suppliers.

Once a supplier's fuel is mixed with other batches, it loses its identity. This big, comingled slug of fuels then awaits its scheduled time to leave the tanks via pipeline. At that point, a batch that is bigger than any one supplier's order—let's say 500,000 barrels—enters a nationwide pipeline system somewhere like Houston, Texas, on the US Gulf Coast, destined for East Coast markets. In any event, as this big slug of fuel reaches Richmond, Virginia, the Navy's 25,000 barrels will be pulled out of the bigger batch at a tank farm there and sent down a smaller pipeline to arrive at Craney Island. In all, the trip from Houston to Craney Island takes about six to seven days.

Brian was thinking, "So far the memo is educational, but what is so important about fuels and their shipping differences with other products?" He hoped there would be a point to all the writing before he dozed off.

The memo continued:

In reality, a supplier like NAPCO rarely refines or purchases a batch as small as 25,000 barrels of aviation fuel. Let's say 200,000 barrels is an average-size batch that it sends in motion on a pipeline system. Let's also assume that NAPCO originally intended to carve out the

Navy's 25,000-barrel order from that batch and deliver it to CIFD (Craney Island). At that time, the entire 200,000-barrel batch of fuel will be placed into play on the commodities market as it enters the distribution chain.

However, NAPCO might find the market demands 200,000 barrels of the same product for a quick sell in New York at a higher price. Instead of carving out 25,000 barrels of its 200,000-barrel batch to CIFD, NAPCO examines the commodity market to see if it can find a replacement for the Craney Island barrels. It finds that Exxon-Mobil has placed a sell order for at least 25,000 barrels of the same product at the same price as the Navy's, and it is available from a tank farm in Greensboro, North Carolina. By substituting the Exxon-Mobil product for what it would have to carve out of its 200,000-barrel batch, it will make more profit by selling its entire 200,000 barrel batch it has at Houston and buying the 25,000-barrel Exxon-Mobil batch at Greensboro to replace the Navy's order. At this point there is a company other than NAPCO supplying the fuel to the Navy. NAPCO made more money, and Craney Island still got the fuel it ordered.

Again Brian was thinking, "Very interesting, but so what?"
The explanation was not over:

Exxon-Mobil might subsequently discover that a

buyer demanding a bigger batch of aviation fuel at a much higher price is needed in Boston. Exxon-Mobil might prefer to make that deal, even if it would need to replace the NAPCO 25,000-barrel batch destined to Craney Island to fill out that order. So it searches for another 25,000 batch of aviation fuel from another marketer that can reach Craney Island on time. If it will make a bigger profit by making that trade, it does so.

The explanation went on to state that

An order for 25,000 barrels made January 30 for delivery February 15 at Craney Island might change hands fifteen times before it actually arrives within the six-day delivery time from Houston, TX, to Craney Island in Virginia. Also, the last shipper-owner may be a petroleum marketer nobody has ever heard of. It can also start out being NAPCO's, change ownership several times, and end up being NAPCO's again as the last owner. And that is why it's nearly impossible to trace.

The memo concluded as follows:

Also, it would require the examination of all of the nomination records considered in the fifteen trades to determine who all the owners of

```
the original batch of fuel are. Got the picture?
I recommend you simply satisfy your audit by
matching the amount of aviation fuel ordered to
the amount that was billed and received and go
no further in your audit.
```

That was the end of the memo. Brian was thinking, "That's it? Why all the explanation for such a meaningless conclusion?"

But that was when he saw it. At the bottom of the memo was a handwritten question: "How do we verify that the fuel did not originate from a supplier that is not on the list of approved suppliers?"

That was when it hit him. It wasn't so much about the transportation of the fuel; it was about its true origin. If the country of origin was not on the approved list, and the shipper (NAPCO) knew it, it would be perpetrating a fraud by being an accomplice to a company that wanted to break through an embargo the United States had imposed or to violate the prohibited and restricted import laws.

Brian did not find anything else in the folders that completed the chief auditor's inquiry. He was now very curious about the memos because the review of approved suppliers for compliance was also an item on the GAO's agenda. Although list compliance was not one of his assignments, he considered that it would be an opportunity to collect some brownie points for his annual performance review if he could find a violation that he could report. Also, Brian was the curious type, and this had the feel of something interesting. The word interesting would not, however, be sufficient to describe the ripples of activity he was about to unwittingly unleash.

4. ON THE WAY TO CRANEY ISLAND

ELI PLACED HIS DUFFELS ON THE GROUND AT THE END OF THE line of bags deposited by Vic and Faith. Pulling into the parking lot was Daneli's fire expert, Dexter Allen, in his new Escalade. He was the most experienced team member. At fifty something, there was nothing he hadn't seen before. He was the old grump on the team, overweight and out of condition.

As Eli walked toward his vehicle to help him unload, Dexter barked, "Keep your distance! I don't want you infecting me with your excitement and enthusiasm."

"Nice to see that you are in your best response mood," Eli remarked.

"I had just fallen asleep, and I think I was about to have a terrific dream. The damn phone interrupted Mary Sue Lannigan's explanation of why it was important that we explore our desires before we return to tenth grade classes in the fall."

"Sorry about that," Eli remarked. "Can I help you with your gear?"

"If you don't mind. My moon suit and boots need to get in the camouflage duffel in the backseat. I didn't have time to pack everything properly."

"No sweat. I'll place it in line with the rest of the bags."

Every team member had a separate color for his or her gear, another one of Eli's OCD requirements.

In a matter of a few minutes, they were all loaded and onboard. One of the great advantages of owning his own aircraft and using an aviation service such as Epps was that Eli had access to twenty-four-hour catering. The last items to load were the trays of food. Anh Nguyen, their Vietnamese rent-a-copilot, placed the tray on the single seat nearest to the cockpit. Vic was at the controls and communicating with the control tower.

"Good evening, fellow travelers," said Anh. "I understand you have an emergency, so I will not delay you with small talk. The air between Atlanta and Norfolk is calm and mostly clear. The temperature in Norfolk is forty-one degrees Fahrenheit. Winds are calm at zero to five knots, and the sky is partly cloudy with little or no chance of rain when we land. We should have a smooth flight. Vic will be at the controls as we take off, and I will be available to assist you in any needs or questions."

After they landed and deplaned, Anh would deadhead the Citation back to Atlanta and await instructions. If he got the call to return with reinforcements or supplies, he would be ready for immediate departure back to Norfolk.

"Are we all set for takeoff?" Anh asked.

Eli looked to each team member and got a thumbs-up. As he looked at each of them, it was gratifying to see the look of real anticipation on their faces. Emergency response is not for the timid, the insecure, or the introvert. The "explorer" spirit is necessary to get past the sleep deprivation, and each team member has to have the soldier mentality to work as a unit with one mind.

"Anh, I think we are set for departure," Eli announced.

Eli checked his watch. It was 2311. As he sat down in his seat next to his fire expert, he pulled out his voice recorder and noted that the wheels were up at 2311 hours, November sixth.

Eli got a rush every time the Citation began its steep climb into the sky. It wasn't like a commercial aircraft. There was no roar or prolonged liftoff. It was a swoosh at a much steeper angle. In a matter of seconds, the Citation was tapering off into a gentle climb that was almost unnoticeable. That was when passengers were free to loosen their seat belts and move about. At cruising altitude, the Citation was eerily quiet except for an ambient buzz that faded into the soft background whoosh. Another feature of the Citation was the ability to swivel one's seat and form a table arrangement where everyone was, more or less, facing one another.

Anh helped with the food for a minute or two and returned to the cockpit. He had ordered egg-and-sausage breakfast biscuits with hash browns and plenty of coffee. The biscuits were wrapped in a thick Saran wrap that kept them hot and steamy—a guilty pleasure to fuel the tough days ahead.

Eli called Hank on the jet's satellite phone for a news update.

The loudspeaker was on, and Hank was advising everyone of a conversation he had had with a Coast Guard buddy stationed in Portsmouth who was responding to the incident.

Hank said, "The Navy and Coast Guard staging sites are positioned along Oyster Shell Road, with the Navy's being closest to the facility. They have helicopters dropping fire retardant from the sky. So far they haven't been able to safely position a fire-fighting barge close enough to the north shore to reach the tanks with foam. The air currents are mild and moving from the west and blowing in a favorable direction.

"This is not a worst-case scenario, but it could grow into one. The supervisory system indicates that a fuel oil tank on the northwest section of the facility was the first to catch fire, and the air currents are pushing the heat and flames in the direction of two other tanks. They might be next to catch fire. None of the twenty jet fuel tanks are involved, and they appear safe from catching on fire at this time. There is a lot of speculation at the moment that two more fuel tanks could succumb to the heat created by the fire and eventually catch on fire or explode."

"Hank, this is Eli. Does anybody know how much product was stored at the time of the alarms?"

"I asked that question myself. My source did not know, but he said everyone is asking that question; we should know soon. Right now they are assuming it's a combination of human and mechanical error. The first reports are that the second high-level alarm on tank seven sounded at 2201 hours. Apparently the first high-level alarm was not functioning properly and never sounded or registered on the supervisory system. That's the mechanical issue. The human issue is that the operator began a new delivery of No. 2 fuel oil at 2127 hours and directed it into a tank that was already at normal full capacity."

Dexter, the fire safety expert, asked, "Hank, Dex here. Has anyone mentioned what the ignition source might be?"

Hank replied, "I asked that as well. So far everyone is scratching their heads on that one. My source tells me that their chief safety officer called the commanding officers of both men on duty and asked, among other things, if they smoked cigarettes. The answers from both were negative."

About this time, Vic turned the aircraft controls over to Anh and joined the rest of the response team in the cabin. They ate their evening breakfast while they discussed the event.

"Hank, this is Mike. Can you get an inventory of all the vehicles and moveable equipment that might have been on the island? I want to know if any were not diesel. Next, I want to see a list of all the water traffic in the vicinity of the island—whose it was and what their missions were."

"I'll get on that right away. Anybody else have a question? I don't hear anyone, so I assume not. Next, I would like to leave you with a tape recording of the latest news report coming out of Norfolk."

"Go ahead with the news story, Hank," Eli said.

The team listened intently as the local late evening news anchor gave a dramatic and emotional account of the obvious. What was important, though, was her account of what she saw on the screen—which was a helicopter's view of the island at eleven o'clock, one hour into the event. Smoke was trailing off to the east, and it was so thick that the view of the tank that was involved was completely obscured. She said that the light from the blaze did provide a partial view of the other tanks to the southeast. Apparently they were still intact.

They hung up with Hank and paused for a moment to contemplate what they had heard.

"Any first impressions?" Eli asked.

Everyone waited for Eli to comment first. That was not his usual style, but he was growing accustomed to opening the doors for comment by making an obvious observation to prime the pump and jumpstart the discussion.

"OK," Eli said. "Let's see what we have so far. Hank says tank seven is the tank on fire."

Eli pulled out an aerial map of the Craney Island facilities that

Hank had faxed to PDK. It was a rough version of an Internet satellite photograph. He remembered that the fuel oil tanks on the north were numbered front to back, meaning tank seven was closest to the north shore of the peninsula. He drew a number seven on the photo over the circular image representing the top of tank seven.

"Let's assume I'm right about this being tank seven. If we have a sabotage potential, let's talk about the ways a perpetrator would ignite the fuel oil on the ground."

Vic jumped in. "If it were me, I would send scuba divers with flares or use a grenade launcher from the water. But whatever the ignition delivery, the person performing the ignition would have to know that a tank had been overfilled and which tank and dike were involved. That would require insider info."

Mike asked, "Is the shore too far away from the tanks to accurately launch a flare?"

Vic replied, "Eyeballing a rough scale of the map looks like we are talking about a tenth of mile or more from water edge to tank dike. Either the device with an ignition potential was launched from a watercraft large enough to handle the recoil of a grenade launcher, or the saboteur came up on the shore to launch it. A flare from the water would be so unlikely to score a direct hit on tank seven that a weapon with aiming capability would need to be employed."

Eli commented, "That's what I am looking for. What's the smallest size of watercraft that would provide enough stability to launch a grenade?"

Vic answered. "We're talking about something larger than a canoe or a small rowboat. They might tip over from the recoil. I would guess a small pontoon boat with a quiet, electricity-powered propeller would do the trick. However, if it were up to me,

I wouldn't risk a watercraft floating around one of the most protected facilities in the world. I would take a bunch of flares, a flare gun, and go scuba diving. You'd have to scale the bank and maybe a fence to get close enough, but that would be my approach."

"Perfect. Let's assume we are dealing with a scuba diving saboteur. Now, how do we know tank seven was his target from the beginning of the plan? What do you think, Vic?"

"Now, that's your sixty-four-thousand-dollar question. If you can figure that out, you can probably finger the bad guy," Vic countered.

"What are the most logical ways to assure it's tank seven?" Mike asked.

Vic answered, "The most obvious is a conspiracy situation with the operator. He pushes the switches that direct the delivery to tank seven and then departs his post. If he doesn't leave the island, he risks becoming a crispy critter. The second alternative would have to involve the computer programming or the circuits of the supervisory panel. Something along the lines of making it appear on your screen you are filling tank eight, but in reality, you are filling tank seven. But before I go into any of these possibilities, I've got to disable the tank's high-level alarms. If I don't, either the operator or the utility disables them by hand. If they are not disabled, the operator or utility will just go to the control panel and shut down the delivery when the alarms sound. So you have to have an accomplice on the ground. Again, if it's me, I would try to involve the fewest accomplices possible. The operator could do it all: disable the alarm, overflow the tank, and then set it on fire before he leaves."

Vic looked at his watch and said, "Excuse me while I land this baby at Norfolk. We should be entering our approach about now. You all need to buckle up."

Vic got up, and everyone obeyed.

As they readied for landing, Eli smiled to himself. He would have loved to know Vic while he was growing up. Eli didn't know his entire story, but he did know that his high school transcript was full of insubordination, pranks, great grades, and high aptitude scores. He went into the marines directly after graduation. He was a highly decorated soldier who was never promoted past corporal. He liked the action, not the politics. He could operate just about anything mechanical, earth-moving equipment, helicopters, and jet aircraft. He preferred a Harley Davidson for transportation and had a pickup for days the weather didn't suit the Harley. He was six foot four and had a body-builder physique and biceps adorned with tattoos.

Eli thought, If I am not mistaken, one is a heart with an arrow through it with the word "Mom" on the heart, and the other is the US Marines insignia. He's old school when it comes to tattoos. He's smart, and he knows it. When he shares his opinions, he does so as one might imagine Moses after he descended from Mount Sinai and laid down the law of the Ten Commandments to the Israelites.

Eli loved the guy. He was the guy you wanted when you needed someone protecting your ass—no matter the situation.

The Citation landed at 0116 hours Tuesday morning. Eli was impressed that Hank was able to find three rental vehicles—two SUVs and a sedan. Usually, an event of this magnitude sucked up all the rental vehicles quickly. Faith and Eli took the sedan; Vic and Clyde took one SUV, with Mike, Blake, and Dexter in the other.

Eli called Commander Hughes as they loaded the vehicles and

continued listening as Faith drove and Vic led them in the direction of Craney Island. Commander Hughes gave Eli instructions on how to pass clearance at the security gate. There was a checkpoint at Hedgerow Street and Craney Island Fuel Road. At the first checkpoint, a decal for the vehicles and credentials for the personnel were awaiting their arrival. They were asked to stay on Fuel Road until the next checkpoint at the Coast Guard staging site, where they would receive another decal that would give them access to the entire response.

The credentials and decals had a chip embedded in them so they could be tracked by computer. In the early days of the technology, tracking was only used for invoicing purposes and billing crew time. That was still being done, but now the military was using it to keep track of all nonmilitary visitors to make sure they could locate them at all times.

As they approached the Midtown Tunnel, they could see the fire-illuminated sky in the direction of Craney Island three miles away. They made it through all the checkpoints and parked at the Navy staging site. It was 0157 hours, and the exhilaration and anxiety of their mission kept everyone alert and champing at the bit. As Eli exited the car, the heat from the blaze surprised him. They were a good half mile away and upwind, but the air temperature had to be ten degrees warmer than it had been at the airport.

Eli led his team toward the buildings with all the lights. The fire lit the sky so brightly that they were walking in twilight. The air was filled with the odor of burning fuel oil. It was all too familiar. The voice of Vic was in his left ear. "Don't you love it? The hair on my neck is at full attention. How about you?"

"If only the rest of the team knew we were disaster junkies. Yeah, I love it. I think you and I were meant for this work. Now, take that smile off your face—we don't need for the Navy to know we're nuts."

"You've got the same smile, amigo!"

The two men looked at each other's faces, turned their grins to the serious countenance of professionals, and walked into the building.

5. GETTING TO KNOW OUR PRINCIPALS

0200 HOURS, TUESDAY MORNING, NOVEMBER 7, 2006

THE NAVY HAD CONVERTED A WAREHOUSE AND TWO SMALLER storage buildings into a makeshift command center. The Daneli team entered the open garage-type door and saw about fifty people milling around cafeteria tables and folding chairs. An enlisted man who looked almost albino gave everyone a name tag to wear on a lanyard, which was included. He led the Daneli team to a small office where a guard manned the doorway. The office had windows on the door and wall. Eli could see the man sitting behind a desk, and he recognized him from when they had met a year ago. The man was on a two-way radio receiving a report. He rose and motioned for Eli and his team to assemble inside his office. He also wore a name tag around his neck. It read Commander Mitchell Hughes.

"Hello, Eli. I'm pleased you made it here so quickly. Is this your crew?"

Introductions were made, and Hughes continued. "I delayed having a full briefing until 0200 hours or when you arrived. The ensign here will show you to your seats."

"This way," a voice from behind instructed.

Eli and the Daneli team sat down at the left end of the second row of tables. "DANELI" was written on a file card in the middle of the table. Military personnel sat in the first row and nonmilitary in the second. The small heating units for the typical metal buildings used by the industry usually didn't meet the challenge of warming the occupants, but with the blazing tanks so close, they were all snug and toasty despite the raw November air. The assembled visitors were now accustomed to the smell of burning fuel oil.

The ensign took the podium and announced that the briefing would begin. "Let the record show that we began at 0202 hours, November seventh."

Then it was Commander Hughes's turn to take the podium. He repeated what the team had heard from the Coast Guard friend of Hank's and continued on that time line.

"At 2249 hours, we completed a helicopter viewing of the event. Only one tank was involved, fuel oil tank number seven. The rest of the seven fuel oil tanks, the four utility tanks, and the aviation kerosene tanks appeared to be undamaged and holding their own. We commenced an aerial fire-fighting operation at that time in an effort to prevent destruction of additional tanks and their contents. We abandoned that effort at 2313 hours when it was observed that tanks six and eight were overtaken by the heat and flames. A series of explosions occurred, but none of the fire-fighting aircraft was damaged.

"We are currently in a standby position until the blaze subsides to allow us to resume fire fighting from the air. It has been asked how much product is in storage at the facility. We have estimated that the eight fifty-thousand-barrel capacity fuel oil tanks were holding approximately two hundred eighty thousand barrels of product. The twenty twenty-five-thousand-barrel capacity aviation kerosene tanks were holding about three hundred sixteen thousand barrels of product. The four utility tanks were holding about nine thousand barrels of other petroleum products. That aggregates to a total of six hundred five thousand barrels. The three tanks ablaze were holding about one hundred five thousand barrels of fuel. The current prediction is that the winds should maintain an easterly drift for the next thirty-six hours. We hope to have either put out the fires or sufficiently reduced the heat and flames by then to prevent any other tanks from catching.

"We are discontinuing efforts to get a fire-fighting barge with foam to the northern shore to tank seven's dike. The distance is five hundred forty-two feet from the water to the dike. That's too far a distance for this type of equipment. When the heat of the blaze subsides to safety standards, aerial fire-fighting methods will be resumed and land-based fire fighting will commence. In the meantime, we must be patient and wait. We are monitoring the air temperatures surrounding the tanks and are getting readings every five minutes.

"I am sure you all are interested in the status of the personnel who were working on site at the time of the incident. An operator and a utility were the only personnel on the clock. We have not heard from either since the incident began. We will not be releasing their names until we can confirm their status; however, we have notified their families.

"As of this moment, the cause or causes of the incident are under investigation, and there is insufficient evidence to draw conclusions of any sort. The NTSB will be heading up these investigations. Its lead investigator should arrive shortly.

"At this time, I would like to inform you of all the agencies and contractors responding and their current roles. A joint command has been established. It is comprised of myself, representing the US Navy, Commander Evan Brockington of the US Coast Guard, Senior Liquid Fuel Systems Investigator Samuel Criss from the NTSB; Captain Jay Nash of the Portsmouth Fire Department; and Michael Ross from the Virginia Department of Transportation. Another agency contributing is the EPA, and its Mid-Atlantic chief, Susan Jones, is on hand. NOAA's Keith Adams is also contributing. The contractors are Adair Petroleum Emergency Response, Bradley Brothers General Contractors, Floating Environmental, and Daneli Crisis Management.

"The incident command will reside here in the main warehouse. The two storage buildings in this mini-complex are being readied as we speak to serve as the emergency responder office and the communications office. The incident command will hold briefings at six hundred hours, ten hundred hours, and sixteen hundred hours. Press briefings will be held daily at seven hundred hours, eleven hundred hours, and seventeen hundred hours. We are bringing in tents to shelter the press, government representatives, and contractor support. They will be positioned adjacent to the storage buildings. We have set up two staging sites for response equipment and vehicles. We are in the process of fencing off these areas here at this staging site and at the Coast Guard staging site to our west.

"Last, all activities must be coordinated through the Unified Command Center office, and your first contact should be through Ensign Volk. The schedule of activities will be posted on the bulletin board to my left. Now, I will turn the podium over to Commander Brockington. Thank you."

Hughes was an impressive figure. Tall and athletic. He appeared to be in his early fifties. He also appeared to be a very confident leader with a little arrogance. If you were casting someone to play a naval commander in a movie, Hughes was your man.

He stepped down and motioned for Eli to come into his office. He asked him to sit down and closed the door behind him.

"As you can see, we have a fluid situation here. I have followed your career somewhat. We have a mutual friend in attorney David Alvarez. He thinks highly of you."

"Yes, Commander, David and I have shared some dynamic projects. I have to admit, however, I didn't know we had this connection."

"He didn't want you to know until it happened. I consulted with him a couple of years ago when I got this command. I felt then, as I do today, that I would need a nonmilitary advisor and consultant should an emergency of this order ever arise. When you left West and went into the consulting business, he called me. Now that you are here, I'll tell you what I need.

"I feel confident about what we do within the military. However, the end of the business that works closely with the private sector worries me. We depend heavily on the petroleum industry, its infrastructure, and its markets. Our focus here is dependability. The military needs to have dependable supplies of fuels to conduct an adequate defense of the United States. When our supply chain is interrupted, we need fast solutions. Needless to say, this kind of event presents a major interruption. One of our needs is your assistance in devising a plan to come up with a substitute for the fuel depot here. The Navy requested backup and replacement plans for all of its major facilities on the heels of the 9/11 terrorism event, but they have yet to be completed. We can't wait for DOD. We need something fast.

"Also, the outrage in Washington and the Pentagon has already begun. I will have enough to do just managing those pressures. I need you to provide me with real information and answers on the energy industry end. Also, I need your counsel in dealing with the politics. David says you are the best at this. I can use that."

"It looks like I owe David a favor. I am at your disposal. Just point me in a direction, and my team will get after it. But if you don't mind, I would like to know what you suspect to be the probable cause of the incident."

"That's as good a place to start as any. It appears as though we have an operator who made two mistakes. The first was that he directed a delivery to a tank that was already full. The second was that he responded directly to the overflow alarm, leaving his post in the control room to inspect the tank rather than following procedure to discontinue the delivery. We have a record of the conversation initiated by the controller at our James River Fuel Movements Control Center and the operator. He called when his board signaled a tank alarm at Craney. The operator at Craney hung up on him in a panic after he insisted on inspecting the tank before he discontinued the delivery. Our controller at James River should have overridden the operator and discontinued the delivery. That means that he failed to follow procedure as well. Our controller waited about fifteen minutes for the operator to call him back. Before that occurred, he was notified that the island was on fire. He never heard back from the operator."

"Tell me about the high-level tank alarms."

"For some reason, the first of the two must have malfunctioned. The tank began overflowing too quickly. The alarm that sounded had to be the higher of the two alarms. We will know that for sure tomorrow when we get a readout of the supervisory data."

"What about the utility? Where was he while all this was going on?"

"At this moment, we are assuming he was gauging tanks. We suspect he tried to investigate the alarm and was overcome by the fumes or the fire."

"Do you have any communication from him?"

"We have no such record in the James River Control Center. Once we access the phone records at the Craney control room, we might find that there were calls. It's too dangerous to enter the island now. We will have to wait until the fire and its heat settle down."

"What's your guess about an ignition source?"

"At this moment, we are all stumped by that question. It's inconceivable to me that there could have been an ignition caused by one of our men."

"That leads me to my next question. Do you have any reason to suspect sabotage?"

"Not at this moment. Our NCIS folks would like to explore that once things settle down here."

"What's preventing them from starting now?"

"Because of the blaze and its heat, we have ordered them to stand down until it's safe to conduct an investigation."

"If you really want my help, you will allow our investigator, Mike Hillendorf, to join the NCIS and a Coast Guard investigator to begin an immediate investigation of the areas that are safe."

"You really think that we might be looking at sabotage?"

"Let me put it this way. I don't think you will want to be answering why you didn't start to investigate it sooner if we do find it's sabotage."

"You have a point. And that's why David recommended you so highly."

"Can you call in the NCIS and the Coast Guard immediately so we can get it started? My other questions can wait."

"Of course; no sense putting it off."

As the commander picked up the handset of his phone, Eli didn't want to cramp the commander's style, so he told him, "My team and I will wait outside while you make your calls."

After a minute or two, Commander Hughes got Eli's attention by tapping on the window between them. He motioned for Eli to enter his office.

"It's done. Your investigator is on the team. They will be arriving shortly."

"You won't regret this, Commander."

The ensign with the fair complexion knocked on the commander's office window.

Eli quickly remarked, "Commander, my team will wait outside while you take care of this."

"You are very understanding. This should take only a minute."

They went back outside while the ensign spoke to the commander with the door open.

Commander Hughes brought the Daneli folks back inside, and they discussed how the firm would attend to the Navy's needs. Eli delegated most of the activities to his team members, but arranging for a substitute for the Craney Island Fuel Depot while it was being rebuilt was one assignment he knew Hank and he would have to handle. He had an idea about what might be available, and he knew that Hank might be one of the few people in the world who could pull it off.

6. RECON

COMMANDER HUGHES BRIEFED USCG COMMANDER EVAN BROCK-ington about the sabotage investigation mission, and he agreed to head it up. The investigation team included the Navy Criminal Investigation Service (NCIS) and Coast Guard. They were assigned to team with Daneli's Mike Hillendorf and Vic Majeski, who would act as consulting investigators. Eli met with them in Commander Hughes's office, the only place at the moment where they could meet and have a reasonable expectation of privacy.

The group agreed to conduct a perimeter reconnaissance of the shoreline for evidence of entry and to investigate the surrounding area for suspicious watercraft or persons looking to enter the water in proximity of Craney Island. NCIS dedicated four investigators led by the NCIS lieutenant, Scott Lemay; the Coast Guard supplied six crewmen, several boats, and other equipment. The Navy also sent two Navy SEALS and eight midshipmen to inspect the perimeter fence. This was a formidable assembly of talent.

The weather wasn't ideal for a middle-of-the-night, water-based recon, but it wasn't awful either. The air and seas were calm, but a low-hanging, light fog prevented long-range visibility, even with the beacons mounted on the two Coast Guard patrol boats. A Navy SEAL and three armed guardsmen were in each boat. Vic was in one boat and Mike in the other. On adjacent properties, the NCIS investigators began a door-to-door search for potential witnesses.

While the recon was underway, Eli asked Commander Brockington if he could try to persuade the NCIS to provide a data and computer systems specialist to inspect the James River Control Center (JRCC) data and supervisory system for any irregularities. Brockington didn't know of Eli's familiarity with the Navy's Craney Island systems, and he was visibly surprised by his question. However, Eli's request was on the mark, and he agreed. After a few e-mails from him and a personnel review by the commander's aide, a Navy IT expert was assigned to the investigation.

Once Eli felt comfortable with the efforts being made to run down the sabotage angle, he turned to Faith Miller, Daneli's public relations specialist. She was watching a DVD of all the news accounts of the incident.

"So, what's your impression so far, Faith?"

"From a media standpoint, it looks like the military has done a credible job in controlling the information about the incident. All the news outlets are running the same scripts and replaying the same videos. The comments by the military spokespersons have also been scripted and consistently vague. In other words, I have seen very little that would require damage control. And they caught a break with the news cycle. The headline is not about the facility fire—it's about further denials by Iran that its reactor development is intended to enrich uranium to make a nuclear weapon."

She continued, "From the standpoint of a person unfamiliar

with this business, I am impressed with their ability to ramp up a response effort of this magnitude in such a short time. I was sitting over there on a lawn chair watching the news accounts, and I had a hard time keeping my mind off what goes into such an effort. However, I was able to focus enough to take notes of all the activity going on around me. You know, Eli, we could use a mobile command post like West's response RV."

"What a great idea! I bet West Industries would jump at the chance to lend their mobile response vehicle to the Navy through us. What a great public relations opportunity. They make a big client happy, and television viewers see their logo on the RV during news briefings. Call West's PR manager at her office in the morning. Unless they have gone through some personnel changes, that person should be Margaret Carter."

Faith excused herself and got on the phone with West Industries to make the arrangements. The mobile command center was usually parked at West's Dorsey, Maryland, terminal just a couple of hours' drive down the road. It turned out it was available, and with a little persuasion, she landed it.

After Faith told Eli of the good news, he led her around the Navy's staging site for a show-and-tell. He identified each response division and described what roles they would play in the overall response. They continued by touring the Coast Guard's command post and staging site. It was closing in on four o'clock in the morning, and no media or news crews could be seen. But that didn't mean they weren't interested. The Navy wasn't letting them on the island until they had their first Unified Command briefing.

When Faith and Eli finished their tour around the response staging sites, the two of them returned to the Unified Command Center. During their walk, photos from the ground and air of the burning facility had been pinned up on the two large cork bulletin boards by the Navy command. Along with several other onlookers, they examined the photos. The photos were as spectacular as the video in the news accounts. There was one striking difference between these photos and the ones released to the press: there were several close-ups at high resolution.

One aerial photo caught Eli's eye. The power substation on the northern shore had an interesting feature. There was a small cove maybe a hundred feet or so from it. It appeared to him that one might be able to land a watercraft in the cove and enter the facility by cutting a hole in the fence without being detected. The substation would block the view from the control building. Eli got Mike on his radio and asked him for his position.

"Eli, I've got the north and northeast side of the island. We're conducting a preliminary perimeter recon. Right now we are looking at a barge-loading site on the northeast portion. What's up?"

"I am looking at some high resolution aerial photos of the incident. One showing the power substation interested me. Did you get a decent look at it?"

"Sure did. The Coast Guard has some terrific spotlights on their patrol boats. It doesn't appear to be in jeopardy of damage from the blaze."

"Did you notice a little cove a couple hundred feet east of it?"

"The NCIS ensign with us had some high-powered binoculars. He pointed it out to us. Our Navy SEAL commented that it looked like a good spot to come ashore."

"That's exactly what I was wondering."

"We're ahead of you on this one. We are in radio contact with the Navy midshipmen inspecting the perimeter fence. We asked them to pay close attention to that area. They are to report back to us when they have done so and are ready to move on along the perimeter. Do you want me to radio you back when we are through with that area?"

"Please do. It occurred to me that the substation might obscure the view of a potential perpetrator from the control building."

"Roger. By the way, the Coast Guard crewman on our patrol boat mentioned that the island uses closed-circuit video security cameras that have a view of about ninety percent of the perimeter fence. He doesn't know if they are backed up by videotape, though. They might be only for real-time viewing. He also doesn't know where the Navy controls the cameras. You might want to get Commander Hughes to help us find answers to these questions."

"I'll get on that immediately. That's all I've got. Unless you have something else, I'm out."

"Nothing else, Eli. I'm out."

Eli spotted Commander Hughes talking casually with some of his staff while drinking coffee at one of the cafeteria tables near his office and approached them.

"May I interrupt you for a moment?" he asked.

The commander replied, "Please do. We were not in the middle of anything."

"I understand that the Navy uses closed-circuit video of the facility for security purposes. Do you know where it is controlled?"

The commander answered, "It is operated from inside the control building on the facility property."

The commander then turned to one of the officers he was chatting with and nodded. That officer was NCIS Lieutenant Scott Lemay, and he said, "Until you arrived, we were prevented from entering the facility for safety reasons. As soon as we heard we were allowed to recon the site, we readied a team of three

Navy firefighters in the highest heat-rated moon suits. They entered the facility about ten minutes ago. The control building is about fifteen hundred feet from the tanks that are on fire. There is a good likelihood that they can enter the building. The video is on a twenty-four-hour taping loop. If the heat hasn't melted the cassettes, they should return with them. I will let you know when they report their findings."

"I'll keep my fingers crossed that they come back OK and have some good news."

Eli's radio was squawking, so he excused himself and responded to the signal. He sat down and turned the dial to active. "This is Taylor," he responded. "Over."

"Hillendorf here. We are too close to the tanks that are burning to complete a fence recon. We have too much heat and vapors. The specifications on our safety equipment won't let us get that close. However, our Navy SEAL put on his wet suit and diving gear and went ashore. He was able to get to the fence for about thirty seconds before he had to get back into the safety of the cool water. He must have great instincts, because he went right to the panel of fence that had been compromised by wire cutters. He had a dry-land-and-underwater camera and took a couple of shots before he had to return. He is back aboard now, and he is talking with Vic. Oh, Vic's patrol boat didn't spot anything interesting, so they joined us when we sent the SEAL out. From the sound of his observations, it looks like your instincts were spot on. We are on our way back to the Unified Command Center. Out."

As luck would have it, the Navy firefighters who had been sent to retrieve the videotapes arrived about a minute before Mike and Vic and the rest of the perimeter investigation team. It was 0440 hours when they all crammed into Commander Hughes's office. The firefighters gave their report first.

"We entered the facility gate at 0351 hours. We were able to reach the control building without incident. Just as the old photos suggest, it's a schoolhouse redbrick pillbox layout with a forty-foot-by-twenty-foot floor plan. The control panel is a U-shaped configuration along the back wall in the center of the building with the gauges, dials, and meters in the center of the U. The fumes were as heavy inside the building as outside, but nothing inside was burned. A paper scroll of tank schematics was unrolled and lying on the map table when we entered. Nothing seemed out of place.

"However, the safety rating of our protective gear did not allow us to approach any closer to the burning tanks than the control building. There was no sign of the duty officer or the seaman whom the schedule indicated to be the ones on duty. All the power was out, so we were unable to eject or unload the security tape. We returned with the entire tape-recording unit. After a comprehensive inspection, we did not find a cassette. Either the duty officer failed to inspect the device at the beginning of his shift and confirm its operating condition, or the cassette was removed before the power went out. As a result, we have nothing further to report."

Mike Hillendorf was the next to report on the recon of the perimeter.

"With the cooperation of our team representing each investigative entity, we were able to identify only one area of interest. However, we hit the jackpot with that sighting. At a small cove near the power substation on the northern shore, a Navy SEAL went ashore and reached the perimeter fence. He took photos, which we have loaded on our laptop, of where the fence was breached with a wire-cutting device. We also have photos of footprints on the sandy shoreline. If we all get on this side of the commander's desk and push it toward the wall, we can all view the photos at once."

The desk was moved, and Mike opened the laptop and fired it up.

Mike continued, "There were six photos taken. With the help of the Coast Guard spotlight, the photos portray the breached fence and footprints in terrific detail in shots one through four. It is clear that the fence had been cut and folded back and then unfolded to appear intact. The triangle of the fold and the cut line approximated a pathway about five feet high and four feet wide at the ground level. We think that's plenty of space for perpetrators to squat and walk through. The two photos of footprints indicate two sizes of feet. The Coast Guard is in the process of pulling the records of high tide to determine how fresh the footprints might be. Our preliminary observation is that we have a sabotage potential in the range of seventy percent of certainty at this time. We are only calling it a potential at this time because there is insufficient evidence to draw a conclusion with a higher certainty."

Commander Hughes was the first to comment.

"Would it be reasonable to draw a scenario where at least two saboteurs entered the facility yesterday evening? They disabled the duty officer and removed the videotape from the security video recorder. They also might have dispatched the seaman gauging the tanks. Is it possible these saboteurs diverted the delivery that was in process to a tank that was full? When it began to overflow and fill the dike, they ignited the fuel on their way out of the facility where they entered. They unfolded the fence and departed the island vicinity by watercraft."

NCIS's officer remarked, "That's about how I see the saboteur angle. Now the question is, do we have a consensus on this scenario being the most likely of events that need scrutiny?"

No one disagreed. Commander Hughes then turned to Eli and asked, "Mr. Taylor, from a private-sector standpoint, how do you see our position?"

Eli correctly recognized the moment as a monumental shift for the fortunes of his firm. He paused to find the perfect tenor of his next remarks to elicit trust and confidence in his coworkers.

"Thanks, Commander. It's a sincere pleasure working with the professionals you have assembled for this event. My thoughts and opinions are primarily to serve you and this effort. Let's first address the press. I liken the problems raised here to a bomb expert who approaches a suspected device that that he must disarm. If he is careful and thinks through every potential, he will disarm the device and save the day. In our situation, the media is the explosive device. You may be on the verge of investigating an event of worldwide importance, capable of exploding headlines. If you get careless with the media and don't think carefully through every question and the implications of your responses, the event reporting will blow up in your face. Nobody goes solo with the media; every request for a response is considered by the entire leadership of the Unified Command.

"I also envision the tightest lid possible by everyone involved to control the amount of information released. Information is parsed out in measured quantities. No speculation, just reports of progress that has been achieved, documented, and analyzed.

"To that end, I can see a three-pronged investigation: one where the military and intelligence branches take full command of the investigation of the potential of terrorism; a completely separate effort where the military enlists the cooperation of other agencies and resources to investigate the potential of corporate and industrial saboteurs; and last, one that continues to pursue the 'accident potential.'"

"Well said. What does everyone else think about Mr. Taylor's suggestion?" Commander Hughes asked.

Coast Guard's Commander Brockington chimed in: "I think Mr. Taylor's advice and division of labor makes a lot of sense. I'm in."

Eli was now on a roll. He next suggested, "If there is a consensus on the approach, then you need to quickly formulate your talking points for your first Unified Command briefing, coming up in forty-five minutes, and the press briefing that follows immediately thereafter. I have some suggestions how you might want to bring up the potential sabotage angle and what to say in answer to the most likely questions."

"Go ahead, Eli. You have our undivided attention," Commander Hughes said.

Eli looked around the room and saw the eyes of receptive minds. Had he not been able to detect support, he would have solicited other viewpoints. However, he felt he had a green light, so he proceeded—full steam ahead.

"It is my experience with the media that you use the approach that you are not ruling out any potentials. You mention the difficulty of making much progress because the continuing fire prevents a closer examination that is required. You also mention you are proceeding on all angles that are not precluded by the blaze. Before they ask, I suggest you tell them you are investigating mechanical failure, human error, sabotage, and terrorism as potential causes.

"Next, you say that it is too early to draw any conclusions on any investigative front. If asked what evidence you have so far, you should respond with something like, 'Our efforts are ongoing, as we are still very early in this process. The evidence we are finding is varied, incomplete, and difficult to interpret. It would be premature to determine what might be meaningful evidence and what might be inconsequential. Until we are confident of what we have, we will withhold revealing these items until it is prudent to release them.

"You may also mention that these investigations will have to be conducted with care and diligence, and therefore, you expect to be providing details as they are confirmed over the next couple of weeks."

Eli continued, "In our industry, we always expect the press to be unfriendly and suspicious. We never let our guard down on sincerity. We always try to be kind and respectful, even to the dumb, clumsy, and downright mean questions. If you do it right, they will understand you are being thoughtful with what you share with them and the public. If you don't, your words will be remembered forever and live in infamy."

Lemay interjected, "I certainly wouldn't say anything more than what you are suggesting. We need to maintain confidentiality and let everyone else know that we intend to vigorously protect that confidentiality. Also, I am grateful to have a contributor as skilled as Mr. Taylor and his team; however, we have to draw the line of that confidentiality between us and the private sector, including his firm. I envision his firm as a contributor in strict conformance to the assignments it is given. That being said, the members of his firm should see only a partial picture of the entire investigation."

Commander Hughes responded curtly, "That is a given, Lieutenant. Mr. Taylor and his firm are aware of how the game is played."

Lemay replied, "I meant no ill will. I suppose I could have said it a little more diplomatically. I just wanted to make sure there was no misunderstanding."

"No harm, no foul," Eli said.

Commander Hughes looked at his watch. "OK then, if you all will excuse me. I need to prepare for the briefings. You may carry on without me."

Commander Hughes asked Faith to stick around and help him with his statement. Eli heard his request and nodded favorably. Eli and the rest of his team got ready for the briefing, and when Faith joined them, they had a planning session.

When they broke up, Vic pulled Eli aside and said, "That NCIS lieutenant is quite the prick!"

"Maybe, maybe not. He is just more turf sensitive than the rest of them."

"Politics!" Vic asserted. "I see the military hasn't changed since Desert Storm."

Eli said, "That's just the way we have to play it. It's their show, and they want to be calling all the shots. We've got to get used to the idea that the sabotage issue will be in their domain and that we'll only know what they want us to know."

"Not so fast," Vic interrupted. "That NCIS data expert they sent to investigate the systems angle is going to need a pipeline systems and supervisory systems specialist before they make any headway on their data at their James River Control Center. We need to be the ones supplying the specialists. That just might be our best and fastest way to get a look at the process. That will be the path to identify the people behind the sabotage."

"I think you're right. That's the ticket! Who do we know?" Eli asked.

Vic thought for a moment and then remembered a guy who had spoken at the American Pipeline Institute conference a couple of years back.

"Eli, what about that guy who recently retired from the Mitchell Companies? He was on the original IBM team that worked with industry IT specialists to develop the early product-movement programs."

"Yeah, I remember him. I have some contacts at Mitchell. I'll call them as soon as it's eight a.m. in Oklahoma."

When Eli called Mitchell's office, their human resources folks figured out that the guy he was looking for had to be Mark Rogoff. They gave Eli his contact info. By midmorning, Eli had spoken to Mr. Rogoff. Without too much pleading, Rogoff was on his way to the Portsmouth Holiday Inn.

7. HALLOWEEN LEFTOVERS

THAT EVENING, AFTER EATING THE REMAINDER OF THE CANDY gleaned from trick or treating, tucking in his son into bed, and reading Goodnight Moon for the umpteenth time to his three-year-old daughter, Brian Matusak went to his basement office and pulled out the copy he had made of the IDIQ memo. On his home computer, he utilized search engines to try to figure out how the commodity-trading energy-supply markets worked. The pickings were slim. He became more frustrated than informed. He decided he needed to talk to someone who understood the business. Brian didn't directly know someone, but he knew someone who could find him an expert. That guy was a personal friend who worked with Enron before its demise. Enron had authored the encyclopedia on trading energy commodities before its house of cards collapsed.

It was 7:30 p.m. in Denver when Brian's friend picked up the phone. He gave Brian two names he thought might help him. One was a woman in Houston who was working for a small investment broker. She sounded the most promising. Alan told him she was recently divorced and living alone. She was very loquacious and always eager to help him.

It wasn't too late in Houston, so he gave her a call. His luck continued. Not only was she home, but she sounded genuinely interested in helping him out. She said she hadn't had a client who wanted to make an energy play in the commodities market for a day or two, and she was hungry for any type of conversation about her specialty.

It was her assertion that the oil futures market was heavily influenced by the big players and politics. Only the real pros, who were hooked up with politicians and energy ministers of foreign countries, could play at such high stakes and rarely get burned. The other energy products were less influenced by politics and foreign countries. And when you got further away from the raw material, like refined gasoline or aviation kerosene, there was even less influence. She was regretful that his interest wasn't in natural gas, because that was where she excelled.

However, she was familiar with NAPCO, and she admitted that she and the rest of the industry were surprised when it won the bid on the 2006 Navy supply contract. She said there were a lot of disappointed big shots, including BP-Amoco, Exxon-Mobil, and Chevron. But that disappointment subsided quickly when NAPCO contacted all the major bidders and promised to enhance their sales revenue with purchases of their products.

"Why were the major oil companies so surprised when NAPCO won the bid?" Brian asked.

"There were a lot of reasons. For one thing, they were surprised that NAPCO qualified to be on the bid list. I think they were shocked to find out just how much business NAPCO was doing. They also were surprised NAPCO had the cash reserves."

Brian's source continued with several more reasons, but it was clear that a lot of what she provided was speculation or opinion. Brian steered her to what he thought was the education he needed most—how to verify the original supplier of the product delivered.

She laughed out loud. "When you find out, I would appreciate you returning the favor! I'd like to know that myself."

Brian got her refocused and asked if she could get closer or narrow it down to a few scenarios.

"Sure. I've done that myself a few times. Here's the deal. When you are dealing with a marketer like NAPCO that refines little or no product themselves, they are buyers first. And it's for this reason I'm surprised they got qualified to bid on a major Defense Department contract. They had to have some impressive insurance and contracts already in hand."

"Who were they with?"

"Quite frankly, the word on the street was that the insurance was not with a regular player, and the contracts were from foreign sources that could ship refined product into the Gulf Coast. That left out only a few candidates due to the US ban on suppliers that were not friendly, yet big enough to handle the volumes requested. When it was discovered the contracts were with Mexico's COMEX, there was genuine surprise. The explanation that made the rounds was that the United States was courting the Mexican government on several political initiatives including illegal aliens, drug trafficking, and arms smuggling. I remember deducing that the State Department might have asked DOD to roll out the red carpet. NAPCO just got lucky they had the right supplier. That made their acceptance on the bid list a political bonanza for the State Department.

"However, we were all surprised that Mexico could afford to export so much refined product, considering its domestic needs. Then the speculation on the street was that COMEX might be the middleman in the deal instead of the supplier. And that is where it gets difficult and complicated. Suppose NAPCO was only using COMEX to launder refined oil from a supplier that was not on the US list of approved suppliers. If that's the case, how is anyone going to find out? Since Mexico would be involved in the scam, certainly it would be unlikely that it would come clean.

"If you want to know that kind of information, you will need to find someone who can determine if COMEX is receiving refined shipments in volumes from a supplier that is not on the US approved list."

"Do you know if there is such an expert?"

"I am sure there is, but I don't know of any offhand. Do you want me to try to find one for you?"

"It sounds like I won't be able to come up with a verifiable analysis without one. Yeah, sure."

"Since there is so little activity in my end of the market right now, I could spend a little time finding you the right source."

"I would appreciate that very much. You are very kind."

"You caught me at the right time. I'm usually not this easy."

The lady energy trader called back the next day. It was an evening call, and Brian had to do a lot of explaining to his wife about who the lady with the sexy voice was. He offered to let her listen in if she wanted. She declined.

"I've got your man," the energy trader asserted. "He's a little weird, but I understand he's one of the few people in the business who keep up with such things. His name is Friedrich Olms. He was a huge player for Dutch Shell back in the day. He went out on his own a few years ago. He made some huge scores early, but recently he's lost some big-time money, but not his friends. He is now a consultant in London. I can e-mail you the information I have."

"Thanks a million. I don't know if I can ever repay you, but if anything comes up and you might need someone in the GAO, give me a chance to see what I can do."

"You bet," she said as they said their goodbyes.

The next morning, Brian received Friedrich Olms's contact information and called him from home before he left for work. It was afternoon in London. Olms was not in, so he left a message.

A day later, Olms returned his call. He was very suspicious about the connection and inquiry. Brian felt it was best to lay all the cards on the table and let the chips fall where they may. That was what opened the door, and Brian learned more than he expected. Friedrich Olms made a connection that Brian did not anticipate.

"I was wondering if I was ever going to hear of an investigation into NAPCO," said Olms.

"This is not an official investigation. I am just trying to understand what's going on."

"It may not be one now, but if you are contacting me, it won't be long."

"Why is that so?"

"My man, let me explain. There are several producers who were blindsided by the award of that contract. I think I know what happened. I never had the time to verify it, and I didn't have the motivation to make time. But you just gave it to me. I'm going to tell you now what I expect I will find. It should take me a couple of weeks to verify it."

"And?"

"And the real supplier of NAPCO products will turn out to be none other than PETGO Oil in Venezuela."

"Really?"

"Yes, my man. I swear, I will find you proof of the honest answer, but don't be surprised if I guessed correctly. I can't explain now why I think it's them. This is going to be enjoyable."

"Why do you say so?"

"My word, the business I will get from the rest of industry when word gets out that I played an instrumental part in reining in NAPCO."

"I can't afford to have the word get out before I finish my report."

"We will try our best. But in this business—at these stakes—it's almost impossible to prevent it. However, if you are not in a position to take the heat, you need to call it off now."

"What do you mean by 'take the heat'?"

"There will be attempts by the interested parties to contain your investigation and use damage-control tactics. PETGO is on the short list of energy suppliers the United States has banned from doing business with its governmental agencies. If your investigation has not reached the highest levels of your agency, the Department of Justice, and perhaps your FBI, PETGO operatives have been known to intervene and erase evidence before it reaches US law enforcement. That means your life might be in jeopardy if they find you before the investigation matures. PETGO has a reputation for using extreme measures to discourage whistleblowers. The FBI can take the heat, and PETGO will usually back off. If it's a lesser person in a lesser capacity doing the snooping, PETGO's means of damage control usually means that heads will roll."

"Are you serious?"

"I'm afraid so. These guys are ruthless when it comes to loose ends."

"Well, that changes things. I just began a preliminary investigation. I've got a long way to go before it reaches the levels you are suggesting."

"I dare say! Until then, it might be best to drop it. If you don't, someone might come looking for you. However, if you take my recommendation and hand it off to your FBI, you may have their investigator get back to me. Now, listen close to what I say—once you have moved this up the ladder, you need to remove your name from the information stream. And if I were you, I wouldn't take credit for uncovering it until it's all over."

"Thank you, Friedrich. By the way, I was expecting a Dutch accent. You sound entirely British."

"I have dual citizenship. I was born in the Netherlands but was schooled in Britain. During most of my employment with Shell, my office and home were in London.

"If I don't hear from you in a week or so, may I contact you? I might want to delve into this matter on my own if you have dropped your interest in it."

"That sounds fair. If I can't push this up and far away from me by then, I will drop it and try to eliminate any mention of my name in the record. After that, I don't care what you do."

"Then that's the way we will leave it. Take care."

Brian hung up, but his brain remained in high gear, contemplating everything he had learned. He knew the saying "curiosity killed the cat," but he had never really thought it could be applied to him, literally. He was at a crossroads. He loved the intrigue of this investigation, and he imagined the reward would be substantial if he found what Olms predicted. Before he went forward on the matter, he knew he had to figure out a method of advancing the audit without anyone knowing he was the guy pushing it.

Maybe, he thought, there is a way to skin this cat before curiosity kills it.

8. JUST ANOTHER DAY AT THE CAPITOL

TUESDAY AFTERNOON, NOVEMBER 7, 2006

JUST DOWN THE ROAD, ABOUT 195 MILES FROM CRANEY ISLAND, sitting in a hallway just outside the House Committee on Foreign Affairs, was lobbyist Sam Nugent of the law firm of Bennett, Bancroft, and Sperling. He was waiting for the adjournment of the Subcommittee on Terrorism, Nonproliferation, and Trade. Sam was wearing his navy pinstriped suit, white shirt, and yellow tie. At forty years of age, tanned, handsome, and fit, he looked like the poster boy for Washington lobbyists. The hallways of the capitol building glowed in an ecru eggshell aura as the florescent lighting reflected off the marble walls and gilded ceiling. The heavy, wooden committee room doors opened at approximately 2:30 p.m. Among those leading the parade to the next committee meeting was Republican Congressman Christopher Findley of Montana.

Sam Nugent stood up and joined the throng down the hallway, positioning himself alongside Findley.

"Not now, Sam. Not here. Catch me after the energy caucus," Findley admonished quietly as he put on his camera face to meet the three reporters patiently waiting behind the roped hallway intersection up ahead.

Nugent slowed and merged into the mass of stragglers behind the pack of congressmen. As chairman of the committee, and leader of the pack, Findley stopped to greet the reporters.

Findley waited for the camera backlight to reposition on him and then made a brief comment: "I can't say much at this juncture, but it looks like we might have a new antiterrorism bill soon. I'm late for the House majority briefing, so I can't give you more than that right now. Our committee will reconvene shortly thereafter and then give its report to the full CFA committee. If all goes as expected, we will take care of any housekeeping chores, and the CFA committee chair will give you his press release. At that time, we can sit for questions."

Matthew Berg, a reporter from the New York Times, asked, "When will that be, Congressman?"

"Immediately after the energy caucus," Findley replied.

With that remark, the throng of congressmen and staffers continued its march down the hallway behind the ropes and away from the reporters. Sam Nugent didn't follow. Instead, he found another row of chairs along the hallway and pulled out his cell phone. He made two calls advising his associates of the recent developments. Sam really didn't need Findley's report now that he had heard what he told the reporters. He could tell his client that the first ingredient to give the president more latitude to react to threats of terrorism was now in play.

At this point in Sam Nugent's career, he had fought so many of these battles he no longer cared about the issues as a matter of personal choice. He was numb to any meaning beyond winning or losing.

Two more congressmen were his next targets on the antiterrorism bill effort. Both were members of the Foreign Affairs Committee. One was facing a tough reelection next year, and he needed the campaign contributions his client could provide. So he was probably in the bag.

The other congressman was a professional swing vote. That was his way of feathering his nest. Swing voters got offers from both sides of the aisle. Currently, he was receiving pledges of support offered by the dove side of the issue, led by a lobbyist who represented several entertainers, movie moguls, and television producers. Sam didn't think his side needed the swing vote king to send the bill out of committee, but he was told to stay in the bidding on his vote so he could find out what the other side was offering. This lobbying tactic usually ensured that one could gauge the strength of the other side. If the opposition was not escalating the bidding, it could be assumed they were confident of a win or a loss. In that case, all you had to do was figure out which one it was.

If the bidding was active and escalating, you could be confident that the vote was close to a dead heat. Simply asking the congressmen which way they going to vote and then tallying up the score was never the answer. There were always too many ambiguous answers and lies among the swing voters. And then there were the congressmen who needed a larger campaign war chest. Even though they might have convictions one way or another, they would put their votes up for bidding simply to feather their nests.

The swing voter is the most difficult type of vote a lobbyist faces. Rarely can a lobbyist be successful by simply putting up the best case and argument. Usually, the lawmaker needs the bill rewritten in a way that eliminates his objections. And that's what the lobbyists do. They present rewrites to the lawmakers until they have one that satisfies them.

Just in case Sam read the committee vote wrong, his firm was drafting several rewrites of the bill in case they determined that the swing vote was necessary to get it passed. One thing Sam got out of his bidding was finding out what the lawmaker didn't like about the bill. The rewrites were being readied to be offered to him if a last-minute push was needed.

Sam walked over to the congressman's office. His door was purposely left open so that anyone could see he was being entertained by lobbyists. Sam walked into the reception room so that the congressman could see him. When he did, the congressman subtly nodded. That was the dance lobbyists and lawmakers conducted in silence. Sam's peek into the office was his sign that he was still competing for the congressman's vote, and the congressman's nod was acknowledgment that he was still in play and that he would let him know if anything changed.

This was the cat-and-mouse game played every day when the House was in session. This was just one of several bills Sam's firm was chasing this session. Sam didn't know it, but it was the most important bill of the entire session. He also didn't know that it was the most important bill his firm would ever handle. The only thing Sam knew was that he was one of three lobbyists from his firm working the same bill. The other two had their own set of congressmen with similar duties. In all his years as a lobbyist, Sam had never worked a bill with more than one other lobbyist from his firm, and that was a senior partner. And the senior partner rarely visited the capitol building. Sam wondered, "What's so special about this one?"

9. THE CAPITOL BEAT

MATTHEW BERG HAD BEEN WORKING THE CAPITOL BEAT FOR THE New York Times for three years. He still wasn't the lead columnist or an on-air reporter. However, he was a sound journalist who had the respect of his colleagues and the lawmakers he followed. He was sincerely puzzled by Congressman Findley's remark that a new antiterrorism bill was in the works. He was aware that it was on the committee's agenda, but he had no idea it was on the move.

After Congressman Findley walked by and gave his remarks, Matthew's eyes caught those of Congresswoman Debra Schuster from New Jersey, a Democrat, as she followed the pack walking down the hall. She put her hand to the side of her head with her thumb and pinky finger extended. Matthew nodded and pulled out his cell phone. A quick search of her number in memory and a press of a button were all that was needed. There was no greeting when the Congresswoman answered.

"I've got ninety seconds before I'm in chambers again. The entire Democratic contingent was blindsided by this one. The subcommittee was in its third round of review on this agenda item. However, after a brief discussion, the chair called for a vote. A quick raise of hands, and it was over. That was probably the fastest I've ever seen a bill get sent out of this subcommittee."

"Where is the push coming from? Is it the White House?"

"Search me. Catch me later in the day. All of us on the other side of the vote will be asking the same questions of our colleagues. If you can get a congressman from the other side of the aisle or, better yet, an insider supporting the bill, to identify a likely source, we can have a private, off-the-record chat that might lead to who that party might be. Got to go now. I'm entering my next meeting room."

Matt's phone indicated she had ended the call. He had other bills and congressmen on his agenda, but they would have to wait for a while. His nose was on full alert. There was a story here, and he wanted to be the first to get it.

After he got the comments from Congressman Findley, Matt called his political editor. Like newspapers all around the world, the New York Times was being squeezed by readers using the Internet for their daily dose of news. However, the New York Times was more plugged into politics than ever.

"Good morning, Matt. You never call unless your nose itches and you can't scratch it. What's going on?"

"A new antiterrorism bill just came out of committee, and it's on its way to Foreign Affairs. Congresswoman Schuster told me it caught her by surprise. Just about the entire Congress is in meetings at this moment, so I was wondering if you had heard who might be driving this bill."

"That's supposed to be your job, Matt."

"Yeah, we know that. But this came out of nowhere. It's been an agenda item and tabled for so long that it was presumed to be there as window dressing to prove otherwise to anyone who accused them of forgetting about it. I expect to catch up with her later in the day. She expects me to be able to shed some light on the matter. I was hoping you might have picked up some party conversation recently that might have sounded innocuous at the time."

"Come to think of it, I did. It was at the social before the planning session for the annual White House Correspondents' Dinner I attended last week. I overheard someone asking the vice president if the White House was going to do anything this year in light of the continuous attacks by lone terrorists acting in the United States. Normally, I would never remember this type of talk except for his answer, which surprised me. Instead of the usual canned reply, he got rather worked up and said, 'If it were up to me, I'd have something in the works.' It sounded a little ominous, and I meant to run it by you."

Matthew pondered the landscape this bill was traveling. A high-ranking GOP congressman takes a bill off the shelf that has been gathering dust and ties a rocket to its ass. The opposition party has no idea why the bill is moving, or they won't say. Findley, the bill's sponsor, is only giving a vague, general explanation that antiterrorism needs are still not being met. The guts of the bill give the president broader powers to direct resources and defensive measures when a threat has been identified.

On the surface, pretty simple stuff. Then why all the mystery?

Matthew's imagination was pretty good, but there just weren't enough clues yet. He had to figure out a way to shake something loose.

10. SORTING THINGS OUT

2100 HOURS, WEDNESDAY, NOVEMBER 9, 2006

THANK HEAVENS FOR ALARM FUNCTIONS IN CELL PHONES. WITHout the alarm, Eli certainly would have slept through his next shift. It was 9:00 p.m., an unfortunate time to start a new shift. As groggy as he was, Eli had to smile at his condition. He awoke fully dressed and sporting a two-day old beard. He was tempted not to shave, but it occurred to him that he was on a military base, and the military still frowned on the unshaven. Eli was also thankful that he remembered to reset his alarm three hours past normal shift change to account for the three hours his shift had overrun the night before.

As bad as motel coffee was, Eli began brewing before he stepped into the shower. On his way out the door, he checked his cell phone for text messages. As he began to read the response updates, it rang and nearly scared him half to death. Vic wanted to tell him he was outside Mike's hotel room. He had met Rogoff, the IT guy, earlier and had driven him to the Navy's Richmond Control Center.

Vic called Mike, but he didn't answer. As he suspected, Mike was so tired he had slept through his alarm or had forgotten to set it. They banged on his door until he opened it.

"Damn, you look bad," Vic announced.

"Sorry, guys. I guess I haven't figured out this shift thing quite yet."

"Do you have a vehicle?" Vic asked.

Mike looked out into the parking lot. "Yeah, I think that white Chevy is my rental. Hold on—let me see if I have car keys."

Mike retreated into his room and announced he did have the keys.

"OK, old man," Vic announced. "We're heading to the Unified Command. We'll catch up with you there."

Thankfully, it was a quiet evening at the Unified Command. The fire at the fuel depot was still burning. While they had been sleeping, the fire-fighting crews got inside the facility, where they were applying foam fire retardant from ground-based trucks. Eli's cell phone rang, and the voice of a weary Hank Fisher in Atlanta started with an apology about any difficulty he might be having while giving his report because of lack of sleep.

"Eli, when you first dreamed up the idea of resurrecting the Charleston Texaco terminal to replace Craney Island, I thought you were joking. I didn't want to say it then, but I thought it was impossible. Well, I think it's going to happen. You were right about it being mothballed but not impossible to make operational. I borrowed a couple of retired operators from Confederated Pipe Line, and we fired up the pumps and let her run for four straight hours. I swear it ran as well as any West terminal. The delivery line to the terminal was left intact and filled with fuel oil, and as soon as we get the EPA go-ahead, we'll start pressurizing the lines and push some product into the tanks. The holding tanks might be a slight issue. They were really rusted on the outside, and the insides had more water in them than we would have liked. However, the tank steel is sound and greater than the minimum wall thickness specifications. Late yesterday, we found an EPA-approved environmental disposal company willing to remove the water and dispose of the waste. If all goes well, I think it's possible we can have an operating facility by 1800 hours tomorrow."

"How about the harbor?"

"Clean Harbor arrived at noon. I'm due a report from them sometime in the morning. They have been testing the old Texaco off-loading equipment. They ordered a bunch of new fittings, hoses, and piping. On short notice, you can't ever find new stuff that happens to fit just right, but we got lucky. A convoy of eighteen-wheelers arrived tonight from BP's Baton Rouge terminal with everything we ordered. BP won't need what they sent us for quite some time. It just so happens their expansion plans that were the target for the parts have been on hold for months due to permit problems. They have agreed to give up what was warehoused there for the cost to reorder them. It's actually is going to save BP a ton of cash. They had run out of storage space and were about to lease space at a nearby yard and erect a metal building just to store the idle parts. Also, they get a break on the time value of money. Now everybody is happy."

"Too much information, Hank. So what is your assessment?"

"Well, I felt good enough to tell the East Coast Navy Fleet Commander that he could start to redirect all refueling vessels to Charleston to arrive by sometime Friday."

"That's less than forty-eight hours!"

"Pretty impressive, huh?"

"Do you actually believe that you can install all the off-loading fittings before then?"

"I've got Hiram Askew's promise."

"You got Askew on the job?"

"We had to pay him double to take a week off at Explorer to head it up. But I have not seen him this excited about work in years. He met the trucks in Charleston when they arrived here today. Hiram, his crew, and Bradley Brothers are working around the clock to get it done. I would never have imagined this was possible, but I think we will make my prediction to the fleet commander. I gave him my estimate for how much it would all cost, and he didn't flinch. I guess when it's the nation's defense on the line, the price tag is irrelevant."

"I told you we didn't need to worry about the costs. They just want to get it done. How about the rerouting of the product?"

"Sorry, I guess I got too excited telling you about the terminal. Provincial didn't like giving Confederated the tariff revenue from Atlanta to Craney, but they did it for the sake of national security. Confederated has had excess capacity on its Atlanta-to-Charleston line ever since the Texaco terminal went off-line. They are eating the cost to reactivate the idle delivery line from their delivery facility to the Texaco terminal. They tested it yesterday, and it held up. That means the reroute is pipeline ready."

"I am impressed. Call me if you run into any snags. I've got to go now. The team is waiting around for our briefing."

Eli checked with Faith, who was putting together her script. She was expecting to be interviewed.

"Do you have a moment?" Eli asked her.

"Yeah, I think I'm ready for the press," she responded.

"Any news on the systems analysis with Rogoff?"

"That guy is amazing. Mack Joyner is with him at the control center. Mack called me about eight thirty and told me that Rogoff has found a couple of major irregularities. He is data mapping it out now and should be here soon. I am not mentioning it to the press. If asked, I am saying that we are looking into the data for evidence of malfunction, but that we have yet to find any evidence of that so far. Which, of course, is accurate."

"Anything else worthy of note?"

"I don't think so. I haven't heard from any of your intelligence buddies. Our agenda for the news briefing does not mention that mission."

"OK. But before I get out of your hair, you need to know that Hank promised the Navy that the substitute terminal in Charleston will be operational and ready to fuel the fleet within forty-eight hours."

Faith had no idea how remarkable that was. She simply wrote it down in her notes to announce when it was her time to give a report. The two of them left to find a seat in the press tent.

The briefing went off without a hitch. The big emphasis from the reporters was the uncertainty of how the Navy was making do with supplying its demands now that its busiest loading facility that was out of commission. Faith responded with a report that the Navy had a contingency backup ready to be online within forty-eight hours. She didn't say anything about Daneli being instrumental in making that happen. She allowed the Navy to take the credit for it. That pleased the Navy, and it put Daneli in better graces with its command. Faith was a very savvy lady.

***

After the press briefing, Eli and his team retreated to the Command Center. Mark Rogoff, their newly found IT expert, was awaiting them there. Eli found him to be quite different from what he expected. He was a good-natured, charming guy with a gift for conversation. He introduced himself when they entered.

"It's so good to meet you all. To be honest, I never heard of you guys before you called me. When I asked around, all I heard was good things. I want to thank you for permitting me to be a part of this most interesting assignment. I bet you're anxious to learn what I have found so far. Do you want me to get right to it?"

"Please do," Eli replied.

"As you probably know, the sequencing and timing of pipeline events are very important to safe and reliable product movements. When things have gone wrong over the years, it has been very important for the industry to determine whether mechanical devices, systems operation, or human error was the cause of these events. This level of importance created the need to add self-monitoring systems that would provide a record that would tell how, why, and when things occurred.

"When I reviewed the monitoring of this event, the first thing I examined was the logs of the controllers from the pipeline operator to the recipient of the delivery. I looked to see if all the commands matched the conditions on the ground. I found the flow of product was commanded to make deliveries at the receiving facilities that matched the written orders as to volume and timing. Since they matched, I looked at the next level of commands. In this case, the delivery matched, but we needed to know whether it was directed to the correct tank.

"At first I found no inconsistencies. The data said that tank seven was set up to receive aviation kerosene and that it had sufficient capacity to receive the entire batch to be delivered. But since we know this could not be true and that this tank was nearly full at the time of the incident, I looked into the timing of the entries of the commands. It is here where I found things that were askew. The entry log showed that the commands to direct the delivery to tank seven were made at three different times.

The first was made about thirty hours before the actual delivery was scheduled, and the other two were at ten minutes before the delivery commenced, and then about twenty-five minutes after the delivery commenced.

"After that process, I examined the nomination map. It did not indicate that any changes to the delivery needed to be made on the day of the delivery. Therefore, I suspected the commands entered then might be telling.

"When the industry devised the self-monitoring system, it was intended to create a record to show how the flow of product was directed. A document trail would be created that would indicate if the operator was trying to cover up its command errors by going into the data files and writing over operating mistakes. The motive for a company doing this is to attempt to escape liability. However, just like written-over data on a PC hard drive, you can recover commands, entries, and data that are altered.

"In this instance, I found tampering. Whoever had access to the system the day of the event replaced the amount of actual volume in tank seven to an amount that was much lower. On the surface, it appeared that tank seven had sufficient capacity when it didn't. The next rewrite made tank seven overflow when it directed the delivery to that tank. The same operator also disabled one of the high-level alarms. The second set of revisions, made after the spill, were designed to hide the fact these commands were given. The monitoring also provides the location of the terminal at which the rewrites were made. In this case, they were made from the terminal inside the Craney Island control room. So far, this only gives us answers to the what and how questions. We are still missing the why.

"I then wondered, 'Why would the operator deliberately overflow a tank?'"

Eli interjected, "Maybe it wasn't he who did it. Remember when I said the answer will be in the details? If you think about how a trained employee would perform his duties, it doesn't make sense that one would have done it. Let me tell you why. Every operator knows about the monitoring and how many alarms are on its tanks. He would know the system would show it was his terminal that made the overwrites. His virtual fingerprints would be all over the place. Also, if he wanted to disable the alarms, he would have disabled both of them, not just one. That part only makes sense if we are looking at someone expert in the programming of deliveries, but not in the safety operations of a terminal.

"And last," Eli continued, "What would have been the operator's motive? What this sounds like to me is we have a perpetrator from outside the current Navy organization who has knowledge of systems before modern monitoring was introduced and before the Navy revamped its high-tank alarms to a dual-alarm system. Mark, when did such improvements become the standard?"

Rogoff replied, "The monitoring began in the late 1980s, but the military-run facilities didn't start to implement their own until about 1991. As for dual high-tank alarms, we started to write them into our programming in the early 1990s. Again, the military lagged behind private industry. I don't think it implemented its until the mid-1990s. So, following your lead, it appears we have a programmer who only has knowledge of your systems from before 1990. I would say that we can rule out that it was an inside job."

"You are so right, Mark," Eli responded. "The story is in the little details about the actions executed by the perpetrator. A trained pipeline employee would not have overlooked this kind of detail."

Mike wanted to get at the big picture. "Now, let me get this straight. We have a saboteur who is knowledgeable about the Craney Island facility to the point that he knows where to enter to be undetected. He also knows to remove the videotape from the security console and how to reprogram the product movement and how to overwrite it. He does this undetected in a span of a half hour or so. However, his planning information didn't reflect modifications made in the last ten years."

"That how I see it," Eli commented. "And I bet we'll find the murdered bodies of the operator and utility if they are not completely incinerated."

Mike then jumped up. "I have got to tell the NCIS to treat the scene as a murder investigation. If you are right, I bet the operator's and utility's bodies are out there on the facility property. We have got to try to find their bodies and any evidence of how they were killed. I'll be back in a couple of minutes."

Mike didn't wait for anyone's reaction. He just ran out of the Unified Command and headed for the equipment shed that had been converted to investigating agencies' headquarters.

They all got a little chuckle out of Mike's reaction. But Vic wasn't interested in anything but solving the mystery of who and why.

"OK, OK, everybody. I'm trying to think. So our perps are knowledgeable up to a time before 1990 or so. That just doesn't make any sense. Why even try a cover-up if you aren't going to do it right? My Lord, the monitoring programming and the dual-alarm systems have not been a secret. For Christ's sake, it's written in the current regulation of best practices."

"I think we are ignoring the obvious," Eli chimed in. "These perps do not care if the investigation discovers the cover-up. We must ask ourselves why they aren't worried. I have some thoughts, but I'd like to hear your ideas."

Mack Joiner, Daneli's failure-analysis expert, entered the discussion. "If you read enough mystery novels, you suspect that the fire and the cover-up are only a ruse—a red herring. That would make the fire only a diversion."

"Hold on!" Mark Rogoff shouted. "I think I might have an idea. When I queried the monitoring program to list the write-overs, the ones near the time of the accident involving Craney Island and its deliveries were the ones I focused on. However, I noticed many other orders to other DOD facilities throughout the country that were also modified. If I wanted to throw someone off the right track and create a diversion, I would write one set of orders for the diversion and then write another set at a different time for the orders I wanted to hide. I would also write some that were dead ends to confuse the analysts and divert their attention."

"So how long would it take to figure out what they were tying to hide?" Eli asked.

Mark replied, "That might not be so easy. I need some sleep to really figure it out, but I would say I should be able to find out in about a week."

"I'm afraid that the military will not accept an entire week for researching. Would it help if we added analysts to work around the clock?"

"Yeah, but they would have to have pipeline programming experience."

"If I got the authority to add a couple more, do you think you could find them and get them here by tomorrow morning?"

Rogoff thought for a moment and then said, "I know of one I could get here tomorrow morning, but finding others will take some persuasion. These guys work full-time for pipeline clients, so you'd have to offer them some big bucks to take time off to come here."

"That shouldn't be too hard to arrange. You call the one you can get here by morning and tell him you will call him back in a short while after we get the authority to add him. Meanwhile, I will be trying to get that authority."

Before Eli could find Commander Hughes, he found Mike talking excitedly with Lieutenant Lemay, who was back from his sleep shift.

Mike saw Eli approaching and asked, "Eli, I told the lieutenant of the murder potential, but he says his men are already on it. He also says that I am not needed, and he won't grant me access to the facility."

"Don't sweat it, Mike. I'm sure the lieutenant and his men can get it right. Follow me."

Mike rose from his seat and said, "If you will excuse us, Lieutenant."

Lieutenant Lemay gave Mike a mock military salute and smiled. Commander Hughes was still on sleep shift, and USCG Commander Brockington was in charge. Since he was the investigation leader on duty, Eli asked him for permission to add the extra analysts and explained why he thought they would be necessary. Brockington called FBI Chief Frank Gilbert, who conferred with his NSA, CIA, and Homeland Security colleagues. In a matter of forty-five minutes, Daneli had approval.

Eli told Rogoff. He called Richard Dugan, a colleague from his days as a consultant. Dugan agreed to join the Craney Island investigation.

Vic needed to get back on other response duties, leaving Mike, Faith, and Eli.

Faith asked, "How many responses have you had in Virginia?"

"Why?" Eli replied.

"It appears the reporters figured out that you were previously at West Industries, and now you're the CEO of Daneli. They have deduced that you must be here, somewhere on the island. They all want to talk to you. It's like I'm chopped liver, and you're filet mignon. I told them that you were busy."

"You did the right thing. Just tell them we have no role that involves being interviewed unless the Unified Command wants it. All such inquiries need to go through the Unified Command. And to answer your question, this incident is my fourth response in Virginia in the past ten years. In those incidents, media relations came under my supervision, and I was the company spokesperson and government liaison. Tell them I wish them well, but I will not be commenting on this matter unless I'm told to do so by Hughes or Brockington."

"Will do. Getting back to our investigation, what do you think the system analysts will find?"

"I have no idea, but I have a strong hunch it will answer the who part of the equation."

The two of them brainstormed for a while, speculating why someone would go to such lengths to alter fuel shipment records and then cover up their alterations. Eli was completely baffled.

***

Meanwhile, out on Craney Island, the NCIS was on the cool side of the lone tank that was still burning. They were combing the charred grounds of the tank farm for clues and evidence. The wind was blowing toward the open sea, allowing closer access to the area between tank seven and the control building. There must have been twenty to thirty investigators searching in a grid-like pattern, wearing fire-fighting protection gear. One of the investigators shouted that he'd found something. Lieutenant Lemay was summoned. The investigator was pointing at a bullet's shell casing lying on the ground. They photographed it and the surrounding area. Lemay took a pen from his pocket, inserted one end into the casing, and lifted it up. Another investigator offered a plastic evidence bag. They placed the casing in the bag and labeled it.

Lemay instructed one of the investigators, "Let's go by the book on this—use strict protocol for chain of custody procedure. Get it catalogued and then carry it personally to the crime lab. I want a full report ASAP."

The wind then shifted dramatically toward the mainland, cutting short the search of the land to the west of the tanks by the NCIS team. Before all the investigators got to the command center, tank seven flared, and an explosion under its floating roof sent the roof and burning fuel toward the retreating investigators. Three of them could not avoid the hurtling mass of steel and burning fuel. Those who could run away did so. The professional firefighters formed a rescue party. They came back with three men on stretchers. Two were conscious, but the other one looked lifeless.

Such are the risks of tank farm fires. A shift in wind can change a contained situation into one of terror. Fire retardant foam being launched on the tank roof had created an uneven tank top surface because the wind had pushed it all to the east half of the roof. When the wind direction changed, oxygen got between the fuel and the roof, creating an explosion-rich mixture of vapor that ignited and exploded.

The investigators unable to avoid the falling debris were rushed from the island to the hospital. The news media gathered quickly in a frenzy, seemingly thrilled to have something exciting to report.

11. RUNNING DOWN THE LEADS

THE NEXT UNIFIED COMMAND MEETING WAS HELD INSIDE THE metal command center building with the doors locked. The time was 0500 hours. There was now a professional videographer recording the Unified Command meetings, and a military photographer was constantly taking shots using flash equipment. The press briefing that followed was held under the main tent, which was located about two hundred feet from the command center. The media onslaught had begun. There had to be at least a couple hundred folks with press badges, cameras, and daylight lighting equipment of all types.

Eli instructed the Daneli members to retreat beyond the notice of the press in case any of them might recognize him or his crew from prior emergency responses. That would be a distraction the military would not want or need.

The meetings went off without a hitch. Half of the Daneli team was sent to the Portsmouth Holiday Inn at 6:00 a.m. for six hours of sleep. After the press briefing that followed, Commander Hughes got a call from his superior, Admiral Conrad Ellingson, who wanted a briefing. That session did not go so well. Hughes came out of his office and sought out Eli.

Upon finding Eli, Hughes whispered to him, "Admiral Ellingson reacted like he was not expecting the sabotage angle. He immediately informed the Joint Chiefs of Staff. I should be hearing their thoughts very shortly. Don't be surprised if more intelligence guys descend upon our little island, and now that we have response casualties, an OSHA team will be joining us."

Eli could only imagine what that might look like. Personnel were already bumping into one another. The Daneli team that was still on duty met at 7:15 a.m. in the parking lot where their vehicles were parked. Eli called Hank Fisher back at the Atlanta office first to see how he was doing on arranging a temporary substitute for the Craney Island terminal.

Hank reported, "It's not easy getting to decision makers in the evening hours. I was persistent, though. Texaco responded favorably to firing up their Charleston facility to help out the Defense Department. Even the Confederate and Provincial pipeline brass were talking about ways to reschedule their product movements to accommodate the DOD and replace the Craney Island volumes with deliveries at Charleston. I actually think everyone is making a serious push to make this happen."

Eli was pumped. Things were going their way, and the team's enthusiasm was pushing away the weariness from the pressure and long hours. Hank's success with the replacement terminal for Craney was impressive. Eli decided to move the meeting off-site to his hotel room and reassembled his team there so they could focus on the sabotage angle.

Vic opened the session with his suspicions about motive and who the perpetrators might be. "Guys, I've got to tell you, there are so many moving parts needed to pull this off. I am having difficulty seeing the terrorist angle. My gut is telling me that there has to be an 'inside the oil patch' element. To get everything arranged just right to make this happen the way it did would take an expert on fuel transportation via pipeline. It's the details. Everything is so precise. Whoever did this was no amateur."

"As usual, you and I are on the same wavelength," Eli interjected.

Mike asked, "If not terrorism, what's the motive?"

Vic responded, "Once we find the motive, we will know who's behind it."

Eli proclaimed, "That's got to be our initial focus. We have got to peel away the obvious clues and look for the oddities. We have to focus on the details of how this scheme was conceived."

At 10:22 a.m., the West Industries RV arrived at the hotel. The West driver was a buddy of Vic's. Vic drove him back to Dorsey, Maryland in his rental vehicle while Faith, Mike, and Eli drove the RV to the Craney Island Unified Command. They were given permission to park it just a few feet from the Unified Command Building. The only issue they had was finding an electrical power outlet that wasn't already overloaded.

While the Daneli team was fiddling with its new office RV and getting ready for the 11:00 a.m. press briefing, representatives from the NSA, FBI, Homeland Security, and CIA arrived at the Unified Command demanding a meeting at 1300 hours. They were sequestered in Commander Hughes's office with the windows now shielded by newly installed curtains. The commander was kind enough to give Eli a heads-up about the meeting before his shift was over. The rest of the Daneli team, including Eli, was scheduled to shut down for six hours of shut-eye at 1200 hours. Vic, Mike, and Eli delayed their sleep shift until after the meeting. Faith was really dragging, so they sent her to the motel to sleep.

News of the heightened profile of the event was kept at a

top-secret level of confidentiality. For that reason, the meeting was moved from Craney Island to the Norfolk Naval Station's Joint Forces building a couple of miles down the road.

The eleven o'clock press briefing went well. Faith and the military PR staff had collaborated well on the talking points, and Commander Hughes and Admiral Ellingson were good at sticking to the script. The real news was that the firefighters were making nice progress with the blaze. They had all but assured everyone that barring an explosion from within the two burning tanks, the blaze was contained, and they were predicting a full extinguish within thirty-six hours.

Mike Hillendorf was watching the news while chewing on a sandwich. West Industries had been kind enough to include lunch for four in the RV's fridge. Mike did the honors of placing it on the RV's all-purpose table while Eli was busy firing up the computers, televisions, and satellite communications. Vic returned from Dorsey at 1215 hours. As they lunched together, they speculated how the meeting with the feds might go. The four TV monitors in the RV were telecasting news from the three major networks and CNN. Mike figured out how to record the shows so they could see them when they returned.

At 1225 hours, the Daneli crew headed over to the naval station. It was a good thing they started out early. The couple of miles distance as the crow flies turned out to be a six-mile drive to the tunnels under the river. There was a traffic backup at the tunnel to Portsmouth, and after passing through two gates, they parked and entered the Joint Forces building at 1251 hours.

The room was set up with nine cafeteria tables arranged in a U-shape. At each table were four chairs. Each table had a pitcher of water and plastic cups. In front of each folding chair at the table was a legal tablet and three sharpened pencils. It looked a little like an SAT test room in high school. All the windows were covered by blinds in the closed position.

Commander Hughes entered from another door, along with four men in suits. To Eli's surprise, the FBI representative was Chief Frank Gilbert from the Baltimore bureau. He made eye contact with Eli and walked over to where he was sitting. Eli stood up to greet him.

"How are you doing, Eli?" Gilbert asked.

"Couldn't be better."

"It's Victor Majeski, isn't it?" Gilbert asked Vic.

"Yes, sir. Good seeing you, sir," Vic responded, as if he were back in the service.

"Chief Gilbert, allow me to introduce our investigation specialist, Mike Hillendorf."

Gilbert turned to Mike and said, "Nice meeting you, Mike. You couldn't have picked better people to work with."

"Thank you, sir. I agree," Mike said.

As they were shaking hands, the other three men in suits approached. Gilbert introduced them as NSA Domestic Antiterror Director Stuart Yarborough, Homeland Security Advisor Derek Trimble, and CIA Counterterror Chief Kent Houck. The fair-skinned ensign at the initial command meeting was there and watching, because as soon as all the handshakes were made, he asked everyone to take a seat so he could begin the meeting. The ensign had placed a lightweight wooden podium to the right of the center cafeteria table. Slightly in front of him sat Commander Hughes. Daneli's new friends at CIA, NSA, Homeland Security, and the FBI took seats bookending the commander.

Along with the three Daneli representatives seated in the meeting were the NCIS and CGIS investigators who had accompanied Vic and Mike on the Craney Island recon. There was an unfamiliar woman sitting next to the NCIS officer. Eli was guessing she was the computer systems analyst who had been sent to look into the James River Control Center data. Also present were Commander Brockington and the NTSB's commander. It was obvious from the appearance of the brass that they were not faring any better on the emergency response shifts than Daneli.

The meeting was being recorded by an enlisted man controlling a cart full of electronic equipment that was plugged into the wall. He was wearing headphones that were wired into the electronics. He was asked if he had run a sound check. The moderator, Ensign Volk, called out, "Testing, one—two—three." The man doing the recording nodded, and the meeting was underway.

Commander Hughes took the podium.

"Outside of a drill, I have never attended one of these. This is our first Craney Island Fuel Depot antiterror briefing."

The commander asked everyone to rise one at a time and announce their names and affiliations, starting with the table to his far right. After everyone complied, Commander Hughes gave Eli credit for urging him to conduct a sabotage investigation of the island's perimeter without delay. He said it had been on his mind, but Eli had convinced him that the safety risk was manageable and that it was outweighed by the benefit of capturing any evidence that might be destroyed if delayed. Eli was very appreciative of the credit, but he had a hunch Hughes was campaigning for Daneli to remain in the investigation.

The commander then recited the details of the recent missions: the perimeter recon and the rescue of the control room's videotape machine sans videocassette. He then turned to the NCIS IT specialist, Sarah Graham. She was somewhat flustered. Maybe it was the magnitude of the event, but it was mostly from her failure to learn anything meaningful from the supervisory control systems at the James River Control Center. In essence, she had nothing to report at the present. The frustration on the face of Homeland Security Advisor Houck was palpable as he tried to pry out of her what the problem was.

After Houck paused for a moment, Eli jumped into the discussion.

"Gentlemen, we anticipated that there was going to be difficulty with an investigation of these systems. Unless you have worked as an IT expert in the pipeline industry for quite a while, you might not be prepared for what you will find. These systems were programmed in the 1960s. They were later layered with modern data systems architecture rather than rewritten. For that reason, I took a chance you might need an expert pipeline programmer. I summoned Mr. Mark Rogoff, our investigative IT consultant. He was one of the original designers of these systems, and he has worked in the industry to diagnose its problems ever since. He has spent some time on the terminal, looking for human error negligence on the part of the operator."

Commander Hughes asked Ms. Graham, "Do you think you could use Mr. Rogoff's consultation?"

"That would be quite beneficial to a swift analysis, Commander," she replied.

Eli glanced over at Ms. Graham and saw an expression of relief.

Houck commented, "It looks like we are going to be stuck with Mr. Taylor's firm for the duration of this investigation."

FBI's Gilbert added to Houck's assessment. "I assure you, gentlemen, being stuck with Eli Taylor and his people can only be a good thing for the investigation. Normally, I wouldn't recommend we go outside the intelligence community for consultation.

Eli Taylor and his company are the exception. I tried to steal him away from the oil industry a couple of years ago to work for me."

Commander Hughes interjected, "Can we accept Daneli Crisis Management Group as a part of this investigation so we can proceed?"

No one objected. Commander Hughes then announced, "Finding no objections, the Daneli Group will remain in the investigation and will be privy to any classified information at the assistant commander grade level."

Commander Hughes did not pause to let in a comment. "Because of Daneli's experience in the industry, they will take the initial lead on the research and data systems, but the FBI will devote agents to join their investigation. And it should also be noted that the Navy will continue to use Daneli as its consultant for overall response of the disaster. That will include many responsibilities other than the industrial sabotage duties of this team.

"Next, I want to focus on our objectives for the next forty-eight hours. The Joint Chiefs want to see real progress by then. My admiral will have to make his report at the end of the forty-eight hours."

Commander Hughes had seized the leadership, authority, and the respect of the gathering. Eli felt confident that it could only be a good thing for the investigation and Daneli's status with the government. They were off to a good start. And now they had to deliver.

One by one, each branch reported its progress and listed its short-term expectations. When it came to Eli's turn, he felt he had good grasp on what he could accomplish, but more importantly, on how Daneli would fit into the entire investigation.

As Eli rose, he cleared his throat and began, "With regard to the information systems, Daneli will assist to unravel the data stream and determine what commands were executed by the automated machinery, when they were executed, and at what terminal. I expect that this process will also provide the best clues as to what entity or entities might be the perpetrators if, in fact, the evidence determines that they contributed to the events to accomplish the sabotage."

Eli concluded his report, saying, "If the sabotage evidence we find is merely a false trail, we will probably find evidence that the incident was either mechanical failure or human error. Either way, we will serve your efforts and objectives and report within the parameters you set."

Eli focused on reading their expressions while delivering his report. It appeared to give everyone some comfort that Daneli would play ball the way the government liked to play it.

The meeting broke directly after Eli's report. He stuck around to take advantage of any socializing opportunity. Gilbert and Eli caught up with each other's lives since their last contact a couple of years ago. They also chatted with the Homeland Security advisor, Houck. Vic and Mike made friends with Ms. Graham, the NCIS IT analyst, and exchanged cards.

As luck would have it, Mark Rogoff called Eli's cell phone as he was driving back from the meeting. It was 2:15, and he was about a couple of hours from the end of his first shift. The two of them then met with NCIS's Sarah Graham at the RV. The rest of team was there, fresh from their sleep shift. Rogoff was certain he could unravel the supervisory data and have something to report within twelve hours after his next shift began.

***

Almost all disaster responses have an unexpected element. And this one was no exception. At approximately 2:30 that afternoon, tank number eight exploded. The concussion was incredible. It rocked the RV and shook up the occupants.

The wind direction changed, and it pushed the flames and heat from tank seven toward other tanks. Although tank eight was covered with flame-retardant foam, the additional heat from tank seven must have turned it into a boiling mixture. And when that occurred, the floating roof let in oxygen. All that was needed was an ignition source. Since the wind was fanning the flames of a nearby tank, burning debris became airborne. In these cases, an explosion is usually the result.

Daneli team members raced out of the RV to look for damage to the RV and command center. Everything was still intact and functional, but the command center's metal wall facing the tanks was now curved and the roof seams were slightly buckled. Some people were knocked off their feet, and a few sat dazed with temporary hearing loss. The battalion of firefighters who previously had been twiddling their thumbs for over a day's time was sent into motion to put out the puddles of burning fuel thrown by the blast.

Luckily, the only injuries reported were from falls and, therefore, were minor. The good news was that most of the remaining product fueling the fire was vaporized by the blast, ensuring a quicker entry for investigation. The other good news was that there wasn't anybody in the press tent at the time. Had there been a press event underway, the casualties might have been severe. The tent was down and burning.

Vic turned to Eli, and with a smirk on his face, he said, "It smells like Bay Town on the San Jacinto. I don't think I'll ever forget that circus. We can't let this one end like that one."

Vic was referring to one of the many disasters he and Eli

worked on together at West Industries, where floodwaters had run so deep and fast that they created a new river channel by gouging out miles of land above the normal high-water mark. In that one, a perfect response execution did them little good. The NTSB had a new chief, and he wanted to make some headlines for himself. He criticized the energy industry for what amounted to just being in the path of a freak "act of God."

It was time for a shift change, and Eli called his wife, Danielle, on the drive back to the motel and gave her a quick rundown of the events of the day. She understood his sleep deprivation, and she assured him that she didn't mind waiting until he had some downtime to carry on a normal conversation. Eli didn't undress before falling asleep, and he didn't remember if the bed was comfortable. He collapsed on his bed in the motel as soon as the door shut behind him.

12. TRUST

BRIAN MATUSAK WAS IN A QUANDARY. IF HE WAS GOING TO CON-
tinue his interest in the NAPCO matter, he was going to have
to trust his department's chief operating officer and the general
counsel. He rationalized that he would proceed with the audit
once he got assurance that the details would be sealed in the attorney's "privileged/confidential" file.

That morning, he made an appointment to see the general
counsel (GC). His secretary demanded he name a reason for the
visit. He chose to mention the investigation of nonqualified bidders for fuel contracts, a choice of words he would regret. He
figured that might pique the GC's interest while omitting NAP-
CO's name from the chain of communication. By 10:15 a.m., he
got a call from the GC's secretary setting a 1:30 p.m. meeting in
their office. That gave him plenty of time to make an outline of
how he wanted to present the matter.

At 1:30, Brian was standing at the desk of Irene Cohen, secretary to Gary French, GAO general counsel. She stepped from
the GC's office and asked him to enter. Gary French introduced
himself as he approached Brian and shook his hand. He asked

him to join him at the cluster of easy chairs surrounding a coffee table to the left of his desk.

Brian sat down and placed his portfolio on the table. He had never been in the GC's office, so he was busy giving it a good look-over. A lot of wood and leather, he thought. As government offices go, it stood out as being decorated much better than most. He wondered if French used his own funds to supplement the typical decoration allowance. Looking at French while he sat down, Brian gathered he was in his mid-forties, maybe six feet tall, and slender. His hair was combed straight back and was an even combination of light brown and gray. In other words, he looked the part of the stereotypical governmental attorney.

"So, Brian, how can I help you today?"

"I've come across an item in my routine audit compliance duties that caught my interest. It's a memo that fell out of the file I was examining, and I found it fascinating at first. I elected to conduct a little research about it, and the more I found out, the more it appeared that I had stumbled onto something that might be a significant violation in the procurement of this year's DOD IDIQ fuels contract."

"You don't say. Do you have a copy of the memo?"

"I do, but before I pass it up to you, I need a written promise of confidentiality under your attorney–client privilege."

French looked at Brian quizzically. He paused, as if his mind were examining a list of possibilities for Brian's demand.

"What led you to become so concerned about confidentiality?"

"I was advised by a research source that I needed to push this to the highest investigative levels of government in anonymity and then get as far away from it as possible. I was told that the likely party of interest is ruthless when it comes to persons looking into the legality of its dealings. He said that this kind of an investigation often backfires if it doesn't reach law enforcement before the party of interest gets wind of it. He said, 'Unless my identity is protected, I might potentially be silenced, permanently.' I chose to start with you because I understand your confidentiality privilege could hide my identity."

Gary French paused, his brain overloading with questions. He thought, Who is this guy? Is he serious? Do I have a crackpot on my hands? And if he is serious, what the hell am I supposed to do?

After French gathered his thoughts, he tried to reply as coolly as he could.

"I see your point. OK, I will promise I will not reveal your identity. I will not retain any documents, written or electronic, that reveal your identity in any way. And if my bosses insist I tell them who you are, I will put them off until I tell you what's happening. If you still insist on remaining anonymous, I will tell them that you will not give me permission to reveal your name. I will tell them that you told me about this on the condition I would not reveal your identity without your permission. How's that?"

"That will do, but I want it in writing, with your signature."

"You really are apprehensive, aren't you?"

"Yes, and cautious, too."

Gary French placed a page of his letterhead stationery in his computer's printer and composed a letter of agreement. He printed it, signed it, and gave it to Brian. Next, he let Brian watch while he deleted the document from his computer.

"Will that do the trick?"

Brian handed the folder to French and sat quietly.

After a quick read, Gary French also found it interesting.

"You have my full attention, Brian. Now tell me how the intricacies of the energy trading market led to a warning that makes you so apprehensive."

"What I found out is beyond the scope of my duties and current assignment. It just fell into my lap. I am free to ignore it completely. I do, however, want to help my agency and my country uncover failures in compliance and illegal activity. But—and this is a big but—I don't think I should be risking my life."

Brian then laid it all out for him, except he didn't provide the names of the people who had connected him with Friedrich Olms.

After Brian was finished telling Gary French the entire story, the general counsel sat quietly looking into space. Brian could imagine his mind mulling it all over. He envisioned wheels within wheels spinning and buttons being pushed.

"So this guy Friedrich says he can obtain the information that will let us know if the fuels actually originated in Venezuela's PETGO refineries?"

"That's correct."

"To be honest with you, Brian, I am not sure that what Friedrich can produce will be enough. It will only be circumstantial evidence. I can't see anyone in Justice getting too exited about this if circumstantial evidence will be the best evidence they can get. However, if they find it interesting and worthwhile, they might see what they can dig up on their own. I know someone there who will give me an honest assessment. I will run it up the flagpole with her and get back to you."

"That sounds fine with me so long as you can trust this person to keep it confidential," Brian said.

"You can count on that, Brian."

French rose and offered his hand. "It's very rare we get anything like what you brought me today. Thanks for trusting me with it. You did the right thing. Now, don't you worry about this. I will take good care of you."

They shook hands, and Brian walked back to his office. Gary French sat at his desk for a while wondering whether he should "dead-end" Matusak's request or continue the investigation. Although his instincts were telling him to drop it, his curiosity got the better of him. The next step would be to contact a Department of Justice officer. After mulling over his contacts at Justice, he called Ann Calloway.

Calloway was busy when her telephone rang. The caller ID read Gary French—GAO. Her greeting was short but courteous. Gary asked if she had an hour for him in the next couple of days. She said she could squeeze him in tonight over dinner. They made a date at the Midtown Grill for five thirty.

Calloway was a tough veteran in the Justice Department. She had the equipment to be a professional model; however, she was a serious-minded person with political goals. She had survived several administration changes because of her pragmatic approach and common sense. Her good looks and tall, slender figure didn't hurt. Gary French knew she would be a hard sell. That was why he had chosen her. If she wanted to pursue the NAPCO matter, then he knew it would be worth the trouble. Little did he know then how wrong he could be.

**

French beat Ann to the restaurant and sat in the far corner booth with his eyes on the door. When Ann walked in, he stood as she scanned the tables and booths. She spotted French and put her

Blackberry in her pocketbook. Ann wasn't the type who needed to walk slowly, looking at each table for faces she might recognize. She looked directly at her target and approached at a pace the patrons would prefer to see the wait staff attempt.

Gary had brought only a copy of the infamous DOD IDIQ memos. After they exchanged pleasantries, she asked, "So, why are we here?"

French asked, "Have you heard of Ryan Rubin and his memo?"

Ann looked back at French with a big smirk on her face. "Why is this coming up again?"

Gary asked, "You've heard of it before?"

Ann relaxed and settled deep into the booth so she could cross her legs. "Yup!"

"And where did it take you?"

"Absolutely nowhere. But it made the rounds at Justice. It is fondly referred to as Rubik's Memorandum—after the inventor of the cube. We actually invited the author of the explanatory memo, Ryan Rubin, to give us a seminar on the energy-trading business. It was entertaining, but nobody in the room had the time or energy to attempt to look further into it. Even Mr. Rubin had no suggestions. He is a whiz kid of twenty-something and just accepted it as business as usual. I will put it in his words. I remember them because I wanted to use them myself when the opportunity arose. 'I consider it as I view electricity. Why try to figure it out? It's been here for a long time. It works, and nobody complains.'

"What he described in the memo has probably been examined and explained over and over again. So why waste time trying to do something that's probably been done before and found to be benign? We're over it. Why is it on your plate?"

"What if I told you I have an auditor who found the energy to take it to the next couple of layers of investigation? He ran across an international expert who says he is confident he can trace the supply chain back to PETGO Oil in Venezuela."

"Really! Now that would be a horse of a different color. Fill me in."

Gary French gave her a quick rundown of what Brian had told him, but without the names.

"Before you get too exited, I need to tell you that this expert can only provide circumstantial evidence of the source. I assume you will want corroborating evidence. We have no suggestions of where to go to obtain that kind of evidence. I brought it to you so you could decide whether it should be taken any further."

"Thanks for the handoff! I used to consider you a friend."

Gary knew she wasn't serious, but he was curious that she might be half serious. "How can this destroy a friendship?" he asked flippantly.

"If only you knew. My boss has a hard-on for NAPCO. When this memo came to light the first time, he was the one who wanted us to pursue it. We persuaded him to put it behind him. He did, but he made us promise to let him know if anything else came up about it. I can only imagine that he will want to talk to your auditor."

"That's going to be problematic."

"How so?"

"Someone told him he could lose his life if it went awry and it was discovered that he was the one who started the investigation. His expert told him to remain anonymous and send it up the ladder to somebody experienced in the business of dealing with bad guys at this level of politics and financial means."

Now it was Ann Calloway's turn to sit pensively.

"This kind of shit is why so many DOJ career lawyers want no part of high-stakes cases. God dammit, Gary! For just once, I needed a term of normal lawyering."

"Ann, I'm sorry. I had no idea this might have legs. I really expected you to tell me to forget about it."

They bitched back and forth for a while. She explained to French that her boss came from a firm that had some litigation with NAPCO. She didn't know the details, but it was apparent that it had left a bad taste in his mouth.

"He is going to jump on this like jalapenos on fajitas."

"Now you're talking," French interjected. "Let's order."

The ball was back in Ann Calloway's court. She struggled with the thought of telling the DAG. She knew he would seize the opportunity to go after NAPCO. She also knew if she didn't tell her boss, she would be deceiving him, and she would have to lie to the GAO general counsel when he asked her about the matter. She rationalized that it had to be done. Her boss was taking a long weekend and was expected back in the office Tuesday afternoon. She figured it might be better to let him in on the news when he returned instead of just before he left on Friday.

Ann wrote a very brief e-mail to her boss that evening. It read, "We need to talk when you get back in the office—Rubik is back."

13. WE'VE GOT TROUBLE

CHARLES BOBICK WAS HOSTING LUNCH AT HAVERBY'S, HIS FAVORite venue for entertaining members of the legislature. The menu prices were so outrageous that only those with deep pockets dared to frequent the establishment. On this particular Wednesday, Bobick was hosting a weekend getaway meal for a few congressmen. Sam Nugent and two fellow lobbyists from their law firm, Bennett, Bancroft and Sperling, were describing an outing they were hosting for this year's Super Bowl weekend in New Orleans.

Walking toward their table was a tall, lean, and well-appointed Latin gentleman. As he brushed by Charles on his way to the restrooms, he subtly patted Charles on the shoulder. A minute passed, and Charles Bobick excused himself for a restroom break. Inside the men's room, the Latin gentleman left an envelope on the washstand and departed. Bobick picked it up, gave it a scan, and placed it in his inside jacket pocket.

When he returned to the table, Bobick apologized to his guests that he had to leave them early. He explained that he had gotten a call from a client with an urgent personal emergency that he felt he had to address.

Bobick appeared to be cut from the same cloth as Cary Grant.

He might be considered debonair. His suit was high-end Italian in the three-to-five-grand range, and he could really make a well-tailored suit look good. On his way out of Haverby's, Bobick turned on his usual smile and focused his view on the occupants of the restaurant to make sure he didn't slight any patrons he recognized. His mind was racing, and his stride was determined. He got this kind of invitation only when there was serious trouble. Although the valet had parked his Lincoln Navigator, Bobick walked toward the steps of the parking deck, up to level two, and right to space C-14, the location described on the contents of the envelope. Parked in space C-14 was a black Chevy Tahoe with tinted windows. The passenger-side panel door opened as he approached, and he stepped inside.

Waiting for him were Simon Flores, the tall, Latin gentleman in the restaurant, and Dan Witherspoon. He was acquainted with both men. They were his contacts with Purified Petroleum Corporation. There was no greeting. Witherspoon was in a hurry.

"Charley, we have a situation. We have picked up a communication that jeopardizes our principal's standing. I am sure you recall the last scare we got a couple of months ago by the Rubik's Memo. Our source says it's back, and this time it might have the horsepower to scuttle our mission. I have been asked to eliminate the risks and to advise you that we will be implementing 'Countermeasure Sanitation.' We regret having to resort to these tactics and the ripples it will create in the Justice Department. You know your assignment. Right?"

"Are you confident your information is accurate?"

"Absolutely. Also, it is my understanding that the legislation we designed has come out of committee and is headed for a vote in the Foreign Affairs Committee."

"That's right. Everything in the legislative arena is on track for quick passage. You can rest assured that our end of the mission is operating smoothly. Dan, I will repeat what I said when this came up the first time. These so-called sanitation countermeasures are not the way to go. Even if you succeed with the sanitation side, there will always remain some well-meaning novices who don't get it. They think they are too clever, and they don't have enough sense to understand they are not bulletproof. You cannot eliminate them all. And, by the way, the news following the fuel depot incident says two Navy operations workers are missing and presumed dead. It was my understanding that no one was going to have to die. I don't like this. I don't like it all. This really bothers me."

"I will pass it on that you have repeated your warnings. Nonetheless, we are counting on you to handle the politics. You don't have any reservations about that, do you?"

"We are good there. I will do my part. Just make sure you use the best professionals in the market. If you screw up your end and this becomes a debacle, you lose my counsel and maybe more. And, yes, I know. I might also lose more clients than you and our benefactor. But that is something I am willing to give up if our mission succeeds. Just remember, our benefactor's name must never be spoken when I am present. I have kept up my end of the bargain so far, and I will continue to do so. Are we straight?"

"Message received."

Charles Bobick stepped out of the vehicle and walked slowly to the valet stand. He could feel his blood pressure rising. When he chose to take on this mission, he acknowledged the risks and that lives might have to be taken. He was learning, however, that even the most careful of plans could fall prey to the unexpected. To him, the news that military personnel were lost was a bad omen. It had been his understanding that the mission could be accomplished without casualties. He just hoped it was an unavoidable outcome instead of disregard for the lives of poor souls who had found themselves in the wrong place at the wrong time.

He had a lot of unexpected work to do when got back to the office. He had to perform his own brand of sanitation. Now that the shit was about to hit the fan, he had to make sure there were no traces of anything in his office that might link him to Purified, its investors, or its friends. His mind drifted back to the thought that the death rate of civil servants was about to increase dramatically. He just hoped none would be friends. Or worse yet, he hoped that none would have links to him. This was all a distasteful business that was getting to him.

***

On the drive back from Washington, DC, to Crystal City, Dan Witherspoon was mentally crossing off items from his list of sanitation duties. His cell phone chimed to indicate a text message. It was from his benefactor's sanitation contractor. He didn't know his real name. He went by Mr. Straight. The message read, "1400 hours, Crystal City Marriott—Room 735."

Witherspoon took a deep breath and exhaled the way he did when he used to exercise. He thought he was getting rather old for all this drama. At fifty-nine, he expected to be the sage advisor valued for his experience. Expectations fell short at age forty-eight when his wife found him diddling his secretary. The divorce left him alone and without a nest egg, and when the scandal became public, he was demoted from his high-paying post in the Department of Energy. He was left to living from paycheck to paycheck.

It was then he sought a higher-paying position, and the Purified Petroleum offer was too lucrative to turn down, no matter the ugly politics that went with it. Now this once-heralded executive was a gray-haired, puffy old man with rotting gums and bad breath covered by a spray mouthwash he kept on him at all times.

***

Room 735 at the Crystal City Marriott was a suite. Señor Flores knocked, and the door opened. A tall man dressed in sweats with a day's worth of stubble appeared and asked him to come in.

"Please forgive me for not introducing my associates," stated the man rising from a chair at the end of the cafeteria-style table in the middle of the room. "My name is Mr. Straight. Please make yourselves comfortable," he said with a Slavic accent.

Dan Witherspoon could not help asking, "Your accent—I thought you were from here."

"That is something I have learned to do when I am speaking on the telephone. I have an ear for accents and dialect. I try to disguise my nationality to avoid attempts to discover my identity."

"Very impressive. So, is this your native accent?"

"Can't say," he answered. "After all, that is the point, isn't it? So—we have little time. I wish to get to our business of the moment. We have been summoned by our mutual benefactor. It is my understanding that we now have a two-pronged mission. One was designed to disrupt the DOD fuel procurement process, to access and alter its historical records. That mission has been accomplished. And now we must focus on our new mission to eliminate or destroy the investigation into our benefactor. Is that correct?"

"That is my understanding."

"Good! If you don't mind, I will begin by recapping the plan to disrupt the fuel procurement process. It was my mission to enter the Navy's Craney Island, Virginia, terminal to set the facility on fire, access its computerized product movement system, and revise the NAPCO fuel batch size orders and delivery volumes recorded in the Navy's records. We called that Operation Junior.

"The second operation was approved this past July, but it was shelved when it was learned it was not needed at that time. It has now been reactivated, except it has been broadened somewhat to account for additional persons in the chain of information. The name assigned to this operation is Senior. Our orders require that accident methodology be chosen to eliminate our targets when possible. If we find that impractical, we will employ whatever means is prudent."

Mr. Straight continued, "It is my understanding that our progress on Junior is to be reported via the Internet on the chosen Facebook account. I was advised that you will give me the approved encryption method for our reports."

"Yes, the encryption code is in this envelope," Witherspoon said as Mr. Flores handed him the envelope.

"Well, then. That concludes my presentation. Any questions?"

"No questions, Mr. Straight. But let me remind you, if your actions do not succeed as planned, there is no 'abort' feature. Do you understand?"

"That is a given. We will continue to adapt our plans to any changes, whether they are setbacks or heavy losses. We will succeed."

"When will Operation Senior begin?"

"To some degree, it is already underway."

"Excellent! And if that's all for now, I will not delay you further."

Dan Witherspoon left the hotel room and headed for the elevator. Waiting for the next car to arrive, Witherspoon was wondering when or if the meetings with the likes of Mr. Straight would ever end. He was growing weary of the clandestine methods, and he didn't like being the broker and intermediary for his benefactor. He mused how fortunate Charley Bobick was that he still had the passion for the mission. Dan Witherspoon, on the other hand, had passed that milestone months ago. If he tried to quit now, he would be just another assignment for Mr. Straight and his henchmen.

Mr. Straight, though, had other concerns at the moment. He was aware of the stakes. If he failed to complete his assignment, he would be dead. He would have it no other way. He had previously tried other pursuits besides the mercenary business, but the thrill of risking his life was a high he could not live without. One of the reasons he was successful and in demand was his willingness to place himself at risk. For him, life was not worth living without his chosen career.

With his assignment orders squared away, Mr. Straight was now in his element. Long ago in Serbia, he had lost his naïveté and the sentimentality of emotion. He and his family had been the victims of obscene and indescribable cruelty. It was there he learned to retaliate with matching brutality. When the fighting was over, he found himself on the side of the international peace-keeping forces. This circumstance was not because of any newfound virtue. They had stumbled upon him, wounded and unconscious. He healed in their hospital. And when he was back on his feet, he returned the favor by volunteering to assist their mission to rebuild and rejuvenate the economy. He figured it was the best way to ensure he would get reliable meals to sustain himself in the short run.

The Americans he met encouraged him to learn English. When he demonstrated a talent for language, he was often placed in the role of the interpreter between the reformers and those who needed reformation. It was in this capacity that he learned to become a valuable agent. He learned to be a facilitator of sorts. And the contacts he made set him on his current career path.

Now he was a dispassionate expert in damage control of the direst of circumstances. He was known as the Janitor. The money was good, and he paid his associates well. They were loyal to him, and he was loyal to them.

The benefactor in this mission was a repeat client, and he paid well. This assignment was particularly dangerous and complex. And because of the danger and difficulty, the fee was extremely high. Mr. Straight understood that the stakes were high as well, and that time was of the essence. Operation Senior was the more time sensitive of the two assignments. This evening, he would be placing Operation Senior in motion. If things went as planned, it would be over within a few hours.

14. TAKING LIVES

WEDNESDAY EVENING, NOVEMBER 8, 2006

THE GEORGETOWN CONDOMINIUM HOME OF ANN CALLOWAY WAS equipped with a security system of the most primitive variety. The complex's management bragged about its value, but in reality, it was easy pickings for a professional criminal. Mr. Straight, the Janitor, was a professional—a careful, meticulous, and organized technician. It was nearly midnight when he and Mr. Othello arrived. It was a cold, drizzly night, and everyone was indoors, warm and cozy. The front security gate took only a moment to bypass. It was commonly known among security companies that a mechanical way to open the gates was necessary for when the electric power connection was interrupted. The Janitor knew it well.

The two assassins waited a half hour in the back of their panel truck after Ann Calloway's bedroom lights were turned off. The Janitor read the agenda aloud for the umpteenth time, and Mr. Othello responded to each item with "Check." His last words before they got out of the truck were "Remember, there are no second chances. Everything must go as planned. Precision and efficiency—now let's go."

Wearing all black, they entered Ann Calloway's condo without being detected after the Janitor disabled the alarm. Mr. Othello spotted her handbag on the kitchen countertop. Among the contents were her cell phone and a pistol. Their intelligence on her was right on target. Within two minutes, Mr. Othello used her phone to compose a text message to Gary French, send it, delete its record from the call history, and return it to her handbag. While Mr. Othello was dealing with her cell phone, the Janitor replaced her pistol with an identical model. The two left her apartment undetected and in possession of her pistol.

Their next stop was at the home of Gary French. They repeated the same tasks there that they had performed at the home of Ann Calloway. The only difference was that they did not need to deal with a pistol. The text messages they sent on the cell phones read, "Emergency! Danger! Meet me in the parking garage at 119 S. Glebe Road, Arlington, space 232 at 10:30 a.m. tomorrow morning. Don't call me. Our phones are tapped, and we are being watched."

Mr. Straight and Mr. Othello returned to room 735 at the Crystal City Marriott at 2:35 a.m. The Janitor opened up his Facebook account and posted this message: "We had a great evening. I wish all my dates went so well." That was their code to all their clients and associates that the first stage of their plans had gone as expected.

THURSDAY, NOVEMBER 9, 2006

At approximately 10:30 a.m., Gary French was standing next to his BMW 535 at the arrival location on Glebe Road. It was another cold and damp Virginia morning. He was agitated and anxiously waiting to learn what had happened. A dark-colored

Lexus sedan slowly approached and parked next to him. Ann Calloway cut off her engine and opened her door. At the same time, a motorcycle turned down the ramp from the next floor up. Within feet of them, it stopped abruptly. The two riders, dressed in black and wearing ski masks, jumped off. Wearing the ski masks were Mr. Othello and the Janitor. The Janitor pointed a pistol at Gary French and fired into his chest three times. In the meantime, Mr. Othello grabbed the shocked Ann Calloway and held her so tightly she couldn't move. The Janitor grabbed her hand and pressed it against the pistol, which was now pointed at her temple. The pistol's trigger was pulled, and it fired. Her body slumped as Mr. Othello released her. She was dead before her body hit the pavement.

As the Janitor checked the pulse on the victims to confirm they were dead, his accomplice placed a crumpled, printed note in Ms. Calloway's left hand and placed the pistol in her right hand. The Janitor opened her handbag and removed the pistol they had planted the evening before. The two assassins departed without being observed. The note left at the scene read: "If I can't have you, then no one shall. Please forgive me."

With that deed done, the Janitor was on his way to dispatch the next targets. In his van, he opened his laptop and connected to the Internet to update his Facebook page. He typed, "I just had a senior moment. That's two for the day. Just one more, and my day will be complete."

***

Thursday mornings at the Matusak home were a panic. Brian and his wife, Dana, had a full day of appointments. Dana worked

Tuesdays and Thursdays at the Red Cross as a grief counselor. Later that day, she picked up their two boys after school for basketball games at the Fairfax County Athletic Complex. She and Brian shared supper at 7:30 with the team's parents. After basketball, they headed for the McDonald's in Centerville.

It was 7:35 p.m. when they sat down in the main dining area. The Centerville McDonald's had three dining areas equipped with flat-screen TVs hanging on the walls. The TVs in two rooms were airing children's shows; the other was broadcasting CNN Headline News. On his way back from the counter, carrying a tray of dinner items to their table, Brian glanced at the CNN broadcast. The photos of two people covered the screen. He thought he recognized the man's photo. He diverted to get a better look.

The photo of the man had a caption underneath reading, Gary French, GAO General Counsel. In bold letters below was the headline, "APPARENT MURDER–SUICIDE IN ARLINGTON." The photo of the other person was a woman. Under her picture was the caption, Ann Calloway, DOJ Attorney.

Brian Matusak's blood pressure spiked. His breathing turned to gulps of air, and his eyes bulged. In a halting manner, he walked closer to the TV to hear the reporter.

"According to Arlington County police, the two were found next to each other in a parking garage off Glebe Road. Details are being withheld at this early juncture in the investigation. Police would only say that they are classifying the incident as an apparent murder-suicide."

Brian struggled to make sure he did not drop the tray of food. When the broadcast moved on to the next story, he headed back to his table as if he were in a trance. His mind was in rewind and fast-forward at the same time. He placed the food tray on the table and pulled Dana away for a private chat.

"Have you seen the news today?"

"Why? What's wrong, Brian?"

"On the way back to the table, I spotted a news story on CNN that might change our lives."

"What happened?"

"It's too complicated to explain right now. All I know is that I don't want us to go home until I have a better idea of what's happening."

"You're scaring me!"

"I'm scared, too."

Dana's mother lived near Fredericksburg, just an hour or so away. Once they got situated in their Chrysler Caravan, Dana called her mother. Her parents, Skip and Joanne Blackmon, were home and questioned their impromptu visit. Dana explained that it was an emergency and that they would explain when they arrived.

They pulled into the Blackmon driveway at 9:30 p.m. Brian told them the entire story.

Dana's dad had retired from the Air Force a couple of years back and had bought a farm near the Dogwood Air Park, where he flew his collection of antique aircraft. Surprisingly, her dad was not skeptical about Brian's story. He convinced his wife, Joanne, and his daughter that he had some contacts in the Pentagon who might be helpful.

That evening at midnight, Brian called Friedrich Olms. Because it was 8:00 a.m. on a Friday in London, he didn't expect to reach Friedrich, but he didn't want to ignore the possibility. Luckily, an answering service took the call. He left an urgent message to call him. He actually used the words, "It's a matter of life and death."

Twenty minutes later, his cell phone rang. It was Friedrich.

"Thanks so much for taking my call, Friedrich."

"May I guess that something bad has happened?"

"I brought the matter to the GAO general counsel yesterday. He said he would run it by a female attorney in DOJ. He promised not to use my name. CNN is reporting he was found dead this morning lying next to the dead body of a female attorney with the DOJ. I think she was the attorney he told my story to at Justice. They were found in a parking garage in metro Washington. For now, they are calling it a murder–suicide."

"Dear Lord! I never expected that kind of retribution or that they would be so close so fast. Let me think for a minute." He paused for a moment. "OK, I have some questions for you."

"I'm all ears."

"Brian, there is no way they would be so close so fast unless they were on a very high level of alert before you started your inquiry. This is not good. Where are you right now?"

"I'm with my wife and children an hour's drive from Washington. We changed our plans for the day when we heard the news story and diverted to her parents' home."

"Good idea. By any chance—did you mention my name to your general counsel, or anyone else, for that matter?"

"No, I just mentioned that my source was an expert in these matters."

"That should buy me a little more time to figure out what to do. I must say, Brian, we have walked into an ambush. My hunch is that your general counsel and his associate at DOJ were also caught off guard. Maybe I have seen too many espionage thrillers at the cinema, but the fact that they were meeting at a parking garage on a Friday morning suggests they were aware of the possibility of danger. Brian, what was the date of the memorandum in the file that started you on this course?"

"I think it was July seventeenth."

"This is another premonition, but it's my guess that whoever is behind this has been aware of the memo and has placed spies or moles in your government, watching for something that would suggest your government hound dogs are sniffing on its trail. We must assume that something was found in either your general counsel's office or the office of his colleague at DOJ. Did you get the impression from your general counsel that he was familiar with the memo?"

"Actually, I was somewhat surprised that he appeared to be totally unaware of it before I brought it to his attention."

"Let's hope that is the case. If the alert arose in your DOJ, then they might not be aware of you and me—yet."

"Yet!"

"If they have the resolve, it is just a matter of time before they trace everything back to the source. Can I call you back on this number? I want to think this over. I will call you back as soon as I find something that might help us."

"Yeah, sure. Just don't take too long. I have nobody else to turn to."

Brian hung up and waited for his wife to start asking questions.

"Brian, you need to tell me what we are going to do!"

"I need a few days with you and the kids safe with your parents while I try to figure this out. Do you think I could borrow your mother's car for a few days while you are in Fredericksburg?"

"How can this be! You are an auditor. What did you get us into? This type of thing doesn't happen to auditors!"

"It might have happened this time, Dana! Look, you are just going to have to trust me. I need your cooperation now, not your criticism. Jesus Christ, Dana! Have a little faith."

15. LACK OF CONVERGENCE

BRIAN MATUSAK AWOKE AT 6:30 A.M. HE WAS GROGGY AND ACHY. While he was making breakfast, Dana's father entered the kitchen.

"Were you able to sleep OK, Brian?"

"Not a bit. How about you?"

"I've been retired now for a few years. Not many things prevent me from my usual eight hours of sleep. But your dilemma got my mind racing. I don't think I got more than five hours in. Last night, I thought of calling my old wing leader. We usually get together for lunch every month or so. He's been a strategist in the Pentagon ever since 9/11. He heads up the coordination of domestic response to air threats like 9/11. He meets with Homeland Security, FBI, and NSA strategists on a weekly basis. I bet he knows somebody who can help us. He usually gets in his office by 7:30. It's seven o'clock now. If he doesn't answer, I'll leave a message. I bet he calls me back before 7:45."

Brian smiled and said, "I guess it wouldn't hurt."

Brian was in a state of fear paralysis. His mind was so consumed with the pictures of how he might be killed he could not think straight. At 7:41, the phone at the Blackmon home rang.

It was Colonel Louis Milton. As Skip had predicted, his old wing leader was offering his old pal his full attention. They talked for over a half hour. When Skip hung up, he told Brian that Colonel Milton was confident that the FBI would be interested in the matter.

Brian and Dana convinced their children that they would be going home soon, but the kids were not too worried because they had their grandparents to dote on them.

At 1:15 p.m., Skip got a call from Colonel Milton. An FBI analyst who worked on matters of foreign espionage on US soil was also on the line. He wanted Brian to visit him at the bureau headquarters on Pennsylvania Avenue at 4:00 p.m. To play it safe, Dana, her mother, and their two children went on a Civil War historical tour to see the Bull Run, Fredericksburg, Locust Grove, and Wilderness battlefields. In the meantime, Skip and Brian drove to Washington and their appointment with Colonel Milton's FBI contact and FBI agent Reginald Wilkerson.

FBI HEADQUARTERS, FRIDAY, NOVEMBER 10, 4:00 P.M.

Brian Matusak and Skip Blackmon signed in at the reception area, and within a few minutes, they were greeted by Colonel Milton's contact, FBI analyst Thomas Thatcher and Field Agent Wilkerson. Thatcher said he couldn't stay long, so he left the matter to Wilkerson. Typical of most FBI agents, it was difficult to determine whether Agent Wilkerson was taking their concerns as legitimate or if he was just doing a favor for a Pentagon official. As Brian told his story, Wilkerson made notes of the names Brian mentioned and entered them in the FBI database for a Nexus query to see if any were part of an active FBI case.

Wilkerson did not have much of a poker face. Both Skip and Brian could tell he was looking at some very interesting information. Wilkerson excused himself and left them in his office for what he said would be a moment. About ten minutes later, Wilkerson returned with two other persons, a female analyst by the name of Angela Cramer and their ultimate boss, District Chief Daniel Greenwood. Agent Cramer was very interested in Brian's visit with GAO General Counsel Gary French the week before.

"Brian, are you certain he said he was going to share your inquiry with a female attorney in the Justice Department?"

"I believe his words were, 'a colleague at DOJ,' and that she would let him know if it was worth pursuing."

"Did Gary French get back with you?"

"No."

"And you are sure he is the only person at the GAO you talked to about your inquiry?"

"That's right."

"Did you know Ann Calloway?"

"I didn't. I've never heard of her."

Agents Wilkerson and Cramer and Chief Greenwood then excused themselves and left the room. Brian and Skip speculated that they had brought something to the FBI that the FBI didn't know of, and that the information was more than just interesting. After about twenty minutes, Wilkerson returned alone.

"Brian, you might have information that is useful to us. We have been trying to figure out all the connections that led Mr. French and Ms. Calloway to meet at the garage yesterday morning. Your story makes the most sense at the moment, and we are trying to determine if there is anything at DOJ that sheds light on this from the Rubik's Memo angle. Do you mind waiting here with me for a little while? Analyst Cramer is talking with DOJ."

Analyst Cramer reentered and advised Brian and his father-in-law that their investigation of the incident had only just begun. Cramer reported, "I talked with the undersecretary at the DOJ. They have no recent account of the matter, there is no mention of the matter on anyone's agenda, and the only record of a meeting between French and Calloway occurred during the previous month."

Cramer whispered something to Wilkerson that Skip and Brian couldn't hear. Then they both excused themselves, leaving Skip and Brian alone. In a few minutes, Wilkerson returned alone.

Wilkerson advised Brian and Skip that they would need to investigate further before they would have a feel for what steps they needed to take and what leads to pursue. He asked them to return to their homes and wait to be contacted by their office.

Brian asked, "That's it? We just go home and wait for a call?"

"Yes, that is how it works. Until we learn more, that is all that can be done. We have your contact information. We will get back in touch once we are confident of the direction of the investigation."

"What if the people who killed French and the DOJ attorney come looking for me? Don't you have places where you can keep us safe while you figure it out?"

"Wait here. I'll ask my supervisor."

Wilkerson returned and related Greenwood's instructions. "My chief believes you are alive now because they must not know about you. He is confident you will be safe until we have a better handle on what is going on. If you can spend the night with your in-laws, we'll have an agent watch your home in Fairfax to see if anyone suspicious shows up. If nobody does, you can be confident they are not on to you."

Wilkerson stood up and opened his office door.

"Please follow me. You needn't worry. You've taken reasonable precautions."

Wilkerson led them to the reception area, shook their hands, and wished them luck. Brian and Skip felt unsatisfied.

In the elevator, they discussed the matter. "What do you think, Skip? Should I be worried?"

"I don't know, Brian. It didn't go down like I imagined. I'm going to call my contact, Lou, and see what he thinks."

Skip dialed Louis Milton's cell phone. They discussed the FBI session in detail. Lou said he would call Wilkerson and get back with him. Brian and Skip drove back to Fredericksburg and had dinner with Dana, her mother, and the children. Still no call from Thatcher or Colonel Milton. They spent the night in Fredericksburg.

After Saturday breakfast, Louis Milton called and said, "I talked with Wilkerson. He said one of their agents sat outside your house all night and nothing happened. Thatcher said Greenwood thinks it's safe to return to Fairfax."

They discussed the matter a little while longer but felt there was little else to do. Brian was exasperated, feeling helpless. Without a better plan, Dana, their two children, and he returned to Fairfax. Back at home, Brian tried his best not to think about the matter, but that didn't work so well. That evening he called Olms in London, but he didn't answer. Brian left him a message to call him back. He fell asleep without hearing back from Olms. He never would.

At 1:10 a.m., the Janitor entered the house and opened the gas line to their fireplace starter. The Matusak home began to fill with natural gas. At about 1:30 a.m., the gas-enriched atmosphere in the house reached a flammable mixture, and the pilot light to their kitchen stove provided the ignition. The Matusak home exploded, and what remained was burned to unrecognizable ashes.

The Janitor fired up his laptop and made another entry on his Facebook page. It read, "I had another good day. Both Junior and Senior have been put to bed."

NOVEMBER 11, 8:05 A.M., SUNDAY MORNING

After trying to reach Brian and Dana and getting nothing but a fast busy signal on the house phone, Skip Blackmon called their cell phones. His call went straight to voice mail. He became very worried. In almost a panic, he dialed his buddy Lou Milton. Lou was not available to answer his call. Skip turned on his computer and opened up the Washington Post website. Clicking on the Metro News section, he saw an article with the headline, "Gas Explosion at Fairfax Home." He frantically clicked on the headline and read, "Home on MacArthur Drive explodes." The article did not provide the address, or the occupants, but Skip picked up the house phone and called the Fairfax County Police Department.

In a matter of seconds, his worries were confirmed. Skip began to sob uncontrollably. The policeman on the line waited for Skip to resume talking, but the line went dead when Joanne Blackmon hung up the phone while consoling and commiserating with her husband. At 9:41, Louis Milton called back. In tears, Skip related the news. Louis Milton was in a state of disbelief that later turned to regret and anger.

Louis Milton had not spoken to Wilkerson since the day before, and he decided to call him. He described the events of the past twelve hours to him. He needed Wilkerson's cooperation and chose not to say anything that might sound as if he was placing blame on the FBI for the deaths of the Matusak family. Since Wilkerson's supervisor was now on vacation, he told Milton he would have to get back with him once he advised the duty chief of the latest developments.

Wilkerson called Colonel Milton back and told him that he had been given authority to investigate the gas explosion at the Matusak residence. He would call him back once he had something to report.

Brian Matusak never saw the news coverage of the Craney Island fire, and he never had the chance to connect the two events. As a result, two separate and disconnected FBI investigations were underway. But what did law enforcement have? It was clear they had a growing body count, but nothing else except talk of a memo that may or may not have any bearing on the deaths. Brian had shown it to French but took it back after he read it. No copies were made. Calloway didn't have a copy of it in any of her records. Brian put the memo back in the audit file, and he put the audit file back on the shelves that held the 2005 records of DOD contracts. He never mentioned to anyone where the file was kept or how it was labeled. In essence, all the evidence of the killings evaporated.

By acting swiftly and decisively, the Janitor had prevented law enforcement from connecting all the dots. He was confident his associates would be pleased that the first phase of their mission was successful and that it had been accomplished without lingering issues.

16. RUN YOUR IDEA UP THE FLAGPOLE

MATTHEW BERG WAS SITTING IN HIS FAVORITE COFFEE SHOP A couple blocks from the Capitol building. It was a little after eight in the morning. This was his time to scan the news stories breaking domestically and around the world to see if there were any connections to what was in play inside the House.

Matt was an analysis junkie. Each morning before he entered the Capitol, he would update his huge computer spreadsheet. On it were three major columns: one for proposed legislation, another for issues being discussed, and a third for headline news events. When a news headline might have a connection to items at the Capitol, he would draw a dotted line connecting them.

He still hadn't heard from his New Jersey congresswoman, and that probably meant she was not ready to go on the record. And although his editor had some inside info to trade on the subject, he still wasn't convinced he had enough to leverage an exclusive interview on what might be driving the movement of the new antiterrorism bill.

One item in the news did catch his eye, and it was kind of local. When he entered the word terrorism into the search field on his paper's website, a headline read, "Navy spokesperson says the investigation of the Craney Island explosion has been widened to consider terrorism and industrial sabotage." Matthew then ran the Craney Island articles backward in time to find the date the disaster started. Connecting the date of the first explosion and the date the antiterrorism bill came out of subcommittee was enough to draw a new dotted line connecting the two.

And that was how Matthew had risen so fast at the New York Times. He had no idea the events were connected, but he now had something to casually throw out during his interview with the New Jersey congresswoman. How she reacted would dictate which direction the interview would take. Most of the time, such a baiting tactic would draw nothing but quizzical looks. But every now and then, he would hit a nerve and get a quote worth the trouble.

At nine thirty, he called the New Jersey congresswoman, and she agreed to sit with him for five minutes if he came by immediately.

"I'm already here. Just buzz the hall security to allow me in." Seconds later, he was sitting at her conference table.

"So, you still want to talk about the antiterrorism bill?"

"Yes, Mrs. Congresswoman."

"Well, I'm guessing you've got more intel than I do. I've got practically nothing."

Matthew related what he had gathered from yesterday's inquiries, but the only thing that piqued her interest was the VP's remarks overheard by his editor. She was interested in the detail that it came from the VP and not a White House or Senate source. He tried a number of spins and angles, and when he saw her glancing at her watch, he knew he had to throw out the terminal explosion.

"I was wondering if you made the same connection I did

about the timing of the bill's movement to the Navy terminal incident?"

"What incident?" she asked in a reflex response.

"Craney Island, Virginia. The tank explosions that shut down the Navy's main East Coast supply hub for its fleet and airbases."

"I thought they hadn't found the cause."

"That's the point. It's unlike the Navy to hold off mentioning the cause unless it's not the usual human or mechanical error."

Matthew handed her his issue of the day's New York Times where he had circled the wire story headline.

After a pause while she read the byline, she looked Matthew in the eyes and remarked, "Now that's more like it. You gave me something to work on. If this leads anywhere, you'll get the exclusive. Have you sent this up the flagpole with another lawmaker?"

"No, Congresswoman."

"Good! Just sit tight. I will probably have something in a day or two."

The congresswoman stood up, smiled, and patted him on his shoulder as she led him to the door to her suite. Matthew walked out and immediately sat down in a hallway chair to compile his notes of the session. He had gotten the ideal response from his toss-out. This was a story in the making, one that might be evolving as he sat there. The congresswoman hadn't had an "aha" moment, but it was close.

Congresswoman Schuster wasted no time finding out as much as she could while she attended to the tight meeting schedule on her plate. She turned to her top aide and asked, "Get a hold of Senator Price from New Jersey. Maybe he knows something about the Navy Fuel Depot story."

When that source came up empty, she didn't stop there. Her

next contact was a US Navy officer she knew from routine exercises in her home state. It turned out he didn't know anything, except he had a friend in the NCIS whom he could contact. She told him it was very important. After some effective persuasion, her Navy officer friend eventually agreed to try to reach his NCIS buddy immediately.

The cell phone of Lieutenant Lemay rang, and the ID screen displayed the name of a friend in New Jersey.

"Hey, Lieutenant, how's it going?"

"Pretty busy at the moment. What's on your mind?"

"My congresswoman was reading about the terminal incident at Craney Island, and she asked me what I knew. Since I knew nothing, I called you to see if there was anything worth saying at this time."

"I can't say much. This investigation has been classified to the commander level ever since I got here."

"Is there anything I can tell her? If I don't come up with something, I'll be in her doghouse."

Lemay paused to think. He then had an idea that would satisfy his friend and the congresswoman, and also serve another purpose.

"OK, I think I've got something you can tell her. Every agency in the US intelligence toolbox is here, and we're all trying to make sense out of things. However, there is a contractor here from the private sector that has the inside track on the cyber angles. The name is Daneli Crisis Management, and their guy is Eli Taylor. If you've got a pen and something to write on, I'll give you his cell phone number."

"Yeah, I'm ready."

"Six-seven-eight five-five-five nine-nine-nine-eight. I can't say anything more than that, but maybe the congresswoman can dig something out of him."

They hung up, and Lemay was patting himself on the back, thinking he had put pressure on Daneli that might yield a misstep. And if it did, he would have something to lobby the Unified Command to take Daneli off the response. He didn't like competing with Daneli for leads. The only problem was, he had just done Taylor a big favor.

17. THE RACE IS ON

ELI TAYLOR'S CELL PHONE NUMBER WAS ON ALL THE CONTACT sheets distributed to the response personnel, so it wasn't a surprise to see the caller ID indicate US Government. He pressed the send button and said, "Eli Taylor here."

"Mr. Taylor, this is Congresswoman Debra Schuster from New Jersey. I'm sorry to bother you, but I'm on the House Subcommittee on Terrorism, Nonproliferation, and Trade. Do have a minute to talk to me?"

"Pardon me, Congresswoman. Are you sure you've contacted the right person?"

"You are the Eli Taylor of Daneli Crisis Management, aren't you?"

"Yes, that's right, Congresswoman, but I can't imagine why you would want to talk to me."

"I was told you and your firm are part of the response effort at the Navy's Craney Island incident."

"That's right, but I have no authority to comment on the response or my role. Before I can discuss anything with you, I'll need to hear from Commander Mitchell Hughes."

"Mr. Taylor, I have no intention of going behind the Navy's

back. I will contact Commander Hughes, but I just wanted to give you a heads-up. An antiterrorism bill just came out of the subcommittee, and it's on its way to the House floor for discussion. The coincidence that this bill came out at the exact time your incident began caught the eye of a New York Times reporter. He asked what I knew about the connection. I could only reply, 'Damned if I know.' Now, if I don't get something soon, he's going to be knocking on your door."

"With all due respect, Congresswoman Schuster, I am under strict orders not to talk to anyone without the approval I mentioned. And that's what I will tell that reporter if he comes knocking. I suggest you talk to Commander Hughes. I hope you understand."

"Sorry I bothered you, Mr. Taylor. My apologies."

"You aren't bothering me, Congresswoman, and an apology is not necessary. I'm just sorry I'm not at liberty to say anything."

After the congresswoman hung up, Eli's mind was filled with all kinds of thoughts. He didn't know where this inquiry was heading, but he now understood that the profile of the incident had just been raised another couple of levels.

1600 HOURS, MONDAY, NOVEMBER 12

Back at Craney Island, Richard Dugan, Rogoff's IT buddy, called Eli at the Unified Command building from the Portsmouth Holiday Inn. His wife had driven him there from Philadelphia, and he was ready to report to work. Since Eli was preparing for the five o'clock briefings, he told him to call Rogoff in his room at six o'clock.

A new tent appeared in the place where the old press tent had stood, and the crowd seemed bigger than before. The facility fire was nearly cold. The sweet smell of burning diesel fuel had been replaced by the acrid odor of scorched earth and a blaze that had been extinguished with flame retarding foam. Only now it was raining.

The Unified Command briefing was held in the control building, and it was mostly operations driven. Eli's ears tuned in when NCIS Lieutenant Lemay mentioned that they had recovered the charred remains of two individuals.

Lemay announced, "One was located not far from storage tank seven, the epicenter of the fire. The other was found behind the control building, between a dumpster and the control building wall. Both body remains were delivered to the NCIS crime lab. The forensic investigators will perform their customary evidentiary autopsy and provide us with documentation as soon as it's complete."

Lemay also reported on the shell casing found. "It's a 7.62 x 51 millimeter M-40 cartridge—standard sniper ammo for Western-world military and police. The lab thinks there is a partial fingerprint on it, but they have to use enhanced recovery techniques because the fire and heat might have compromised the image. That means additional time before we know if the print identifies anyone in the database. And for that matter, we won't know whether it was left by perpetrators of this event or merely someone who was out here for target practice in the past. Obviously, if it's not from a US enlisted man, we might speculate that it's related to this event."

Vic and Mike spotted Eli and sat in the chairs to his left. Eli hadn't seen Vic for a while, so he asked him where he had been.

"I think I'm on to some interesting shit. I'll lay it all out after the briefing."

Mike whispered, "They aren't going to say so yet, but the body by the control building has been identified as the operator, Paulding. The other remains will probably never be identified. All they have are ashes in the outline of a body."

When Commander Hughes called on Daneli to give their report, Vic took over and delivered the only real news they had, which came from him working with the fire-fighting effort.

Hughes then went on to report that the cause of the incident was still under investigation and that it would be premature to conclude anything. As if taking a cue from Faith, he looked right at her when he announced, "I will not speculate on the cause. Instead, we all need to be patient and wait until the investigation team reports on its conclusions."

Eli got with Faith after the briefing. She agreed to take their places during the press briefing that followed. Vic, Mike, and Eli retreated to the RV and poured themselves some coffee. Vic told Eli that he didn't have to spend much time with the fire-fighters. He had used the free time to look over the nomination logs that had been extracted from the James River Computer memory discs. Rogoff had converted the raw data to a series of six compact discs.

Vic sheepishly looked at Eli and stated, "I never told management at West Industries that I learned how to be a controller. If they knew I could do it, they would have transferred me to the operations room. I wouldn't have ever seen the outside of the control building again. I couldn't have taken that.

"Well, anyway," Vic continued, "from the CDs, I pulled the names of all the shippers on the Navy's system and all of their origin points. One hundred percent of the deliveries destined to Craney Island traveled on just two pipeline systems, Provincial and Confederated. Those companies don't provide shipper information without a subpoena. If you want to save time, I suggest you ask the Navy who they use at DOJ for subpoenas."

"After your career as a controller, are you thinking about practicing law?"

"If all you had to do was pass the bar exam, I'd give it a shot. Since they now force you to get a JD degree from a certified law school, and that takes three years off your life, I'm gonna forget about law as a career. Besides, I wouldn't want to be a threat to you."

"That's very thoughtful of you. But I cannot deny that we will need to verify Rogoff's finding of any alterations by comparing the records of pipelines. I will get somebody to work on the subpoenas. Now, is that all you found?"

"Kind of."

"What kind of an answer is 'Kind of'?"

"Well, do you remember how Rogoff told us the perps altered shipping records to other destinations?"

"OK."

"We might not have to go through all the shipments and to all the other Navy destinations to find our perpetrator. Just like you've been saying, there are details on top of details. This is tedious work. But I may have hit on a shortcut. By just focusing on Craney Island deliveries and the two pipeline systems utilized, we should have enough evidence to rule out all but one shipper or all but one origin—whatever the perps were trying to disguise. It is complicated to explain. You are going to have to trust me on this part."

"Are you trying to weasel your way into Rogoff's investigation?"

"Kind of."

"You and he are on different shifts."

"Only for six of each twenty-four hours."

"What about your other duties?"

"Whatever the Navy and Coast Guard needed my advice on, they are past that stage for now. Besides, I will still have my cell phone. If they need me, they will call me."

Eli was all out of reasons why it was a bad idea. So he let him do it.

"It's against my better judgment, but I am going to say OK— for now. But you can bet I will be making sure you are not distracting them or slowing them down."

"Whatever. You won't regret it."

Vic gave Eli a salute and left the RV. Eli could sense that Vic would sell his mother to be the one who cracked this mystery. Eli figured Vic wanted their team to beat the NCIS and the other government agencies to the bad guys. He loved making the higher-ranked guys look bad. In this case, Eli didn't think that was all a bad thing.

Faith was walking in as Vic was walking out.

"Eli, do you have time to go over the news coverage and PR with me?"

"One moment. I need to visit with Commander Hughes for a moment. Can you wait here until I get back?"

"Sure. I'll grab a bite while you're out."

Eli left the RV and found Commander Hughes and Commander Brockington in Hughes's office. He told them about the subpoenas. They agreed with the request, and Brockington said he would call their DOJ liaison and get it done pronto.

Back in the RV, Eli found Faith waiting for him.

"What you got?" Eli inquired.

Faith looked at Eli a little oddly. It was like the look your dog gives you when it's perplexed.

"Your speech pattern is regressing to military-jock lingo."

"Sorry about that. It happens whenever I spend a lot of time with Vic. Don't ask me why. It just happens."

Faith had reviewed all the major news coverage of the incident. She was convinced that the military had satisfied the media's thirst for facts and answers. Their questions were getting softer, the on-scene credential requests were down fifty percent from the first day, and the story had been taken out of the first five minutes of the network news TV scripts. They were also off the front pages of the newspapers. And the military brass was happy. Life was good for the folks in her line of work.

Next was the bad news. She was becoming bored. The thrill was gone.

"Don't worry," Eli told her. "I've been down this road too many times to be deceived that the worst is over. The mania comes and goes in waves. Besides, boredom in our line of work is a confirmation that you have done your job well."

Eli didn't want her to lose her edge, so he gave her a tease.

"I'll let you in a little secret that I was going to cover at our next team briefing. Something is going to break the news within forty-eight hours that will restore the panic in the media. It has to do with our sabotage investigation. It will say that the incident was not the result of mechanical failure or human error. I have no idea what it is going to be. I can only say that we are investigating evidence and clues that should point to a perpetrator. But because we are still far from drawing conclusions, we must keep a very tight lid on our investigation. We cannot even say we are pursuing leads of potential sabotage. Absolutely no mention of it to anyone—not the press, not your friends."

"So your instincts were on target. And with that shell casing they found, it's starting to add up that you were right!"

"I wouldn't go that far just yet. Between us, I'd say that the odds are better on what my instincts were telling me than on the other options. However, we are in a race to discover what the plot is and who the players are. The military intelligence agencies are keeping their investigation close to the vest as well. Only a handful of military officers are even aware of our investigation. If the bad guys find out that we might be on to them before we have it all figured out, they might slip away, and the rest of the investigation might crumble.

"Oh, and there are a couple of other things I should let you know. Commander Hughes is not going to mention the shell casing to the media until they get the fingerprint report. And also, you might hear of a New York Times reporter looking for an interview. I got a call from a congresswoman telling me he might look us up for a story he's working on. So don't let the lull fool you, and keep on your toes. All this lurking stuff could come up at the same time."

"I hear you. Oh, I forgot to tell you this, Eli. The press has been hounding Commander Hughes, begging him to allow them to interview you. The commander told me that that he would make you available at the next news briefing."

Eli sighed. "I was hoping I might have gotten lucky that the press had enough meat that they'd lost interest in me."

Eli was not looking forward to that. There simply wasn't anything to gain by him talking to the media, and a minor misstep could result in the military losing faith in Daneli. Besides, they always wanted to know how he and Danielle had been doing since they had had to defend themselves two years ago when the Russian Mafia invaded his pipeline project. He was tired of the questions and the distractions they always created.

Eli heard someone entering the RV. It was Rogoff and another fellow.

"Good morning, Eli. I wanted you to meet Richard Dugan before we headed to the James River Control Center."

Eli stood up and extended his hand.

Dugan offered, "Good to meet you, sir. Mark filled me in on our mission. I'll do my best to deliver the information you're seeking."

"Good to meet you, and welcome to our team. This lovely lady is Faith Miller, our media relations expert."

They all shook hands as Eli gave his usual offer: "If there is anything you need to get the job done, please do not hesitate to ask me."

Dugan turned to leave and looked back. "Thanks for the opportunity. I can't wait to get started."

As they left, Eli was considering telling them that they might encounter Vic, who was already there and joining their investigation. Instead, he thought it might be fun to see how they would handle that on their own.

***

When Rogoff and Dugan arrived at the control center, Vic told them that he had persuaded Eli to let him join their effort. As Eli had imagined, within a very short time span, they were all best buddies looking to solve mysteries together.

Vic explained to his new best buds about his reasoning that they only needed to focus on the movements on Provincial's and Confederated's systems. Rogoff and Dugan embraced his strategy and were off and running with it.

By five o'clock, the Navy had its subpoena to search the pipeline records at Provincial and Confederated. An assistant attorney general contacted both pipeline companies, and arrangements were being made for them to produce data files to be electronically transmitted to the Navy NCIS offices.

Eli and Faith headed to the press tent to attend the 5:00 p.m. briefing. As they sat in the back of the tent, Commander Brockington walked over to where Eli was sitting and told him he had just received a message that the pipeline data files would be transmitted by 1800 hours.

Eli texted Vic the good news. Vic texted him back that they were making terrific progress. After Eli read the message, he noticed Commander Hughes was wrapping up his presentation. He announced, "Daneli Crisis Management was instrumental in finding a temporary replacement for the fuel depot. And now I am turning over the podium to Eli Taylor. He will deliver the report on peripheral matters."

Eli walked to the front of the room and delivered a report describing how Daneli was supporting the military's efforts. He excluded any mention of the sabotage or terrorism angle. When he was through with his part of the briefing, the press turned to the questions he had been dreading. They wanted to know how his company had come about and how Daneli had come to take a prominent position in the military's response. When he satisfied them with detailed answers to those questions, they wanted to know more about his personal life, his wife, Danielle, and how he and Danielle had been doing since the South American pipeline project two years ago. As usual, he refused to comment on those questions. That was when Commander Hughes rescued him and announced the briefing was over.

As everyone was dispersing, Commander Hughes approached

Eli. "I've been getting calls from a congresswoman, Debra Schuster from New Jersey. I gave her what we have been telling the press, but she wants to talk to you. I think I can trust that you won't tell her anything classified."

Eli got the impression that Hughes wanted Eli to get her off his back, so he relented.

"If you want me to talk with her, you can be confident that I won't say anything that you wouldn't want me to say."

"OK, then. I'll call her back and tell her to call you."

"Yes, sir," Eli replied.

Eli exited the press tent and headed for the response RV, leaving Faith to take any follow-up questions the press might ask.

The Navy was now serving full meals in a tent adjacent to the Unified Command building. Eli took four take-out meals with sodas and headed for the James River Control Center for a dinner meeting with Vic, Rogoff, and Dugan.

Congresswoman Schuster called him en route. "Eli Taylor," he answered.

"Hello, Mr. Taylor. I just spoke with Commander Hughes. He told me he had given you permission to talk with me. I really only have one question that your commander couldn't answer. Have you been contacted by anyone from Congress, the Senate, or the White House about your investigation?"

"Just you, Congresswoman."

"Thanks, Mr. Taylor. You see, that wasn't so bad."

"Yes, ma'am," he answered.

And true to her word, she thanked Eli and hung up.

Eli's shift and Vic's were scheduled to be over at 1800 hours. Eli hoped that the data file would reach the control center by then, and he wanted to be there when they started to run the data files so he could check that Vic left when his work shift was over. He feared Vic wouldn't want to leave. He needed Vic to keep his shift aligned with his so he could make sure Vic didn't wear down. He had experience with Vic overextending his shifts and becoming ornery. That didn't work well in the consulting business.

However, Eli was puzzled by the congresswoman's interest in him only to ask him that one question. "What did it mean?" he wondered. It left a foreboding cloud in the air above him. He was wondering if he and his team were a little out of their league in this investigation. Everything seemed to be heading in directions he had never gone before. He was getting a little worried.

18. TOO MUCH INFORMATION

ELI GOT TO THE JAMES RIVER CONTROL CENTER IN ABOUT AN hour. The control building was circa 1960, brick and stucco. Rain was coming down in buckets as he pulled into the parking area. The air temperature was almost balmy, and the thunder sounded like a light drumming, as if it was far away. Odd weather for that time of year. Once inside, he felt as if he had come out of his Wayback Machine and had been transported back to the 1960s. Linoleum on the floors, Steelcase furniture, and CRT monitors on tabletops. Even the hanging fluorescent lighting was perfect period stuff that one could not find anymore. The military's no-frills attitude for infrastructure was "if it ain't broke, don't fix it." In a way, it was kind of refreshing to be reminded of the "built to last" designs of that era.

He sat and listened to the three of them explain that they were really close to figuring out the mystery. After a couple of bites into his submarine sandwich, Mark Rogoff brought Eli up to date.

Pointing at Vic, he said, "You know, you've got a real gem in this guy. He saved us a lot of needless steps. Once we get the shipper IDs and proprietary data from the pipelines, all we have to do is run one more set of queries we have set up, and it will tell us whose shipments have been altered, when they were ordered, when they entered the pipeline, where they originated, and where and when they were delivered. All that and any alterations to the numbers can be produced in seconds."

Eli commented, "It looks like the pipeline data file should arrive about an hour before Vic and I need to take our sleep shift. Is there any chance you could have answers before we leave?"

Mark replied, "Unless the pipeline data arrives in an unexpected format, we should be able to plug it in and get answers in a few minutes."

Eli waited with them for the data file, deciding the information was more important than their shift change. He asked Rogoff about the military programming expert. "How's that NCIS IT specialist working out?"

"You mean Sarah Graham, right?"

"Yeah, that's her."

"She left last night. She convinced her superiors that she was just getting in the way of our progress because we had to train her as we went on pipeline supervisory systems. These programs were written before she was born."

At 1844 hours, the data file arrived at the Control Center. Rogoff imported the shipper identification data into their computer and ran a set of queries. Before 1900 hours, the monitor screen lit up with the results. Rogoff announced, "All twenty-six instances where data was altered, there was one shipper that was involved or common to every instance: NAPCO. All of their shipment sizes were adjusted. Sometimes the adjustment reduced the size of NAPCO's contribution to the batch it was a part of, and at the same time another shipper's contribution to the batch would be increased by the same amount. Other times, the reverse was achieved—increasing NAPCO's contribution and reducing another company's contribution."

After a pause to study the data, Mark continued, "This was done to every shipment of NAPCO on Provincial's and Confederated's pipeline system. After all the adjustments, the total amount NAPCO shipped remained the same. All the alterations amounted to a net of zero. There are alterations to shipments on other pipelines to other destinations, and, if necessary, we could run queries for all the alterations if you think you need it."

"We may need it later," Eli replied. "But this is plenty of information to digest at this time."

Eli turned to Vic and asked, "Got any ideas what might be their objective?"

"Shit! This is not what I expected. I would have expected a shipper's identity might be changed or an entire entry might be erased. At the very least, I expected the total amount of what NAPCO shipped would be adjusted. Why would anyone go to all this trouble just to alter the size of one set of shipments in one batch only to make the same alteration in reverse in a later batch?"

Eli sat quietly, letting his mind sift through potential scenarios.

Rogoff chimed in, "OK, the only thing I can come up with is either someone is trying to match a schedule or trying to eliminate a match to an existing schedule. Does that help anyone?"

Vic scratched his head. Dugan stared blankly into space. Then Vic said, "Let's backtrack. The shipments match a series of nominations made months before. We know that in the private enterprise world, the nominations are simply reservations a company makes to place its expected production or imports on a pipeline system to be delivered to market. The only sanction for not meeting your expected shipment schedule is that you make other arrangements in the transportation industry that most likely will increase your cost of transportation. That would be such a minor penalty that it would hardly be noticed. Certainly not something you would go to drastic measures to cover up."

"Does it work the same way on the government's side of the street?" Vic inquired.

Eli added, "Product movement in the Defense Department was not one of my stronger suits in the pipeline industry. But I can try to estimate the equivalents. Most, if not all, DOD shipments are governed by existing contracts. The DOD's estimated needs for a year are placed up for bid in preceding years. I am not sure, but I think they break it down by where the DOD terminals are located. For instance, the volume needed at Craney Island for a year is estimated and put up for bid. Suppliers that are qualified bidders will then bid on filling the volumes. I suppose the government accepts the bids based on price. The low bidder might be able to fill the needs of an entire terminal for a year. I imagine you found the names of more than one shipper?"

Rogoff answered, "There are several shippers in Craney Island's nomination file, but only one company's shipments were altered. That shipper is NAPCO."

"Let's assume then that several shippers were either needed or desired to fill Craney Island's needs. That would mean there are several contracts. I still cannot get to the place where a supplier would need to consider such drastic measures as murder and mass destruction to adjust or hide the size of its batches or the dates it was shipped. And when you add the fact that they did not alter the net amount of the total, it makes less sense. Unless you guys have some ideas, I'm afraid we are going to need the advice of an expert in the government procurement world. But in any event, we can report that the evidence you found points to NAPCO's involvement, or to someone else's desire to make it look as if NAPCO is involved?"

Rogoff rubbed the back of his neck and nodded. "I can't say any more than that. We can continue to analyze the shipping data to the other terminals where there were alterations. I don't know if it would lead to anything, but if that is what you want us to do, we will continue to analyze it."

"Yes, I want you continue that process. I am skeptical we will learn any more than what we know now, but we need to complete the task to answer any question that might arise about what we found elsewhere."

"Oh, by the way," Rogoff mentioned, "besides the shipment alterations on the Provincial and Confederated systems, we found almost as many alterations on movements to DOD facilities other than Craney Island and on other pipelines."

"I don't know if that's relevant at this time," Vic suggested. "Maybe we'll need to get back to Eli on that later."

Vic and Eli left Rogoff and Dugan, allowing them to write up their findings. Vic and Eli were exhausted, and they had drifted past their shift change, but they needed to report their findings before their forty-eight-hour deadline passed. Eli also needed to see if the intelligence agencies wanted to change Daneli's assignment. They headed back to the Unified Command and briefed Commander Brockington.

As soon as Brockington realized they had a likely corporate espionage perpetrator rather than a terrorist, he led them into Commander Hughes's office. In a matter of minutes, they were all part of a video conference with Admiral Ellingson and the four intelligence team leaders, FBI's Frank Gilbert, NSA Domestic Antiterror Director Stuart Yarborough, Homeland Security Advisor Derek Trimble, and CIA Counterterror Chief Kent Houck.

Brockington repeated what Eli had reported to him. And when he suggested that the evidence pointed to NAPCO's involvement, there was an eerie silence. Frank Gilbert broke the silence with the question Eli had expected.

"Eli, who or what is NAPCO?" he asked.

Eli replied, "NAPCO is North American Products Company. It's a diversified energy company. I believe it came about some ten years ago or so. I don't believe it owns or drills oil fields. However, it has grown significantly by the purchase of distribution and marketing companies in the oil industry. Apparently, it has a contract to supply the DOD with petroleum products.

"Everyone needs to be aware that there is a huge caveat on our findings. We have concluded that whoever committed the sabotage manipulated only the NAPCO shipments; however, we can't say for sure if it was done at their direction. Heck, we haven't figured out why the perpetrators needed to make the alterations. We only know that all the shipments to Craney Island by NAPCO were altered. We can only speculate on what are the most logical conclusions.

"However, it doesn't make sense that a terrorist would go to the trouble to acquire the know-how to hack into the programs and alter the shipment data on your computer records if terrorism was their overall objective. However, if altering the shipment data was their objective, the diversion of the fire would provide them with the time and the opportunity to make the shipping alterations. That's the logic we pursued. And if that is what they were after, it appears an investigation into NAPCO and why someone might want to alter its shipment data is logical as well."

After another long pause, Commander Hughes asked, "What progress has been made on the terrorism angle?"

NSA Antiterror Director Yarborough replied, "The latest reports from the intelligence community are inconclusive at this date. There was not enough light for the satellite imagery to detect any activity before the terminal burst into flames. However, afterward, the light created by the blaze was sufficient to expose a small, unidentifiable watercraft departing the area. After a few seconds, the watercraft disappeared. Either it traveled beyond the light from the blaze or beyond the range of the satellite, or it was scuttled. However, no debris washed up on nearby shorelines. Attempts to determine the origin of the watercraft have not been fruitful. There is no record of a military or civilian watercraft in the area, and there were no sightings by potential witnesses in the area."

NSA Director Yarborough continued, "A blanket examination of the chatter from e-mail, telephone, and Internet-based communication devices did not detect any existing language, markers, or code for terrorist activity aimed at this event. But that doesn't mean the people involved aren't using other means of communication or that they are not using coded messages.

"Active surveillance of known terror groups also came up negative as to this event. Prior to our meeting, we placed a rating of thirty percent confidence of terrorism activity as the cause and seventy percent for all other potential activity. Upon hearing the Daneli report, I would not recommend we revise the confidence rating. However, it would be my recommendation that we consider reallocating our emphasis and resources at this time."

FBI Director Gilbert cleared his throat and weighed into the discussion. "If we are going to concentrate on industrial sabotage and Department of Defense energy contracts, it appears our investigation will rely heavily on the cooperation of the Department of Justice and the DOD Procurement Office. I can advise my director, and we can expect he will confer with the attorney general to recommend how DOJ wishes to proceed. What can we expect from the DOD?"

Admiral Ellingson responded, "I will brief the Joint Chiefs after we adjourn. They have been following your efforts. I expect they will agree that the Navy and DOD Procurement Office cooperate to appoint an investigative team to take over where Daneli left off. Frank, do you think you can get a recommendation from the AG this afternoon?"

"That would be my goal," Gilbert replied.

"I will try to do the same," said the admiral. And then he continued, "I don't like not knowing what precipitated this attack on the fuel depot. And I can assure you that the Joint Chiefs feel the same way. They are going to be disappointed that although you found a company that is the likely focal point of what transpired there, any accusation at this time would be circumstantial at best. And we haven't come up with a motive yet or the answer to the question of why. I am not saying that you all have not done a great job of dealing with this event. I will try to defend your efforts. But they get really impatient when an act of this magnitude occurs to their vital resources.

"Mr. Taylor, I understand that your firm is providing assistance on developing a substitute for the fuel depot. I also understand you and half of your company's on-site team is overdue for a sleep shift. I will be expecting a progress report from Commander Hughes on this matter two hours after you are back on duty. Gentlemen, we have a lot to accomplish. I appreciate your dedication."

The meeting ended, but before Eli returned to the hotel, he made sure everyone from Daneli had his or her assignment. On the way back to the hotel, Vic had a lot to talk about.

"Eli, I can't believe we are being nosed out of the hunt. We lead these bozos to the correct scent, and they kick us off to the side. They won't catch a cold without us. Don't get me wrong. I enjoy the work that Daneli gets. We have the most fun of anyone in our industry. But this kind of fun comes only a few times in a lifetime. Besides, we are really good at solving mysteries and finding the bad guys. How are we going to get back in the hunt?"

Eli got the message loud and clear. "They are very grateful for our help. They are the principal. We are the contract help. And besides, this is the military and our nation's intelligence branches. What would it say about their capability if they allow some oil industry contractor to lead their investigation? Come on, Vic, you've been in the military!"

Eli pulled into the hotel parking lot. As he was about to get out of the vehicle and tell Vic to play it cool, he found Vic was still in the debating mood.

"OK. I know you are right. You always know best. You know how grateful I am for you rescuing me out of the rat race at West Industries. And then you gave me this great opportunity when you went on your own. I owe you a lot. I want a chance to make it all up to you."

"You don't owe me a thing. I don't do charity work. I do what I do for my own self-interest and to do the right thing. We need to show the Navy how much we appreciate this opportunity. They put their faith us. We don't need to do or say anything that implies that we think we are better than they are. That would be an insult, and we would never be asked back."

"OK, Eli, I'll lay it all on the table. I've got a hunch about what went down here. Ever since you let me work with Rogoff and I got to look into the fuel movements and saw that NAPCO was involved, a bright light has been blinking in my brain. This goes back to the summer when I was dating that Justice Department lawyer chick. You remember her, don't you?"

"Yeah, but what does that have do with anything?"

"It just so happens that I met her when I was testifying in that damage prevention regulation case against BP. She was recently divorced. I had just left Shari. We had a few drinks..."

"I'm real tired, Vic. You can tell me about the great sex part at another time. Just get to the heart of the matter."

"Sorry, just thinking about her again reminded me of how sexy she is. Anyway, it turns out she heard from a colleague who was litigating it that I was a pipeliner. She was working on something that had some pipeline issues. She wouldn't say, but I am almost sure that NAPCO was the company she was looking at. Anyway, she asked me how pipelines kept track of who owned the product in the pipeline. Either our romance went stale, or her interest in pipelines diminished. That was when we stopped seeing each other. The point is, I'd like your permission to talk to her about our little mystery. I won't divulge anything about the investigation. I would just like to ask her out and casually inquire about her pipeline matter. That's all. If nothing is connected, I will drop it. If it is, I will place it back in your lap without going any further. What do you think?"

"The issue is—do you know when to shut it down, and should I trust you to recognize when that is, and to resist temptation to go it alone without my counsel?"

"That's brutal, man. I thought you were on my side."

"I'm on your side, Vic. I just want to make it abundantly clear that I am not authorizing you to use your judgment on this."

"Then I have your approval?"

"Reluctantly, yes. But you better not let me down."

"Great! I'll give her a call before I hit the sack."

19. A CHANGE IN COURSE

ELI AWOKE FROM HIS SIX-HOUR SLEEP A LITTLE MORE GROGGY than the day before, but still within the tolerable range. Since this was his third straight "eighteen hours on, six hours off" shift, it was time to go to a "twelve hours on, twelve hours off" broken-day shift to avoid sleep deprivation. He called Vic's cell phone. As usual, Vic was waiting for Eli in the restaurant. A call to Mike was a repeat of the day before. Eli woke him up. He had slept through his alarm. He wasn't used to keeping emergency response hours. That's why first-responder shift mates are like soldiers. They are in it together, pulling for one another and resisting the urge to judge their bunker mates. Making sure everyone is ready for the next shift change is just part of it.

Eli's cell phone was flashing. He had a text message from Hank: "At 2300 hours yesterday, the temporary fuel supply depot at Charleston was filling the first Navy aircraft carrier. Two destroyers and another carrier are in place and about to receive fuel. All is well."

Eli wasn't going to be able to wash the smile off his face for quite some time. Hank was a miracle worker.

As Eli entered the motel restaurant, his eyes captured a familiar sight. Vic was sweet-talking a cute waitress, and she was all ears.

"Hey, boss. Please say hello to Heather," Vic said.

"Hello, Heather. Nice meeting you," he replied.

Heather smiled and told Vic she had to tend to her other customers.

"Not bad, huh?" Vic interjected. "I'd say she is a low first-round to a high second-round draft choice."

"You never cease to amaze me."

"I get lonely, you know. I need companionship. Oh, by the way, I called, e-mailed, and texted my Justice friend. Not a word back in return. I figured out how to reach her at work before I tucked myself in and left her a message. I should hear from her soon."

"Maybe you are losing your touch. Or maybe she only needed you because she was getting information from you. Maybe she doesn't need you anymore."

"Get real, man. Remember who you're talking to. She is either out of the country, in the hospital, or dead. I'm going over to her condo as soon as we finish our breakfast. If I remember correctly, she leaves for work about eight a.m. If she's not there, I'm going to DOJ."

"You want to hear some great news?"

"Shoot."

"The temporary Navy fuel depot at Charleston began fueling a carrier last night."

"No shit! Hank is a freak. I'm going to have to work hard to top that one."

"Just don't do anything too crazy. Remember what we talked about earlier."

"You're beginning to sound like my ex. Nag, nag, nag!"

Vic's drive to Georgetown took about two hours. On the way, he called Ann Calloway's cell phone but only got her voicemail. Vic left her a message saying he was coming by to visit. Of course, he couldn't resist telling her that he missed seeing her in that white lace negligee she wore the last time he spent the night with her.

When Vic arrived at the gate to her condo, he called up to let him in. There was no answer. He remembered her passcode was her mom's birthday: 070241. He pushed it into the keypad, and the gate slid open. He prided himself on his memory as he drove to her row-style townhome. At 8:05 in the morning, it was barely past dawn. He didn't notice the yellow police ribbon that was draped across her stoop until he was about to climb the three steps leading to her front door. An immediate sinking pain in his gut and a hard swallow was his reaction. Police ribbon only meant one thing to Vic. Her condo was a crime scene, and the fact that Ann hadn't answered his calls led him to the most morbid conclusion. She was either dead or in the hospital. He turned around and walked slowly to his vehicle. He sat inside and contemplated his next move and Ann Calloway. The Department of Justice was less than a half hour away. He had no reason not to visit there next.

Vic had visited DOJ more than once when testifying in the BP matter this past summer. He knew the way and where to park. He contemplated whether he was too early for normal business hours, so he decided to grab a cup of coffee. He stopped at Casey's Coffee and Doughnut Shop on Twenty-Third Street. Vic picked up a Washington Post and bided his time until 9:00 a.m. When he arrived at Justice, he signed in at the visitors' window and indicated his visit was with Ann Calloway.

The woman attendant asked, "Sir, do you have an appointment?"

Vic shook his head no. She asked that he wait a moment.

Vic stood off to the side of the visitors' check-in and figured if something really bad had happened to her, someone would be sent down to tell him the bad news. That was close to what happened. Only instead of a single someone, two men in suits and a security guard approached.

One of the suited men stopped at the visitors' window and looked in at the sign-in attendant. She pointed to Vic.

"Are you Mr. Majeski?" he asked Vic.

"Yes, sir, Victor Majeski."

"Please walk with me. Ms. Calloway cannot meet with you, and we want to talk to you about your visit."

Vic dutifully followed, and the two other men walked behind him. They led him to a room adjacent to the security office on the first floor. The room was textbook. A wooden table stood in the middle with four metal chairs, no pictures on the walls, a sofa against one wall, and a two-way mirror in the other. The man who had greeted him asked Vic to take a seat at the table.

"Mr. Majeski, my name is Oliver Rudd. I work with Ann at Justice. Have you spoken with her recently?"

"I suppose the last time we talked, it was in person. That would be sometime in August. However, I did try to reach her last night and this morning. I wanted to see her again."

"Why did you want to see her?"

"While I was a DOJ witness for the government's case against BP Oil, we started a social relationship. We hadn't seen each other in a while, and I missed her."

"One second, please."

Mr. Rudd asked the other suited gentleman to open up his laptop computer. After a couple moments of typing, he looked up and resumed his interview.

"Mr. Majeski, I didn't see you on Ms. Calloway's recent visitor list. But as you suggested, I just looked up the visitor list for BP legal team. I see your visits now. I regret the formality here, but we are tightly screening all contacts to Ms. Calloway. You see, this past Tuesday, the seventh, Ms. Calloway was shot to death."

Vic just stared into the dark eyes of Oliver Rudd and shook his head. He had expected the worst, but confirmation was much more dramatic and emotional than he expected. His eyes swelled with tears. As he reached into his back pocket for his handkerchief, he cleared his throat and asked, "Can you tell me what happened?"

"She and an attorney with the Government Accounting Office were found shot early Tuesday morning in an Arlington parking garage."

Vic was trying to imagine the scene when Rudd interrupted his thoughts.

"You wouldn't have any idea why she was there that day, would you?"

Vic collected himself.

"Uh, no. Sorry. I can't help thinking of her. I don't have a clue. We really didn't know that much about each other. She was single. I'm single. We hit it off and had a few dates. We made a promise to each other not to talk shop when we were on a date."

"So why come by to visit her at her office?"

"When she didn't return my calls, I went by her condo early this morning. I thought I could catch her before she drove to work. I saw the police crime-scene tape on her stoop. I got worried. I impulsively came by here hoping to see her or find out what might have happened."

"Do you have a habit of visiting your girlfriends at work without talking to them first?"

Vic peered at Rudd, realizing that he was being interviewed as a possible suspect.

"What were the circumstances of her death?" he asked.

"What do you mean?" Rudd replied.

"You know what I mean. Are you considering her death a murder?"

"We don't know what to make of her death. The scene in the garage appeared to be a murder–suicide. A pistol registered in her name was found in her hand. A note was found in her other hand. The note indicated they were lovers, and she was ending it all."

"That's not Ann. I can't see her losing her mind over a lover and choosing violence as a solution. There has got to be another reason."

"Well, we agree on one thing, Mr. Majeski. We have yet to find anything to suggest that she was involved with the GAO general counsel. They were colleagues. Let me ask you something. It's about the last communication we have from her. It's a message to her boss. What do you know about Rubik's Memo?"

Vic immediately recognized the term, but couldn't place it. "You said Rubik's Memo, not Rubik's Cube?"

"That's right, Rubik's Memo."

At that moment, it all flashed before his eyes. That was the document that had started her interest in the pipeline business. That was why she had wanted to visit with him when he was here working on the BP trial. That was what had brought him to see her today. He was connecting the dots between her and Craney Island. Then his instincts kicked in. He didn't want to lose control of this investigation, and he didn't want to get his boss in hot water with the military.

"Mr. Majeski! Victor Majeski, are you there?"

Vic looked directly into Rudd's eyes, just the way Eli had told him honest people answer questions. "Sorry, I was scanning my memory to see if I could remember anything about Rubik other than the cube. Ann and I initially talked about our jobs, but I was under the impression she was using that as an icebreaker. Trust me. Our relationship was more social than business.

"And before you ask me the obvious question; we had a great relationship. It didn't really end; it just became squeezed out and a lower priority. I live in Atlanta. She's up here. When my BP testimony was over, I stopped coming to DC for a while. The only reason I am here now is that I have a business assignment with the Navy in Chesapeake. I am going to be here for a couple of weeks, and DC is only a few hours' drive away. I got to thinking of her, and how we might hook up again. That's it."

Rudd examined Vic—his eyes, his overall body language—and he reflected on his choice of words. Vic had him flummoxed, and Vic could see it in his body language as Rudd dragged his fingers through his hair and squirmed in his chair. To seal the impression, Vic took over the offense.

"Ann was a great gal," he said. "I'd like to be a part of the effort to bring to justice the son of a bitch who killed her. Is there anything I can do to help?"

"I can't think of anything at the moment."

"Look, I'm staying at the Waterfront Holiday Inn in Portsmouth. Here's my business card. It's got all my contact information. By the way, are you heading up the investigation?"

"I'm a contributor. The Arlington Police has the lead as long as there is no link to any case or client the two were working on. Justice and FBI are assisting."

"Do you have a card you can give me? You can count on me

going over our conversations in my mind. If I remember anything that might be of help, I'd like to call you. Oh, and one more thing: since I'm here, is there a chance I could talk to Richard Fleming? He was the other attorney I worked with on the BP matter. I'd like to pay my respects to him with regard to Ann."

Rudd replied, "I suppose so."

Rudd used his multichannel radio to see if Fleming was in. He was. Rudd told him Vic Majeski was in the lobby and wanted to know if he had a moment for him. Fleming approved. Rudd gave Vic his card and stood up, and they shook hands.

"I'll walk you back to the visitors' window to get you a pass."

Rudd got a pass on a lanyard from the attendant and accompanied Vic up to the fourteenth floor. They talked some more in the elevator, and Vic promised he would look through his BP file notes to see if there was any mention of Rubik's Memo. When they got off the elevator, the receptionist notified Fleming that Vic was there. When Fleming arrived, Rudd left them.

As Fleming walked Vic back to his office, he asked, "So what brings you back to DOJ?"

Before Vic answered, he made sure he was out of earshot in Fleming's office. Both Fleming and Vic sat down in the chairs surrounding the coffee table off to the side of Fleming's desk.

"I was trying to reconnect with Ann Calloway. You know we dated for a while when I was working with you on BP."

"Oh, I didn't think about that. We are all in a knot about what happened."

"I'm up here on business with the Navy, and I've been trying to contact her. When she wasn't returning my calls, I got worried. So I thought I'd try to catch her at the office. When I checked in downstairs, they told me she was shot to death. I'm pretty messed up about it. What do you think happened?"

"It's like something out of a movie. We don't buy the crime-scene evidence that indicates it was about a lovers' breakup."

"I am with you there. I was just wondering if it might have something to do with that oil movement puzzle she was working. Rudd, the guy who was just questioning me, told me her last written words were about some memo."

"Do you mean Rubik's Memo?"

"I think that was it. While we were seeing each other, she asked me how petroleum product shipments moved in pipelines and how the pipelines kept track of the ownership of the batches if they changed hands."

"We have been wondering about that. One of the other attorneys is looking into it. I believe it's Neil Driscoll."

"Well, when they told me about Ann, I thought I'd come up here and pay my respects to you and to offer my assistance. If she was murdered, I'd like to think I did everything I could to help you catch the son of a bitch. Don't hesitate to call me if there is anything at all I might be able to help you with."

"I'll pass that on to Driscoll."

Richard Fleming walked Vic back to the reception area, and Vic was back in his rental car in a matter of moments. He drove out of the parking garage at Justice, pulled into a side street parking spot, put the vehicle in park, and cried. He had held his emotions in check for the last half hour, but the dam that held them back broke, and they poured out as he sat there and sobbed. After a few minutes, he was back in control of himself to the extent that he could call Eli.

"Hey, amigo, do you have a few minutes?"

"Yeah, Vic. Where are you?"

"I'm sitting in my vehicle just outside of Justice. You won't believe what I found out. It's sad, man—real sad. Are you ready?"

"Hell yeah, I'm ready. Don't give me the song and dance. Just tell me about it."

"Slow down, man. Can't you see I'm hurting?"

"OK. I'm sorry about that. I guess I'm just in an impatient mood. So what happened?"

"My Justice gal—she's been murdered. She was found dead next to an attorney from GAO. And guess what the last communication she had with colleagues was about?"

Just as Vic got the words out of his mouth, lightning appeared in the sky and a loud clap of thunder shook his bones.

"I'm sympathetic that you might be broken up about this. I know this is not what you were expecting to find. However, I'm not in a guessing mood."

The rain was coming down harder now than when he had arrived. He had to yell into his cell phone so that Eli could hear him over the sound of huge raindrops pelting his vehicle. "OK," he shouted, "I'll skip the drama. In so many words, she said the NAPCO oil shipments mystery is back. If what she was working on and the Craney Island event are linked, I don't think it would be a reach that whoever is behind Craney Island has something to do with her murder. I wonder if the GAO attorney found dead next to her was also investigating NAPCO. Whatever it is, I'm getting a strong feeling we need to find out if there is a connection. All we have to do is figure out what is so damn important about the shipments."

"That's not going to be easy, especially with all the law enforcement and intelligence guys on the trail. Look, Vic, we don't have any authority to look into this, and if anyone finds out we are, we'll never get a military job again. I'm also worried you could get your fingers caught in the cookie jar. The feds don't take kindly when they find somebody snooping around their cases."

"I'm way ahead of them, boss. Everything we need to know is in a memo that was circulated in Justice. And I think I know how to get a copy of it without anyone being the wiser."

"If you are sure you can get the memo without raising any suspicion about what you're after, then I might be willing to go along."

"Just leave it to old Victor. This is going to be a slam dunk."

"All right, Sherlock, be very careful. And keep me posted."

"I think I can do that."

20. THE RIDE OF THE POLISH COWBOY

VIC WAS BROKEN UP ABOUT ANN, BUT HE KNEW HE WAS ONTO something. He had to push Ann and her demise out of his thoughts so he could think straight. He was now more determined than ever to find out what was so damn important that so many people had to die. Maybe the memo held the key, and if it did, he knew where to find it.

Vic had a hunch when he left Portsmouth that he might be spending his sleep shift in DC. However, he was completely wrong about what would keep him overnight. He had thrown his duffel in the trunk of the rental car. In the duffel were his bar-hopping duds. Vic was no cowboy, but being in the oil business meant you were around guys from Texas. He soon found out that women in bars were drawn to men who looked great in jeans and cowboy boots.

Raised in New Jersey, and after a couple of tours with the Marines, he settled in the Baltimore area working for West Industries. At first he didn't know you could buy steel-toed safety boots that look like the best alligator-skin cowboy boots you could find in the old west. And nobody looked better in Levis, cowboy boots, and a western shirt than Vic. If you think actor

Sam Elliot looked like the classic American cowboy, then Vic was a close second.

Vic had with him a close facsimile to what he had been wearing when he met Patricia O'Galvin. She was the executive office manager at the GAO. He met her when West Industries was holding its annual management meeting in Baltimore a couple of years ago. It was Vic's first invitation after qualifying by his promotion to supervisor status. In the Wyndham Hotel bar before a dinner meeting, he spotted three attractive women getting sloshed at a nearby table. Miss O'Galvin was one of the three. He couldn't resist making their acquaintance. Vic strolled over in his best cowboy amble and introduced himself. At six foot four and with tattooed forearms that were exposed by his rolled-up sleeves and his bodybuilder physique, Vic was a city girl's dream.

He and Patty had a fling that never got too serious. Patty was the name Vic called her. She was crazy about Vic, but she realized that he wasn't going to be husband material. He was a creation of her imagination. And he knew how to fulfill all her fantasies. He had talked to her just about a month ago. He had heard she was getting married, and he wanted to wish her well. He said he would stop by and take her to lunch the next time he was in DC. Kismet, he thought. He called her cell phone.

"What you doing, dreamboat?" she answered.

"How you doing, sweetheart? Guess what. I'm in town, and I was wondering if you might be available for that lunch I promised you."

"I have a manicure appointment, but I can reschedule. What did you have in mind?"

"I was thinking of treating you to lunch where we first met—at the Wyndham."

"That would be irresistible. But isn't it a little extravagant?"

"I am putting the bill on my company credit card. But I'm feeling a little guilty."

"Why is that, Victor?"

"To be honest, I thought about you when I realized that the assignment I am working on requires some information about a GAO matter. Would you mind if I mixed a little business with the pleasure of dining with you?"

"No, I won't mind so long as you can give me a preview."

"This is very hush-hush. The assignment I'm on has to do with liquid fuel supplies to the Navy. There was a memo that has been referred to as Rubik's Memo. I am investigating the fuel shipments delivered to the Navy this year. One of the suppliers is NAPCO."

"You are working on that! That's been a hot topic around the office for the last few days. The FBI has been talking to everyone. Tuesday, our general counsel was found murdered. And just yesterday morning, one of our auditors died in a natural gas explosion at his home. I've got a copy of the memo. I'll bring it with me, along with anything else that you might find interesting."

"You'd do that for me?"

"I don't want you to get too big of a head, but there isn't anybody I trust more than you. I am so glad you called. This is so exciting! And, of course, it will be so nice to see you."

There was no convention or event in town that attracted cowboys, so when Vic entered the Wyndham, he turned a few heads. He got a room for the night and left his duffel in his room before he headed for his rendezvous with Patty. He sat at the bar, ordered a Jack Daniels, and smiled back at any fetching woman casting her gaze on him. He was expecting Patty O'Galvin, and he didn't want to offend her. So Vic did nothing more than smile back, returning not even a wink or a long look.

Patty arrived at about 11:45 a.m. One step into the main dining room, she directed her gaze at the bar. When she looked in that direction, Vic spotted her and stood up. That was all it took to put a smile on her face, and she walked in Vic's direction. Patty was a blond-haired, attractive gal in her mid-thirties. She could turn a few heads as well. As she approached, Vic grinned and opened up his arms, expecting a big hug. And that was what he got.

"Ooow, you great big hunk. You look better than ever," she purred, still caught up in Vic's embrace.

"Let me get a good look at you," he said, releasing her from his arms. "What a vision of classic beauty you are. How did I ever let you get away?"

They spent the next moments catching up, and then the hostess approached and advised Vic that his table was awaiting them whenever they were ready. Vic asked if he could transfer his bar tab, and upon getting an affirmation, he ordered Patty a gin and tonic, her favorite libation.

Their meeting went just as Vic had imagined it. Patty showed him a picture of her fiancé. Vic approved. Patty gave him a copy of Rubik's Memo from her pocketbook along with a copy of the police report of the Gary French–Ann Calloway homicide.

Patty looked around the room in a measured scan, then leaned closer to Vic and whispered, "I can tell you something nobody has asked. I haven't said anything to anybody yet because it has me a little worried. The GAO auditor who was killed in his home yesterday, Brian Matusak—I saw him in Gary French's office a week or so ago. Yesterday I asked Gary's secretary, Irene Cohen, if Gary and Brian were working on anything together. She said she didn't think so, and then she said something that didn't jibe with what I had seen. She said she didn't believe they had ever met. She quickly walked away and turned down the hallway. I saw her burst into tears when she thought she was out of my sight. I know she was lying because Gary French didn't meet with anyone who did not get recorded in her notebook."

Vic was paying close attention, but he asked, "Patty, do you mind if I write this down?"

"Not at all," she replied.

Vic pulled out a pen from his jeans, turned over the photocopy of Rubik's Memo, and jotted down all of Patty's story.

When she asked about Vic's role in it, he knew he had to give her a taste of it, but he had to draw the line so she wouldn't be able to connect all the dots. Vic was not afraid that Patty would do or say anything purposely to get him in trouble. He was more afraid of her innocently saying something to the wrong person.

"My company's assignment has more to do with what the Navy is trying to figure out. We're down in Chesapeake at the Navy Fuel Supply Depot. We are helping them reconstruct some shipment schedules that were lost in their data bank. Someone we talked with mentioned that there was a memo circulating in GAO this summer that might help us figure out who owned what. There is probably no connection to my investigation. I need to see if I should rule it out. But what that secretary told you is a little odd."

They soon got off the subject, had a nice meal, and parted after another hug and a meaningless kiss. Vic could not wait to get to his room and read the memo.

The first time he read it, he was surprised that it was nothing that he didn't already know. He was beginning to read it again when he focused on the handwritten scribble at the bottom: "How do we verify that the fuel did not originate from a supplier that is not on the list of approved suppliers?"

Then it all came back to him. That was the question Ann asked him when they were working together on the BP matter. She wanted to know how the original owner of the product could be verified for compliance to the approved shippers list. Maybe, Vic thought, the auditor was wondering the same thing.

"That's it!" he screamed. His mind was now in high gear. Vic thought, What if NAPCO is delivering fuel that originated from a country not approved by our government? What if NAPCO's contract specifies countries of origin that are off limits? He thought for a few moments how revising the size of the batches might throw somebody off the trail. He imagined a few scenarios that explained how altering the batch sizes might disguise the true owner.

Vic sat there mulling it all over and over again. "And Patty mentioned that the auditor was also found dead. That's a lot of killing for just trying to sell some energy to the Navy," he said out loud. Vic didn't think the gravity of the events had an even balance. He tried to imagine scenarios in which everything made sense, but he knew he needed some quiet time to figure it out.

Here he was in the nation's capital, so he took a walk along the National Mall. It was a good morning to do just that. He could be alone among thousands of tourists, and nothing would bother his concentration. He first sat on a bench near the Lincoln Memorial until he got to a place in his deciphering he needed to get to. He got up and paced nervously. He stopped suddenly and then looked for another place to sit and contemplate again for a while. He repeated these maneuvers several times until he seemed to wake up, as if after a nap. He looked around, and he found himself in front of the Vietnam Veterans Memorial.

My God! he thought. "What a coincidence. I start to figure things out, and I'm back to where the world started for guys like me. Just like when I got back home after my tour of duty in Desert Storm. We've got the military involved and people pushing buttons in high places that don't make a lot of sense, but they fuck with our lives."

Vic was ready now to resume his role in this drama. He called Eli to tell him about it.

"So, this is why I'm here. It's all about this memo that explains why it is impossible to trace the ownership of fuel shipments once they are nominated to be shipped on a pipeline. Everyone calls it Rubik's Memo, like the cube. I'm not sure why they call it that. It's authored by a guy named Rubin. I'm guessing that it's a play on the name because they are both puzzles.

"Anyway, I got the memo from a friend who works at the GAO. On the surface, it seems to be no more than an explanation of why it is nearly impossible to trace the ownership of the fuel once it enters the supply and transportation chain. NAPCO is the only shipper used as an example of a company who has a Defense Department contract and whose fuel shipments might be traded several times before they reach Craney Island. I find it interesting that the author singled out NAPCO and the Navy's shipments to Craney Island, but that is not what caught my eye.

"At the bottom of the memo is the handwritten question, 'How do we verify that the fuel did not originate from a supplier that is not on the list of approved suppliers?' What do you make of it?"

The edge on Vic's voice communicated drama and enthusiasm, and Eli was catching the enthusiasm. "OK, let's parse this out. We've got two arenas of activity where things are happening at about the same time frame. At Craney Island, we have the destruction of an important military asset that is planned merely as a distraction so an energy supplier can safely access the military database to alter the size of shipments it made to the Navy. At the other arena, this memo arises that deals with the same energy supplier who ships to the Navy at the same facility that is destroyed, and someone is questioning how one can trace the ownership of the supplies and shipments. And there is a handwritten comment on the memo asking how one can confirm that the fuel didn't originate from a supplier that is not on the approved list. And once this memo arises, the DOJ attorney working on it is murdered along with the GAO general counsel. Is that right?"

"You got that right, but let me clarify one fact. The memo originated some five months ago, in July, but there is more. An auditor at GAO recently dragged it up again, and he was killed along with his family in a natural gas explosion at his home on Thursday. My contact saw him visiting with the GAO general counsel last week. And when my contact asked the general counsel's secretary what the auditor and general counsel were working on together, she replied that they didn't know each other. Here is my question. What is so damn important about the size of shipments and their link to a supplier that might not be on the government's approved list?"

Eli responded, "My instincts tell me that you are on the right track. I suspect that the approved list of suppliers does not include companies whose crude or product originates in certain countries where the United States has broken diplomatic relations, or countries the United States has imposed economic sanctions or restrictions against. And at the top of that list would be countries the United States has established an embargo against because of recent human rights violations. We are probably talking about countries like Cuba, Iran, Sudan, North Korea, etc. Of those, only Iran is an oil exporter. From what little I know of NAPCO, I have no idea of how it gets the fuel it markets in the United States."

Eli continued, "I think I need to do some more research into NAPCO. I've been doing some research on my own about them, but what you found suggests I dig deeper. When you get back to Craney, we can pool our information and brainstorm. But before I let you go, let me congratulate you on some fine investigative work. Now get your ass back here at Craney as soon as you can."

* * *

Vic strolled into the RV at Craney Island about four in the afternoon. The entire Daneli team happened to be on duty and somewhere near the RV. Eli called everyone together for a conference.

"Listen up, everybody! I know Vic and I have not been obeying our shift rules, but I think you will understand once you hear why. As you know, the Navy has taken us off the industrial sabotage investigation. Well, Vic came to me with a persuasive plea to let him continue to investigate it on the sly. I agreed. Most of Vic's response duties were no longer needed, so he had time to devote to this hunch he wanted to follow.

"I'd like your thoughts on what Vic and I have been working on. First of all, Vic's hunch had to do with a company whose shipments we discovered had been altered during the event here at Craney. That company is NAPCO. They are an independent distributor and marketer of energy products. NAPCO won a bid contract with the Department of Defense in 2005 to supply the military with refined petroleum products.

"When our preliminary investigation revealed that the fire and explosion here were the likely result of industrial sabotage, we hired Mr. Rogoff, who verified our suspicions. And just so everyone is up to date, Mark Rogoff is now working as the Navy's IT specialist as of early this morning, since his research for us was complete. They are working to revise and update their programs to make it more difficult for an unauthorized person to alter their shipment schedules.

"But getting back to what Rogoff discovered for us, he found further confirmation that additional NAPCO shipments have been altered. Besides the Craney Island deliveries, he found US government shipment alterations to Fort Richardson in Anchorage, Alaska, and at Fort Bragg, North Carolina. All the alterations were performed during the first hour of the fire, and they were made from the Craney Island terminal when controllers were busy trying to determine what might have gone wrong at Craney Island. We don't know how the saboteurs knew they could perform the alterations in that way; we just know that is the way they did it.

"Vic followed that lead, which was based upon a loose coincidence I will elaborate on later, by trying to visit with an acquaintance who might know something about NAPCO and the DOJ's recent interest in their fuel movements. He discovered that this acquaintance was shot to death this past Tuesday along with the general counsel for the GAO while they met in a parking garage in or near DC. We now know that the DOJ attorney had recently begun working on the NAPCO matter once more. We are not sure about the GAO's general counsel, but we suspect they were working on the matter together. On top of that, the home of an auditor at GAO was set on fire, killing the entire family. Vic and I suspect that their deaths and the Craney Island event are directly related.

"So it is our conclusion that this is all the result of bad guys, some really bad guys, working on behalf of NAPCO to hide something. First of all, this is all conjecture at this point. Do not assume that any of what I am saying has been verified to the extent that we can turn it over to the Navy. The military intelligence community is aware of Mr. Rogoff's findings, but they know nothing yet of what Vic has discovered.

"As of twenty-four hours ago, that's all we knew. Since then, I had someone help me with my research of NAPCO. A colleague of mine who is an energy industry consultant worked for the firm that NAPCO hired to assist them in their formation. He enlisted the recollection of his coworkers who were assigned to the NAPCO formation. The rest of what I now know was taken from them.

"NAPCO was formed in 1991 by executives who broke away from Bronco Petroleum. According to my sources, the only CEO NAPCO has had never worried much about investment capital. He quickly found funding for all their acquisitions without difficulty. It was as if he had a secret sugar daddy ready to spend money on all of their projects. The money came from all over—foreign banks, brokerage houses in the United States, and abroad. And some from individual investors.

"This was not so much an unorthodox approach, but it was the way it came about. There was never a public offering or placement of stock. This is an all-equity, privately held stock company. In case you are wondering, there are only a few other modern energy companies formed in this manner. The rest of NAPCO's funds are derived from profits and short-term debt. I know what you all are thinking: this might be interesting, but how does it enlighten us about the fuel shipments to the Navy? I'll try to tie it together as we go.

"While this info came from one source, I went on the Internet to see if I could find the fuel purchases NAPCO made. Luckily, most of it is published in Platt's Oilgram, to which I subscribe. About eighty percent of NAPCO's product was purchased from a Mexican oil producer, COMEX. The rest is from a patchwork of small producers that presented bargains. When I got to this point, I expected that I was at a dead end. After all, it has always been near to impossible to look into the dealings of Mexican producers.

"But it just so happens that my Internet search presented a host of articles about COMEX and its recent issues. Apparently, the denationalization of Mexico's oil industry in 1993 didn't favor all newly privatized companies. COMEX either sold or lost almost all of its exploration business and became more or less an independent refiner. In 2004, ninety-four percent of the product it refined was purchased from other sources. Now here is the quirky shit. By the end of 2005, it had fallen behind on most of its production orders due to a series of problems at its refineries, and it was in desperate straits. So when the NAPCO contract was made with DOD, COMEX didn't have the production to supply it. So COMEX became a purchaser of refined products to fill the NAPCO orders. I searched through all the published trades and transactions in Platt's to determine who was COMEX's supplier. There were only three: AOPC out of Nigeria, the country of Sudan, and PETGO, the nationalized oil producer from Venezuela.

"What made that information relevant was what Vic uncovered in DC. Vic told me that his DOJ contact was investigating NAPCO's shipments to the Navy, and there was an issue about verifying that the shipments originated from countries that were on their approved list. It was then that we began to wonder if the Craney Island event and the killings might be the result of hiding the identity of the originating country. Then I found out that NAPCO had to sign a pledge that none of its supplies for the DOD contract could originate from energy producers on the US embargo list.

"Since Vic and I talked early this morning, I found out which oil-exporting countries are not on the US approved list. They are Iran, Sudan, and Venezuela. I then tried to see if I could eliminate any of these countries through data on the Internet. I ruled out Iran because COMEX hasn't traded with companies that buy Iranian oil products. I then ruled out Sudan because the volumes COMEX purchased from Sudan were insufficient to satisfy the contract NAPCO had with the DOD. That process eliminated everyone except Venezuela and its exporting company, PETGO.

"For the sake of argument, let's assume that Venezuela is supplying COMEX with one hundred percent of the volumes needed for the DOD contract. My question is, how does NAPCO not know that? It is the one whose neck is on the line if it's true. I expect we won't discover what NAPCO knew or should have known. I know of no source for that information. I also don't know NAPCO's motivation for either ignoring the possibility that COMEX's product originated in an unapproved country, or being aware of it and trying to hide it. I also don't know if Justice is also conducting an investigation into this angle. My question to all of you is twofold: do we continue to investigate this on our own, or do we turn everything over to Justice and the military intelligence community? I am asking you because all of you are vital to the future of this company, and I felt you should have a say."

Mike was the first to comment. "Wow, that is a lot to digest. My first reaction is to get rid of it. It appears at least five persons are dead because they might have known too much. That strikes me as a police matter and not one for a private company. Now, if DOJ and military intelligence ask for our assistance, then we have a different question to answer."

Within the next few minutes, everyone except Vic took Mike's position. Eli looked at Vic and asked him what his thoughts were.

Vic replied, "I'd like to know more about NAPCO, and I bet I can find out who its sugar daddy is. But Mike might be right. What you and I uncovered might be best suited for the government to pursue. I'd like to be a part of it, but I am not going to be upset or stand in your way if you turn it all over to them."

"But on the other hand"—Vic paused—"there is something that has me worried. And I'm worried because no one else seems to be worried about it enough to mention it. I'm going to throw this out for you to think about. What if we are right about the facts and wrong about the motive?"

"What do you mean?" Mike inquired.

"I'm talking about something that's bigger than NAPCO and industrial espionage. Think about this: if all you wanted was a contract with DOD to sell your fuel, would you be willing to murder people and blow up a US military asset just to protect who you really were? I can't stop thinking this is too much evil and skullduggery for something of that scope. It doesn't add up! There is also a lot of risk. The US defense establishment considers attacking one of its military bases as an act of war. Why would a government, especially Venezuela, risk being in that situation?"

Mike prodded. "What exactly are you suggesting?"

Vic responded. "I wish I knew. All I know is that I can't get it to add up in my mind. Eli might be right about staying as far away as we can, but what if this is not about who originally owned or produced the oil?"

After no one commented, Eli interjected, "Except for Vic's hunch, it appears we are close to exhausting the Navy's need for Daneli's expertise. As soon as Commander Hughes gets back on shift, I intend to discuss with him his interest in keeping us around. I expect he will agree that our services will either no longer be needed or at least be scaled back significantly. I want to thank you all for doing such a fine job. I have received nothing but praise from all our military counterparts."

"But before we get out of here, do any of you have thoughts about Vic's theoretical dilemma?"

Again, no one commented. It appeared that no one except Vic, and maybe Eli, had the curiosity or the thirst for that kind of risk.

Eli added, "Well then, I guess I'll go tell Brockington what we discovered and try not to suggest what we might be thinking. These guys are supposed to be the experts on finding the bad guys and defending the country. Why don't we let them figure it out?

"Vic, I want you to accompany me. Everyone else, continue working on whatever you were doing, but stay close by so I can advise you of the Navy's response."

With that, Vic and Eli visited with Brockington. As Eli began to get into it, Brockington looked at his watch and interrupted him.

"Excuse me, Eli, Commander Hughes is due in here shortly. This sounds like something we both need to hear. Do you mind waiting?"

Eli replied, "No, sir. If you don't mind, we will find a seat outside and wait for you to come and get us."

"Very well."

After a short wait, Commander Hughes arrived, and Eli relayed to him the events of the past twenty-four hours.

21. PREMATURE CELEBRATION

SIMON FLORES ASSEMBLED THE PAGES HE HAD COPIED AND PRINTed from Facebook. He then picked up his cup of coffee from his hotel desk and called Dan Witherspoon's hotel room from his cell phone.

When Witherspoon answered, Flores announced, "I have a report from the Janitor—mission accomplished. The cleanup is complete, and he is monitoring all communication channels. So far, so good."

Witherspoon hung up with Flores and dialed Charles Bobick. Witherspoon relayed the news as Bobick pulled up the project Facebook page and confirmed the report. The first phase of their mission was over. They felt it was time to celebrate and blow off some steam.

Witherspoon made arrangements to meet at Bobick's yacht in Baltimore's Inner Harbor East Marina later that evening at seven o'clock. Charles Bobick's yacht rarely left the dock. He used it for parties and meetings of the most private nature. The harbormaster was also very discreet. He kept an official and unofficial visitor record. Also, for a pretty penny, a daily maid service cleaned it to his lofty standards.

The weather was a balmy fifty-four degrees, so Charles Bobick and his guests entertained on the deck. The bar was open, and seas were calm. The sounds of stereos playing music and voices partying could be heard throughout the harbor. His yacht was not the only one in the harbor that was celebrating something. Bobick was feeling frisky and asked his invitees if anyone was interested in female companionship for the evening. He knew that Dan Witherspoon delighted in spending the night on the yacht with an escort service beauty, so Bobick made the call for a 10 p.m. arrival.

After a couple of rounds of cocktails and small talk, the discussion turned to the mission. Witherspoon opined, "You know, when I signed up for this mission, I was an easy recruit. I believe in the objective. Now that I can see the finish line, I have to say that I am impressed with the resolve of the men leading it. They are relentless micromanagers. You know them. Is this the way they run their enterprise, or is this mission special?"

"This mission is very special," Bobick averred. "They lost key business associates on 9/11. That really stung them, but when they lost family members stationed in Iraq, they became obsessed with the idea that we are allowing the barbarians of the world to determine our future. They decided to take on the responsibility of making the world a safer place. They felt they had the resources and contacts to make a difference. In fact, early on during the conceptual phase, Charles told me he believed he was blessed with great wealth to make such a difference."

While they talked, the stereo played the Reprise collection of Sinatra hits in the background. The harbor waters rolled with the tide. The yacht was influenced by the motion of the waves. Facing the open sea and feeling the effects of the liquor and the waves gave the two men the illusion that they were miles away from the complexities of the world.

They continued to discuss their benefactor and his emissaries, especially his relationship with the Janitor, Mr. Straight.

Witherspoon was in a particularly jovial mood. "I think we can all agree that we never want to be caught in the Janitor's crosshairs. That man never fails to fulfill his mission. Hah! He performs a clean, precise, and lethal janitorial service."

Bobick asked, "What nationality is he?"

Witherspoon responded, "I think he is Italian."

Otherwise silent and invisible, Simon Flores interjected, "Serbian. He is Serbian."

Bobick and Witherspoon gave Flores a stare as if he were an intruder, having forgotten for a moment that Señor Flores was within earshot. On the surface, one might imagine that Simon Flores was Dan Witherspoon's manservant or bodyguard. In reality, he was two things: an intimidator and an apprentice learning the in-house security management craft.

Simon Flores was a nonnegotiable ingredient in the Purified arrangement. Witherspoon had no choice. He was essentially training his replacement, a fact of which he was acutely aware. But at the age of fifty-nine, Dan Witherspoon had few options. He used to send Flores away when he was partying, but the years had jaded him. He'd rather be sent packing for being an old fool than be considered irrelevant and without pleasures. He began testing the limits of his freedom a few years back. He assumed his benefactor knew about his company-paid philandering. Since he had not been punished for it, he had drawn the conclusion that his benefactor did not give a damn. It couldn't be further from the truth. Witherspoon's lascivious behavior disgusted him; however, he had learned to put up with it because he had discovered that it took such a man to do the dirty work that was demanded.

But his benefactor was no fool. In the early days of their political activism, his benefactor learned the benefit of collecting dirt on opponents as well as collaborators. The reason—you never know when it might serve your agenda. Señor Flores served as the curator for the dirt on Purified, its employees, and its collaborators. For tonight, Flores merely observed and kept a mental note.

The conversation between Bobick and Witherspoon returned to their schemes, the participants, and the victims.

"It always hurts to see a good-looking woman like Ann Calloway get chewed up in the machinery," Witherspoon lamented. "What a waste of such a body and alluring mind. Do you think she was too sexy to be an attorney?"

Charles Bobick didn't know what to make of the question or how to answer it. He knew that Witherspoon had exceeded his alcohol limit, and he was now in the vulnerable posture many of his yacht guests attained.

Bobick replied, "Don't forget I knew her. She was a fine attorney and a patriot. I will miss her and mourn her loss all the days of my life."

"Don't get sentimental on me. You know the nature of our work. I just wish I had the chance to know her better, if you know what I mean."

"Yes, she was a finely appointed lady. It's a shame."

"So what do you think about that French guy at GAO?"

"I was also acquainted with him. My career and his crossed paths many times. He was a decent lawyer and a solid, but unspectacular, politician. When the last administration went out of office, his days as general counsel were numbered. I think he saw the Rubik's Memo as a possible horse he could ride to keep himself in the political mix. I think Ann was just doing her job. Neither of them had any idea what they were dealing with. I expect they had imagined there were people out there with the skills and experience of the Janitor but never really imagined one would be after them."

Witherspoon commented, "I bet the Janitor could entertain us for quite a while with stories of his exploits. What a skill set he must have to execute the murders and make a defense department facility literally blow itself up. And he does it flawlessly, without any evidence that he was the perpetrator. By the way, have you had the chance to read about the Craney Island fire?"

"Oh yeah! I had no idea what the effect of losing a tank or two to a fire would do to the military. They were scrambling for a replacement. Had the energy industry not stepped up and devised a temporary patch, our defensive capability would have been crippled. That facility has been out of service for almost a week. I saw a classified report from the Joint Chiefs to the White House. DOD had no internal answer for losing Craney Island Fuel Depot. Homeland Security was all over DOD for not being able to protect such a vital and irreplaceable asset."

Witherspoon added, "Everyone in my industry was aware of its vulnerability. We all face it every day. Accidents can create the same result the Janitor accomplished at Craney Island. Actually, DOD was plumb lucky Commander Hughes hired a firm that knew the oil transportation business. They got right on the substitution job, and Daneli had the clout to pull it off. Had they not been on the job, there would have been no temporary industry patch. They were lucky, all right."

"Who is Daneli? I don't think I've heard of them," Bobick inquired.

"They were formed just a year ago. The executive VP of West Industries left his position as heir apparent for the CEO post to form his own consulting firm. It's all about Eli Taylor. His career must have crossed the path of Commander Hughes. Trust me, this was a one-in-a-million connection. If we had picked any other DOD facility, it is very doubtful Daneli would have gotten the call to respond. Hell, his company is not even listed in the current year's publication of emergency responders. It takes at least a year for new companies to reach the industry publications. It even takes longer for the military to find them."

"This Daneli company—what all do you think they are doing for the Navy?"

"Eli Taylor is best known for being a big-time project leader and an emergency response guru. I suspect they are helping the Navy cope with putting out the fire, getting the facility back online, and finding a temporary substitute for its role in the military supply chain until it is entirely back online."

"You don't think he is helping them on investigating the cause?"

"Good heavens, no. Maybe his company could, but the military almost never lets an industry contractor into that sphere of activity. The military intelligence and the Justice Department are too afraid of what an unvetted contractor might learn about their vulnerability and bumbling to let them inside an investigation. Our mutual benefactor thinks we should set Daneli up as a scapegoat if the mission starts going south on us. Ellingson was given the lead on that potential. He says Daneli's input ended when they determined the cause was not human error or mechanical failure. However, I doubt Taylor's talents are so diverse that he can work effectively inside and outside the military and intelligence framework. And don't forget, we have the Janitor.

Taylor and his group would be no match for his kind of treachery."

"So, where do you think the Janitor goes when he is not working a job for our benefactor?"

"That's a question I do not want to know the answer to."

***

Later that evening in his farmhouse at Horseshoe Bay, British Columbia, just outside Vancouver, the Janitor was not in a condition to celebrate. After another day off his antipsychotic medication, he was fighting the same old demons that had plagued him since his late twenties. Although his surroundings did not resemble his landlocked hometown of Zvornik, that was what his eyes were seeing. Everywhere he looked, there was death and disease. His skin was crawling with imagined creatures.

Mr. Straight was a borderline schizophrenic. When medicated, he could control his mind and function like a normal person, but when he was taking his medication, his life was robotic, and he was incapable of feeling any emotions. When he was not taking his medication, he could experience exhilaration, joy, and the pleasure of a woman. However, away from medication, he was vulnerable to the dark side of his imagination. And that meant that he was incapable of fighting the hallucinations that clouded his reasoning.

To the left, he saw his family being raped and murdered in gruesome detail. To the right, fearsome animals were chasing him, and serpents were crawling underneath his clothes. Only when his live-in companions were there to reassure him could he muster the strength to momentarily push the bad thoughts away so he could enjoy the good emotions. He referred to his companions as Sodom and Gomorrah. They provided his pleasure and catered to his every need. They had a routine. Mr. Straight would let them know when he stopped taking his meds. And when his job commitments demanded he be ready for work, they had to force him to get back on them. And that was his life when he was not on an assignment.

This night, the hallucinations were particularly frightening. He could be heard saying to himself, "You are not real," and at times, his mind could not differentiate between a door and the edge of a cliff. He had been afraid of heights and insects as a child, and this night he was walking on a window ledge thirty stories high, and the ground was crawling with roaches and centipedes.

The Janitor had been successful in keeping his sickness a secret to his employers. If he had not, he would be unemployable. However, as he grew older and was under more stress, it became more difficult to control the disease. The issue now was how much longer he would be able to control it before it controlled him.

22. NEW ORDERS

AFTER LISTENING TO ABOUT FIFTEEN MINUTES OF EXPLANATION, Commander Hughes sat motionless in his desk chair with his head resting on his hand and his elbow on the armrest.

Eli was thinking, If I didn't know better, I would think he was in a trance.

When he finally moved, he sat up straight and looked directly at Vic.

"Well, gentlemen, I don't know if I should scold you or congratulate you. On the way here, I had a brief conversation with Admiral Ellingson. Our Unified Command intelligence report as of twelve hundred hours does not make the connections you allege. You are not going to make any points with the intelligence guys, and I can promise you that the brass will not like you going off the reservation to pursue an unauthorized investigation. And they will not be happy if you are on the right track, thereby showing up the intelligence branches.

"However, if you are right, there is a small possibility that they will forgive you. You have forced me to call another conference call meeting like we had the other day. You know, just because an incident response operation has no time off or weekends, that doesn't mean everyone else in the world has the same agenda or schedule. It's Wednesday morning for them, and I promise you, they will be in a cranky mood. Run along now while I try to set it up, but do not leave the island."

An hour and a half had passed when Vic and Eli were called back to Commander Hughes's office. The FBI was busy verifying Vic's assertions. When they entered Commander Hughes's office, the video-conference monitor displayed all the participants. Each military and governmental branch was represented by either an admiral or district chief accompanied by the highest-ranking case officer working the investigation. It didn't take a close look at the faces to see there was not a happy camper among them.

Commander Hughes opened the meeting. "Thank you for reconvening. I didn't expect we would ever need to revisit assignments. I trust you have my brief explanation of what this is all about. And before I let Mr. Taylor explain his actions, I want you to know that I made it clear to him and his employee Victor Majeski that I am not pleased that he conducted an unauthorized investigation into matters he understood were in the government's domain. All that being said, he and Mr. Majeski stand before you now to cooperate in any manner you see fit."

Admiral Ellingson took over. "Mr. Taylor, you tell me if any of what I am about to say is not accurate. After our last conference, I revised the assignments that omitted your firm's participation in the industrial sabotage investigation, but you ignored my instructions and followed your nose, or your employee's nose, because of a hunch. Is that true?"

"With all due respect, Admiral, that's a part of it."

"What part am I missing?"

"The part that was so speculative and remote. Had we suggested you pursue it, you would have laughed in our faces and ignored it. And if anyone was capable of getting anywhere with this investigation trail, it could only be Victor Majeski. If you permit me to explain, I think I can convince you of it."

"Continue, Mr. Taylor."

"Just as the intelligence community enlists attractive women to be spies who learn how to use their looks and feminine guile to get access to information nobody else can, Victor Majeski has the same effect on women. One of his recent lady friends happened to be an attorney in the Justice Department. She mentioned to him in July that she was working on a matter about which he might know something that could help her. He couldn't remember the details, but what he did remember was similar to the issues our IT guys were facing. He was wondering if there might be a connection to her matter and the records that were altered during the Craney Island event.

"All Mr. Majeski was going to do was ask her a couple of questions that were designed to provide a link or a failure of a linkage. When he discovered she and the GAO general counsel were killed a couple of days ago, and the last communication she had before her death was about this issue, he looked a little deeper. He discovered it involved the same shipper issue we were working on. That was when he felt he was on to something. But he still didn't have enough facts or linkage to turn it over to the FBI or military intelligence. I asked him if he was confident he could find out enough to present it to the FBI. He said he was sure of it and that he could do it safely and without anyone knowing what he was doing.

"He told me that he was confident because of what was told to him by another old girlfriend who worked at the GAO. I have a lot of confidence in Vic that goes back many years. I told him to follow it up to see if it was productive, but to make sure he didn't screw up. She had access to the information he needed, and she gave it to him.

"And that's how we fell back into the matter. Now, one thing I want to make clear. We had only good intentions here. We were certain that the lead we started with was so insignificant that it would not be pursued by the FBI or military intelligence. However, in Vic we had the only person who had the connections that could get the info needed to find the linkage, if there was one, without causing a stir.

"Vic used those connections to get a copy of the document that is probably the focal point of what transpired at Craney and what got people killed at DOJ and GAO."

"Chief Gilbert, what is your assessment?" Ellingson asked.

"First of all, when I first heard of this barely an hour ago, I was pissed. But I have a history with both Eli Taylor and Victor Majeski. They possess instincts and skills that are rarely found anywhere, including the intelligence community. And now that I know how they got started on this path and reentered the investigation, I agree that they probably were the only persons who could have found this trail so quickly."

"How about you, Director Trimble?"

"NSA's investigation was going nowhere. I wish Mr. Taylor could have kept us better informed, but I think I get why he didn't. Why didn't you let us know what you were up to, Mr. Taylor?"

"I considered it, but until we got where we are now, I didn't believe that we had enough that would prevent you from ridiculing us and demanding that we stay away from the investigation."

"Well," Trimble replied. "That is exactly what I expected; and I can't disagree with that assessment."

Ellingson then asked everyone else, "Does anyone disagree with Director Trimble and Chief Gilbert?"

Nobody spoke up.

"OK, it looks as though we are back to where we were a day and a half ago, only now we are finally onto something that might produce who is behind this mess," Ellingson proclaimed. "I guess we should be thankful you guys are working on our side. You are only working on our side, aren't you?"

That got a chuckle from Vic and Eli and a few of the others.

"Yes, Admiral. That is correct, and we wouldn't have it any other way."

"OK, I'm over my shock and indignation. At least now we have something the Joint Chiefs will be pleased with. And, by God, I will not be telling them that our contractors who were told they were taken off the investigation are the only persons who have made any progress. So don't let that out. That will be our little secret, and it will be Daneli's punishment for disobeying an implied order. You and your company will not get credit for any of it, Mr. Taylor. However, I am ordering the FBI to lead the rest of this investigation and to keep Daneli on as special advisors. Any final words from anyone?"

Nobody spoke, and Ellingson adjourned the meeting and cut his video connection. Gilbert stayed on and asked Vic and Eli to come to his Baltimore office as soon as they could get there Monday morning.

***

After the conference call, Commander Hughes met with NSA Domestic Antiterror Director Stuart Yarborough. They recommended that the National Terror Alert System color be changed to amber. That revision created a level of moderate anxiety at all agencies—FBI, CIA, DOD, NSA, etc.

What followed was a matter of protocol. All branches of the military revised their schedules and orders to begin regimented maneuvers. The unwritten result was that all DOD leaders began to get a little edgy, and that meant a lot of questions were asked. In this case, there were few answers, only suspicions. The anxiety and questions ran all the way to the executive branch in the White House. The news media was asking questions. And since no one had any reasons or other plausible answers for the higher level of alert, the anxiety was directed back to the FBI and the leaders of the Craney Island emergency response.

The Daneli team was unaware that the level of alert had been revised, but they were feeling the stress.

23. WHAT HAVE WE STEPPED INTO?

LATE WEDNESDAY EVENING, A CONFERENCE CALL TOOK PLACE among the leaders of the conspiracy behind the events being investigated. Some were corporate executives, some were their operatives who were orchestrating their orders on the ground, and some were politicians and military leaders. The subject of the discussion was Daneli Crisis Management Group. The person explaining the reason for the meeting was one of the military participants.

"Gentlemen, I asked for this meeting to inform you of events that came to our attention today. As you know, operations Junior and Senior went as planned, without complication. Earlier today we delivered the fire- and heat-resistant suit we used at Craney Island to NAPCO's Houston terminal, and as expected, it went off without a hitch, nobody the wiser.

"As for the sequencing of our mission, we got some unexpected news. It was anticipated that at some time in the not-so-distant future, it would become known to law enforcement that the two operations were connected. In fact, we expected to secretly leak the linkage at a time convenient to when it would be optimum for the completion of our mission."

He continued, "However, quite unexpectedly, a contractor for the military discovered the linkage and reported it this morning.

This contractor was chosen because of its expertise in responding to disasters, not investigating crimes. This team was also chosen to assist in finding a fuel supply substitute for Craney Island. We were aware of the Navy's hire. We also knew the company had expertise in terminal and pipeline operations. We think the commander chose them because he hoped they would be useful in finding a substitute temporary fuel terminal that the Navy could use while Craney Island was out of commission. When we learned of their hire, we expected that their expertise in pipeline transportation would eventually be useful to NCIS and the FBI, and that would lead the investigation to where we wanted it to go.

"They discovered the Junior and Senior link by sheer luck and happenstance. In fact, we didn't know they had any knowledge of Operation Senior, much less the ability to link the two together. If it wasn't for the fact that their operations expert was a witness for the DOJ on an unrelated matter when Rubik's Memo came to our attention in July, they would have no basis for even knowing of the memo, the government's interest in it, or the persons involved on the government's side. It was a matter of pure luck.

"However, now that the linkage has been reported, we need to discuss if and how we need to revise our timetable and plans."

The principal benefactor took over from there.

"Gentlemen…"

There was a long pause, as it was obvious that he was controlling his emotions and collecting his thoughts.

"I am very disappointed that you miscalculated this aspect of the mission. Someone drastically underestimated the capabilities of this vendor. This does not bode well for the success of the remainder of our mission. We cannot afford a wild card invading our operation and adjusting our timetable. How do you propose to avoid this?"

Art Daniels, Purified's CEO, was one of the parties on the conference call, and he responded. "I believe we can adjust our schedule and be prepared to undertake phase two of the mission. However, I don't think we can afford to have Daneli sticking their noses into it. I recommend that the Navy take them off the response and replace them with another contractor."

One of the military participants responded, "I'm afraid it's too late for that. Daneli has already made operational the temporary terminal that was designed to replace the lost capability of Craney Island. The Pentagon is depending on their advice and counsel to keep it working. Besides, it would be impossible to convince them that Daneli should be relieved of its duties before Craney Island has returned to full operation status."

With that remark, the leader could no longer restrain his anger. He pounded his fist on his desk with such ferocity that most of the people on the call jumped in their seats. "That's not the type of reply I expect to hear! I can't use commentary. I expect solutions."

Daniels replied, "We can place additional operatives on Taylor and Majeski. And we can bug their phones, cars, and hotel rooms. If we find that they are threatening the success of our mission, we can eliminate their involvement."

The principal reentered the discussion. "If you are confident we can place ourselves in a position to make that call without jeopardy, then so be it."

Daniels responded, "We have the resources and the connections to do that. I will prepare a revised timetable for the rest of the mission and advise you of what measures we have taken to ensure Daneli does not come between us and the success of the mission."

One of the military leaders added, "It should also be noted that the Daneli investigators who have figured prominently in their linking the events have been placed under the thumb of the FBI investigation. That means we will know what they are doing and thinking from now on."

That statement seemed to give the attendees added comfort and ended the call.

THURSDAY, NOVEMBER 16, 0700 HOURS

It had been a week and a half since Daneli was hired to respond to the Craney Island event. Vic and Eli were sitting in a conference room at the FBI's Baltimore District Office. Chief Gilbert and a number of others walked in. Some were setting up a breakfast, and four others, three men and a woman, sat down at the conference table.

"Good morning, Eli. Good morning, Vic. I want to introduce to you the investigative team that will be working this matter for the FBI. To my left is Assistant Chief Daniel Greenwood. And to his left is Agent Angela Cramer. To my right is Agent Thomas Thatcher. They are all from FBI headquarters in Washington. We have a lot of things to cover this morning."

Eli looked over the crew Gilbert had brought in. The two guys in suits looked like FBI stereotypes and were not very interesting. The female agent was a different story. It was difficult not to notice that Agent Cramer was an attractive, thirtysomething, dark-haired beauty. Instinctively, Eli looked at Vic, who was looking her over.

Eli looked at her, and she was looking back at Vic. It was comforting to see that even FBI agents were affected by Vic the same way waitresses were. His story about his liaison with the DOJ attorney was being confirmed before their eyes.

Gilbert brought Eli out of his focus on Agent Cramer as he began to speak. "Since you and Vic have been assigned to assist us in this matter, we have been busy finding new links and tying up loose ends."

Gilbert picked up a remote control from the table and pointed it at the wall to their far right. A flat-screen monitor descended from the ceiling, and a picture appeared. It was the video of the fully engulfed Craney Island Fuel Depot from the air.

Gilbert narrated as the video played. "Monday evening, November seventh, the Navy terminal at Craney Island, Virginia, explodes and catches fire. The military responds and calls in Daneli Crisis Management Group to assist it."

Gilbert clicked the remote again, and another scene appeared. "This is a photograph of the crime scene at the parking lot in Arlington where Ann Calloway and Gary French were found."

Vic turned his head away for an instant once he realized he was looking at Ann's body.

Gilbert continued, "The very next morning, Tuesday, November eighth, Gary French, the General Counsel for the Government Accountability Office, is found shot to death next to Ann Calloway, an attorney working for the Justice Department. These two separate events occur, and two separate investigations begin in different FBI offices.

"The FBI's Washington, DC, headquarters assists the Arlington police in its investigation of the shootings at the Glebe Road parking deck. The same day, the FBI's Baltimore office is asked to assist the military in its investigation at Craney Island to determine whether the cause of the fire there is terrorism or industrial sabotage. These investigations are barely underway when Brian Matusak, an auditor at the GAO, enters the FBI HQ on Tuesday morning, November ninth."

Gilbert clicked his remote again, and the GAO employee directory picture of Brian Matusak appeared on the screen, along with a photo of what was left of his residence.

Gilbert continued his narrative.

"Matusak tells us he brought a memo to Gary French on the previous Friday, November third, that he ran across in his audit of DOD contracts with fuel suppliers. He was advising us that he was afraid that Mr. French and Ms. Calloway were dead because he reopened the audit of NAPCO, the company mentioned in the memo. He says he has been working with an energy marketing expert who tells him his life might be in danger. Before the FBI HQ office can run down Brian's suspicions—his home explodes. That investigation suggests natural gas had filled his home while he and family slept and ignited. There were no survivors. The investigation of the explosion has not yet uncovered sufficient evidence to determine if the explosion was the result of foul play; however, right now, we are assuming foul play was the cause.

"The same day, Mr. Taylor tells the military working the Craney Island incident that NAPCO is the prime suspect behind the explosion and fire. He and Victor Majeski are taken off the investigation, but Mr. Majeski wants to discuss it with a woman attorney at DOJ he dated this past summer who was working on a matter that involved NAPCO. Coincidentally, she happens to be Ann Calloway. Majeski begins to suspect her death might be related to the Craney Island event, so he talks to another woman he knows who works in the GAO office. She tells him about the memo and Brian Matusak.

"So what we have now, due to the efforts of Daneli and their Mr. Taylor and Mr. Majeski, is a combined investigation to connect the crimes and determine who the perpetrators are. And as of yesterday, I did a routine peek into the life of Mr. Matusak. We obtained his office computer and all of his phone records. It just so happens that he had been investigating NAPCO and that he did have some recent conversations with the GAO general counsel. So what he did say to our DC bureau, we substantiated. As of early this morning, before you arrived, we had a telephone interview with one of the persons to whom Mr. Matusak made several recent calls. He is an energy consultant in England. His name is Friedrich Olms. We corroborated that he was the person who told Brian Matusak his life might be in danger. Do either of you two know Olms?"

"I know of him," Eli answered. "He used to work for Shell, and I believe he consults under his own flag these days."

"Why am I not surprised that you know him? What can you tell us about him?"

"Not a whole lot. He's a little eccentric, but he knows his craft. He has a solid reputation and is knowledgeable of energy dealings in the world market."

Gilbert then announced, "Don't try to contact him. He is going undercover until we tell him that it's safe to resurface. He also corroborated your suspicion that Venezuela and PETGO is NAPCO's supplier. He was working on that linkage for Brian Matusak. He told us he doesn't have all the ducks in a row, but he is so close that he predicted he could send us a completed analysis with all the facts within forty-eight hours."

"So what do we know?" Vic asked.

"To start with, you were justified to gloat about being spot on. But your period of gloating is over. We have a lot to do if we are going to bring the bad guys to justice. My first duty is to get you to tell me of any other hunches you might have. So we are all ears."

Vic looked at Eli and asked, "Do you want to go first, boss?"

"You've got the hot hand. Why don't you take the first swing at it."

"OK, the first thing that keeps bugging me is how PETGO or NAPCO knew what was going on with the investigation of the things in Rubik's Memo. How did they know about Ann Calloway and the GAO connection with its general counsel and auditor? Before I give you my hunch on that one, I need to mention the other thing. And that is how the bad guys knew they could alter the DOD shipments by accessing the computer in the control room at Craney Island. That kind of knowledge is only known by very few people. This is very sophisticated stuff. I suppose we can brainstorm on this one later."

Vic continued, "Now for the first puzzle, I think the person who is the inside snitch at the GAO is Gary French's secretary. And if you can dig up her phone records, I bet you will find out who she is squealing to."

"What leads you to her?" Gilbert asked.

"My contact there told me she saw Matusak visiting with French in French's office last week. And when she heard both were dead, she asked his secretary if they were working on anything together. The secretary responded, 'I don't think they knew each other.' My contact says French's secretary knows of all of French's meetings and keeps records of them in her notebook. And to top that off, my contact heard her burst into tears as soon as she thought she was out of sight of my contact. Now I tell you, if these bad guys are killing off everyone they suspect is onto their schemes, my contact will probably be in danger once you start poking your nose into the secretary's business. And before I give you her name, I want your promise you will protect her better than you protected Matusak."

"You have my word on that," Gilbert stated. "I will arrange for a safe house for her today. And if you are right, we should have a name of who is being fed the inside information from French's secretary. By the way, do you have the secretary's name?"

"I wrote it down. Here it is, Irene Cohen."

"Thanks, Vic. If you don't mind, I want to get her name to one of our analysts so we can start looking into her contacts."

Gilbert asked Thatcher to find an analyst to start the research on Irene Cohen. "Is there anything else we need to look at in the GAO or DOJ?"

Vic and Eli shook their heads no, and Gilbert continued, "Now let's focus on how we need to search for those who hacked into the Navy's computer. Vic, where do you want to start with the brainstorming you suggested?"

"It seems to me we are looking at someone from inside the Navy with this special knowledge, or an outside contractor. It would be too easy to identify an enlisted man who knew he could access the data at Craney Island and also how to alter the data. I spent a good day with the original programmer of the Navy's system in their control center. I didn't see anyone in Commander Hughes's group capable of doing it all. I also understand that NCIS couldn't find anyone at the Navy who was providing information and know-how to any unauthorized conspirator. However, the Navy did have a systems maintenance contract with a division of Harbitron. Their office is in Norfolk. If it were up to me, I'd start snooping around Harbitron."

"How did they get access to the Navy's system?"

Vic responded, "That's the interesting part about this. The Navy has a closed, dedicated system that does not communicate on telephone lines. No Internet or public telephone-line access is involved. You have to be at one of its terminals to access it. And there are only two terminals on their system that can alter the data. One is at Craney Island, and the other is at the James River Control Center. That is why the bad guys had to create a diversion and tank fire at Craney. They needed the time at the Craney terminal to access the system and alter the data without someone coming after them.

"The fire at Craney provided them the time and the diversion. They had to know that the safety procedures prevented anyone entering the island until the fire burned itself out. That provided the time at the terminal without fear of interruption. They also had to know that the control center at the James River facility would be busy trying to figure out if the system had operated properly. Their focus would be diverted to their supervisory system, which coordinated with the pipelines and the tanks. Therefore, the Navy operators would not be noticing or expecting that their data files were being accessed. The only risky part was protecting the perpetrator at Craney from the heat of the blazing tank. He had to be wearing very special gear to survive the temperatures created by the fire."

"Anything else?"

Eli looked at Vic and shrugged. Eli then gave them his thoughts.

"There is one thing that jumps out at me. The bad guys had to be planning this for quite some time. If the GAO auditor didn't start his investigation until a week or so ago, I can't imagine the perpetrators could put in place a mole at the GAO or DOJ and also find a co-conspirator at the Navy or Harbitron who could carry out this complicated scheme in such a short time. They had to be planning this back in July when the Rubik's Memo was initially making its rounds, or even before then. The obvious clue to me is the protective suit the guy at the Craney terminal needed. You just don't find those in a store and pull them off the rack. They are usually a special order to a very short list of manufacturers. Most big-city fire departments only have one or two of them. And they are quite expensive. Imagine the planning that was necessary to get one without leading a trail to the buyer."

Gilbert commented, "To a similar extent, that is what I have been thinking since I got involved in the Craney Island investigation. The execution was too slick for amateurs or the usual terrorists, and it was planned out to the tiniest of details. No evidence was left behind. No trail was evident. Had your company not been brought in to assist at the onset, I can't imagine that the investigation would be anywhere near where we are."

"You know what," Eli interjected. "It just occurred to me. I bet that was not a part of their planning. They were not expecting the Navy to bring in an energy industry expert to respond. Commander Hughes told me that this incident was the first time the Navy had gone outside its usual list of responders. The perpetrators were not expecting us. I wonder if they have any idea that we might be so close to finding them out."

"That's a good point," Gilbert remarked. "If we keep our investigation off the grid, we might sneak up on them. The FBI investigators will be looking closer at NAPCO. We need to find out what their motivation is and who they have working for them who has the capability to pull off these crimes.

"Vic, before we start digging into the GAO, we need to know all your movements and contacts when you were gathering your research in Washington the last few days. We need for you to let us interview you before we send out agents. While all that is going on, we could use Daneli's insight into what NAPCO's motives might be."

With that, Gilbert broke up the meeting and asked Greenwood to take over. Vic spent the next half hour walking the FBI through every step and communication he made during his research trip to DC. By the time he was through, the FBI had a much higher opinion of Vic and his talents.

Gilbert and the rest of his FBI team excused themselves and left the room. A few minutes later, Gilbert came in and asked Vic to huddle with Thatcher and Cramer in another office to record all the details of his investigation and suspicions. While Vic was out of the room, Gilbert asked Eli about Vic.

"So tell me, Eli, how does a guy with only a high school diploma and a pipeline inspector background end up being Vic with all these other talents?"

Eli replied, "That is a part of Vic's mystique. You see this tall guy with a muscular physique and tattoos, wearing a T-shirt and jeans. He prefers his Harley Davidson for transportation, and his speech is basic New Jersey dialect.

"He expects you to profile him as an uneducated, simple-minded biker or greaser. What most people never get about Vic is that he wants people to get that impression of him. It's what he wants you to see. Underneath, he is an über IQ performer, a thoughtful and sensitive guy. You only get to see that part of him once he sees you are a straight shooter. If you're not, you never see that side of him.

"And if you don't have the opportunity to work next to him, you don't realize how versatile his mind is. If something is mechanical and he's never seen it before, it takes him just a minute to figure out how every part of it works. He has a license to operate heavy equipment like cranes and backhoes, he has a pilot's license, and he fixes washers, dryers, refrigerators, vacuum cleaners, and, of course, automobile engines. He holds about every designation given to experts in explosives. And if it shoots bullets, he can break it down, put it back together, and hit the center of a bull's-eye at any target range."

Eli continued, "One of the many things that make Vic different, besides the biker persona and his talents, is his power of deduction. It isn't your ordinary common sense. He is your quintessential out-of-the-box thinker.

"I have learned not to be surprised by his intellect. However, I marvel at his decisiveness. With all that calculating going on, one would expect him to be slow to action. But this is when his instincts kick in. He often selects the best choice immediately, and he reacts with precision. All these talents and skills make Vic the perfect bunker-mate."

"The two of you are so different. How do you get along?"

"I have often read that the success of many of the world's greatest leaders is usually the result of the people they choose as collaborators and advisors. I owe a lot of the successes in my career to Vic."

"Don't you compete?"

"Hell, yeah, we compete—in everything. In my early days, the most fun we had was competing over women. I eventually met a woman who changed all of that for me. But, in all honesty, I could never hold a candle to Vic.

"I've been around people who think he's cocky. Yeah, he's cocky all right, but not the way most people think. If you can differentiate sarcasm and self-abasement from bragging, then you know his cocky act is actually a comedy act. It's all done for the sake of humor, not self-aggrandizement. And when it's all said and done, it's his intelligent sense of humor that keeps the babes devoted to him. He initially attracts them with his looks and his big galoot act, but that's not what hooks them."

That ended Gilbert's lesson on Vic. He left Eli alone to check in on how his team was faring with Vic.

Eli sat there thinking, And now the FBI is getting a taste of life when Vic is around. Eli was tempted to say the one thing he admired about Vic that few people ever saw. He was the classic existentialist, a single voyager on a journey through life. He saw the world and his role in it differently from most people. His eyes saw without prejudice or influence. He didn't need anyone, and those who couldn't live without him, he wasn't interested in.

Eli was contemplating how this relationship with the FBI was going to turn out. He mused, The stories that are going to come out of this arrangement are certain to be legendary. When I retire, I know what I will be doing. I will be writing novels about my experiences riding shotgun at Vic's side.

Eli left Vic with the FBI and told him he'd call him later to arrange dinner together.

***

About the same time of Eli and Vic's meeting with the FBI, another party tangentially involved was grieving. Colonel Louis Milton, the great friend of Brian Matusak's father-in-law, was having difficulty dealing with the guilt from failing his best friend in the worst of ways. He was lamenting that he might not have done enough to protect his friend Skip and his family. He became worried that his feelings of guilt might be affecting his military duties, so he shared his difficulties with his boss, General Forest Detwiler. Detwiler appeared to be interested, and he asked Milton to send him a copy of the file he had prepared for his buddy Skip. After Detwiler examined the file, he offered Lou time off to put the matter behind him.

Following his conversation with Milton, Detwiler became consumed by all the coincidences with another matter he had been getting reports on in his capacity as a member of the Joint Chiefs of Staff. On a hunch, he opened his folder on the reports. The most recent entry was today's progress in the Craney Island disaster. He laid it beside his recently received copy of Lou Milton's file on the Matusak matter. Within a few seconds, his hunch was rewarded. Both folders included a mention of NAPCO, and both suggested irregularities in fuel shipments to Craney Island.

The general was suspicious of coincidences. He called his Joint Chiefs counterpart and overall lead on the Craney Island investigation, Admiral Ellingson. Ellingson was more than a little concerned about Detwiler's findings. In short order, Ellingson told Detwiler he would look into it for him and give him a call back when he was satisfied that a thorough investigation had been made. Detwiler didn't like the way Ellingson ended the call. He felt he was owed more of an explanation than what was offered. He wondered if he was feeling like Brian Matusak had when the FBI told him to go home because their agents were on top of things.

General Detwiler called Milton to let him know he was going to look into the matter personally. That seemed to give the colonel some comfort.

24. THE HUNT

VIC STAYED WITH THE FBI IN DC WHILE ELI CHECKED BACK IN AT Craney Island. On the way there, he called Hank in Atlanta to see how the substitute for Craney Island Fuel Depot was holding together. Hank's emotions were riding as high as he could remember.

"Not one damn hitch," Hank blurted out. "It's running like a sewing machine. We have fueled three carriers and a slew of smaller craft. As a matter of fact, Daneli is now in the terminal operation business. It may not be for long, but we are fully operational. And I am the fleet commander's new best friend. And I gave myself a new title: interim director and vice president of terminal operations."

"Something tells me you are going to want a raise when I get back to Atlanta."

"I am already working on my presentation and argument."

After some more banter, Eli hung up with Hank and joined the rest of the Daneli crew that wasn't on sleep shift. Eli spent the rest of his shift reviewing the status of the systems research and observing the Navy's cleanup of the terminal. Vic arrived at Craney Island about the time Eli's and his shift was to end.

Before heading back to the hotel, Eli walked over to Commander Hughes's office. There were only a few responders milling around—nothing like the madhouse of the past few days. The press tent was down, and the feel of crisis frenzy was totally absent. He glanced back at the staging area. It had been previously packed with fire-fighting vehicles but was now filled with energy industry construction equipment, perched and eager to enter the terminal as soon as it was safe enough to allow for the repair and reconstruction of what had been damaged or destroyed.

Hughes was on the phone but motioned for Eli to come in. Eli sat down on one of the three Steelcase chairs facing his desk. Hughes was feeling pretty good about himself, and Eli could tell there was a different tone to the commander's voice. His face looked relaxed, and he spoke with a half smile. He hung up with the signoff, "Very well, Admiral."

Commander Hughes said, "That was Admiral Carpenter of the Joint Chiefs. We are all up for sainthood now. And the only thing I've really done was call you to respond. He just got off the phone with Texaco. They are going to lease their Charleston Terminal to the Navy on a year-to-year basis with several renewal options at the Navy's discretion. Daneli's efforts in finding an operational substitute for Craney Island allowed the Navy to look a lot smarter than it had a right to imagine. We always needed an East Coast backup facility if either Craney Island or Jacksonville went out of commission. Now we have one.

"The cleanup of Craney Island is still a day or so from completion, and as you know, the rebuilding of the terminal is already underway. That Rogoff guy you brought in to do the IT investigation is going to work with us to modernize our supervisory and product movement systems and programming. It looks like Daneli has already achieved 'favorite son' status."

"I am as pleased as I can be that we came through for you and the military. Is there anything else we can help you with to rebuild and refurbish Craney Island?"

"I think we have got that under control."

"Then I'd like to talk to you about pulling back consultants who are no longer required to be on-site. Except for Vic, who is assisting the FBI, I think we can complete our remaining duties from Atlanta."

"Well then, I want to thank you personally. It's been a pleasure working with you."

They said their goodbyes, and Eli assembled his team for the last time on the incident site. He called Hank to send the company plane to pick them up. However, someone had to drive the RV back to West's Baltimore facility, and Eli insisted he would take care of it.

Vic volunteered, "Hey boss, I'll come with you if you don't mind. I'd like to touch base with the station hands working the night shift. We can grab a bite and find a hotel room before the plane returns in the morning."

That made sense to Eli. Everyone dispersed, and Eli cranked up the RV. It took a few moments as he tried to remember how to drive it. It had been a couple of years, but it all came back to him.

It was a little difficult maneuvering the RV around Portsmouth's streets, but he managed. Vic and Eli were both in a good mood as they made their way to Baltimore.

When they arrived at West's Baltimore tank farm, it was just before dinnertime. Vic went inside to visit with his West Industries buddies while Eli spent the idle moments on the phone with his old mentor at West, Harry Meeks, to see if he was able to make any progress looking into NAPCO. Harry was their general counsel back in the day, and Eli followed him in that position when Harry retired in the 1990s. Harry was in his seventies now, but his mind was still as sharp as a tack.

After the usual small talk, they got down to business, but not before Meeks told Eli he had bought a new toy.

"Eli, did I tell you I've got Skype on my computer?"

"How do you like it?"

"I've been playing with it as much as I can. I bet you never would have believed I'd become so computer literate."

"What was the occasion?"

"Now that six of my grandchildren live out of state, it's the only way I can stay connected with them, so they don't forget who I am. The semiannual trips just don't allow that to happen."

"I hope I didn't catch you at a bad time."

"Heavens no, I was going to call you later anyway. I think I found what you were looking for. Although NAPCO is entirely a private-stock company, its four major investors are on record. Three are foreign investment houses, and one is an American funding firm. The foreign investment houses are difficult to penetrate to find out how they became private stockowners. However, one of them is Australian, and I have done work for the law firm that represents them. I was able to find out that their investment in NAPCO was made possible by a private financier out of Panama."

"Panama?"

"Yeah, Panama. I had the same reaction. Before I tell you who it is, I want to tell you about the American funding firm. It is known as AFA, Ltd., American Funding Alternative. It is a small player that has never made this kind of investment in any other company. It's out of Miami, Florida. All of its executives had Latin names, so I called our friend David Alvarez to help us out. David had never heard of them. He did a little digging and found out they have placed a lot of small investments for Central and South American investors. There were no public records on them, so David made some inquiries. He found that they are owned by a company with three investors: PETGO, COMEX, and VENGAS. All are Latin oil companies. Both the Panama company and this company have a common investor, PETGO."

"The plot thickens," Eli commented.

"You've got it. We are talking about Venezuela, one the countries on your oil embargo list."

"And who is VENGAS?" Eli asked.

"I'm still working on that one. But it looks as if it's an offshoot of the Horatio Ramirez empire."

"You're talking about the president of Venezuela?"

"That would be affirmative."

Vic drove up, and Eli told Harry to continue to dig up the origins of the other NAPCO investors. Harry said he would and hung up.

"Hey, amigo," Vic said as he pointed to the West regional office building. "The guys in the control building said my old RAM Team crew is attending a meeting there. Do you mind if I say hello?"

"Come on. I'll join you."

They visited for a while with the West employees on the job. West's Baltimore tank farm was the site of the main office for its Atlantic Division. The area manager and the crew Vic once supervised were there. It was enjoyable watching them interact with Vic. It was obvious they missed him.

Walt Davis was the manager. He had never taken a shine to Vic, and he didn't care too much for Eli either. Walt never got over Eli selecting of Vic to work for him when they were at West Industries. What made matters worse was that Vic's crew never stopped telling Walt how much they missed Vic or that the way Walt wanted things done wasn't the way Vic would do it. The only words exchanged were to give him their respects and to thank him for the loan of the RV—never mind that Walt had no say-so in the deal.

Vic called them a cab while he was in the facility. On the way into town, it was time to think about dinner. Eli asked Vic if he had anything in mind.

"Oh yeah, amigo. You are in my world right now. We are heading for the Blue Oyster on the waterfront. And by the way, I got you a room at the Waterfront Wyndham."

"Great food?" Eli asked sheepishly, knowing that Vic rated his restaurants by the quality of the female clientele.

"Not bad," Vic replied.

"And the scenery?" Eli continued to inquire and keep the cat-and-mouse game going.

"Oh yeah. The best scenery in the entire state of Maryland."

"And what do you like about the scenery?"

"Besides its natural good looks, it's so friendly and eager."

"So how do you want to play it?"

"Let's do it straight up this time."

"Serious?"

"Yeah. It will be more of a challenge. I will say I'm in a pickle because my friend here is a married man whose eye stopped wandering, and I'm horny as hell."

"So you want to go the pity route?"

"I've never gone there before, but I think I can pull it off."

Eli didn't want to go much further with this banter, so he changed the subject.

"So are you going to bring me up-to-date on where you are with the FBI?"

"Did you have to bring that up? I was getting my mojo on about tonight. If you absolutely have to know, I hung around there and twiddled my thumbs while they ran down a few things. They came back to me just before lunch with a list of calls on the secretary's phone at the GAO.

"They found three calls to prepaid cell phones, two incoming from one number and one going out on the day before Ann was killed on another. They don't have a valid name of the cell phone users, but they have a picture from a security camera at the cellular dealer. The buyer of the second phone was getting out of a Chrysler 300 when the store camera captured his image. They haven't made an ID, and they didn't get the tag number. However, they were able to identify all the cell towers of the calls made on the phones. The first two calls came from Florence, Italy. The last one originated near a cell tower very close to Craney Island.

"They did the same thing with the auditor's contacts. They contacted that Olms guy from England again. They are moving him around the British Isles so the bad guys can't find him. He said he told the auditor that Horatio Ramirez of Venezuela was one of the money men behind NAPCO."

"That's what Harry Meeks thinks."

"I figured you'd get Harry back working for you. How is he?"

"Same old Harry. Now, what else?"

"Let's see. Oh yeah, they took your lead about Harbitron and ran with it. Apparently, the guy who serviced the Navy's system has been missing for the past week. His name is Eric Parma. Gilbert thinks he's dead or permanently out of the country. My money says that he's pushing up daisies somewhere. He was recently separated from his wife and kids. They sent a couple of agents to his home. He lives alone in a duplex in Surry. We should be hearing from them sometime this evening on what they found."

"Anything else?"

"Nothing except the feeling that we are missing something big."

"What do you mean by big?"

"Something huge! I know you think I'm a conspiracy freak, but dammit, Eli, everywhere we look, this thing gets wider, deeper, and darker. And everything is so neat and precise. This is no amateur-hour operation. I get the feeling we could be looking at something the CIA should be looking into. What's your take?"

"I just don't know. I don't have your instincts."

"How about the other FBI folks Gilbert brought in?"

"The Thatcher fellow seems OK, but that Greenwood guy is a dickhead."

"How about Agent Cramer?"

"That's what this interrogation is all about. Isn't it?"

"I saw her looking at you and you looking back. I was just curious."

Vic declared, "I've got my eye on Agent Cramer. She's got the full package. She didn't say much when you were there, but she's got the kind of personality that appeals to me."

"Oh, I didn't realize it was her personality that you were looking at."

"I didn't mention her good looks because that was rather obvious. I have to admit that a great figure hidden in a habit, a nurse's uniform, or a business suit gets my immediate attention. When we got down to the busywork, she took off her blazer to get more comfortable. She definitely is a first-round draft choice, and maybe even a lottery pick."

"That's what I figured. What's your take on her?" he asked.

"You know the plot. She'll play aloof and disinterested."

"She may be a little out of your league. She has some serious good looks."

"I guess that explains why she was flirting with me after you left. I saw that look in her eyes. She wants to know me better. And I'd like to know her better."

"It's good to see you have gotten over Ann Calloway."

"Hey, now, that was a little below the belt. But I get it. You just want me to talk about it because you miss the action and can't do anything about it."

"Something like that."

"Well, we came to the right place tonight. But let me warn you. You better muster up all your strength to keep it in your pants. The gals who frequent this joint are home wreckers."

The taxi dropped them off at the entrance to the Baltimore Waterfront development, and they walked down the main drag. It was a cool night, about fifty degrees. Vic was sporting a Levi's jacket over a black T-shirt, jeans, and cowboy boots. Eli was in a turtleneck, khakis, and a wool sport jacket. They were the 2006 version of the "odd couple."

When they made their way into the Blue Oyster, Vic walked up to the hostess, and she said, "Mr. Majeski, how nice to see you again. Would you prefer to start in the bar?"

Vic kissed her on the cheek and said, "You know me too well, Christine."

The music coming from the restaurant's speaker system was the Nora Jones's hit Come Away with Me, a favorite of Eli's that transported him to romantic memories. A quick scan of the joint revealed that Vic's assessment of the scenery was dead on. Eli estimated the ratio was three to two, women over men, and most had some redeeming physical appeal. A few were spectacular.

They strolled up to the bar, and the two barkeeps were a man and woman combo dressed in black, stretchy attire.

The female barkeep gave Vic a smirk. "Howdy, cowboy. Got your Vic-troller on?" she asked as she winked.

"For you, Cindy, I'm on twenty-four seven," Vic replied as he leaned over the bar and kissed her on the lips.

The male barkeep interrupted and said, "Hey, Vic, you know the rules. No ticky-no-touchy."

Vic extended his hand to him and said, "Hey, Wil, how's my favorite master mixologist?"

"Can't complain. You want to start with the usual? And is this guy with you?"

"Sure is. Let me present to you my boss and great friend."

"No shit!" Wil exclaimed as he looked at Eli. "Vic said he'd lure you in here one day. You must be Jesus Christ!" Wil announced.

Eli laughed. "Most people just call me Eli."

"Eli Taylor," purred Cindy. "We've been waiting for you." She then shot Eli an air kiss.

"What have you gotten me into, Vic?" Eli asked as he played along.

"Don't worry, boss. They only play with other couples."

Wil smiled and asked, "What can I pour you? The first one is on the house."

"Jack and soda, please," Eli replied.

"Except for the way you look, you guys are like twins."

"Not really," Eli said as Cindy poured them two Jack Daniels and soda.

Vic asked, "So, you got any recommendations?"

"If you like a threesome, the gals next to the window are stock-brokers from New York."

"I dig stockbrokers," Vic remarked. "Come on, Eli, I think I can make this work," Vic said as he saluted Cindy and Wil.

"Thanks for the tip. We'll be back shortly."

Vic grabbed Eli's arm and pulled him away from the bar.

"Hey, man. Have you been working out? You're not on the prowl, are you? You know that is one of the things wives say they notice when they think their guy is cheating on them."

"Afraid not," Eli said as they headed for the three babes in the booth next to the window. "Lifting a child can build you up just the same as lifting iron."

"Now, you just smile and go along with my lead."

As they approached the table with the stockbrokers, one was looking at them, and the other two were deep in conversation.

"Hello, ladies, how did the market do today?" Vic inquired as he stood next to their booth.

They all looked in Vic's direction. Two giggled while the other measured Vic with her eyes.

"I'm Vic, and this guy is my dad. To whom are we looking at so adoringly?"

The one who had measured Vic made the introductions. Her opening salvo indicated that Vic and Eli were about to meet a playful mind with a wide range of interests. It's not often that the Archie comic book characters are brought back to life.

"That's Betty. This is Midge in the middle. And I'm Veronica."

"Very cute. Where's Archie?" Vic inquired.

Veronica replied, "Finally, a man with sophistication. Archie and the boys are nursing Hot Dog back home."

The Veronica gal introduced to them as Betty asked, "So, Dad. Do you have a name?"

"Just call me Mr. Tibbs."

They all looked at Eli as if he was from Mars.

"Mr. Tibbs was a role played by Sidney Poitier in the 1960s," he remarked.

Vic jumped in. "Don't mind him. He's been away from the game for quite a while. So really, how did the market do today?"

Midge responded, "It's down twenty-six. Are you a player?"

"Yes," Vic replied. "But not so much with investments."

That comment got the expected response as the ladies giggled and smiled alluringly at Vic.

Veronica inquired, "So how about you, Dad—I mean Mr. Tibbs?"

Vic answered for Eli. "To be honest, he used to be a player, but he's got a wife and kids back in Atlanta now. We're here on business. We're both looking for some fine-looking ladies to join us for dinner. Afterward, my dad has to go to bed alone."

"How about you?" Veronica inquired.

"Me, I've got a different after-dinner mind-set."

"I bet you do!" Betty remarked.

"Seriously," Vic commented. "The evening is young, but we'll be hanging here in the bar before we get too hungry. We're straight shooters, and if you like witty repartee over a great meal, we can deliver the mail. If you want to stick with us, I'd like to buy your next round."

Veronica looked at Eli and inquired, "What say you, Dad? Do you let your son do all your talking for you?"

"He does a pretty good job, doesn't he? Truth be known, Vic is no bullshitter. He's single and always on the prowl. I'm just along for drinks and dinner conversation."

Veronica huddled with her cohorts and turned to them and stated, "We're in the mood for seafood. How about you?"

The evening began just as Vic had imagined it would. He asked them what they were drinking and walked to the bar as

Eli kept them company. They asked if they were really there on business. Eli started to answer, but Vic was already back at the table advising the group that Christine was moving them to a large booth overlooking the harbor.

By the time they were about to sit down, Cindy arrived with a tray of cocktails. "Hey, Veronica," she asked, "how did I do?"

"Just what the doctor ordered," Veronica replied.

As the evening progressed, Vic and Eli discovered that Veronica was the boss of the other two, and relating their real names was not on their dance card. They were in Baltimore for a conference on trading shorts, "stock shorts." Vic and Veronica were sitting together on one side of the table, and Eli was sandwiched between Betty and Midge on the other. As the evening progressed, it became clear that Veronica was looking to get laid, and her companions were only along for the preliminaries.

After the first round of drinks was served, Eli caught a glimpse of Veronica's hand dipping below the table every now and then. Vic's face made it pretty obvious when that happened that she was checking out his equipment. Vic soon had his arm around her and gave her occasional squeezes. This went on through a couple more rounds of drinks and the meal. The ladies on Eli's left and right were both married and lived in Manhattan.

Betty was a blonde and a real talker. She was definitely not in the market for a liaison. Midge was a busty brunette who became less reserved and more amorous as the evening progressed. She placed her hand on Eli's thigh a couple of times but apologized immediately. Eli also got a few breast facials when she got up twice to visit the ladies' room. It was difficult to imagine how her movements were not intentional. Eli was struggling to keep his mind off of the sexual sidecar and back on the husband train. Watching Vic and Veronica was like being teased by a porn movie as an appetizer.

Eli kept thinking to himself that this was a test to his commitment to marriage. About ten thirty, it was time to leave the Blue Oyster. They got in a taxi that drove them to the Hilton Inner Harbor at the Baltimore Convention Center, where the girls were staying. To avoid the obvious, the girls got out and went directly to their rooms. Vic walked over to the bellman. He slipped him three fifties and told him to bring a bottle of champagne and Jack Daniels to room 827. Eli and the taxi headed for the Wyndham to crash for the night.

***

Vic knocked gently on the door to 827, and the vivacious Veronica appeared in a black-lace negligee. Her long auburn hair had been pulled around to rest across her left shoulder. Vic didn't utter a word for the next minute or so. Veronica was a tall, tanned, statuesque beauty with a slight freckling on her shoulders. Vic was a sucker for freckles, and he gently caressed her shoulders and drew her to him for a languid kiss on her dark, red lips. Her hands were busy with his belt and zipper.

Vic whispered in her ear, "Don't rush, my darling. You will mess up your manicure."

He took her hand and led her to the edge of the bed. He sat down, reached around her hips, and pulled her to him. She raised her legs and mounted him as Vic buried his face in her ample breasts. Their lovemaking extended well into the early morning. The last round ended at about one thirty.

It was only then that Veronica appeared to be distracted enough to make conversation. "My lord," she sighed. "Can I take you home with me?"

Vic replied, "I love to visit New York, but you've got to be partly insane to live there. We can always get together for an 'I miss you' visit. Sometimes that kind of arrangement is better than any other."

"Lover boy, right now you can count me in."

"Veronica, are you going to give me your real name and phone number?"

"I'm not there yet. How about you give me your phone number?"

When Vic got up and handed Veronica his business card, she asked for another and wrote her phone number on it. Veronica drawled in her best attempt at a Southern accent, "Now don't you lose this, darlin'. It would be a shame if we never got a chance to hook up again."

25. ARE WE THERE YET?

AT 0730 HOURS, ELI CALLED VIC ON HIS CELL PHONE. AS USUAL, he was waiting for Eli in the restaurant, eating breakfast. It was one of the rare times when there was no cutie pie keeping him company or waitress making eyes at him. With only four hours of sleep after a week of incident response, the toll on Vic's energy was starting to show.

"Did you hear from Gilbert last night?" Eli inquired. "I forgot to ask you."

"He sent me a text while we were at the Blue Oyster. I didn't notice it then. I must have been getting groped by Veronica while my cell phone was vibrating. Speaking of last night, how did you resist Midge? She was all over you."

"At times like last night, I wish I was a eunuch. I hadn't had a case of blue balls like that since high school."

"If Midge was anything like Veronica, you really missed the boat."

"Don't tell me the details. It's not a good way to start the day. Besides, what did the text say?"

"Oh yeah. That computer guy from Harbitron. Well, according to Gilbert, there was a four-day-old unfinished plate of food sitting on his kitchen table. He says his television in the kitchen was on, and there were signs of a struggle."

"It sounds like we won't be interviewing him in the future."

"You could say that. They found him in the bathroom wearing a bullet hole in his head. My guess is that his usefulness expired. And when he spilled the beans about his job being done, they spilled his brains."

"Did I ever tell you that you have a way with language? Was that poetry or prose?"

"Just call me Lord Byron."

"Of all the poets, that was an unusual call."

"I know. And that's why you love me so much."

"All right, you're getting a little weird again."

"So when is the company jet arriving for you?"

"About noon."

"Then let's go visit Greenwood. I'm thinking he didn't tell me everything. Do you think he might be holding back?"

Sarcastically, Eli replied, "Our new best friend? Nah! The FBI withholding important details? It would never happen."

The FBI had given them credentials that would gain them access to the reception area on Agent Thatcher's floor. He wasn't in, but Agent Cramer was. She met them in one of their conference rooms. Vic asked her what details they had picked up in the home of Eric Parma. She opened her file and gave him a sheet of paper with a list on it.

"Did they find his cell phone?"

"If it's not on the inventory list, it wasn't there."

"How about his phone records?"

"Not here. Let me check on that. I'll be right back."

"You see, they are hiding things from us," Vic remarked. "That reminds me, I asked my old firefighting school instructor, Mark Durant, what vendors sell the kind of gear Parma must have been wearing. He said there are only two in the world. He said he would check to see if they got any orders recently for a single suit. That's the lead I want to follow that the FBI hasn't thought of yet."

Agent Cramer came back in the room with a couple of pages of paper. "We ran a search on it Monday. It just never got in the folder."

Cramer handed it to Vic, and she continued. "The numbers that are circled are our way of singling out those that need following up. The calls with a check mark are insignificant. The others have the names of the owners listed at the bottom."

Vic did not find the identified calls helpful, so he focused on the circled numbers. In his mind, he compared them against the unidentified numbers on Irene Cohen's phone. There was a match, but he kept it to himself.

"When do you expect to hear from Greenwood?" Vic asked.

"He said he'd call in before noon."

"How about Thatcher?"

"He is supposed to be interviewing the rest of the people on Matusak's, French's, and Calloway's call list. He'll call in. What are you two working on?"

"I'd like to visit Harbitron, if that's OK," Vic replied.

"Yeah, that's more up your alley."

"OK. I'll report in when I'm through with them. Come on, Eli. Let's get moving."

Vic and Eli left, and, once out of the door, Vic pulled out a notepad from his shirt pocket and wrote down a phone number.

"We don't need to go to Harbitron. I got what I was looking

for. I don't think they have cross-checked the phone numbers on everyone's call list. I did, and I saw a match. We need to see my old buddy at the Fairfax County Police Department. If anyone can track down a junk cell phone, he can."

Eli had a plane to catch back to Atlanta. Vic drove him to Dulles Airport, and Eli left him on the hunt. Eli could see Vic was doing just fine on his own. Vic promised to call him if he or the FBI came up with anything interesting.

Just sitting around waiting for the FBI to call wasn't Vic's idea of collaboration. He realized he was out of his element, but he was having fun trying to be as good as any agent without the resources of the Bureau at his beck and call. So he was off to see detective Fritz Reynolds at the Chrome Diner in Fairfax. He called Fritz and gave him the matching cell phone number. Fritz was an old buddy he met while working an oil spill in Centreville in 1988. He said he'd bring the phone research with him.

Fritz was waiting outside the diner, pulling on a cigarette when Vic drove up. Vic greeted him with, "How ya doing, amigo?"

"Not bad, you old son of a bitch. You're looking like you still work out."

"Oh yeah. The girls like the guns and six-pack. Hey, can I bum a smoke?"

"Don't tell me you are still bumming cigarettes?"

"It's like the memory of an old girlfriend. You can't wait to see her again, and when you do, you wonder what you saw in her."

"So what kind of shit are you working on?"

"You wouldn't believe me if you didn't know me. You remember I left West to work for the guy who mentored me there."

"You mean that lawyer in Philadelphia?"

"Yeah, but now we work out of Atlanta."

"How do you like it?"

"It's been a blast so far. And this assignment is so cool. We've been working the Craney Island fire for the Navy."

"How did you get from putting out a fire to running down the calls of bad guys?"

"That's the cool part. We think the fire might be a deliberate act of sabotage. Two of the people we think might be linked to the conspirators have calls to the cell phone number I gave you. I'm a step ahead of the FBI, and I want to see if I can beat them to the punch."

"Let me tell you. From my experience, there is no greater satisfaction than beating the feds. I've got the information in my jacket pocket. Let's go inside, and I'll help you make sense of it."

They got a booth in the back, and Fritz asked the waitress to keep the booths around him vacant as long as she could. Fritz pulled out several pages of paper that were folded in his pocket. "The number you gave me is to a throwaway phone. Since we don't know who owned it, we simply tried to identify every call to it or from it.

"We queried the computer to identify every cell tower a call was made from or received at that number. We started with November first, and we had no calls until Thursday, the second. There was an outgoing call to a Marriott in Crystal City, and the next was from a cell phone off a tower in Crystal City. The next call was from a cell phone belonging to a Daniel Witherspoon. The next two calls were also outgoing and made the same day. And the same cell tower was used. The calls were made to two other throwaway cell phones—no identification and untraceable. Another call was made to Witherspoon again the next day. But this time, a cell tower in Curtis Bay, Maryland, was used."

"Where is this guy—Witherspoon?"

"Let's see. Oh, the first day Witherspoon was in Houston,

Texas. The second call, the one made on the third, was received in central Washington, DC. The next two calls that day were made to throwaways again and are from Crystal City; however, the next call is made from Chesapeake, Virginia. Isn't that where Craney Island is?"

"You betcha, it is!"

"And here is another that same day made from Portsmouth, Virginia. This one is to a retail establishment, the Oar House. The next one is that evening to another throwaway. And then, later that day, one is made from Crystal City to Surry, Virginia, to an Eric Parma. On the next day, the fourth, we have another from Crystal City to Witherspoon in DC. Is any of this helpful?"

"It's a surprise that we have all of this. This is dynamite information. This cell phone might have been used by the henchman doing all the dastardly deeds. What else do we have?"

"Let's see. The next call is made on Monday, the sixth. I've got two calls to throwaways and another one from a cell tower near Richmond. It's to this guy Parma again. It appears he is on the move to Portsmouth or Craney Island because here is another to the same throwaway made from Portsmouth about an hour or so later. And here is another made to this Parma guy that evening, but it's to a cell tower in Portsmouth. Do you want me to keep going?"

"Yeah, we're hot."

"OK, the next call is late that night from Portsmouth to Witherspoon in DC. Then the next morning, the seventh, he gets a call from a throwaway at a cell tower in DC while he is in Crystal City. Then he calls that same throwaway from Arlington, Virginia."

"What time is that call made?"

"Let's see. Five minutes after nine in the morning. And then at eleven twenty, he calls Witherspoon in DC. This guy Witherspoon sounds like his boss, and he keeps letting him know how things are going."

"We're both on the same wavelength. What else do you have?"

"I've got three more phone calls he made that day, all to throwaways. One is from DC, and the other two from Crystal City. Then on the next day, the eighth, I've got more from Crystal City to that same throwaway. Now here is one that interests me. He made a call late that evening from Fairfax to Witherspoon. And then again to Witherspoon at two o'clock in the morning the next day. Something tells me he did something bad in Fairfax that night."

"Again, we are thinking alike. Can you leave me the lists? And this guy, Witherspoon, can you get a list of his calls?"

"That's a roger on all counts so long as I get a piece of the collar."

"I cannot control that, but I can promise to lobby for it with the FBI."

"That's all I can realistically hope for."

Vic and Fritz caught up with each other's lives and went their separate ways. Vic was excited about what he had found out. A lot of ideas of what to do next raced through his mind. The first thing, however, was to find out if this assassin was still in town. As he was driving into DC, he called Maryanne Madison at the Greater Washington Visitors Bureau.

"Hi, Maryanne, this is Vic Majeski."

"Well, speak of the devil. Julie was just asking about you the other day at lunch. What's on your mind, big guy?"

"I need a really big favor. A friend of mine is in some trouble, and we need to find a guy who is in town and staying at a Marriott in Crystal City. If I gave you his check-in date, do you think you could find him?"

"Is he still in town?"

"He was as of last night."

"That should be doable. When did he check in?"

"We're pretty sure it's November the second."

"Just hold on the line a minute or two, and I will check it out."

True to her word, Maryanne was back with the information in a couple of minutes. "I've got a woman and a man who checked in that date who have yet to check out. The man is Eugene Kravitz. The woman is Lucy Lin."

"Did I ever tell you how good looking you are?"

"Yeah, yeah. When are you going to see me?"

"What are you doing tonight?"

"That depends on what you have in mind. As long as we can take care of it between five and seven-thirty, I'm available."

"Oh yeah, baby. We have a deal. Can you meet me at the Wyndham for a quick meal and a race up to my room to get ravaged?"

"I am looking forward to it. See you then, you big hunk."

Vic was thinking, This is a hell of a profession. I solve crimes by day and get laid by a different babe each night. I could get used to this shit.

26. THE START OF FISHING SEASON

AS ELI WAS WAITING FOR HIS FLIGHT TO TAKE OFF, HE GOT A CALL from Commander Hughes. "Eli, do you have a minute?"

"Yes, sir. What's on your mind?"

"I just got a call from a reporter for the New York Times. He's following some story having to do with an antiterrorism bill in the House of Representatives. When I told him I would not be able to talk with him, he asked my permission to talk to you. Apparently, he thinks there is some chain reaction linking the events here with the bill. I also got a heads-up from a congresswoman about the same matter. I've contacted Admiral Ellingson, and we think you should talk to the reporter. We can't say anything, and Ellingson is thinking it will only increase the profile of the investigation if we stonewall him and the congresswoman. We expect you don't know of anything with regard to this bill. If you don't, we want to know if you would be comfortable answering his questions in a way that won't say anything, but will satisfy him."

"One thing I can assure you of is that I know zero about what might be going on at the Capitol, and I know nothing of the bill the reporter might be following. So in that regard, I can't say anything to worry about because I don't know anything. And by the way, I also got a call the other day from Congresswoman Schuster from New Jersey. I'm assuming she's the one who contacted you. She was wanting to ask me questions about Craney Island. I told her I wasn't at liberty to say anything unless she got permission to talk to me from you. Apparently, that didn't discourage her."

"Apparently not. She said she tried to talk to you and told me what you told her. Can I trust you to satisfy these folks without saying something that will backfire on us?"

"I think I can do what you want, sir."

"OK, then. I'll have this reporter call you. His name is Matthew Berg. Please call me as soon as your interview is over."

"Will do, sir."

As Eli considered the task, he could not overlook that one of the best friends he ever met in the media was the editor of the New York Times, Isadore Andropolis. He figured he could always contact him if this guy Berg was barking up the wrong tree. About ten minutes later, Eli's cell phone was ringing. It was Matthew Berg.

"Mr. Taylor, my name is Matthew Berg. I am a reporter for the New York Times. Do you mind if I record this interview?"

"I don't mind," Eli replied.

"Thanks for taking my call and allowing me to record our discussion. This won't take long. I'm following the antiterrorism bill that recently came out of the House Subcommittee on Terrorism, Nonproliferation, and Trade. No one was expecting this bill at this time, so I have been looking at acts of terrorism all over the world against US assets. Our paper recently reported that terrorism has not been ruled out as the cause of the Craney Island incident. Would you care to comment?"

"In my company's role as a consulting contractor to the US Navy, our scope is limited to our assignment. While causation is one of our areas of investigation, we are bound by the kinds of causes that would be a part of our expertise—human and mechanical error. So far, our investigation has not uncovered any definite evidence of these two causes. We have not ruled them out, but we have reported no findings of such causation at this date. I am aware of the statement by the Navy to the press that it has not ruled out sabotage or terrorism either. There is no inference that I know of that suggests these statements favor any potential cause at this time. On the contrary, until the US Navy is satisfied that it has found the actual cause, it is leaving all options open."

"Is that what you have advised them to say, or is that the opinion of the Navy?"

"Actually, neither. It is the consensus of all the investigating agencies and consultants. We all agree that it is premature to settle on a cause at this time. Also, I have been a part of the discussion, and I can assure you that the press will learn of the cause as soon as the Navy finds it."

"Mr. Taylor, can you tell me why it is taking so long to find the cause? Has there been an attempt to cover up or remove the evidence?"

"Actually, the investigation is not taking a longer than usual time to find the actual cause. The agencies involved are simply trying to avoid speculation of the cause. Our research into disaster investigation suggests that when a quick determination of cause is reported, it is usually more speculation than fact. The Navy and the agencies assisting the Navy's efforts don't want to make that mistake. It's really that simple."

"So you haven't seen any evidence of terrorism?"

"I didn't say I have or I have not. My focus has been on the evidence of human or mechanical error causes."

At this juncture, Matthew Berg was reviewing his notes and trying to think of a line of questions that might actually get Eli to slip up and reveal something he was trying to conceal. After pausing for quite some time and getting nowhere, he ended the interview.

"Thanks, Mr. Taylor, for taking the time to answer my questions. I realize you are on a tight schedule, so that will be all my questions for now."

"You're welcome, Matthew."

Matthew told Eli he had stopped recording the call, but he was not finished with him.

"Mr. Taylor, off the record, do you have a feel for when a cause might be found?"

"I really don't. We are making progress in a methodical manner. I've been quite impressed by the professionalism I have observed from all the agencies involved."

"I know you know this, but you are really quite good at answering questions in a way that is respectful and articulate while revealing nothing. Where did you get your training?"

Eli realized that the reporter was now attempting to get him to relax and make a mistake. He wasn't going to let that happen.

"Matthew, there is no agenda on my part to conceal information or divert your questions away from your needs. My experience is in the energy industry. A lot of that experience has come from disaster response. You don't stay in this business long if you start making up stuff or speculating. I try my best not to do any of that."

"Very well."

"Do you mind if I ask you some questions off the record?"

Matthew froze, not knowing what to say. "Uh, I—I guess not. What do you have in mind?"

"What's the connection between you and Congresswoman Schuster?"

"There is no connection. I was fishing for any congressman

or woman who might know why this bill was coming out of committee. She was willing to talk to me, and when I saw the news piece on this incident, I just threw it out in our discussion. She seemed to be as interested as I was. I think when she talked to you, she realized that she wasn't going to get anything further from you, so she told me about your conversation."

"Do you know how she identified me as a possible source?"

"I believe one of her aides knew someone responding to the incident from the government. I think that's how they found you. Is your role supposed to be a secret or something?"

"No. I was just curious who referred me to you or the congresswoman."

"Were you trying to avoid being in this spot?"

"Not exactly. Hey, maybe you could do me a favor, and if so, I would do one for you."

Now Matthew was intrigued. "Sure, if the request is reasonable."

"I would like to know who made the referral to me, and I would like to hear anything from you that you might think I would like to hear."

"That appears reasonable. I'll see what I can learn about the snitch."

"That's not how I would characterize my inquiry."

"Please excuse me. That's what I would call him."

After the call was over, both Eli and Matthew felt they had made some progress and the potential of a relationship that might prove beneficial.

27. THIS JOB ISN'T SO HARD

ABOUT TWENTY MINUTES AFTER HE GOT THE INFORMATION FROM Maryanne, Vic drove into the Crystal City Marriott and parked his SUV in the valet line. He gave the redcap a sawbuck and told him he would be back out in less than ten minutes. Once he got inside, he went to the front desk and asked the cute, perky attendant to ring the room of Eugene Kravitz. At the same time, Vic intentionally knocked over the penholder on the counter, sending it cascading over the side of the counter where the attendant stood. In a planned move, Vic attempted to grab it before it hit her or the floor, giving him the opportunity to lean over the counter and see her monitor's screen. It was displaying the guest details for Kravitz, revealing that she was ringing room 1132.

"Sorry about that," Vic apologized. "I've been doing dumb things like this all day."

"I think it missed me and fell on the floor," the attendant remarked. "Oh well, nobody seems to be answering Mr. Kravitz's room."

"If you don't mind, I am supposed to meet up with him. Is it OK if I wait in the lounge?"

"Help yourself," she replied.

Vic called Agent Cramer on his cell phone as he strode toward the lounge.

"Hey, Angela, this is Victor Majeski. I located the perp who did French, Calloway, and Matusak, and started the Craney Island fire. I am outside his room right now at the Crystal City Marriott, and he is not in the room. If you hurry over here, you can plant a bug in the room before he gets back."

"What?" she said with incredulity.

"You heard me, right?"

"Yes, but how do you know his name? I'm not going anywhere just because you think you know who he is."

"He's traveling under the name of Eugene Kravitz, but it's probably an alias. Does that ring a bell?"

"I can't believe you're ahead of us on this. Yes, that's the same name we've got."

"Then get cracking. You won't want to be late for this. I don't think you want me to take him on by myself."

"Don't do anything! I'll be right there."

"Make sure you bring someone who can bug the room," Vic said just before he hung up.

Vic chuckled at his arrogance, and he thought, I wish I could have been at her office so I could have seen her reaction. I'm a very naughty boy.

Vic looked at his watch, and it was a couple of minutes before one o'clock. He then walked to the main restaurant in the hotel and approached the hostess. "Hi, I was just called to help wait on tables. Where is the cloakroom?"

The hostess directed him to a hallway and said, "It's the second door on the left. But don't you want to check in with the supervisor first?"

"No, I'm running late, and I want to look like I'm ready to

work. Thanks," Vic said as he turned and headed for the cloakroom, thereby not giving her a chance to complain.

He used to do this as a kid, and he knew it still might work. Sure enough, the cloakroom door was unlocked, and there were all kinds of linen uniforms for the staff. He picked out a bartender's gold linen tux jacket that was an extra long. Under the rack with the jackets were the shirtfronts. Among them was a sixteen-inch collar with a black bow tie clipped to it. He quickly grabbed the new duds and walked out of the cloakroom undetected.

Vic took the elevator to the eleventh floor and looked down the hall. A room-service tray with leftovers sat on the carpet outside one of the rooms. "Perfect," he thought. He scooped it up and carried it to the stairwell. Once inside the stairwell, he changed into the hotel garb, picked up the tray, holding it like the most expert waiter, and walked down the hallway toward room 1132. There was no activity, no shadows under the door, nothing. He continued to the end of the corridor and turned around and walked back past 1132. He figured he'd do this until either the occupants of the room walked in or out, or Agent Cramer arrived. But his cell phone rang, and he jumped, not realizing how nervous he was.

It was Mark Durant calling back about the moon suit.

"Hey, Mark, were you able to come up with anything?"

"It was a piece of cake. There were only three orders worldwide to private companies since the beginning of the year. One was to BMG Response, another to Sentry Chemical, and another to NAPCO."

"I owe you big time, but I have two questions: Where did the NAPCO uniform ship to? And can you fax me the data on the orders?"

"NAPCO's suit went to its main Houston terminal, and yes. Where do you want it faxed?"

"To my attention at the Wyndham Hotel in Washington, DC."

"You got it, pal. And before you go, whatever happened to that Rachel gal from Denver that you shacked up with at the conference in San Diego? I'm heading that way for an extended assignment, and I thought I'd look her up."

"Bad news. She became obsessed with Fred Couples, the golf pro. She started stalking him. I think she served two stretches in jail because of it. What a shame. She could really party."

"Whoa, I guess that rules out trying to reconnect with her."

"If you do, I expect you'll have little competition. She's gone completely whacko."

Vic usually steered moochers like Mark away from his lady friends with fibs about them getting married or the like, but he didn't have to fib about Rachel. He was telling Mark the truth.

After his conversation with Mark, Vic thought, Do I feel lucky? Stealing the line from the first Dirty Harry movie, he pulled the telephone records Fritz had given him out of his pocket and looked up the number for the Oar House.

The person answering announced, "Oar House."

"Hello, my name is Victor Majeski. I'm investigating the fire at the Navy Fuel Supply Depot. Can I speak to an employee who would have been working the week before last Monday?"

"I'm the owner. I worked the entire week."

"And your name, please?"

"Fred Meltzer."

"Fred, do you recall if anyone might have rented or purchased a small watercraft that week?"

"We weren't having a great week for business. I don't recall selling any, but we rented a few."

"Did anyone pay you in cash?"

"Funny you mentioned that. Almost all our sales are credit cards, debit cards, or check. But we did get a rare cash sale. I remember it well. It was a tall Latin-looking gentleman. He rented a two-seated Bozeman pontoon boat, an electric motor, and a trailer. I had to get it out of the warehouse. He couldn't wait around. He left me a phone number, and I called him when it was ready for him to pick it up. The guy has yet to return it."

"You said he was Latin looking. What kind of an accent did he have?"

"You know, I never did figure it out. He almost had no accent, but it appeared that whatever it was, it didn't sound like English was his first language. Did he have something to do with the fire?"

"I don't know. Could be. How much did he pay?"

"Three hundred fifty for the rental and a thousand dollars deposit. If he never comes back, he paid about as much as the whole thing was worth."

Vic's phone was indicating that Agent Cramer was calling, so he said goodbye and picked up her call.

"Vic, we are entering the hotel. Where are you?"

"I'm wearing a bartending outfit, and I'm walking the eleventh floor hallway."

"Normally, I'd have some follow-up questions, but they can wait," she remarked. "We'll be there in a minute or so."

In a few minutes, the elevator door opened, and Agent Cramer, Thatcher, and two other agents walked out.

"What room, Vic?" Cramer demanded.

"Eleven thirty-two—it's about halfway down on the left. It

looks like a suite, so you'll need to check the unnumbered doors on each side."

"Thanks, Vic. We'll take it from here. Please wait for us in the stairwell."

"That's a roger," Vic replied. He walked to the stairwell and watched through the window in the door.

The two FBI agents used fiber optics to look into the rooms undetected. They poked the optic wands underneath the door and scanned the room. They must not have seen any activity because Thatcher pulled out a master hotel key card and inserted it into the door slot. Cramer and two agents entered, while one stayed in the hall. Vic was watching to see if anyone might try to leave by another suite door. Nothing happened, and after about two minutes, they all exited and walked toward Vic.

In the stairwell, one of the agents pulled out a handheld device, powered it up, and dialed in some kind of code, and within a split second, a four-scene video picture popped up. It appeared to be the view inside of room 1132. The operative powered it off, and Cramer instructed the group to walk down to the tenth floor and take the elevator down from there. Vic picked up his shirt and jacket and followed. Once in the elevator, Cramer looked at Vic, felt the cloth of the lapel on his barkeep jacket, and asked, "So, what's the story with the outfit?"

"In case the bad guys walked out of the room or elevator and could see me, I wanted to look inconspicuous, like a hotel employee, so they would not recognize me if I ran across them again."

"Not bad," Thatcher commented. "How did you get it?"

"I just walked into the cloakroom and found my size on the clothes rack. As a kid in high school, we used to do the same thing. Obviously, it still works."

"Unbelievable!" he remarked. They all walked out of the hotel, and Cramer insisted Vic follow her back to FBI headquarters. Once there, Chief Greenwood joined the party, and they put Vic on the hot seat about what he had been doing to find the bad guys. He told them the entire story about noticing the matching cell phone numbers and getting the call list from a cop he knew. Vic explained how he had narrowed down the suspects by when they arrived in town based upon the date the cell phone was activated and so on.

Greenwood just shook his head. "You are brilliant, but you are a loose cannon. I don't know what I am going to do with you."

Cramer said they pulled prints from the hotel room and took some pictures of the items in the room. "I'm afraid he is dead on the mark. The photos we took inside the room included the addresses of Gary French, Ann Calloway, and Brian Matusak written on slips of paper pinned to a cork bulletin board. No names, just the addresses."

Thatcher came in and announced, "We called in the scanned fingerprints from the car on the way here. Two of the prints matched known operatives in the intelligence community. One was that of Mariano Cota and the other was Dieter Hoff. Hoff has a long rap sheet, but nothing ever stuck. Cota is a fairly young, recent player."

Greenwood walked directly into Vic's gaze and asked, "So, what else do you know that you haven't told us?"

"Nothing, really! I got so excited about this lead, I acted immediately just in case they were about to leave."

"I don't know if I should believe you, but for now, you have given us plenty to go on. Now sit here while we set up everything in a separate situation room. When it's all set up, we'll come and get you."

When they walked out of the room, Vic called Eli in Atlanta. He was home with the nanny and the kids while Danielle was on her way to Hilton Head to coach her tennis circuit clients. Eli couldn't believe how far Vic had gotten since he left him a few hours ago. Vic told Eli about Witherspoon and why he thought he was running the show. Eli told him he expected he could find out more about him since he was in the oil industry.

Vic also told Eli about the moon suit. "I want to visit NAPCO in Houston tomorrow to see if they have it available to see. I've got a plan how to do it without creating suspicion."

"What are you doing tonight?" Eli asked.

"Don't worry—you're not missing anything. The gal who gave me the hotel and the name of the bad guys is joining me for dinner and sweaty sex up in my room."

"You are special, my friend. I swear you are giving me material for at least ten roasts at our first annual employee meeting."

"Uh-oh, Agent Cramer just walked in. I'll check with you tomorrow when I crack this case wide open."

Vic said that last part loudly enough so Cramer could overhear it. She just smirked at Vic as he hung up on Eli. She took Vic by the hand and led him out of the door of the conference room.

"Come along, dear," she said. "We can't do anything right without you."

"Yes, dear," Vic responded. "But can we play together without the others being there?"

Angela Cramer let go of Vic's hand and gazed at him as they walked down the hallway. "You know, Victor. You need to learn how to play with the other children so that when you grow up, you won't be so awkward around them."

Vic just smiled back at her and purposely undressed her with his eyes so that she would notice. "Maybe I only want to learn how to play with you," he said coyly.

Agent Cramer smiled back as they entered the situation room the FBI had set up for what they called Case USN 23A. There were a number of video screens on the wall and people seated at a long countertop facing the screens. There were computer keyboards in front of them. They sat poised waiting for instructions. There was an unfamiliar man in the room who approached Vic as he stared at the screens.

"Mr. Majeski, I am Deputy Director Raymond Inge. I've been anxious to make your acquaintance. Chief Greenwood has spoken well of you. But I also understand that you are not much of team player. Because of that, we are hesitant to take everything you say as truthful. I hope you understand that. However, we are willing to put up with your eccentricities while we help our country catch some very bad people.

"We are about to give you a live peek into what we do. However, I will need your word that you will keep everything you see and hear in this room completely confidential. And just to let you know how serious we are, we will arrest you for obstruction of a federal investigation if we discover you did not heed this warning. That is a felony, and it will incarcerate you for a minimum of fifteen years. Do you understand me?"

"Yes, sir. I understand, and I promise I will not disappoint you. But I have to say, I have been having a lot of fun while we have been investigating these incidents. This is a great life you lead here in the FBI. However, I don't want to be an FBI agent. I prefer my job with Daneli."

Director Inge stared at Vic for an awkward moment that was intended to intimidate him, and then he turned away and said, "Carry on." Vic's return look suggested he had won that stare-down confrontation.

When Inge left the room, Greenwood ordered that the first screen flash the pictures of the persons known to be dead. Within a heartbeat, the photos of Calloway, French, and Matusak appeared. The second screen began showing footage of the Craney Island fire, the charred facility after the blaze was put out, and the chalked outlines of the bodies of the facility's operator and utility. The third showed photos of NAPCO's officers and Board of Directors. Another screen showed the employee photos of Irene Cohen of GAO and Eric Parma of Harbitron. And finally, the last screen displayed the recent mug shots of Dieter Hoff and Mariano Cota, along with the security-camera shot of the person who had bought the throwaway cell phone. Vic gathered it was their best likeness of Eugene Kravitz. Another screen showed the live-streaming video of the room 1132 of the Crystal City Marriott.

Greenwood began giving a rundown of where the bureau was in the investigation.

"We have contacted everyone on the call lists of French, Calloway, and Matusak. All are safe and apparently ignorant of the events of the past few days, except for Matusak's in-laws. This provides additional credence to Irene Cohen being the mole who alerted the perpetrators. Her call list is somewhat problematical.

"As Mr. Majeski so brilliantly pointed out, he was able to identify one of the suspects by finding a phone number match on Eric Parma's call list. A further inspection of her call list, however, suggests that the call to Eugene Kravitz was too late in time to be her initial communication of the NAPCO investigation. Since that was her only call to Kravitz, she had to contact someone else first. We have run down the remainder of the calls, and we have narrowed it down to only two possibilities: her initial communications were in person, or it was a call made to a party who appears to be a routine business associate.

"Ms. Cohen's call list also has some calls that we could not identify earlier or ones that did not appear to be from a co-conspirator. We have since determined that the first two unidentified calls were to a son who is studying overseas. That means that her co-conspirator is either somebody else on her call list or someone she communicated with by other means. We have checked her emails, and she does use an Internet social networking site. We think her communiqués before her call from Kravitz were with someone to whom she only passed on information in person or an attorney in the Bennett, Bancroft, and Sperling law firm. All other calls are from family or friends.

"The lawyer she contacted at BB&S is Sam Nugent. He's an associate who reports to lobbyist Charles Bobick. Now here is the kicker. Bobick is a lobbyist for the Organization of Oil Exporting Countries—OPEC—and some of Bobick's major clients include NAPCO and PETGO.

"To this date, all we have is a mountain of circumstantial evidence. Although all the cracker crumbs lead to NAPCO, we don't have anything that can support an arrest. I can't help but think the longer it takes to find a smoking gun, the further away NAPCO is from an indictment. Bobick and his BB&S buddies remain persons of interest. We intend to look into their past dealings and watch them very closely.

"We are also looking for Kravitz and his henchmen, but the only thing that might trip him up is returning to the hotel room or using his throwaway cell phone that we are monitoring. And since there has been no call activity on that phone for twenty-nine hours, we suspect that phone is toast and that he is using another.

"We are going to follow the connection to the law firm by seeing if we can get a match on the call lists of Bobick and Nugent with Kravitz. Other than that, we will continue to look for coincidences. What are you investigating, Mr. Majeski?"

"I'd like to go down to Houston tomorrow to check into the potential that the purchase of the moon suit will lead us somewhere. Other than that, I've got nothing."

Agent Cramer commented, "Tomorrow is Saturday. Won't the facility be closed?"

Vic replied, "Pipelines don't close facilities when shipments are going in and out. There will be a regular staff there, and facilities located around refineries have shipments around the clock. Actually, it's the best time to make this kind of a visit. Only the weekend employees will be handy. If anyone is unsure of why we're there, they'll be hesitant to bother a superior on a weekend."

Greenwood then gave out assignments. "Angela, I want you tagging along with Vic, and I don't want him doing anything you don't know about. And that means we need to approve his movements in advance and approve revisions."

Vic interjected, "I've got a hot date tonight with the gal in the Visitors Bureau who helped me locate Kravitz. Does that mean Angela will be joining us as a threesome?"

Greenwood looked at Angela and then the both of them looked at Vic. "I can tell this assignment is going to be challenging for the both of you. And, no, you are not going to get an answer from me on questions such as that one. I am just asking that you exercise common sense when it comes to this investigation."

Vic turned to Agent Cramer and remarked, "My date has to be home by eight, so I'll be free by seven-thirty or so. We can have dessert in my hotel room."

"Don't flatter yourself," Cramer replied.

Vic smiled as she turned away, but he was reading the signals loud and clear from her. She was into him. The chemistry was there, and Greenwood may have been picking up on it as well.

"OK, you two. You are temporarily working as partners, and that means you have to be professionals. The cute repartee must stop here. Now, go and find us something that will help us catch these guys."

Agent Cramer and Vic worked out an agenda. She would meet Vic in the morning at his hotel restaurant at eight thirty. They booked a Continental Airlines flight to arrive in Houston at 12:40 p.m. central time.

"How come you didn't book a return flight?" Vic asked. "Are we staying in a Houston hotel room indefinitely?"

"I didn't book a return because I don't know when we are going to be finished there. We can always book the return at the airport."

"Does that mean there is no chance we'll share the night together?"

"That depends on how you play your cards," Angela said as she got up. "Now you run along to your Visitors Bureau honey."

Vic said goodbye, but he was thinking, Now you're talking!

28. CHECKING OUT THE SIGHTS

BEFORE VIC WENT BACK TO THE HOTEL, HE CALLED THE FERC (Federal Energy Regulatory Commission) and asked to speak to his old buddy there. He used to work for Colombia Gas in Baltimore before he became an enforcement and compliance officer. They started a friendship at industry conferences and local pipeline association meetings. When he left Colombia, they continued their friendship, even though he began making compliance inspections at West Industries when Vic was there. They had a pretty good relationship, and Vic was comfortable asking him a big favor.

"Hey, amigo, Vic Majeski here. I need a favor, old buddy. Do you have time to visit with me?"

His old buddy was happy to hear from him, and he invited Vic to come by his office. Once there, Vic told him about his need to inspect NAPCO's Houston facility to see if they had the Inferno fire suit that was used in the Craney Island fire.

Vic inquired, "I was wondering if you had a problem with me masquerading as an FERC inspector."

"I don't have a problem, just as long as you can pull it off. If it goes south, I will disavow ever knowing you."

"I can live with that. Now there is just one more favor. I need to borrow one of your hard-hat decals with the FERC insignia."

He opened a drawer in the credenza behind him and pulled out a sheet of decals and gave Vic a couple.

"And by the way, I need your contact with NAPCO so I can call him from here and make an appointment tomorrow for an inspection visit."

"Let me look that up for you. You realize you are going to owe me big time for this?"

After a minute or so diving through a directory, his regulatory buddy declared, "OK, you need to contact Robby Vickers at 710-555-1303. Just remember one thing. I want to know how your meeting turns out just in case he calls me, and I need to log it in as an inspection conducted. You can use the phone in the conference room next door."

Vic made the call and got an appointment for the next day at 2:30 p.m. He stopped by his friend's office to say goodbye and reached into the business card holder on his credenza and grabbed a couple of business cards without him noticing as they shook hands.

The compliance officer said something about cashing in on the return favor. "Hey, I've got a quid pro quo that will set us square. I've got an inspection at West scheduled that's a conflict with a trip my wife insists that I take with her. I can't reschedule the West inspection because it's the only time I can visit before the two-year inspection time period will elapse. That's a violation my boss won't accept. Can you fix it with the West guys in Philly? I'll need their signatures on the inspection form."

"No sweat. I'm on good terms with the operator. Send me the paperwork, and I'll take it by there. I'll mail you back the completed form."

They shook hands and parted ways. With that mission accomplished, Vic made his way to the Wyndham. He called Eli to tell him about his Houston trip.

They brought each other up to date. Vic was really on a roll. There were just a couple of things that were bothering Eli. What was this guy Kravitz doing right now? And the other thing was the stuff Greenwood wasn't telling Vic. Eli was betting that the FBI was soon to know about Witherspoon and drawing the same conclusions Vic had drawn.

Eli also expected the Bureau was trying their best to crack Kravitz's real identity. He mentioned all these things to Vic for him to digest. Although Vic was aware of them, Eli had a hunch Vic's mind was on other matters.

"Vic, you can't lose your focus on what the bad guys might be thinking or doing. They like to eliminate people who stand in their way of reaching their goal, whatever that is. I don't want them to find you."

"You are trying to get me out of the mood to ravage Maryanne this evening. I made a lot of progress today. It's time for me to unclutter my mind so I can be at my best for Maryanne."

Sarcastically, Eli remarked, "Maybe you're right. Maybe doing it your way works best for you. After all, the bad guys might find it more difficult to find you than Ann Callaway or that French fellow. And maybe they won't be carrying any weapons when they come across you. Yeah, just forget I said it."

"No, no, no. It doesn't work that way. You can't just take back something like that. You are trying again to have one of those discussions that eventually fucks up my brain. Once said, that kind of shit stays in play. I won't be able to erase it from my mind."

"I'm just trying to tell you to be careful. You need to watch your backside," Eli retorted.

Vic looked in his rearview mirror as a reflex to Eli's warning. He noticed a silver SUV was behind him, and two men were in the front seat.

They hung up on that thought, but Vic's mind had been diverted from Maryanne. Eli's warning stuck in his head as he turned into the Wyndham parking deck. Instinctively, Vic glanced into the rearview mirror again. The same silver SUV pulled in behind him. He made a mental note of the vehicle, but then it dawned on him: Fritz was supposed to call him back on the results of the calls listed on Witherspoon's cell phone. So, before he got out of his vehicle he called Fritz.

Fritz told him that his lieutenant noticed he was doing a lot of call searching and asked him what it was all about. Fritz was a straight shooter, so he had to tell his boss. His boss wasn't too happy, and he told him he could only help out another investigation on one condition—that they get something just as valuable in return.

Vic paused for a moment and then told Fritz, "OK then, I've got something for you."

"You do?"

"Yup, I sure do. Do you remember that call we found on the throwaway phone that came from Fairfax?"

"Yeah."

"Well, it is a damn good bet that it was made the night my suspect blew up the house of Brian Matusak."

"Matusak! That incident is related?"

"That's what I'm saying. Check out the Matusak crime scene log. It matches perfectly with this guy's phone calls. Now, you can't let on to anyone, except your boss, that I gave you this. You have got to make it look like you figured it out with a little help from me. That ought to be a quid pro quo, don't you think?"

"If that means an equal trade, then I'm good with it."

"Even Steven."

"OK, I'll give it a shot. If he agrees to cooperate, where should I fax the list?"

"Send it to my attention at the DC Wyndham Hotel."

"You got it."

Vic hung up and got out of his vehicle confident that he had satisfied Eli's attempt to keep his mind on the investigation. As he walked toward the hotel elevator, he whispered to himself a play on the lyrics of an old Rick Nelson song: "Good-bye Eli, and hello-o-o Maryanne."

As Vic walked away from his rental vehicle, he remembered the silver SUV that followed him into the garage. He decided to walk up and down the aisles of cars in case it was still around. He didn't see anything, but before he went inside, he looked underneath his rental from near the rear bumper.

"Son of a bitch!" he exclaimed as he tugged on a magnetized GPS tracking device attached to the carriage. He pulled it off and placed it under the vehicle next to his. Afterward, he gave the entire vehicle an inspection for other devices and found none.

Vic called Eli and filled him in.

"Boss, I guess this is a sign we are getting pretty close to the bad guys. You should perform an undercarriage inspection of your car as well."

As Eli and Vic continued, Eli walked out of his office and into the parking lot.

"Look under the rear bumper first to see if you can spot something that looks out of place."

"I don't see a thing."

"Don't give up. Feel under the bumper with your hand. If you come across anything that protrudes from the smooth surface, pull on it to see if it's attached by a magnet."

"I got something!"

Eli inspected the rectangular device. It was about the size of a deck of cards with a green light shining from it.

"Was yours black with a glowing green light?"

"Son of a bitch! You've got the same thing as mine. I'll tell Cramer. Why don't you call Jim DeFoor and get him over to the office to see if he can find any surveillance shit in the office."

"Good thinking. I'll do that. I guess we have graduated from trying to find the normal corporate screw-ups to investigating serious bad guys. I'm going to have to reconsider our interest in continuing this line of work. Why don't you lie low for a while until I get a better idea how we should proceed?"

"Is it OK if I resume my plans to go to Houston tomorrow with agent Cramer?"

"You should be out of harm's way. Yeah, go ahead. Check in with me as soon as you get back here."

"That's a roger, boss."

SATURDAY, NOVEMBER 18

Agent Cramer picked up Vic at his hotel, and they proceeded to Ronald Reagan International Airport to catch their flight to Houston.

Cramer told Vic, "We swept your vehicle for eavesdropping devices as well as your room at the Wyndham. We found bugs in your dome light in your rental car and under the desk phone in the hotel. It looks like you've become real unpopular with the enemy. Greenwood has been on the phone with Gilbert, and Gilbert ordered a protection detail until this business is concluded. Gilbert seems to have taken a special interest in your safety."

Vic told her about their last encounter with the FBI while working on the Bolivian project when they were with West Industries. After hearing Vic's retelling of the last couple of years, and how Eli had worked with Gilbert before, she had a better understanding of why Gilbert was so willing to protect Eli and Vic.

***

Continental flight 722 arrived at Houston at 12:01 p.m. central time. The flight was smooth, and Vic slept the entire airtime. Agent Cramer had arranged for a Houston bureau agent to meet them. Vic hadn't counted on that.

He pulled Angela aside and told her, "I wasn't counting on anyone but you and me visiting with NAPCO."

"The agent is just accompanying us to the office, where a pool car is waiting for us. You don't have anything bizarre planned, do you?"

"No, it's just that I told them just two of us will be visiting with them."

Vic took Angela to lunch at Ruth's Chris Steakhouse on Richmond Avenue, his favorite restaurant anywhere. To Angela's surprise, Vic ordered the blackened shrimp Caesar salad. She ordered the steakhouse salad.

"I can't believe it! You take me to one of the best steakhouses in the world, and you order the shrimp salad, and I am the one who orders steak."

"This ain't no average shrimp salad. Besides, it's lunch. We can come back tonight, and you can watch me down the Cowboy Ribeye. What you ordered isn't too shabby. I used to order it until they started serving this."

"You are an enigma, a contradiction, and a paradox. Does anybody really know who you are?"

"The ones I call my friends know me."

"And who would they be?"

"For one, nobody knows me better than Eli."

"Two peas in a pod, aren't you?"

"You can't be serious. We are as different as night and day. The differences just don't get in the way of our respect for each other."

"How in the world did the two of you ever hook up, anyway?"

"I hope you mean 'hook up' in the old vernacular?"

Angela laughed. "Yeah, the old meaning."

"I am not sure I know. It just sort of grew. We met while we worked a couple of emergency responses. Also, he was the guy you called when you had legal issues. I seemed to have more than my share of those."

"I bet!"

"It was never like that. I just didn't shy away from controversies. Besides, Eli was the best at advice and protecting you. I guess what really sealed our friendship was him taking up for me against my boss. I think I may have helped him with 'street cred' with the peons of the company—guys like me. Since then, we share the knowledge that when called upon, we will take a bullet for the other."

"You two seem to work well together when it comes to an investigation. How did that start?"

"That's when we just have a lot of fun. He is crazy smart, and I have a nose for how this business works and 'doesn't work' from the ground up. Most industrial disasters are the result of human mistakes and neglect. We can sniff out most incidents, how they occurred, who made the mistakes, how to find the bad guys, and how to nail them for their dastardly deeds. We love to catch the screw-ups or evildoers so they don't get away with their crimes!"

"So, what surprises are in store for us at NAPCO?"

"Not so fast. I told you something about me. Now it's your turn to tell me about you."

"What do you want to know?"

"How did you end up with the FBI? What do you do when you are off the job?"

"You are going to be surprised how easy those questions are. My dad is a cop in Jackson Hole, Wyoming. My mom died at an early age. I had few friends and role models who weren't boys or men. My dad didn't want me to be a cop, but he suggested the FBI. And when I'm not on the job, I garden."

"Seriously, you garden?"

"Yeah, what's so unusual about that?"

"Where do you live that you have room to garden?"

"Two years ago I bought a little place in Arlington."

"What are your favorites?"

"Are you really interested, or are you setting me up?"

"Don't be so suspicious. I really want to know. My specialty is shade plants."

"Now I know you are lying. You are just trying to hook me."

"Hah!" Vic chuckled. "You think you know men. Well, this man grows autumn ferns, river begonias, caladiums, New Guinea impatiens, and hosta, just to name a few."

"My God, you are a freak!"

"I will take that as a compliment."

"Next you're going to tell me you read for enjoyment."

"Do you want to know what titles I've read in the past couple of weeks?"

"OK, I give up. I have never met a Vic Majeski before. Now I know I am in for more surprises at NAPCO this afternoon."

"No surprises. You just need to follow my lead. If we walk in there saying who we really are and what we want to know, we'll get nothing. They are expecting two new, inexperienced FERC safety compliance inspectors. And that's what we will give them."

Vic and Angela arrived at the NAPCO gate at 2:20 p.m. The gate slid open after they announced themselves at the call box, and a voice instructed them on how to find the visitors' parking area. Aaron's description of the facility was on target. It looked as if it could use a huge investment in paint and general maintenance. Vic put on his hard hat with the FERC decal on it and took his time looking around before an employee approached them.

"Howdy, are you Mr. Majeski?" asked the employee. "I'm Robby Vickers."

"Sure am. And this is Angela Cramer."

They shook hands.

"I'm afraid I forgot to pack a hard hat for Ms. Cramer. Do you have one she can use?"

"Not a problem. Come with me to the control building."

"As I mentioned to you on the phone, I'm new at the job," Vic remarked. "I've worked in the business for many years, but new with FERC. Angela just started last week. She's in administration and is along for the experience."

"Glad to have both of you. This place is about to be transformed starting next month. Everything runs like new, but we need a cosmetic overhaul. So if you can look behind the surface rust, I think you will find that we run a good ship. Where do you want to start?"

"As long as we are in the control building, we can start here."

Robby showed them around and answered all the feeble questions the inspectors had asked Vic over the years. When they got to the door on the other side of the building, they walked amid all the protective gear. Several pairs of boots lined the walls. Hard hats of various colors and vintage appeared on the shelf above the rack holding all the protective outerwear. Breathing apparatuses were stored in a cabinet next to the clothes rack. And, as Vic had hoped, the white Inferno suit was hanging at the end of the rack.

"Holy shit! Is this one of these Inferno suits? I guess you guys are serious about safety. How much did that set you back?"

"Actually, I have no idea. It just arrived the other day. I don't even know who ordered it. Some guy came by with a delivery truck and dropped it off. I guess I need to find out what exercise the company has in mind for it."

Vic pulled one of the sleeves to his nose, and he sniffed for the smell of No. 2 fuel oil.

He and Angela spent the better part of an hour at the facility as Vic took notes in a portfolio he brought along. When he had approximated the inspections he was accustomed to when he worked at West Industries, he and Angela said their farewells, advising Robby he needed to run so they could inspect the Provincial Pipeline facility down the road.

On the way back to downtown Houston, Angela asked if he had found what he was looking for.

"Sure enough. That white Inferno suit was what allowed their IT guy to withstand the temperatures at Craney Island while he messed with the Navy's systems. You don't buy one of those just to have it available in a facility if the need arises. It's too expensive. And the money they have invested in their plant suggests they would never buy one just in case you might need it. The manufacturer knows of no other energy companies that have bought one this year."

"Why did you sniff the sleeve?"

"I wanted to see if I could smell fuel oil on it. But the odor was so faint that what I was smelling could have been the ambient odor from the facility."

"You got what you were looking for, right?"

"Oh yeah. So do you want to hang around here, have a meal, and then catch our flight back to DC? Or do you want to try to get on an earlier flight and have dinner in DC?"

Agent Cramer replied, "I'd rather get back on an earlier flight, but what makes you think we'd be eating out together if we did take the earlier flight?"

"I guess it was more of an invitation than me taking you for granted. Forgive me. I don't even know that you might be married or have a regular guy that you see."

"That is not exactly what I was thinking."

"What were you thinking?"

"I was thinking that I'd like to cook for us at my place."

"Now you're talking. I don't think I could resist that offer. Do you want me to call Continental and see what kind of flight we could catch?"

"It depends on how badly you want to make it."

"I'll make the call."

Angela sped to reach the FBI office to return the pool car and get a ride to the airport in time to catch the 5:40 flight to Washington. Had she not been an FBI agent and flashed her badge, they would not have reached the gate in time. They got a ride in a golf-cart-type of vehicle, and the Continental gate attendants waited to close the doors after they boarded.

It was after eight o'clock when they pulled into Angela's driveway in Arlington. Her home was a quaint cottage, just as she had described. Once inside, she poured Vic and herself a glass of Cabernet. Vic followed her into the kitchen and sat down on a stool that cozied up to an island bar. He was now following her every move. From the fridge, she pulled out two precooked Cornish hens sitting in a pot. All kinds of vegetables soaked in the broth at the bottom of the pot. She looked at Vic and winked.

As the meal cooked, Vic was inhaling the aromas of the wine, the Cornish hens, and Angela. His eyes were feasting on her smile and her body parts as she squatted to peek into the oven and check the progress of the hens. He winked back as she glanced back at him. She had taken off her navy blue blazer. Her whiter-than-white blouse and tight navy blue skirt gave her a smart look that promised some dynamite equipment underneath. It was then that he figured out who she reminded him of.

"Angela, have you seen the movie The Jackal?"

"Which version?"

"The 1990s version with Richard Gere."

"Yeah. Why?"

"I've been trying to figure out who you remind me of. Do you remember the Russian KBG major? I think her role name was Koslova or something like it. I am not talking about the scar on her cheek. What reminds me of her that I see in you is her dry but sexy wit. I really dug her."

Angela turned away from the oven. She approached Vic in a slow, sultry saunter. With her eyes on his, she nestled up to his side, with her mouth inches from his. Vic was anticipating a kiss or a tender touch, but instead Angela struck a match on the strike plate next to the candle on the island, lit the candle, and turned her back on him. She was also a hell of tease, he thought. He wanted to grab her or spank her but resisted the urge, just in case she was a different kind of bird. He didn't want to disrupt the drama she was manufacturing.

Angela asked, "Are you familiar with an iPod?"

He answered affirmatively, and she pointed to a stereo unit on the kitchen étagère.

"Find something you like for a little ambiance."

To Vic, looking at the playlist of someone's iPod was a revealing invitation. He felt as though he were swimming in her pool of intimacy. As he scrolled through the list of artists, he realized Angela was humming a tune. Vic wondered if the tune was a hint of what he should be looking for. He listened intently. It was familiar. He waited a little longer, and the title jumped out at him. He scrolled to the song titles and found it. He looked over at Angela as she was making two place settings on the island. She was swaying with the melody as she set the cooking timer.

Vic selected "Lady in Red" by Chris de Burgh and moseyed over to Angela, placing her right hand in his left hand as the song began. She looked intently into Vic's eyes as he put his right arm around her waist, gently pulled her close, and moved in step with the music in a rhythmic slow dance. The mystery of Agent Cramer was beginning to unravel. She was a true romantic. He mused, "She must have a vision of how romance with her partner should take place." He was looking into her eyes for clues, but he was only falling deeper under her spell.

Vic was in unchartered territory. His love life was filled with women who catered to his every move. Almost all of his initial encounters moved at an ever-increasing pace. Angela was in no hurry. Her languid motions and words played havoc with his hungry desire. Even in dancing caress, Angela was not succumbing to him. Her breasts pressed gently against him, and his pelvis had found a comfortable spot against her, but she was following her own agenda, not his.

Vic slowly bent down to kiss her lips, and Angela raised up on her tiptoes to meet his. Vic was in a hypnotic trance as Angela's tongue danced with his in a rhythm of its own. "The Cornish hens had to wait," he thought. There was something going on here. The dancing also had to wait. Vic's instincts took over again. He picked up Angela, cradled her in his arms, and carried her to the sofa, where he sat down with her on his lap. Angela calmly disengaged her mouth from Vic's, opened her eyes, and took a deep breath.

As if on cue, the oven timer sounded the alarm that the hens were done cooking.

"Supper is ready," Angela announced as she struggled to stand up and escape from Vic's arms.

"You've got to be kidding," Vic remarked.

Angela was smiling coyly, but Vic was confused. Angela was not kidding. She donned a pair of cooking mittens, pulled open the oven door, picked up the pot, and placed it on the stovetop. A couple of fork jabs into the breast of one hen, and she declared, "It's ready!"

Vic walked over to the kitchen and stood in amazement as Angela prepared each dinner plate as well as any presentation found in a DC restaurant. She placed the plates on the island and pulled out a box of matches from a drawer. Her match struck the strike plate on the box with the poise of a lifetime smoker. Two candles were lit, and Angela killed the overhead lights.

"Dinner is served," she declared. "Now take a seat while I pour the wine."

Vic obeyed, and as Angela placed the bottle on the island countertop, she bent toward Vic, kissed his forehead, and sat down.

"So, what makes Mr. Majeski who he is?" she asked.

"What makes you think I know?"

"I've got no doubt about that."

"Can I trust you to can keep a secret?"

"If that's the way you want it, yes."

"It's pretty boring."

"Let me be the judge of that."

"Well, if I can't get out of it, here goes. I always had a hard time picking just a few interests. Everything seemed to appeal to me when I was young. I tried them all. My mom started me out with piano lessons. My dad was a mechanic and liked sports. So I did that, too. I was always bigger than most in my class, so I was pushed harder in that direction.

"In many ways, I never saw the drawbacks in the things that interested me. I only saw the advantages, the adventure, and the anticipation of learning something that I never imagined.

"Sometime in my junior or senior year of high school, my father asked, 'So, what's it going to be? What kind of career do you envision?'

"I had no clue. I ended up in a junior college, working nights as a mechanic, when the guys I hung with talked me into enlisting in the Marines. I came out a much more mature guy. And I learned something about myself that I didn't expect. I learned that I got what I wanted faster and easier when I acted naive and unrefined. In many ways, I'm the guy people want me to be. I adapt to their expectations. So, in a way, I've been building the Vic Majeski most people expect. So, you see, I'm not sure who I am."

Angela just smiled. She opined, "I think that whoever you choose to be, that person will always be interesting."

Vic replied, "I do know one thing. You interest me."

It was eleven p.m. when they finished eating. By then Vic realized that Angela had had the evening rehearsed in her mind before they left for Houston. Even three glasses of wine did not deter her from her plan. Whatever signs he thought he was getting about lovemaking were merely a tease. While Vic was thinking about her bedroom, Angela was picking up his coat and handing it to him.

"It's late, and I've got to report back to Greenwood. I enjoyed your company."

Vic was in shocked disbelief, but he didn't let it show. What wasn't a tease was everything else about Angela. Her cooking was exceptional. She was definitely smart. She had the kind of looks that get better the closer you were. And she was delectably alluring. Vic realized he was falling for her. He wanted to get to know her better. He figured he would get another shot at romance with her if he played his cards right.

To that end, Vic did not want to spoil the good time they had had that evening. So he chose his words wisely and mentioned to her how much he had enjoyed himself. Angela walked over to him and hugged him. It was an embrace of gratitude and understanding.

Angela asked, "Will you be coming by the FBI office in the morning?"

"I expect to, but I will have to check in with Eli before I know if and when."

Vic got another harmless kiss as he opened her front door to leave. He told her goodnight, and he sped away, feeling as though he were seventeen again. At least he had gotten to first base on their first date.

29. STIRRING THE POT

ON HIS WAY TO THE HOTEL FROM ANGELA'S HOUSE, VIC GOT A CALL from Fritz in Fairfax. He wanted to thank him for the information about the investigation of Brian Matusak.

"Our DA announced yesterday that we are pursuing the matter as a homicide. And he's not too happy with the FBI for holding back information. And just this afternoon, the FBI called to say they were taking over our investigation. Ain't that just like the feds!"

He continued, "After I got over the indignation, I thought about what you are working on. If I were you, I would visit with Brian Matusak's father-in-law, Skip Blackmon. He says he and Brian visited with the FBI the day after seeing the news report that the GAO General Counsel was murdered. Matusak told the FBI that he would be the next logical target and wanted to be put in a safe house or at least get around-the-clock protection. Greenwood ordered them to go home."

"No shit!"

"Blackmon is looking for someone to help him find out who did it. Our hands are tied since the FBI took it over."

"Would you mind if I talked to him?"

"Not at all. Let me give you his contact info. Also, I faxed the phone records you requested over to your hotel."

Once inside his hotel, Vic checked with the desk and picked up the fax. Back in his room, he examined the list for owners of the phones Witherspoon had spoken to. Many of the calls were to employees of a company called Purified Petroleum. Then he saw Fritz's note saying that Witherspoon was the head of security for that firm, not NAPCO. Vic made a mental note to mention this inconsistency to Eli. Reading further, he found that Fritz had already cross-checked a few phone numbers to owners on the other phone lists. The one that stood out was the lawyer with BB&S law firm. He was on Irene Cohen's phone list and Witherspoon's.

Vic had a lot on his mind, but he understood the significance of that connection. He preferred to pick it back up in the morning when he wasn't so exhausted. However, as tired as he was, he had trouble sleeping. He felt the investigation was getting more and more confusing. And then there was the female FBI agent he couldn't stop thinking about. He thought, "Maybe it will be much clearer in the morning."

The first thing next morning, while on his way to the FBI office, a rejuvenated Vic Majeski called Skip Blackmon. Vic explained that Fritz had suggested he call. Blackmon appeared grateful that someone was trying to get to the bottom of things. He had some interesting news that Vic was unaware of. He told Vic that his friend Louis Milton had briefed his superior, General Detwiler, about the case. He was the Air Force member of the Joint Chiefs. He said he was aware of Daneli's role in what he called 'the industrial sabotage matter.'

Skip asked, "So do you think the two investigations are related?"

Vic replied, "I don't just think they are related; I know they are related. Look, I'm not sure who I can trust with the information I have. Also, the way people are dying because they knew too much—the same could happen to you. And I don't know if I want to shoulder that guilt if you suffer the same fate. Now on the other hand, if you convince me you are willing to accept that fate, then maybe I would share what I know if you can also convince me I can trust you."

"How about this for a convincing argument: my daughter, my only child, and my only grandchildren, are now dead because she trusted me. Other than that, I've got no involvement in your investigation. I know I can trust Colonel Milton and his superior, General Detwiler. I've known them my entire military career. With or without your help, we are going to get to the bottom of this. If you don't want to combine efforts, we'll do just fine without you."

"You're a persuasive guy. I'm going to trust you. I may be crazy for doing so, but I like your style. OK, so here goes: Brian stumbles onto NAPCO's attempts to disguise the fact that Venezuela's and PETGO's oil is fueling the US military in violation of US policy. He tells French, who shares it with a DOJ attorney. NAPCO has a mole in the GAO office who discovers the early signs of an investigation and tells her liaison.

"The next thing that happened is this: a plan that had been hatched four months ago is launched by NAPCO's henchmen. That plan was ready just in case such an investigation reappeared. They eliminate all persons in the information stream and use whatever methods are available to destroy any trail of information that might lead to how PETGO is involved. That meant getting onto the Navy's data systems. And the method they used was the only way they could have done it. They had to log onto the Navy's system at Craney Island. And to accomplish that, they had to eliminate the workers and create a diversion. The fire was that diversion."

"Jesus Christ! What an operation!" Skip said in disbelief.

Skip then asked, "So where is the FBI with the investigation?"

"I should find out this morning. I am on my way there right now for a meeting. Hey, do you mind if I call you right after the meeting?"

"Please do. I'm anxious to find out anything that might make sense of this."

As Vic approached the FBI's office, his cell phone rang. It was Skip Blackmon again.

"Sorry to call back so soon. Have you got a minute?"

"If it's important, I've got all the time in the world. What's up?"

"I called Louis Milton when we hung up earlier. I thought you should know what he said. I have him on hold, and I can conference him in. Do you mind?"

"Like I said, if he's got intel I could use, I'm all ears."

Skip patched Milton into the conversation. After a brief introduction by Skip, Milton explained what was so important.

"My boss is General Detwiler. He called me early this morning. He's been interested in the investigation ever since I mentioned it to him a few days ago. He's been busy. The attorney general is now on the case. He and General Detwiler have initiated a highly classified review. Only the two of them and the three of us know about it. Before they move forward, they want to talk to you and your employer, Eli Taylor. I think they have some information they are willing to share with us. Do you think the two of you can get over here this afternoon?"

"I'll call my boss and call you back," Vic replied.

30. RESIGNATION

RESUMING HIS DRIVE TO THE FBI OFFICE, VIC CALLED ELI WITH THE news of the developments. He began with the most interesting.

"Hey, amigo, I've got some interesting shit to share with you this morning. But I don't have long before I need to hang up. I'm on my way to the FBI office for a 10 a.m. meeting. First things first: can you meet with me, a member of the Joint Chiefs, and the U.S. AG this afternoon in DC?"

"You're kidding, right?"

"Afraid not. I talked with the father-in-law of the deceased GSA auditor, Brian Matusak. His name is Skip Blackmon. When the FBI failed to protect his son, Blackmon called his buddy who works for General Detwiler, the USAF member of the Joint Chiefs of Staff. Detwiler didn't like what he heard, so he talked to the attorney general. The AG wants to limit who knows of his interest in the matter to us, Detwiler, Blackmon, and his buddy Louis Milton. So that leaves out the FBI and the military, except for Detwiler. I spoke to Milton. He thinks Detwiler and the AG know something they don't want to share with the rest of the investigating agencies."

"Doesn't that strike you as odd?"

"Oh, yeah! Most definitely! Should we go?"

"What do you think?"

"I should know more after I meet with the FBI, but my instincts tell me yes."

"To be honest, if the AG says he wants to meet with us, I don't think we have much choice. Tell them I'll fly up this morning. We own this jet for a reason. It makes impromptu meetings six hundred miles apart a reasonable consideration. Anything else I should know about?"

"I've been a busy guy. We found the moon suit used at Craney Island at the NAPCO facility. The Fairfax DA determined the Matusak explosion is a homicide; however, the FBI took over their investigation. And Matusak went to the FBI with the Rubik's Memo link to French and Calloway, asking for protection. But instead, they told him to go home. And I got the phone records off Parma's cell phone."

"That's a lot to digest. Anything else?"

"I think that's all. Oh yeah, I found the place where the Craney Island perps rented the boat that got them from the mainland to the island. I'll tell you more, but I'm pulling into the FBI office. I'll call you when the meeting is over."

"I'll roger that. I'll be anxious to find out how it goes."

Vic's drive to the FBI office was melancholy at best. It was raining. It was cold and windy. He might not be able to unwrap the enigma of Agent Cramer. And he might be off the FBI case by lunchtime.

After passing through a couple of layers of FBI security checkpoints, he headed for the FBI break room on the fifth floor for a cup of coffee. Thatcher was there sneaking a second doughnut.

"Hey, Vic, what you know?"

"Good morning Tom," Vic replied somberly.

"Did you hear we caught a break and have Dieter Hoff detained in Barcelona?"

"No, I didn't."

"We've got a briefing at 1000 hours in the situation room. Angela's and our supervisor, Daniel Greenwood, will give the briefing. If you think Director Inge can be a hard-ass, he can't hold a candle to Greenwood, and he's in a bad mood this morning. He doesn't like coming into the office on Sundays."

"That's just what I need."

Thatcher disappeared out the door. Vic moseyed past Angela's office. She was on the phone with her back to the door. Her door was closed. Vic peeked at his watch. It was 9:55 a.m. Before he entered the situation room, he strolled down the hallways just to see what he could see. He walked past several offices. He heard the voices and stopped in a doorway that was obviously the situation room. Thatcher was talking to an older guy, and an array of operators was sitting at keyboards, ready to receive commands. Thatcher motioned for Vic to come closer.

Greenwood was one of the types who tried to impress you with how firm his handshake can be. However, Vic's hands were enormous, thick, calloused, and always ready for a challenge. Vic reacted to Greenwood's overzealous squeeze with a reactionary vice grip that drew a wince from Greenwood's face.

Instead of uttering a word, Greenwood just nodded. Vic smiled back widely and a little over-the-top. Agent Cramer walked in, and Greenwood announced, "I guess we are ready to proceed."

Greenwood quickly ran through what Angela reported about their trip to Houston. Greenwood was anxious to get to his side of the investigation and ordered an operator to pull up the photos of Kravitz, Hoff, and Cota.

Greenwood continued. "We are confident that Kravitz is an

alias. We believe him to be Emile Montag. Montag might not be his real name either, but it is the one Interpol uses for him. He is a renowned assassin and facilitator for various nefarious organizations. He has a nickname in the underworld community. They call him the Janitor. He is either of Serbian or Croatian origin. And if we run into him and his cronies on this matter, we can expect a resourceful and well-equipped adversary. He has no fingerprints on record, so we cannot be certain. However, we enhanced the photo from the phone store, and from his prior association with Hoff, we have a high level of confidence that he is the one carrying out the assassination orders. His whereabouts are unknown at this time.

"As for Hoff, he wandered into our purview when he used an identity we had in our database. Spanish intelligence had been alerted to let us know if they had a sighting, and they confirmed he was checked into the Grand Marina Hotel in Barcelona. We picked him up for questioning yesterday. He thinks we are interested in him for a South African matter last week where there was an unsuccessful kidnapping. He was not held for long, but he remains under surveillance."

Greenwood paused. The director was wearing an earpiece of some kind, and it appeared he was listening to something coming from it. He then walked over to Angela, bent over, and whispered something in her ear. Greenwood, of course, just might as well have shouted; Vic could read his lips. He whispered, "We don't need him anymore."

Vic tuned back in and heard Greenwood say, "And that's about it. We will continue to monitor Hoff's movements and communications."

Vic remarked, "That's it. You call a meeting on Sunday morning, and that's all you got?"

Greenwood was not amused and replied, "What were you expecting, Mr. Majeski? Right now, we just don't have enough evidence on anyone to make an arrest, much less get an indictment from a grand jury."

"How about the other guy in the suite at the Marriott? I think his name is Cota. He's the least experienced. I'd think you would be all over him by now."

"The fact that he is new actually makes him more difficult to locate. We have no history to use to track him."

"I'm sure you guys have been doing something while I've been digging up the good stuff. How about Sharon Ogden, Matthew Greene, and Ryan Rubin?"

"Who are they?" Greenwood asked.

"You've got to be kidding!" Vic deadpanned. "You do know Rubin's the guy with the memo, not the cube. The other two are the other GAO parties on the memo. I expect you've got an update on them."

Greenwood looked at Thatcher, and Thatcher responded.

"I have their statements in my file. Let's see, I think I've got it right here. Yup, here it is. Sharon Ogden—she's the DOD deputy director of procurement and acquisition, and Greene is the GAO chief auditor. Ogden said it's in Justice's hands, and she's awaiting instructions. Greene said he never got a follow-up from DOD, so he's in the dark. And Rubin said he was told by his supervisor not to spend any more time on the matter."

"And?" Vic implored.

"And nothing else is in the file," Thatcher replied.

"Those notes sound old. When were they made?"

"Let's see. July thirtieth and August second."

"You've got to be kidding me! It's late November. Where's the recent stuff?"

Greenwood reentered the discussion. "We have nothing more on that side of the investigation. There was nothing more to get."

"You guys are special. Back in July, I suppose it was just a curiosity. But now that people have been murdered because of the memo, a moron would know to take a more recent and closer look."

Cramer could see that Vic was heading into a fight he could not win, so she tried to mediate the matter before it got out of control by mentioning reports she was ordered not to share with Vic.

"I tried to get back in touch with them on my own a couple of days ago. Ogden said she never followed up, and she said she knew nothing about Calloway, French, or Matusak. Greene was reassigned to HUD. He said he was told that DOD was no longer interested in the matter and that he hasn't heard a thing since. And Rubin left the DOD in August. Our office has been trying to locate him, but so far nothing has come up. We think he's consulting somewhere, but so far, nothing."

Greenwood snapped, "Now you know more than I did. Are you satisfied now?"

"What about Witherspoon?"

The room became silent. Vic wanted to talk with Angela first about Witherspoon, but it was now out of the bag.

"Maybe you should educate us about him," Greenwood said as he glared at Vic.

Vic peeked at Angela, but she was staring at the floor. "Don't tell me you didn't check out all the calls on Kravitz's cell phone?"

"Please continue," Greenwood answered.

"I don't think that is an answer," Vic retorted. "Did you or did you not investigate his phone records?"

Greenwood was pissed. That was something Vic did quite

well—piss people off. Interestingly enough, he usually worked it to his advantage.

"Who the fuck do you think you are?" Greenwood yelled. His face was beet red, and the veins in his neck were bulging.

"I'm an ignorant, novice, son of a bitch who's not even trying hard. I thought you guys were supposed to be the clever ones."

"You asshole! You're holding your own personal investigation, withholding information and playing coy, little mind games. We've had just about enough of your charade."

Vic borrowed a line from Dan Aykroyd on Saturday Night Live. "You ignorant slut!" he proudly remarked. "It's you guys who are holding back and not sharing. You're so afraid I'm going to embarrass you again by beating you to the bad guys. Normally I'd be pissed, but you guys are pathetic. I think I'll just conduct my own investigation without your help. Then we can have a real contest."

"You don't think I can fuck you over, do you? Right now I have half a mind to arrest you for obstruction."

"Now you've finally identified the problem. You only have half a mind! Go ahead and arrest me, you idiot!"

Greenwood's face and neck were now past red, bordering on maroon. And his hand gestures suggested he had lost control of his motor functions. He took a deep breath that must have been his way to trigger his body to return to some semblance of control.

"Get him out of here!" Greenwood ordered to Thatcher and Cramer.

Angela grabbed Vic's arm and tried to pull him toward the door. Thatcher was a second behind her. But that didn't stop Vic from responding.

"You won't have to worry about me showing you up anymore.

I'm on my way back to Atlanta. Call me if you get stuck. I'm always available for a good joke."

Once out of the door, Vic was smiling ear to ear.

Thatcher asked Vic, "What the hell was all that about?"

"You can take your hands off me now. I'm neither angry, upset, nor agitated."

Angela and Thatcher complied as they walked toward the lobby.

"Look, guys, this partnership was not going to work out in the end. The only person I can work with, or for, is Eli Taylor. I called him this morning and told him I would be coming home today. As far as the scene I made in there, he deserved it, and I wanted him to know that I was on to his incompetence. As for you two, I really enjoyed this…"

Vic paused and looked affectionately into Angela's eyes. "But I was getting too interested in you, Angela. I'd like to date you, but we were working together, and I don't think it's appropriate or smart to continue like that. This way, if you are interested, we can date without worrying about how it might affect the investigation."

Thatcher commented, "I've got to hand it to you, Vic. You are an interesting fellow. The way you chewed up our boss in there was very entertaining. I don't think anyone has gotten under his skin like that before. I'm going to miss having you around."

Angela took Vic's hand and led him out past the reception area, past security, and on to the elevators. "Do you really want to date me?" she asked.

"What do you think this was all about? That's a promise."

Angela kissed his cheek just as the elevator was stopping on their floor. "I want to hear from you again," she demanded.

Vic stepped onto the elevator car and blew a kiss to her as the elevator doors separated them.

In Vic's heart and mind, he knew this thing was not over for him. However, he knew he didn't want to work again with the FBI. "It's just like the military," he thought. "The higher you travel up the food chain, the bigger the assholes."

Vic called Eli as he was on his way to PDK Airport. "Eli, what the FBI told me is that all of these connections are circumstantial, barely enough to get a grand jury indictment, and insufficient to get a conviction. Is that true?"

"I'm afraid so. They will either have to find the henchmen or something like an eyewitness testifying that a PETGO or NAPCO official ordered the murders or the fire at Craney Island. You've done more than any law enforcement official can reasonably expect. If they can't do the rest with the information you supplied, then the bad guys will go free. We will just have to accept that as a potential."

"I guess I'm all right with that. I hate it, but I see your point. Well, I told the FBI that I'm done with the investigation. That will probably mean I will be heading back to Atlanta with you tonight."

"That's probably the best thing for all of us."

"Yeah, but I learned one thing that doesn't add up. My Fairfax policeman buddy says this guy Witherspoon doesn't work at NAPCO. He's got him at a company called Purified Petroleum."

"That's not what I expected. What the hell is Purified Petroleum?"

"Shit, if you don't know them, they've got to be tiny or brand-new."

"I'll have to run that down. I'll get Harry to check it out."

"You know, this whole thing has the feel of something more

convoluted and sinister than what everyone is letting on. I sure would like to know who the mastermind is. But I suppose we'll never know."

"You sound like you're going to miss being a part-time FBI agent."

"It's a little bit of that and the fact that I'd like to see more of Agent Cramer."

"I thought I sensed a little something between you two just before I left to come home."

"She cooked dinner for the two of us last night at her home. She's got a lot going for her. And here's the weird part—I only got to first base."

"Uh-oh. She's got her hook in your cheek. You better get back to Atlanta soon before she becomes the second Mrs. Majeski, or you the first Mr. Cramer. Hey, I like the way that sounds. Hey, Cramer, where's Newman?"

"Very funny. Don't hold your breath waiting for that to happen."

"Have you heard anything more about our meeting?"

"Not yet. I'll call Louis Milton right now and call you back."

Vic paused for a few seconds. He was wondering what Greenwood had heard in his earpiece that meant the bureau didn't need him any longer. He thought that he needed to come back to that issue later, but now he needed to contact Milton.

Lieutenant Milton passed on to Vic the meeting time and place. It would be at the Department of Justice at 3:00 p.m. Milton said he would meet Vic and Eli at the Dulles general aviation hanger at 2:15 so they could ride together and get acquainted. Milton asked Vic how his meeting with the FBI had gone.

"You need to know that I walked away from their investigation."

"Why do you want to walk away from the investigation?" Milton inquired.

"It's complicated. The bottom line is that my company was asked to work with them on the investigation. I was my company's point man. The FBI was not willing to share all its information with me because I had been beating them to all of the good leads. This morning it all came to a head. I got into an argument with the director. I think his name is Greenwood. I heard him say they didn't need me anymore."

Louis Milton asked, "Would you be interested in knowing what my boss, General Detwiler, thinks?"

"I can only imagine. Another guy with stars on his shoulder straps that thinks I need to be stifled."

"I think you would be surprised just how much you two think alike. Let me ask you: if you were in charge, what measures would you be taking?"

"There are a couple of folks I would like to put the heat on. One is this guy that we know nothing about. His name is Witherspoon. Another is...hold on a second while I find his name."

Vic pulled a small flip pad out of his back pocket and sifted through its pages.

"Here it is. This guy is a lobbyist in Washington. His name is Charles Bobick."

"Does the FBI know about them?"

"They haven't said so, but if they are doing the basics, they have to be aware of them. But without the resources of the FBI, there just isn't anything I can do. We would just be placing our lives in jeopardy by alerting the bad guys to the fact that we are on to them."

Skip uttered in frustration, "This multiagency stuff is so far beyond anything I know."

Vic remarked, "Tell me about it! My usefulness was just about at its end, but this supervisor Greenwood is a major prick."

"That's the guy that Skip blames for the deaths of his daughter, her husband, and their two grandchildren."

"Are you saying he's the one who called the shots on refusing to find a safe house for them?"

"I was in the room when it went down, and that's the way I saw it."

"I don't get it. Why was an FBI district chief taking a personal interest in your case? They've got tons of agents, supervisors, managers, and upper-level administrators to deal with cases. I wonder why he would want to be personally involved."

But even Vic was questioning his words. He thought, Maybe he's on the other team.

He tried to get more out of Milton about Greenwood and Detwiler, but Milton just didn't know anything Vic didn't already know. They ended the call, and Vic was getting an uncomfortable feeling about all the coincidences in both investigations.

Vic scratched his head and tried to recollect Eli's warning about coincidences. "Oh yeah, I got it!" He thought out loud. "Coincidences and danger—they always go together."

It turned out Vic wasn't the only one who didn't like convenient coincidences. After what Milton told General Detwiler about what happened to his friend's daughter and son-in-law, the general started to look into the matter. He called his colleague Admiral Ellingson. He had contacted the admiral about his review of the Craney Island event and his take on the murders of French, Calloway, and Matusak. Ellingson said he would have to get back with him after he reexamined the file. After several attempts to contact Ellingson and not receiving a reply, he got a call from NSA Director Yarborough. Yarborough told him to stay out of the investigation. Detwiler was never fond of Yarborough and his ultraconservative views. That warning only ticked him off and inspired him to look into it on his own.

When you are the member of the Joint Chiefs of Staff, you have friends in high places. Detwiler chose to visit with the attorney general, Adam Goodman. He'd known Goodman for a while, and they had developed a relationship of trust. Goodman was also not a fan of Yarborough's. Goodman and his office reviewed the FBI's handling of both matters. To say the AG was not pleased was an understatement.

Goodman told Detwiler his biggest criticism was the high-level involvement of a civilian consulting firm with no prior track record with the bureau or DOD. According to Goodman, not only was it odd, but to have them play such an important role in what should be a highly classified matter was absurd to him. He expected that there had to be some favoritism, nepotism, or political clout involved, but the dossier he had on Daneli and Eli Taylor didn't show any connections in high places.

Goodman was tempted to visit with Ellingson, Greenwood, and Yarborough, but his instincts told him to work it backward, a favorite ploy of his that he had developed over decades of lawyering.

What Milton failed to tell Vic was what Detwiler had told him about Goodman and his reason for visiting with Daneli, which was, "You start your investigation with the one person involved who is the least likely to invent a cover story and the persons most likely to be intimidated. Also, Taylor is an attorney, like him. He figured he had a lever that might be valuable—Taylor's license to practice law—and that he could take it away if he didn't cooperate."

Vic checked out of the hotel and had a late lunch at a diner on his way to Dulles to meet Eli at the airfield. He was traveling west on Highway 267, the Dulles Parkway, in Fairfax County, a route he had taken more times than he could count. As he came upon an eighteen-wheeler, he looked in his outside mirror to see if the lane was clear. About three car lengths back was a silver SUV, and it was coming on fast. At the moment it was about to pass, Vic recognized it as the SUV that had followed him to into the Windham Hotel parking lot the other day.

This time he was going to look inside the cab to see if he recognized anyone inside. As it was about to pull even with his vehicle, the passenger side window of the SUV was rolling down. As Vic focused on the person behind the window, the afternoon sunshine reflected off a metallic object moving toward the window. Vic realized he was looking down the barrel of a micro-Uzi submachine gun.

Vic's reflex reaction was to hit the brakes and duck. A splash of bullets broke through his side window and shattered his windshield. The aim was high and too far forward to find Vic. The vehicle behind him was braking as well, just missing his rear bumper as he regained control of his vehicle.

"So you want to play rough?" Vic shouted as he wiped shattered glass off his dashboard. He floored his vehicle and pulled behind the silver SUV with his GMC Yukon. Before the Silver SUV cleared the eighteen-wheeler and before the driver could aim his weapon on him, Vic rammed it and kept his gas pedal on the floorboard. The first impact fishtailed the SUV, but he rammed it again, and the second impact sent it flying into the median, crossing it diagonally. Oncoming traffic was braking and swerving to miss being hit. It bounced across the eastbound lanes and into the barrier cyclone fence, where it crashed into an embankment.

"Take that, you motherfucker!" Vic yelled at the top of his lungs. After a couple deep breaths, Vic cried out, "Ooow weee! That's a rush!" As he slowed down to nearer the speed limit, he was thinking, "That might make the evening news."

31. THE MOST IMPORTANT MEETING OF OUR LIVES

THE DANELI JET CARRYING ELI TAYLOR WAS TAXIING TOWARD THE general aviation terminal at Dulles. It was cold and windy. Louis Milton arrived about ten minutes behind him. Milton was meeting Vic for the first time, assuming the only other guy in the general aviation terminal was him.

"Victor Majeski?" he inquired as Vic got up and walked toward him.

"And since you are in uniform, you must be Colonel Milton."

"That's right. Sorry I'm a little late. There must have been a wreck or something on the parkway. I didn't see anything, but it came to a standstill about a mile or so before the airport."

"I'm afraid I had something to do with it. Some guy driving an overloaded truck in front of me dropped some of his load on the highway. It flew into my windshield, shattering it. The glass just missed my head. I was pretty lucky, but my rental isn't drivable now. Can you fit the three of us in your vehicle?"

"Holy cow! Are you sure you're all right?"

"No worries. Just little bits of glass in my jeans. I'll be fine."

Just about that time, the Daneli Citation was taxiing in front of the terminal. Colonel Milton and Vic went to meet Eli as he deplaned. They shook hands and headed directly for the parking lot where the colonel's car was waiting.

In the car, they chatted about Vic's mishap and what they might be expecting at the meeting. Vic said nothing about what really happened. It was a friendly conversation, but not revealing. They arrived at Justice ten minutes early for their three o'clock appointment. They were escorted into the attorney general's office, where Adam Goodman and General Forest Detwiler were awaiting their arrival.

After introductions and pleasantries, they got down to business. Attorney General Goodman was the first to break the ice.

"Gentlemen, the general and I have been following this matter ever since Colonel Milton brought it to the general's attention. I believe that was the day after the family of Brian Matusak was murdered in that awful explosion at their home.

"As a member of the Joint Chiefs of Staff, General Detwiler had been briefed on the Craney Island matter. So when Victor Majeski told Colonel Milton that he was sure the two investigations were linked, the general became intrigued. He contacted Admiral Ellingson, but the admiral wasn't cooperative. Then Stuart Yarborough told the general to stay out of the investigation. That didn't sit well with us. It's not the NSA, Homeland Security, or the Navy's place to withhold details to members of the other branches that share the highest security level.

"But before we start barking up their trees, we need to bark up yours. So tell me what makes you so sure you have connected the two matters. Mr. Taylor, I would like to hear from you first."

"We are pleased to find someone with an open mind and a sense of urgency," Eli said. "At this point, all we know is now a matter of record with the agencies we have been reporting to. It's in the case records of the Navy and the FBI. The only thing we have done is taken that information and drawn a conclusion that is undeniably the one and only one that fits.

"NAPCO is the connecting entity. We have identified a guy who must be working for them as an independent contractor and connected him to all the crime scenes. His name is Dan Witherspoon. It's all in the telephone records collected by the FBI. There's a new twist to this guy's story. He's also listed as the director of security for a company called Purified Petroleum. As we speak, I have a man looking into how the companies are linked, if in fact there is a linkage."

Adam Goodman was taken off guard by Eli's matter-of-fact proclamation. The FBI was under the AG's jurisdiction. But no briefings from the Bureau had included Eli's assertion. Whatever pressure he had planned to put on Eli and Daneli to have them reveal speculations was now off the table. Goodman knew that Taylor was no fool, and only a fool would lie about facts in the FBI's possession that would be readily available for him to verify.

Goodman was now sitting in motionless contemplation. Eli had shifted the doubt from him and onto Ellingson, Yarborough, and now Greenwood. For the first time since Adam Goodman was sworn in as the AG, he was truly worried he had a problem of monumental proportions.

Goodman wondered to himself, Am I being lied to by my own department heads? Are Ellingson and Yarborough hiding something rather than just being the Neocon assholes I despise?

Vic looked at Eli as he usually did when he wanted to say something that was not a reply to a question. Eli nodded.

"Mr. Attorney General, I was under the impression that we were going to share information at this meeting. We are anxious to hear anything we might not know about."

Goodman was still reeling from the implications of Eli's assertions. "Uh, sorry, Mr. Majeski, I was immersed in thought. Your Mr. Taylor has given me an idea. Eli, have you found any tangible evidence other than the Rubik's Memo and your computer tracking investigation that links NAPCO to Craney Island?"

"How is this for direct evidence," Vic interjected. "I found the high-temperature protection suit worn by the perp who blew up Craney Island hanging in NAPCO's cloakroom. Greenwood knows it. And if anyone wants to verify that assertion, they can go to NAPCO's Houston facility, pick it up, and scope it for DNA. I'll bet you'll find it matches the DNA for Eric Parma, Emile Montag, or one of the henchmen working for Montag. The DNA I'm talking about is what the FBI accumulated from the DC hotel room they used as their headquarters in DC. It's all currently in the file at the FBI."

Again Goodman was at a loss. His reports did not mention anybody named Parma or Montag, any protection suit, or findings from a hotel room of the perpetrators.

Summoning all the strength that he had, the kind that is necessary for one to reach high political status such as the office of US attorney general, Goodman managed to hide his shock and anger in his reply. The only way not to look foolish or surprised was to pretend that he knew what Vic knew.

"Mr. Majeski, I don't believe you could have made a more compelling argument. My notes were not clear as to who possessed that knowledge. I thought I knew something you didn't. What you just told me was the intelligence I was going to share, but now that I see you know as much as the FBI, I am at a loss. Do you mind that I call you Vic and Eli?"

"Please do," Eli replied.

"Gentlemen, this matter is larger than we predicted. And it seems to grow by the hour. We are in your debt for being so vigilant. I wish I knew more."

And that was when Vic started to say something he shouldn't. He was feeling frustrated again.

"Well, here's something else that might be news," he declared. "Have you considered both matters are only a part of a larger scheme or conspiracy? Because if you haven't, you might find yourself behind an eight ball you can't get around. Do you catch my drift?"

Eli jumped in to protect his friend and employee. "Mr. Goodman, sir, I must apologize for Vic's outburst. He gets carried away sometimes, and he has a fondness for conspiracy theories. What he just said is not a part of our firm's suspicions. We have discussed it while brainstorming, but we have absolutely nothing to support it."

Vic, however, was not willing to be silenced.

"I thought you invited us in here to share thoughts as well as intel. Eli is right about me being not as circumspect as he or our firm. But if you gentlemen are really on the same side as we are, you better not ignore the possibility that there might be more to the coincidences and connections than what is obvious. It's all from the same playbook. It's slick, professional, and well funded. And they have their hands on information that can only come from inside the government.

"Let me give you an example. The fire at Craney Island. Who told the bad guys when to show up? The Navy only averages two shipments a week at that facility. That shipment was scheduled by a computer. No human involvement. You don't randomly show up and expect to see a delivery underway. They were told when to show up. Somebody within the Navy. Got it?

"And I could go on and on," Vic said.

"Please do. I haven't heard anyone else mention that."

"OK, how's this? Ryan Rubin, the guy who wrote Rubik's Memo, is unaccounted for. No one seems to care. His boss got reassigned after the memo first surfaced in July. The DOD procurement officer who originally asked about NAPCO and provoked the explanation provided by Rubin—she was told by her superiors to forget about it.

"And tell me if this is standard operating procedure. Eli's and my vehicles had tracking devices placed on them without our knowledge. We found eavesdropping and surveillance devices in my hotel room and our vehicles. How do the bad guys know we are even on the investigation or might know anything worth hearing? The FBI and the NSA are the only agencies besides the military that should know that, unless they told the bad guys or they are the bad guys."

To Eli's surprise, Detwiler and Goodman seemed genuinely interested in Vic's remarks. However, the meeting came to an abrupt end.

Goodman ended it all by saying, "You have given us a lot to work on. We need to step up our efforts. We appreciate your candor and faith that we would take your words as your trying to help us out. Due to your insights, I'm seeing this matter a little differently than before we met. If you don't mind, I'd like to get back with you after we do a little investigating on our own."

***

On the way back to Dulles, there was little conversation between Vic, Eli, and Colonel Milton. It was obvious that they were mostly stunned by the meeting. At the airport, they pledged to stay in touch.

On the plane ride back to Atlanta, the conversation between Vic and Eli was nonstop. It started with Vic's observation of the meeting.

"OK, I let things get out of hand, but did you find their reaction was like, 'OK, I believe you'? Didn't you think they were supposed to say that I was losing my mind?"

"Vic, when they didn't act surprised or angry, I realized that we were further ahead of the information curve than they were. I think they were in shell shock. I also think that the AG is going to start asking Greenwood some tough questions."

"I've got one for you. What is the connection between NAPCO, Witherspoon, and Purified?"

"This is what Harry was able to dig up in the few hours he's been on this angle. Witherspoon worked for the Department of Energy for twenty years and was let go because of improprieties. He eventually hooked up with Purified Petroleum, a small operator working under the Doss Petroleum conglomerate shield. In between, Witherspoon did some consulting for NAPCO. And that's the only connection linking the two companies as far as we know. Harry is trying to figure out whether Purified and NAPCO are linked in any other way."

Their discussion went back and forth for a while before Vic told Eli the real story of his drive into Dulles. All the way back to Atlanta, they debated what they should do. They settled on calling Gilbert. After Gilbert cussed Vic out, he said he'd send a crime-scene unit to examine his rental vehicle, which was parked at the airport, and have an evidence team check the parkway where the confrontation occurred.

After they hung up on Gilbert, both Eli and Vic felt that they had been dumped into a pressure cooker. The stakes had been raised in a land of unfamiliar territory. Eli asked, "Were you able to identify the shooter?"

"Afraid not," was Vic's response. "But we must be getting pretty close to the real bad guys if they resorted to killing in broad daylight."

Eli was shaking his head because he was watching his good friend shake off being shot at the way most would ignore bad weather.

Vic declared, "I expect we will be hearing back from the AG, for better or worse, without much delay. What do you say we keep the rest of the Daneli folks in the dark about today until we know more?"

Eli had to focus really hard to step back and consider Vic's proposition with a clear mind. After a long pause, Vic was goading Eli for a response.

"What's wrong, amigo?"

"I'm thinking, damn it."

"You're a little edgy, wouldn't you say?"

"Think back a couple of years," Eli said in an agitated state. "How did you feel when I was shot in that bus in Peru? Afterward, you told me you felt like you let me down by not taking him out before I had to put myself in that position. Well, I don't want to be wondering the same thing. You could have been killed today."

Vic was starting to get it, and he gave Eli more slack. After a little more debate, they decided to keep the shooting incident and their meeting with the AG to themselves, with the exception of Harry Meeks, until they heard back from the AG.

32. DESPERATE MEN

DANIEL GREENWOOD SAT IN HIS OFFICE MULLING OVER WHAT
had happened in the situation room. He was trying to figure
out whether Victor Majeski had made him look like a fool.
There is an old axiom among poker players: if there is supposed
to be a fish or a donkey—an inept gambler—at the table, and
you are not sure who it is, then it's you. Greenwood was the
donkey, and he didn't know it. In any event, Daniel Greenwood
was pissed. He was afraid that it might look as if the bureau
was following cold trails and leads that went nowhere. He had
kept his bosses, Chief Gilbert and Attorney General Goodman,
from knowing about Vic's latest discoveries. He was afraid how
it might reflect on him if Goodman knew everything. More
important, he didn't want Gilbert and Goodman looking over
his shoulder.

It is often said that desperate men take desperate measures.
After hours of deliberation, Greenwood determined that his best
strategy was to eliminate Vic before Goodman caught wind of
Vic's findings. Unfortunately for Greenwood, he had no idea that
Vic and Eli had already met with Goodman. Nevertheless, Vic
was in his crosshairs. And now he heard that Mariana Cota had
failed in his attempt to silence Majeski.

There were too few real crime fighters in the ranks of the modern FBI. Their legions were staffed by marksmen and tactical fighters at the bottom of the food chain and administrators and politicians at the top. They had impressive gadgetry and manpower. But long gone were the career investigators. The few who were left were considered dinosaurs, and their ideas, warnings, and advice were rarely considered valuable. The same dysfunction and malaise had occurred in many government agencies and in many corporations. It allowed them to be beaten by small groups of clever and agile adversaries.

Inge and Greenwood had achieved their status by playing the political game better than their competition. Their crime-fighting deficiencies allowed Vic and Daneli to make them look bad. As for Greenwood, among his flaws was being a bad loser. He desperately needed to exact revenge on Vic for humiliating him in front of his troops. His only problem was that he was running out of ideas how to do that without creating a trail that would lead to him.

7:45 A.M., MONDAY, NOVEMBER 20

Vic entered the front door at Daneli Crisis Management Group in its office at Perimeter Center in suburban Atlanta. The receptionist was not at her desk yet. Just about every employee had gathered there for the ceremonial morning bullshit session. Erica Davis, the office administrator, was the first to greet him. She ran toward him with open arms and gave him an "I missed you" hug.

Hank Fisher was sipping on his morning tea. When Erica let go of Vic, he approached, carrying a box wrapped with ribbon and a bow in his left hand and extended his right hand for a shake.

"Welcome home, Investigator Majeski. In honor of your investigative exploits, we have proclaimed you the first recipient of the Daneli Sleuth award."

They shook hands, and Hank handed over the box. While Vic was standing there, not knowing what to do, Faith Miller approached and gave him a half hug.

"I poured you a cup of coffee so you can sit down and open the box without suffering caffeine withdrawal."

She handed Vic a mug of coffee, and he sat down in a chair at the break-room table. Inside the box was a houndstooth Sherlock Holmes hat with a brass-colored ribbon hatband that bore the inscription, "November, 2006—US Navy Response—Victor Majeski—No. 1 Sherlock." Vic smiled broadly as Blake, Mack, Clyde, Mike, and Eli took turns at shaking his hand.

"I don't want to sound like an ungrateful clod, but why am I more deserving than any of you? We're teammates."

Mike responded in a way that captured the moment. "In this, our first really big assignment, you were our most valuable teammate, and we appreciate your efforts."

"OK, under that scenario, I am honored to be the first MVT—most valuable teammate. By the way, has anybody heard from the FBI about my parting?"

Erica responded, "Would you consider a call from Agent Thatcher saying that the FBI was thankful for our contributions, but they have determined that the investigation should proceed without our counsel anymore?"

"Ooh! That sounds more like a firing than a divorce by mutual consent," commented Hank.

"I guess I wore out my welcome in my usual fashion," Vic remarked. "So enough with the FBI. What's next on our agenda?"

Eli replied, "We're going to give you a couple of days to get back into the swing of things around here. Nothing but easy stuff. We've gotten a number of requests for nonemergency assignments because of the notoriety we received for our efforts assisting the Navy. We need you to contribute to our efforts to prepare our responses. We have received so many that we'll need to add contract employees. I scheduled a 'workshop' meeting for all of us after lunch where we can separate the wheat from the chaff."

When the socializing dispersed, Erika followed Vic into his office. "From what I gather, you had a rollercoaster romantic life while you were on assignment."

"I guess you could say that. You've known me long enough to know that the women in my life are not conquests. I care about them. I can't explain how I felt about Ann Calloway. It was bad enough knowing she died so young and vibrant. But to be murdered in such a meaningless way. And then on top of it, her death was a part of my investigation. I haven't had enough time to process it yet. But I promise you one thing: if I ever get a chance to take revenge on her murderer, it's not going to be a pretty sight. I owe her that."

"You know, just hearing you talk about her let me know that your mind is in the right place. I came in here because I was a little worried that you might be messed up about her. I was also wondering if what I heard about you and the female FBI agent might be a substitution thing."

"Is it Eli that's spreading that around?"

"I can't say for sure, but I wouldn't blame him. I'd look at a different gender if I wanted to know the culprit."

"Faith? I wouldn't have guessed that."

"For a guy who knows so much about women, you really don't know shit."

"Well, I don't think you need to worry about that. The only reason I'm attracted to Agent Cramer is because she reminds me of you."

"Oh my god! Now I really know that I don't need to worry about you because of Ann Calloway. You're just on the prowl twenty-four seven."

"Hey, I was just having a little fun. Besides, you're taken."

"I think this where I get off. Yup, this is my stop. See you later."

"Don't go yet," Vic said. "To be candid, I am feeling a little anxious about whether these perps are going to leave me alone. I told Eli not to spread this around, and I know you won't either. The bad guys tried to take me out the other day. I got him before he got me. But if it's one thing that I've learned about these assholes, they can't take a joke."

"Now you've got me really worried for you. What are you going to do?"

"Eli and I are working on something. You needn't worry. Honestly, we've not going to let anything happen. You know how Eli has a way of protecting us. Go on now."

As Erica walked out of his office, Vic said, "Tootles! You know I'm crazy about you."

To get his mind back to being the old Vic, he called an old biker friend to see if he wanted to catch lunch with him. His old friend was happy to oblige; besides, he wanted to hear all about Vic's latest assignment. And that was OK with Vic.

***

While Vic and Eli settled back into old routines, the axis of evil that was the reason for their anxiety was striving to stay one step ahead of any attempts to discover their agenda. Witherspoon felt the need to tie up loose ends. Irene Cohen was no longer a useful asset in their scheme, so it was time to make sure she was silenced.

Witherspoon called the Janitor, but his call did not go as expected. The Janitor was off his medication. His associate who answered for him told Witherspoon that Mr. Straight was on another assignment that required his full attention. Witherspoon had few other reasonable options. He made it clear to Mr. Straight's associate that unavailability was not an acceptable answer, and that there would be hell to pay. His last words before he hung up were, "I will be expecting to hear from Mr. Straight before midnight."

In Horseshoe Bay, the Janitor had already begun taking his antipsychotic medication. During a period of clarity, he made a call to Mariano Cota, asking him if he was available for a job that would be solo, without him. Although Cota was banged up pretty bad from his run-in with Vic on the Dulles Highway, he was willing to take the assignment. Upon receiving an affirmative reply, Mr. Straight felt he might be able to satisfy whatever need Witherspoon had. Through the cloud of medication and the delusions of his invisible demons, he summoned the strength to talk to Witherspoon.

He reasoned that if this psychotic episode tracked what he had experienced in the past, his demons would be vanquished in a few days to the extent that he would be able to maintain enough control to resume his responsibilities for his benefactor. However, the Janitor was now in his late thirties. With each year and episode, more medication was needed than the last time to arrest the demons. And with each episode off his medication, the intensity and duration of his delusions grew. He was also at the maximum safe dose of his antipsychotic medication.

As the evening drew close to midnight, Witherspoon was in a panic. He was contemplating a call to his boss, Art Daniels, at NAPCO. That was a call Witherspoon did not want to make. Luckily for him, he caught a break. The Janitor had mustered enough control to carry on a short conversation.

Mr. Straight told Witherspoon that he had told Mariano Cota to remain in the Washington area just in case loose ends needed tying up. Witherspoon explained that Irene Cohen and Dieter Hoff were the loose ends. Mr. Straight said that Cota could handle Cohen while he took care of Hoff.

Irene Cohen would be an easy mark. She had been carrying the guilt that she might have been responsible for the death of her boss, Gary French. It was preying on her mind and interfering with her ability to think rationally. She had considered suicide; however, the reasons that led to her agreement to be a mole remained with her. Her drug-addicted daughter and her two grandchildren were living with her because they had no other alternative. They depended on her, and she could not refuse.

She had recently told her contact at Bobick's law firm, Sam Nugent, that she needed more money. They agreed to help her out. She had just gotten a call from Nugent to come to the office and pick it up. Sam had also told her he had some good news for her that would help her deal with her anxiety, and how his firm could help her daughter. Irene was excited to meet with Sam and arranged to see him the next day.

TUESDAY, NOVEMBER 21, 1:33 P.M.

Mariano Cota limped across the GAO parking lot and placed a homing device on Irene Cohen's Toyota. Cota had not recovered completely from the hurt Vic had given him on the Dulles Parkway, but he was feeling well enough to do the Cohen deed. He waited in his vehicle just beyond the parking garage exit, waiting for it to signal that it was moving. His orders were to tail Cohen until an opportunity arose to dispatch her in secrecy.

At two in the afternoon, Irene Cohen told her supervisor that she had received a call from her daughter. In truth, she had an appointment with Sam Nugent. Her Toyota started to move, and Cota was alerted. Irene drove directly to a pharmacy she used that was situated in a small downtown mall on Massachusetts Avenue. She needed to refill her Xanax prescription and take the medication before meeting Nugent. The mall had a parking deck, and she found a parking spot near the back of the lot.

Mariano Cota parked near Irene's Toyota. She was a nervous wreck. As she composed herself, reapplying her lipstick and combing her hair, she did not notice the man who had approached. The man fired his silenced weapon, and a bullet passed through her windshield and into her skull. The door was opened, and Cota checked for a pulse. Feeling no pulse, he emptied her purse and removed her wallet to make her death look like a robbery. Cota closed her car door and left, but not entirely undetected. A witness got a good look at the shooter. An artist's sketch matched the appearance of Cota.

33. ADJUSTMENTS

ART DANIELS WAS ASKING FOR AN UPDATE ON IRENE COHEN. WITHerspoon called the Janitor's new cell phone number posted on his Facebook page. The Janitor said he was en route to find Dieter Hoff. But that was not the truth. He was still in Canada, having difficulty controlling his disease. His periods of delusion were less often, but he was still impaired. His handlers would not let him leave yet.

The Janitor, however, had good news for Witherspoon. Irene Cohen was no longer an item of unfinished business. However, Witherspoon had more assignments for the Janitor—Victor Majeski and a visit to Elmendorf Air Force Base in Anchorage, Alaska.

Both Greenwood and Witherspoon wanted Vic out of the way. They needed some time and breathing room. However, they were running out of available soldiers capable of fulfilling their needs. The Janitor was still a few days from being ready for an assignment, and Cota's right ankle was in a brand-new plaster cast. It got to hurting him so badly, he wound up in an emergency room. He was diagnosed with a fracture. Dieter Hoff was still in Europe. That meant the hit on Vic would have to wait.

***

Back in Atlanta, it had been only one day since Vic had left the nation's capital. He was already getting a little bored with the paperwork and analysis work Eli had left with him. He was happy about all the new work coming their way, but he'd rather be doing it than scoping it out. His mind started to drift. Within seconds, he was wondering if there was anything he didn't follow up on in Washington.

Vic opened up his note pad and scanned the pages. He crossed off the Oar House in Portsmouth and resumed his scan. And when he saw Angela's cell phone number scribbled at the bottom of one of the pages, he picked up the phone and called her.

She was in the office.

"Hello, magic man. Are you back home in Atlanta?"

"That's where I'm holding up for the time being. I can't believe I'm saying this, but I missed the sound of your voice. Anything breaking up there?"

"The trail has gotten so cold on NAPCO that they assigned me other cases. How about you?"

"Apparently, the word got out pretty fast that we were the ones helping the Navy at Craney Island. It's already created some potential new business for us. Eli has got me chained to a desk to look over some of the requests."

They talked about hooking up again when Vic was back in town, and how next time Vic would do the cooking. They talked a little longer but hung up when the conversation grew stale. Vic was beginning to feel the same way he felt when he returned to Atlanta after dating Ann Calloway. The difference was that he and Ann had consummated their affection, but he and Angela were only at the beginning. However similar, he did not want to be done with Angela.

Four o'clock was the end of the office day at Daneli, and Eli stopped by Vic's office. Vic was looking out the window and appearing a little forlorn.

"Hey, man, are you contemplating the cosmos or are you homesick for your sweethearts in DC?"

"Hey, Eli. I don't know, maybe a little of both. You know I really dig it here. This is the best job I've ever had. There are as many, or maybe more, great-looking women in Atlanta than in Baltimore and DC, but Agent Cramer might be my chosen one. All we had was dinner together, but there was something special happening."

"I was wondering about that. I guess that means you're not still bummed out about Ann Calloway."

"They both have been on my mind."

"Do you have plans for dinner tonight?"

"I haven't thought about it."

"Why don't you come by our place? I was going to throw something on the grill anyway. Danielle just got back from Hilton Head this afternoon. She's dog tired, and she is not in the mood to cook."

"I don't want to impose. Heck, you two probably need some alone time."

"I'm not inviting you overnight! This is just for dinner and conversation."

"OK, but I need to go home first, feed the dogs, and run an errand."

Vic drove his pickup truck to the home he had recently bought in suburban Atlanta. He really didn't have to feed the dog. He had a self-feeder and water gizmo that took care of that. What he really wanted to do was pick up his 1995 Harley Davidson Heritage Softail with the ape hanger handlebars. It had been at the shop since before he got the call to head for Craney Island.

His pickup was rigged with a ramp so he could drive it up onto the bed and secure it. Eli lived about three miles away, a perfect distance for him to take it for a spin to see if the mechanic had fixed the transmission problem it had.

When he got home, he exercised his dogs a little and then cranked up the Harley. It was comforting to Vic to feel that rumble throughout his body and the wind in his face. It was a cool, clear, November evening in Atlanta, probably in the mid-fifties. Being back on his bike was a calming influence. He had his favorite bike-riding gear on, and as he coasted down the highway toward Eli's place, he could feel the old Vic coming back to life. People in the cars around him were taking a gander at him, just like always. He might have been alone in the world, but that was all right with him. He had gotten used to life as a man apart. He might not be an easy fit in the world around him. He was, however, satisfied with who he was.

At 5:30 p.m., the sun was setting on a golden-and-pink horizon. He was heading due west, right at it. As he crested a hill, the sun's glare nearly blinded him. His eyes adjusted to it just in the nick of time to notice that the slow-moving vehicles ahead were braking because of the glare and lack of visibility. Vic immediately thought about the cars that were behind him. He didn't want them to rear-end him, so he gunned the Harley's throttle in neutral, creating its loud signature growl. He wasn't certain whether that alerted the driver behind him, but the driver jammed on the brakes of his sedan, barely stopping short of Vic's back tire.

Vic looked in the rearview mirror as this drama unfolded. With the sun illuminating the interior of the trailing sedan, he could clearly capture the stress on the face of the male driver as he approached, standing on his brake pedal. Vic sighed in relief, feeling thankful that he wasn't meeting his maker just yet.

The adrenalin of the near miss invigorated Vic. He arrived at Eli's door juiced, a completely different guy from what he had seen when he left the office. Danielle greeted him at the door. She gave Vic a big "I missed you" hug. And when their black lab, Igor, got in the mix standing on his back legs with front paws on Vic, it was like old times. Vic bent down and hugged Igor, getting a slobbered lick in return. Vic loved it. He asked Igor, "Where's your ball?"

On cue, Igor tore out of the foyer searching for one of his tennis balls to bring to Vic. Danielle and Vic headed for the outdoor patio, where Eli was grilling the steaks and talking to his infant daughter, Samantha, as if she understood him. They ate dinner and drank a little too much for a weeknight. After Danielle put Samantha to bed for the night, Vic entertained them with his exploits in Washington and his stories of working with the FBI.

Danielle faded about nine thirty and left for the bedroom. Vic and Eli sat in the den and chatted for a while. It was obvious that the unfinished business with the Craney Island investigation and his suspicions about the motives were weighing heavily on Vic's mind.

"Eli, I wish I could tell you that I am over with that business," he sighed. "It just didn't work. I can't be a consultant like that. Taking a backseat to all the decisions and not being given the intelligence the agents were getting was just too frustrating. It was cool hunting the bad guys, but they got to do all the fun things while, metaphorically, I was waiting in the car. This might sound silly, but being the only one not carrying a piece made me feel impotent."

"I bet that was scary."

"Seriously, it was scary."

"I'm sorry. I know you're being candid. But I couldn't resist the temptation. It's a shame we don't get to call the shots in our role as a consultant. But it's something we all have to get used to. But I have a feeling we will have another shot at how it all ends."

"Do you know something I don't?"

"I do. That's one of the reasons I wanted you to come over tonight."

"Spill it out, man! What did you hear?"

"I got a call from Greenwood just before we left the office. He told me Irene Cohen was murdered. My first impression is that the bad guys are tying up loose ends. That got me thinking that whatever the end game is, they will be going for it earlier than we anticipated."

"Oh, my God!" Vic blurted out. "That is just perfect! If they murdered Irene Cohen, they might be on to Patricia."

"Don't worry. I've got that covered. I'll tell you about that later. All this is bad enough, but I had some questions I was afraid to ask Greenwood. Maybe you know the answer.

"He said Cohen was murdered in the middle of the day when she normally was at work. I didn't ask where the assassination took place, but I bet it wasn't at the GAO. But that's not all that's got me worked up. Why was Greenwood calling me to tell me what had happened?"

"This is why I love working with you. You can smell a rat faster than anyone I know. I bet we can figure this out. What exactly did Greenwood say?"

"I was wondering when you would ask that question. I think that's our first order of business. I took notes. The first thing he mentioned was that he wanted to keep me informed as a matter of courtesy. You know that matters of courtesy are never on his mind. The second thing was that he wanted to know how you and I were doing now that we weren't working the investigation. It's awfully sweet of him to worry about us, but we both know that's bullshit.

"He also said you and he had a little disagreement when you withdrew from the investigation, and he wanted to know if I had any complaints with the FBI. I figure there is something in that question that is begging to be analyzed, but before we do, you need to hear his last question. He wanted to know whether you had heard anything or seen anything since you left that morning."

Vic responded, "If we assume he had an ulterior motive for making the call, we need to know why he asked those questions. OK, let's talk about Greenwood. That idiot accused me of holding back information. I was definitely guilty, but so was he. The stuff I didn't tell them about was stuff they already knew. I just didn't want them to know I knew it. So, in reality, it was the FBI not sharing. I don't think that should count against me. But that's the way Gilbert was working it as well. So that shouldn't be a complaint that would interest him."

Eli asked, "If that's not it, could there be something Greenwood is doing that we don't know about, including Gilbert? Don't try to answer now, but keep that in mind when thinking about his last question. His last question was, Have we heard or seen anything suspicious since I left DC? I haven't heard or seen anything, except our meeting with Detwiler and the AG. Have you?"

"Not a thing."

"OK, here's the other thing. I also got a call from Gilbert. He said the attorney general advised him of our meeting. He said that Goodman wants us to go through him only at the FBI. He mentioned that, just to be safe, Ms. O'Galvin was being moved to a safe house only he knew about.

"And that's what had me surprised. I'm now wondering if he and Goodman suspect that Greenwood has done something that would affect you or is in bed with the bad guys. Do you think there is more about the murder of Irene Cohen that he didn't tell me?"

"OK, Eli. Let's backtrack. We suspect the AG was caught off guard when we told him of everything we knew that wasn't in Greenwood's reports to him. Could it be that the AG called Gilbert, not Greenwood, wondering about the missing intel? Could Gilbert have some doubts about Greenwood's role in all of this? For that matter, our talk with Goodman might have been the first time the AG started to wonder if Greenwood was a part of it."

"That's what I have been rolling around in my brain. And I've got some more questions. Why is Gilbert worried about Greenwood and you? I might be a little paranoid, but when I add it up, it comes out like this. Goodman must trust Gilbert, and told him to check up on us to see if things were OK. That puts Greenwood and Gilbert on opposite sides. So that might suggest that Greenwood is a part of your conspiracy theory. And that would be how the bad guys know about us and what we've been doing. He might be working for whoever is behind it, and Gilbert and Goodman are now suspicious of Greenwood. So, maybe Greenwood's call was about being suspicious about what we were up to. If he's on the other side, he might be wondering why we haven't told anyone about your drive to Dulles."

Vic replied, "It sounds like you are beginning to see things my way."

"Let's just say that I'm not discounting it anymore. How do you see Gilbert in this?"

"OK, let's say it's Greenwood's role to continue the hoax that the NAPCO investigation is making enough progress to satisfy the AG and anyone else who might care. Let's assume that strategy buys the bigger conspiracy more time to work out the end game."

"That makes sense. Let's say Attorney General Goodman confides in Gilbert about his suspicions of Greenwood's role. Let's also assume Gilbert is thinking as we are, that the conspirators killed Cohen because the conspirators are tying up loose ends. Might Gilbert be thinking that the conspirators have the same plan for you?"

"Holy shit, Eli! I think you're right. I bet Greenwood and his pals placed a contract hit on me after I left the investigation. Those assholes!"

"All right, this is nothing more than conjecture. I might have it all wrong. I have been thinking about it ever since I got the call from Gilbert, but it wasn't until I was home and getting ready to grill that I started to put it all together. Believe me, if I had figured this out before I left work, I would have discussed it with you then."

Vic asked, "What do you have in mind?"

"First things first: do you have a gas furnace at home?"

"Sure do, and I also have a carbon monoxide detector and alarm."

"You'll need to turn off the furnace pilot when you get there. And before you enter your doors, you need to examine them closely, looking for unfamiliar wires or contacts in the doorjamb. Do you have a burglar alarm system?"

"Yeah, it's connected together with the other alarm."

"Make sure it's on when you get inside. If everything goes well tonight, we can work on a comprehensive plan at the office. For just tonight, why don't I wait for you to leave and then follow you home at a distance. If someone is tailing you, we might be able to do something about it."

"Are we being paranoid or just careful?"

"Either way, there's no harm in it."

"You've got a point."

Vic got up to leave. Eli told him to put on his Bluetooth earpiece, and he would call his cell phone once he was out of sight. Before Eli left, he looked in on Danielle. She was sound asleep. Eli collected his shotgun and a box of shells that he kept in the garage. He figured he would bring them with him in the car, just in case.

In the unlit garage, Eli watched Vic head out toward the entrance of the subdivision. He waited a few moments. Seeing nothing, he opened the garage door and drove off in pursuit of Vic. Vic called him on his cell phone.

"Hey, amigo, I am rolling down Friendship Road. You might want to get a good look at the white sedan that's between us. Just as I pulled away from the entrance of your subdivision, I noticed its headlights turn on as it pulled out behind me."

"Just to be safe, why don't you try to time the next traffic light so you will stop at the red. Maybe he will get close enough for you to see if he looks familiar."

"I'll try my best."

Eli spotted the white sedan once he got on McEver Road. Vic timed the light at the next intersection perfectly so that all three of them would be stopped. The streetlights at the intersection were bright enough to get a decent look at the driver of the white sedan. Eli's cell phone rang. It was Vic.

"You ain't going to believe this. The guy behind me almost ran into the back of me on the way to your place tonight. Do you think he could be a hit man or the FBI?"

"I wish I knew."

The light turned green, and Eli told Vic to stay on the phone line.

They all started moving forward again.

"Vic, I've got an idea. What do you think about me lightly tapping his rear bumper at the next red light? It might be interesting in how he reacts."

"You've got to be kidding! What if he's the guy doing all of the killing? That would be suicide."

"I've got my shotgun on the front seat, but I think you're right. Instead, I think I'll follow the both of you and see what happens. I wrote down his tag number. We can check it out in the morning if nothing else happens."

The three vehicles continued until Vic pulled into his driveway. The white sedan passed, and Eli followed him. The sedan eventually pulled out of Vic's subdivision and back onto the highway heading for downtown Atlanta. Eli called Vic, told him what had happened, and said he would park a few houses down from Vic's, just to see if the white sedan returned. Eli waited for about fifteen minutes and called Vic. They agreed that this guy was probably FBI keeping track of Vic's whereabouts and that nothing else would probably go down that evening.

Although Eli felt Vic would be safe for the night, he was more than worried. Whoever the bad guys were, they were now after Vic, and they had a habit of eliminating their enemies. He thought, Why didn't I see this coming? I've endangered the one guy who means the most to me! I've got to find a way to protect him.

Early the next morning, Eli called Vic to see if anything had happened after he left. Vic said he hadn't noticed a thing.

"Vic, I'm going to call Harry Meeks. He can run down this tag number for us. After that, I'm heading for the office."

"Roger that. I should be in about 8 a.m."

***

Eli caught Harry at home when he called. Harry agreed to make a visit to the Atlanta FBI office and visit with his old comrades who were still around and run the plates through their database. Just before lunch, Harry called. They were spot on. The guy tailing Vic was Evan Wilson, an FBI agent. Eli asked Harry if he would come by the Daneli office and visit with Vic and him.

Harry arrived about 12:15 p.m. "Do you mind that we take this conversation down the hall?"

"Dammit, Eli! You're starting to worry me."

Vic and Eli walked to the staircase well, where they told Harry about their theory. He didn't know Greenwood, but he knew Gilbert. Nevertheless, he was visibly sickened by the suggestion that someone in the FBI would be part of such a conspiracy.

"Eli, I cannot fathom that an FBI section chief would resort to such tactics. How sure are you that Gilbert suspects it?"

"Pretty damn sure. About as sure as I could be without him writing it down and sending it to me."

"If Vic is the latest target in such a high-stakes cat-and-mouse game, I don't like the way this is going."

"Any suggestions?" Eli asked.

"Not offhand, other than to send Vic into witness protection."

"No fucking way," Vic exclaimed.

"How do you guys always seem to wind up in life-and-death situations?" Harry asked as he shook his head.

"Just lucky, I guess," Eli replied. "And this isn't all the worst of the situations Vic and I are in. Two days ago, we got an invitation to talk to the US attorney general and a member of the Joint Chiefs of Staff."

"Seriously!"

"Yes, seriously."

"Before I say anything more, I'm afraid I have to ask you to keep it confidential between us. I only ask that because that is what they asked of me."

"If you have to ask, then I suppose I'll have to honor that with a reply. The answer is yes, of course."

Eli relayed the entire meeting details and then told him about Irene Cohen. Harry paused just like Goodman did.

"Eli, you weren't kidding. This is a hell of a situation. And I thought the Bureau tailing Vic was scary. Let me think about this for a while.

"How about we try to brainstorm our alternatives with all of the Daneli folks? I think we need to bring everyone at Daneli into this discussion. We have a lot of brainpower in our company. It looks like we are going to need it."

"Before we get to that, what did you find out about NAPCO and Purified?"

"It's not what you'd expect. There is nothing at all linking them except what little work Witherspoon did for NAPCO before taking the Purified job offer. In fact, the only thing I found was what you might consider gossip, and it's bad blood instead of a reason to be coconspirators. Some insiders say that the Doss brothers were really surprised that NAPCO got the Navy supply contract instead of his banner firm, Doss Energy."

Eli looked at Vic, and Vic winked.

"Now it's starting to make more sense," Vic asserted. "It looks like the Doss boys might have decided to exact a little revenge on NAPCO. Whatever the Doss boys are up to, they chose to set up NAPCO as the fall guy. Oh yeah, we've got to have a brainstorming session about all of this."

Harry agreed, and Eli set up a meeting for later in the afternoon at PDK Airport, where Daneli had a small office in the hangar where it parked the company jet. Harry drove, leaving Vic's and Eli's cars in the parking lot, just in case someone was keeping an eye on them. They sneaked out the back door, got in Harry's car, and headed for PDK.

Before they left, they contacted the rest of the Daneli employees. He told them to drop by the office and leave their cell phones there before heading to PDK. It sounded a little paranoid, but Eli didn't think they had the luxury of being naïve enough to think that someone might not go looking for them. He didn't want their phones to give away their location.

34. PLANNING TO SCHEME

ARRIVING AT THE SEASIDE RESIDENCE OF WINGATE AND TRAMMEL Doss were the attendees of the Hero Club. That was the name this group chose to flatter themselves. Under the guise of philanthropy, they met for the purpose of changing the course of the history of the world. There may be private clubs that have more funds, or maybe there are ones that have more political and military influence, but none come to mind. Besides the financial resources of the Doss brothers, whose joint wealth ranked them among the top ten wealthiest persons in the world, they had recruited the likes of two other entrepreneurs who also ranked in the top twenty-five wealthiest; one an American owner of casinos throughout the world and another a hedge fund manager whose personal holdings and board memberships influenced the major defense contractors in the world.

Making up the rest of the club were Congressman Christopher Findley, who had recently run against David Bennett for the US presidency—and lost; lobbyist Charles Bobick; Stuart Yarborough, NSA domestic antiterror director; Admiral Conrad Ellingson; Norman Shearer, deputy attorney general; General Carl McEwen, USAF; and Daniel Greenwood, FBI division chief.

How this group became devoted to their cause was a product of Charles Bobick's intuition. He had represented all of them at one time or another. He became familiar with their needs, biases, and agendas. When the Doss brothers approached him about the potential for doing something bold and dramatic, he knew they could be counted on, especially if the price was right. The Dosses made sure the price was appealing.

The attendees were assembled in the grand dining room of the residence. The size and scale of the Doss East Coast residence was such that there were more chairs at the table that were unoccupied than were occupied. It was a cold day of sleet and freezing rain. The surf crashing against the rocky shore, though four hundred feet from the residence, provided a calming cadence that belied the seditious plans underway in the Doss dining room.

Charles Bobick called the meeting to order. Admiral Ellingson served as the recording secretary, taking notes on a laptop that would remain in the hands of the Doss brothers at all times.

Bobick opened the portfolio in front of him and requested that Stuart Yarborough provide a progress report on Operation Scalawag.

"So far, all operation centers report that better-than-expected progress has been made. Operations Junior and Senior have been completed with resounding success. We have even stumbled upon some good fortune with respect to some unexpected bad luck. This comes by way of the selection of the response contractor for Operation Junior, Daneli Crisis Management.

"The negatives Daneli created came in two forms. We wanted the defense establishment to experience the effects of the loss of its most vital fueling terminal for a longer period of time, thereby growing the vitriol for Islamic terrorists. Not only was Daneli able to quickly find a substitute for Craney Island, the DOD now has the backup facility it could not find on its own. The other negative created by Daneli is that it was able to link our two missions faster than our plan anticipated. While both developments are unsettling, we can adapt to the inconvenience without the need to scuttle the mission.

"The good thing that has come from Daneli is that it has provided us with the opportunity to cast them as a backup fall guy if the main objectives of our mission cannot be achieved."

Congressman Findley inquired, "How so? Please elaborate."

"As you recall, Commander Hughes selected Daneli because of its energy industry background as emergency responders, not its experience working with the high command of the military establishment. We expected law enforcement and the intelligence agencies would uncover the deception we created by manipulating the NAPCO shipment data. And we expected someone would eventually discover the veiled attempt to mislead investigators into thinking the mastermind behind the shenanigans was President Ramirez of Venezuela. However, we didn't expect anyone had the investigative skills to find the trail so fast. And, of course, we knew we would be able to influence the progress because of our well-placed people in authority throughout the expected investigative mechanism. But as you know, we didn't expect a firm with the wherewithal and instincts of Daneli. We also had no idea how ambitious and radical they could be.

"There is a silver lining, however. Without our prompting, Daneli started several unauthorized investigations. Most were leading nowhere, except their lead investigator was beginning to unpack our layers of deceptions faster than we expected. And here's the good part: their radical methods suggest we can successfully portray them as the real bad guys behind the terrorism if we need to. We are confident we can paint them as an overly ambitious contractor wanting to make a big splash in the response field, creating the disasters so they could get the response contract. We are making good progress creating an evidence trail that leads to Daneli."

Admiral Ellingson interjected, "I've seen the Daneli group in action. We cannot underestimate their capability. Painting them as patsies will not be so easy."

Daniel Greenwood responded, "I have also seen them in action. They are clever and resourceful, all right, but they are also impetuous, egotistical, and careless. In other words, they can be led into a well-conceived trap. If we play our cards right, they will also rid us of any disposable underlings without us getting our hands soiled. I have begun implementing a frame scenario that has great promise. I have the complete details in the report we handed out today. Take it with you so we can discuss it at our next conference call."

Ellingson continued, "Well, I'm thankful that the man in charge of performing that bit of business is also the man making that assessment. I will only say that if we have to go down that route, you had better be on your game. These guys don't miss much. In fact, I came here today to say that we need to take them off the job before they find out too much and decide to act upon their conclusions."

Greenwood replied, "Let me assure you, Admiral, they are not as close as you might think. And also, their top investigator, Victor Majeski, has recently walked out of the investigation of his own volition. I've got a man watching his every move. You let me worry about Daneli's role.

"Also, we have withheld the identification of the fingerprint on the shell casing found at Craney Island. That went exactly as we predicted it would when we decided to plant that bit of evidence at the terminal. We transferred a fingerprint of Majeski's from their response trailer to the shell. Once that is announced, any speculation of an inside job will be deflected."

"I'm warning you. Don't underestimate that Majeski guy," Ellingson replied. "I'd like to know how he connected Operation Junior and Senior. We never counted on anyone doing that. No average guy connects those two operations in just a few days without serious smarts."

"Don't worry, I've got it covered," Greenwood replied. "And besides, we've established NAPCO as the perpetrators. Before anyone will find out that is also a ruse, we'll have all of the potential whistleblowers so apparently guilty as accomplices that no one will take up for them."

There were plenty of faces in the room showing a lack of confidence in Greenwood's assertions, but no one was willing to push any further.

Wingate Doss gave the next report. "First, let me say that I am very pleased with the progress we have made and the professional performance of our operatives. While we still have several more acts in our drama, I am more optimistic that we have the ingredients to be entirely successful. The Purified Petroleum team, playing the role of our generals and commanders in the field, has not missed a beat. Team reports to me have been timely and thorough. My brother and I are very impressed with the organization all of you helped to create. For specifics on our agenda, I turn the chair over to my brother, Trammel."

Trammel Doss was not as imposing as his brother. He was only six feet two and looked smaller because of his slender and slumping build. And he looked older than his age of fifty-seven. Wingate was the athlete in the family. Trammel was the scholar. Their Dutch grandparents, whose real name was Doschler, were big investors in energy stocks after the stock market crashed in the 1920s. The brothers came to the United States for college in the late 1960s and never left.

"Good evening, gentlemen. Our monitoring headquarters indicates the time is prime to execute Operation Husky. Elmendorf Air Force Base and Fort Richardson, located near Anchorage, are the military's West Coast command headquarters and fuel-supply depot. There is no other military base that is more strategic west of the Mississippi. While as true patriots we are saddened that we must destroy valuable military assets and sacrifice additional lives, we continue to be committed to our goal to awaken the US military establishment to the greater threat growing in the Middle East.

"Starting Monday, at about twelve hundred hours, the fuel depot will experience an incident that will rival the Craney Island event. Perhaps as many as two or as few as one tank will be destroyed. After we confirm the success of this mission, an anonymous text will appear in the inboxes at the CIA and all Pentagon agencies, the State Department, and at the headquarters of international news organization, Al Jazeera. It will announce that the attacks on US military assets will continue unless the trade sanctions are removed from Iran and that nine specific Islamic detainees at Guantanamo are set free.

"This communication will originate from a site in Tabriz, Iran, that we created specifically for this deception. And based upon the demands that are listed in the text, it will be difficult to argue that the source is a country or terrorist group that is something other than Iranian. Based upon the new legislation about to be signed and our knowledge of the new procedures written to cover a multiple threat, Homeland Security and NSA will take command of the response, and the Pentagon will consider the threat as more than a single terroristic act. With our collective urging, we expect the administration to consider the attacks on two of its military bases as an act of war.

"The actual 'boots on the ground' plan to overrun the tanks at Anchorage will be carried out by a small detail of three men: General McEwen, who could not be with us today because he is en route to Washington; PFC Raymond Baker; and our operative, the Janitor. PFC Baker will be the unfortunate accomplice who will order the tanks to overflow. When he leaves the delivery facility, it will be by the jeep assigned to him as the fuel movements operator. A cell phone-triggered explosive device has been hidden in the jeep and is set to go off when the phone receives a call. PFC Baker will not know about this part of the plan. The Janitor, who will be observing from a vantage point overlooking the fuel depot, will dial the cell phone as the jeep passes the overflowing tank. The explosion will be more than sufficient to ignite the rich gas atmosphere and set the tank on fire.

"Furthermore, we expect the type of chaos that ensued after 9/11. That will give us time to remove any trace that the two events were created by internal forces. If all goes as expected, the political outcry that will be fueled by Congressman Findley and his friends on the Hill will fill the airways with talk of retaliation.

"That retaliation reaction will now be easier to lead due to the expected passage of the new antiterrorism law. Congressman Findley and Charles Bobick have assured me that the amended law will be enacted before the president will need it.

"That, along with the expectation that the Joint Chiefs and the Pentagon will recommend an invasion of Iran, should seal the deal on a military solution based upon these terroristic acts and Iran's aggressive uranium enrichment program. We have two additional allies in the State Department and on the Joint Chiefs of Staff to ensure the momentum will be too overwhelming not to act.

"That ensures our mission will be complete, and we will not need to proceed further, except for taking measures to remove all traces of our involvement. The ball will be rolling toward the destruction of all Islamic influence on world affairs. I know I share everyone's aspirations that our intervention will finally remove the threat of an organized Islamic jihad aimed at the United States and also end the energy stranglehold this region has on our economy. We will never be recognized for our part in ridding the world of this evil, but we will always have the satisfaction of being the real heroes."

Admiral Ellingson queried, "And if our plans fall short of our goals?"

Wingate Doss replied, "Of course, if we have to abort, we will undertake Operation Freedom."

"And that's our last agenda item," Charles Bobick declared. "As mentioned earlier, the Daneli Group has been targeted as the patsy. Evidence indicating they staged the events to get the response and investigation business has already been placed strategically to suggest their company was the mastermind behind the events. And with all your collective influence to direct the investigation at Daneli, we should be successful in escaping culpability."

The gathering discussed much more as they drank cocktails and socialized. But it soon became clear that the group was split as to the danger that Daneli Crisis Management posed. Greenwood and Ellingson even got into a shouting match over Greenwood's tactics.

Leaving the residence together were General McEwen and

Admiral Ellingson. Their drive back to Washington was filled with trepidation. Ellingson asked McEwen, "What do you think about the Doss Brothers?"

"I see them as men willing to risk their fortunes and reputations to make the world a better place."

"It seems to me, Carl, with their money and influence, there are other ways to get that done without putting so much at risk."

"Don't you think it's a little late in the mission to question their motives?"

"Perhaps I'm just getting a little nervous now that we are getting so deep into the plan. We're putting a lot of faith in these guys, and I'm a little worried about whether they have the right stuff to make sure we don't expose ourselves to the unexpected."

"From where I stand, I haven't seen them sparing any expense to make sure that doesn't happen. Besides their political objectives, they also have a lot to gain monetarily. They have designs that their oil business will be in a terrific position to take advantage of the political results. With all that at stake, I can't see them overlooking anything that will stand in our way. Don't worry, they've got it all covered."

35. THE MIRROR MEETING

THE ENTIRE DANELI ORGANIZATION AND HARRY MEEKS SQUEEZED into the enclosed area alongside the Citation aircraft at their hangar at PDK airport. The agenda of meeting: to discuss the fallout from the Craney Island response and investigation.

Before a retelling of the events of the last couple of days, Eli got everyone's promise of confidentiality. In the center of the room was a big, two-sided, dry-erase whiteboard. Eli flipped over the board to the hidden side, which displayed the issues he had prepared for the meeting. After a lot of discussion and expressions of concerns, the group settled down to focus on a list of ideas about how to get out of their predicament. Not unexpectedly, Vic came up with the craziest story of all. And after all was said and done, the group kept coming back to it.

It went something like: Ramirez and PETGO were not the real bad guys. They were a patsy. The real perp was a master of deception. The fire was his diversion to hide the programming changes made at the Craney Island Terminal. The pursuit of the Rubik Memo was nothing more than another ruse, though incredibly convoluted, diabolical, and creative, to divert the entire US intelligence establishment away from whatever was the true "end game." Eli then brought everyone up to date with the developments of the last few days.

The major problem with where he was leading the group was that they had no idea what that end game might be. Vic then took them on a free-fall brain drain of a journey.

"OK," Vic declared in a calm, authoritative voice, "I'm going to list all the obvious, potential bad guys who might have something to gain by all of this, and which of them has the capability to pull it off. The list includes Hezbollah, the Lebanon-based Islamic party; al Qaeda; Muammar Gaddafi, Libya; Iraq; Iran; Afghanistan; Pakistan; North Korea; Russia; China; and so on."

Vic continued, "Now we eliminate all countries or enemies that don't have extensive petroleum backgrounds and interests. Remember, this event is all about petroleum. That leaves out Hezbollah, al Qaeda, Afghanistan, Pakistan, and North Korea. Iraq is out of commission due to the US war there and Saddam Hussein's death. That leaves Gaddafi-Libya, Iran, Russia, and China. I don't see Russia and China having a real motive, and I can't see them using such tactics. That leaves Gaddafi and Iran. Gaddafi seems like a long shot to me. Quite frankly, he's old and has not shown any inclination to stir the pot. I like Iran because they have a reason to get even with us. Our financial and trade boycott against them makes them the obvious frontrunner to consider this type of operation."

Hank interrupted. "Vic, I love your logic, but it can't be that simple. Also, there is the obvious: such matters are for governments to work out."

"As we are all aware," Vic insisted. "But it's my ass that's in their sights at the moment!"

There was a long, silent pause. It would be a good guess that they were all contemplating Vic's dilemma. A look around the room made it apparent that everyone was waiting for Eli to say something. Instead, Vic continued.

"Now you see what's been driving me lately. Rather than waiting around for something to happen, I did some research last night. I felt I could trust Agent Cramer, so I called her. She told me the FBI has been investigating the killing of Irene Cohen, and they found some interesting fingerprints on her car. When the Bureau checked it out, the prints didn't match the guy they suspected. They matched a known bad guy, Rahim Abdulla, a mercenary of Afghan or Iranian background. The last time this guy's name hit the FBI's radar was from a CIA alert a couple of years ago. He is identified as a freelance muscle operative working North America. So Cramer thinks that it's either been Rahim all along and not Cota, or that the bad guys somehow were able to obtain Rahim's prints and transfer them to the surface of Cohen's vehicle.

"Now here is where it gets a little sketchy. You all remember the last words from Rogoff when he left us. He said that other DOD fueling terminals also had shipments that were altered. At the time we were focused on NAPCO and chose not to follow that route. Also, if you remember, Rogoff told us he was hired by DOD after leaving our assignment. I spoke to him last night as well. I asked him about the other shipments that were altered. You won't believe his response. He said he was advised by the top Navy systems guy they were top secret, and he was not to discuss those shipments with anyone, and that included Daneli. He apologized, but he said he had a fantastic contract with the DOD, and he didn't want to jeopardize it.

"Well that really piqued my interest. So I called Dugan, the other IT guy who helped Rogoff with Craney Island. Dugan said Rogoff called him last week and told him about his new assignment. Apparently, the Navy high command doesn't know we added Dugan to help Rogoff. And from what Dugan says, Rogoff didn't mention Dugan's contributions when they offered him the redesign contract. Rogoff told Dugan he was afraid the Navy would change its mind and not hire him if they knew he needed someone else's help. Also, Rogoff didn't tell Dugan to keep his mouth shut on the other altered shipments.

"In the meantime, Dugan filled me in on what they found. It appeared to Dugan that the DOD's terminals at Fort Bragg, North Carolina, and the joint Elmendorf Air Force Base/Fort Richardson bases in Anchorage, Alaska, also had the same kind of alterations. That got me thinking. Now, remember what I said earlier about the 'real end game'? What if the bad guys had something bigger on their mind than hiding oil shipments? What if Craney Island is only the first of three targets on someone's radar? What if the Venezuelan oil connection is only a ruse to keep the intelligence agencies off the track?"

Mike Hillendorf interjected, "That's a pretty convoluted and clandestine ruse. I don't know much about Iran and their clandestine operations, but I would guess what you are suggesting is a pretty big stretch for its intelligence capabilities. More than likely, it's an organization wanting to point a finger at Iran."

"Bingo. You got it, Mike."

"I got what? What did I say?"

"It's not about Craney—not about NAPCO—not about Venezuela, PETGO, or Ramirez. It's about something else, and maybe that something else makes us think it's about Iran. But whatever it is, it might include Elmendorf and Fort Bragg."

Another long pause ensued. And then it hit Eli like a bolt of lightning.

"Hey, everyone, I think I've got something. When I was at West, I remember there was an antiterrorism task force to respond to the DOD about possible terrorism targets. They were compiling a list of all potential targets for a Homeland Security database. I worked on that with a friend of mine at Provincial Pipeline here in Atlanta. The CIA was going to download the list into their keyword surveillance programs. These keyword programs search emails, Internet communications, and the like, and when they find keywords next to other keywords, like 'bombing,' 'target,' etc., an alert appears. They then monitor further communications that might suggest a plot or terrorism.

"West had no deliveries to valued military bases that might be considered targets, so its role was merely in-house compliance. West was eventually eliminated from being an active terrorism response member, but Provincial was the highest volume of all the strategic carriers to military facilities, and their guy was really involved in their response plans. I just now remembered something he once mentioned about it. He said if anyone wanted to cripple the US defenses, the most vulnerable target was the fuel supply. He said the DOD data suggested that the most harm would be the destruction of the largest and most strategic fuel terminals of the Army, Air Force, and Navy. You all keep working on this while I call my Provincial buddy from the hallway."

Using the satellite phone Daneli used for emergency response communications, Eli called him. He caught a lucky break. His buddy was in and answered the phone. A couple of minutes later, Eli walked back into the hangar. Everyone stopped talking and stared at him.

"According to Provincial's general counsel, the three most strategic targets would be Fort Bragg, Elmendorf, and Craney Island. Is that a coincidence or what?"

There was an audible gasp from Faith and an "uh-oh" from Hank.

That was when Harry joined the discussion. "I have been listening with keen interest. But now that you are on a huge conspirator operation track, I need to counsel you. I'm getting a little nervous just listening to where this is going. Let's pause a minute to reflect."

Then Harry continued, "As you know, it's been a long time since I was active with the FBI. However, I never miss a reunion of the Atlanta chapter of retired agents. When the 9/11 hits occurred, Islamic terrorism was our favorite topic of discussion. I can tell you right now that from what the other guys have said, Iran cannot be the source of such an operation. They are not that sophisticated. We need to make sure we don't go off the reservation and start a panic."

Vic was next to re-enter the mix. "Harry, I hate to say it, but you are missing the point. It's not Iran. It's a plan to make it look like it's them. After I rolled it around in my brain a few times, it sounded ludicrous to me that Iran was the mastermind. The only other idea I have sounds ever crazier than the Iran angle. However, listening to Eli and thinking about why the US Attorney General is conducting a separate investigation, things are beginning to make sense. I think there is a bigger picture that we cannot see. You might think I'm losing it, but I think I might know what the end game is. My warped brain is telling me that we have not been looking at an event that is over. Instead, we are looking at a series of events that are at the beginning of something bigger."

Both Harry and Mike jumped in together and tried to tone down the big conspiracy talk. Harry said, "Let me say this again: if you are going to look down this road, you need to do it in a way that the car doesn't hit a pothole and run off into the ditch. Are you willing to do that?"

Eli then reentered the fray. "Are you suggesting that we need to place limits on where this discussion is going?"

"Not exactly, but yes, in a way. You need to make sure you don't end up in a place that you can't get yourself out of. We all have limits. Daneli Consulting has limits of what it can do."

"OK, Harry, I think I know where you are coming from. You don't want to inhibit our discussion—you just don't want us to end up in a bigger hole than we are in now."

"That's a way of saying it."

"I've got faith in these folks. I don't believe we will ever end up in that kind of predicament. And I think I can make sure we don't lose sight of reality."

Vic then dove back in. "OK, now that we got that out of the way, I'd like to continue."

Harry remarked, "I want you to continue, Vic, and I am hoping you will place it all in perspective."

"I think I have the perspective. I just don't have enough facts. That being said, I'd like everyone to imagine this bigger thing and where we might be along the course of where it is heading."

The room seemed smaller, quieter, and dimmer as Vic took the group down a path only his mind could imagine. Vic walked toward the dry-erase board on the wall, picked up the marker, and started writing as he continued talking about his theory.

"First thing, we've got a highly sophisticated group of bad guys. Next, they blow up USN Fuel Depot at Craney Island. While they are there, they alter the shipment logs to Craney and two other military fuel depots."

After writing all that down, he started to write another column of events.

"Immediately after that, they murder two GAO employees and a DOJ attorney to hide the NAPCO connection. Or so we think. What if they did all this to focus everyone's attention on NAPCO and away from their real goal?"

"Next—and don't forget this—the mercenary Cota was first believed to be Latin. However, the FBI says his prints match an Islamic mercenary. At first this seems like odd bedfellows. But why the deception? Maybe it's intended to look like Islamic terrorists all along. And maybe the timing of everything was essential to preparing the stage for their end game."

Vic turned away from the white board and addressed the gathering.

"The more I learned about our investigations at Craney Island and the murders of Calloway, French, and Matusak, the more I see the mind of a highly sophisticated, cold-blooded, monster with a master plan designed to appear to be so convoluted that nobody will be able to connect all of the dots before it all plays out.

"No, I don't see Iran as being behind this. But if we believe all of the above is an accurate assessment, then what do we have? Why would anyone go to all this trouble and scheming to point the finger first at NAPCO, then Venezuela, and then finally at Iran? So we have to ask ourselves, who would gain from all this deception ending up with Iran looking like the bad guy? Is it Israel? Not likely. It doesn't need the United States to do its bidding, and it's not its style to risk its success on the expectation that the United States will understand why it had to destroy valuable US military assets to prompt us to wipe out their enemies.

"So, who does that leave? If it's not a country, could it be a person or a group? The only thing I came up with is someone here in the United States wanting the American public and the intelligence community to think the threat is from Iran or a foreign Islamic power with designs on fucking us over. I'm going to say this as dispassionately as I can. Could we be looking at a conspiracy by the US Neocon movement to incite the United States to widen its military goals to include the Islamic-controlled countries of the world? Could energy be behind it? Are we looking at a plot so insidious to anger America to the extent that it will consider a military action against Iran or all Islamic countries that are not our allies?

"That's the way I see it. It's the only possible reason the US AG is conducting a separate, secret investigation. They must have some intelligence that suggests such a conspiracy. And one more thing. I promised Eli I would keep this confidential between him and me, but you have got to hear this. I vaguely suggested this theory as a possibility in our meeting with the AG. And here's the scary part. Neither the attorney general or Detwiler acted surprised by my suggestion. It was like they were on to the possibility already."

Dead quiet. Nobody stirred. This was no pregnant pause. Instead it was a combination of wild thoughts and foreboding.

Vic was not done.

"So you are probably wondering why we are caught in the middle of this. It's my guess that we have been manipulated all along. All of our new buddies in the Navy are not really our friends. Have we been chosen as their unwitting accomplice? Have we been manipulated and deceived and become the instrument of the bad guys to perpetrate the deception to the maximum extent? And if that's so, are we the patsy if the scheme needs a fall guy?"

Eli looked around the room to see his employees looking at him. He was as hesitant to say something as they were. Vic was staring at the floor, intentionally avoiding Eli's gaze.

Finally, Eli responded.

"I have to give it to you, Vic. When I ask you to think outside the box, you don't disappoint!"

Hank had been sitting quietly observing until now. "Vic, do you have something other than circumstantial evidence and deductive reasoning to suggest that we make such a leap in faith? Because if you don't, I think we need to avoid writing conspiracy novels and treat this matter with the dignity it deserves."

"No, I don't have anything more than what I have mentioned, but there is one way to find out if I am right without much risk. We simply give the AG the facts on the computer software hacks on Elmendorf AFB and Fort Bragg. I bet we get their attention big time. And guess what? If I'm right, they will be looking at how to prevent what happened at Craney Island for those two bases. We might be back on the job, but with a different boss."

The entire Daneli team debated the matter for another half hour and then came to a vote. It was unanimous that they wanted to move on Vic's plan.

36. HELLO, MR. ATTORNEY GENERAL

WITH EVERYONE WITNESSING, ELI CALLED COLONEL LOUIS MIL-ton and advised him of some new, important information he thought the AG should hear. Within minutes, a conference call was arranged on secure lines in Washington and, with Daneli using their satellite telephone.

"Hello," Eli beckoned. "Can you hear me, Mr. Attorney General?"

"Yes, Mr. Taylor, I can hear you. I understand you have come across some new information. Is that correct?"

"I think so, sir. We've known about it for a while but didn't act on it because it appeared to be irrelevant at the time. But since your interest in the matter, we have been reexamining what we knew to see if there was something we were overlooking."

"I was hoping that was something you might do when you left here the other day. So what have you got?"

"When our programming experts examined the shipments to Craney Island, they found alterations to Craney Island's shipments that led to the tanks overflowing. What we didn't mention at that time was that we also found alterations that affected fuel shipments to military bases in other parts of the

United States. At the time, we were focused on Craney Island and who might be performing the alterations and whose shipments were altered.

"At that time, we were not focused on other facilities. Yesterday we talked to one of the programming experts, and he told us that the other bases where shipments were altered are Elmendorf Air Force Base/Fort Richardson, and Fort Bragg. Following a hunch, we verified that these two military fuel terminals were mentioned in a Homeland Security report just a few years ago that determined that the destruction of these bases would cripple the US military more than any other kind of attack except a nuclear strike."

After another long pause, Goodman asked, "May I call you back using this connection in a few minutes? I want to discuss this with General Detwiler."

"Certainly, sir. We will stand by awaiting your call."

In a matter of ten minutes or so, Daneli's satellite phone was buzzing and flashing, indicating a call. Eli answered the phone and put the conversation on the speaker box.

"Mr. Taylor?"

"Yes, this is Eli Taylor."

"Adam Goodman here, and on the phone with me is General Detwiler. General, please say hello so we can be sure that you are patched in."

"Mr. Taylor, this is Forrest Detwiler. Can you read me?"

"Loud and clear, General. Can you hear me?"

"Yes, I believe we have a full connection."

Adam Goodman proceeded. "After conferring with the general, we have some questions. How are the base deliveries controlled?"

"We are not familiar with Elmendorf, but we are with Bragg. At Bragg, the deliveries are controlled from the fort's control building adjacent to Provincial Pipeline Company's Fayetteville Delivery Station, just inside the fort's property. We understand that the control panel is only operated manually by fort personnel."

"What can you tell us about Elmendorf?"

"We could look it up on the pipeline system schematics."

"How long will that take?"

"We should be able to access the database momentarily, but it will only show the private company side of the connection. If you are aiming at shutting down the deliveries, you will have to find someone familiar with how the military system is controlled. Without such authority, we can only speculate how it's done by reviewing the industry side of the fence."

"Tell me what you can surmise."

"Roger that, but Vic will have to take over for me. He's our expert."

"Thanks, Eli."

"Victor Majeski here. I've located the products pipeline system maps indicating the delivery line to Elmendorf. It originates at the Haines deep-water port and travels a few miles to the Fort Richardson Fuel Depot. This appears to be a military-owned and operated pipeline. It would be my guess that a military or privately owned terminal located at the deep-water port has a manned control building that directs shipments to tankage within the fort's premises. That would require an additional manned control building inside the fort that monitors deliveries and operates the tank valves. But I must admit that this is only conjecture based on my knowledge of similar operations elsewhere. To be certain, you would need someone familiar with the Fort Richardson Fuel Depot."

General Detwiler interjected, "How would an operator shut down the system or revise the delivery schedule?"

"Any system can be hacked from an outside source if it communicates with the outside world, but I don't think that is what you would expect because of the Craney Island experience. Therefore, you can expect a private communication system with no lines of connection to the outside world. That means that persons inside the control building, either at the port or the fort, are the only persons capable of influencing the deliveries into the fort."

"Thanks, Vic. I think that's all I need at this time."

"Eli, if we needed a civilian to operate these pipelines inside the control buildings, could you supply the personnel and expertise?"

"Yes, sir. Vic would be one operator, and if you needed another deployed at the other location, we could find someone to do that within a 48-hour window."

"If you don't mind, please find another operator to be placed on standby."

"I will arrange for that. Anything else?"

"I think that's all for now. I want to thank you for your cooperation and expertise. I am beginning to understand how valuable a resource you can be. I'm pleased that you can anticipate our concerns. And just one thing: our communications must remain confidential between us."

"You have our promise of our loyalty to you and to maintain the strictest of confidentiality of all matters between us."

"Thanks. You will be hearing from us shortly."

The Daneli phone was hung up, and the hangar became so quiet all one could hear was the forced-air heating system delivering warm air to the hangar. The air vent rattled with a steady tapping refrain, a sound never noticed before.

Eli looked around the room, but this time he didn't wait for someone else to comment.

"It appears you were right, Vic. They sure sounded like they were thinking along the same lines as you. You know, I was pretty scared when Andrew Johnson was trying to kill me a couple of years ago. I don't mind admitting that right now I am a little terrified. We might be talking about a Seven Days in May kind of conspiracy. For all you nonconspiracy nuts, that was a book and a movie about the military's attempted coup of the United States' executive branch.

"I'm afraid Vic and I are inextricably attached to this drama. That probably means the rest of you can choose to be left out. I certainly won't blame you if that is your choice. I want you to think about that right now. Because if my hunch is right, that satellite phone is going to ring again pretty soon. It will be the US Attorney General asking that we assist him in preventing something similar to a coup—or at least an overthrow of our foreign policy that will result in the United States going to war against Islamic jihad. In either case, it will be one faction of our government against another."

Vic remarked, "I can't believe I might have been on the right track. This is nuts!"

"I'll need to know who wants to continue on this assignment if things go similar to what Vic was imagining. As soon as you know, please let me know. It's almost two o'clock now. We should take a break. I haven't had lunch, so I'm going to order in. You may order as I am or take a break and go somewhere where you can think about this away from the pressure of the moment.

"But before we break, I must insist that none of what we have discussed here today is shared with anyone. And I mean family and spouses included. And in your consideration of whether you want to continue to pursue this matter, you need to be aware that in doing so, there will be significant safety risks and potential charges against us if we end up on the losing side."

To Eli's surprise, just about everyone stayed. Only Faith and Blake Cooper left. As one might imagine, the conversation at the hangar was lively and creative. Eli called Richard Dugan to see if he was up to another emergency assignment. Eli didn't tell him what the assignment was, but Dugan was definitely interested. As it turned out, he really enjoyed working with Daneli and its employees. While this was going on, Vic was compiling a list of pipeline operators who might be interested in assisting them if they were needed.

At 1550 hours, the satellite phone was flashing. It got quiet when Eli answered the call.

"Eli Taylor," he announced.

"Eli, this is Adam Goodman and General Detwiler. I'm afraid we are going to need your expertise. I think we have a complicated and difficult situation. I'm not going to beat around the bush. With your help, the general and I believe we have uncovered a plan within the US government to incite the public to demand military retaliation and ask questions later. Their goal is to punish and take control of the Islamic nations of the world harboring terrorists with intentions to do harm to US assets and its allies. We think the terrorist attack at Craney Island Fuel Depot was the first strike. We believe Elmendorf and Bragg are next.

"We also believe that we must act immediately to save valuable defense assets. Since our last conversation, we have confirmed that all product movement at Elmendorf tankage is controlled from its control building, just like at Fort Bragg. We need you to help us reprogram the delivery orders for these two bases without being detected. We also need to know if you and your company are willing to take the assignment. And we need to know your answer by 6 p.m. Eastern Standard Time, today. And if this is a consideration, under the War Powers Act, we can authorize to pay you at a rate of five times your existing contract rate, an amount we are offering at this time."

Eli responded, "This will sound presumptuous, but we have anticipated this potential before we called you today. After your call, the core of the company sat around and debated it. We are all in."

"I am very happy to hear your response. You realize this could be dangerous for those deployed at our direction, and there is also the possibility that we might fail and suffer the consequences."

"Yes, sir. We do."

"We will need you, Victor Majeski, and your systems programming expert to arrive here in DC by 2100 hours. Is that doable?"

"Yes, sir. Where shall we meet?"

"General Detwiler has set up an office at the National Pollution Funds Center (NPFC). We will leave you directions and credentials at the general aviation terminal at Dulles.

"Next, we will need to have an operator available at Elmendorf in Alaska within 48 hours."

Eli asked, "Is that the only person needed in Alaska?"

"We believe so."

Eli looked at Vic, and Vic nodded.

Eli said, "Mr. Majeski wants to be that guy."

"Very well. We will see you then."

And with that, the call was ended. Vic called Dugan back. For five times his normal pay, he was willing to suit up and go anywhere. He would meet Eli and Vic at Dulles at 2000 hours. Erica arranged for the plane's arrival and two rental cars. Hank, Mack, and Clyde were to stay back in Atlanta with Erica. Vic arranged for a copilot from Epps. And since no one knew they were at the hangar, there was no FBI tail to report that anyone had left Atlanta for DC or parts unknown. Vic told Hank to make calls from his and Vic's cell phones every now and then in case someone was trying to track their location. Hank was also tasked with monitoring the calls to their cell phones, then alerting Vic and Eli about return calls they might want to make because of their importance.

Once they were in the air, it was apparent that something was bothering Eli. He pulled Vic away from the copilot's seat and looked him in the eye. "You know, we don't have a backup plan. What if Detwiler and the AG are in on it? What if this is all a setup for us to be the fall guys? They pull us back in just in time to complete the frame-up. We need to come up with something."

Vic was now the one without a clue. "Look, when we go this far up the ladder of authority, I'm useless. I think this is where you do the planning and I act the part of the trusted partner."

Eli just nodded. Vic returned to copilot the Citation, and Eli remained in a thoughtful pose in his seat. He ran through his list of trusted friends in high places. Although he felt Gilbert was a potential, he ruled him out because he was too close to the issues and conspirators. He needed someone totally out of the loop.

After ruling out just about everyone he remotely knew or trusted, only one person remained a candidate: Isadore Andropolis, the editor of the New York Times. He took a chance and called him.

After the call, Eli sat there grateful he had made a number of expensive acquisitions when he started his response practice. The satellite phones were a pricey item. And it wasn't that they could not be hacked into, but the state of the technology at the time was such that there just weren't enough of them for the marketplace to spend the money to find bugs or hacking devices. That made conversation on the satellite phone a secure communication.

37. WE ARE DEPUTIZED

DUGAN WAS WAITING FOR ELI AND VIC AT THE DULLES TERMINAL, and as Goodman had promised, an envelope awaited their arrival that included credentials and directions. The NPFC building was no more than an inconspicuous office building in Arlington, Virginia. They passed through security and were escorted to the auxiliary command center used for disaster response. General Detwiler, Louis Milton, and US Coast Guard Commander Evan Brockington, who was part of the Craney Island Response Command and a longtime acquaintance of Eli, were awaiting their arrival.

Detwiler rose, offered his hand to Eli, and stated, "I bet you know Commander Brockington. He's been consulting with Goodman and me since this matter landed in our lap. He's the reason the AG and I had the confidence to make you a part of our plans. He trusts you and your organization."

After a round of handshakes and introductions, Detwiler laid out the mission.

"In two of the cubicles along the far wall are two researchers who are now working on the electronics we will encounter. The terminal setup in the middle of the room is operated by Lieutenant Furman. He's controlling the videos on the array of flat screens hanging from the ceiling. Two Coast Guard intelligence officers will be assisting us, and you will meet them soon. I will explain their assignments later.

"We have developed an operation plan. Its code name is EPA, for reasons I will explain as we go along. Our strategic objective is to physically tap into and connect to the two delivery controllers, one at Fort Richardson and the other at Fort Bragg. This will be a physical, hard-wired, electronic connection at the sites that will allow us to override any pipeline or delivery commands executed at the two forts.

"We plan to make the physical connections under the cover of two visits. At Fort Richardson, past US President William Bailey has scheduled a speaking engagement in Anchorage in two weeks. And if you are wondering, President Bailey has been informed of our mission, and he is entirely on-board. When an ex-president visits a military site, there is always a previsit advance team that coordinates arrangements with the host base command. One of the Coast Guard intelligence officers assigned to our mission, Petty Officer First Class Kirk Darnell, will be a part of that advance team. He will connect a minicomputer to the dedicated lines or the actual controller, leaving it hidden there to transmit the shipping commands to our terminals here, allowing us to control the product movement and storage commands remotely to this site.

"At Fort Bragg, the Coast Guard is teaming up with the NTSB on a compliance visit to its fuel depot. Eighteen months ago, they had a small leak event at the depot that required a significant repair and facility upgrade along with the spill cleanup. Random site visits were part of the follow-up order. We have scheduled such a visit for Friday, four days from now. An intervention to its control system identical to the one planned at Fort Richardson will be performed at Fort Bragg.

"From here, your Mr. Dugan will team with our computer programmers to write the commands to override the systems at the two forts. Once operational, we will be monitoring each delivery command as it is directed by the local controllers. We will have the capability to see the actual fill volumes of the tankage as they appear in real time. When a local command is given that we know will overflow a tank, we will override it by directing the delivery to go to a tank that has the capacity to accept it. Thereby, we will prevent any spill from occurring.

"Once a local delivery is about to occur, we will launch a drone to video the fuel depot, looking for attempts to ignite the prospective spill if we cannot prevent it. Here is where it gets a little dicey. We have a Coast Guard assault team standing by on alert awaiting our order to capture or eliminate anyone attempting to ignite the anticipated spilled fuel, whether they are outside the fort or within it. If the perpetrators are within the fort, entry and access will be tricky. We have a cover story arranged that should provide the necessary access, but forcible entry is not ruled out."

Eli commented, "I take it that the fort command will not be notified of your intentions."

"We cannot do that, and here's why. The reason we are at this decision point and why we created such a mission is that we believe we have identified some of the major conspirators. Two of them are believed to be the generals commanding Fort Richardson and Fort Bragg.

"And as you might imagine, there will be a high price to be paid if we cannot capture or kill the perpetrators and connect the conspirators to them. Just so you will know who not to contact or who to give a cover story to if you are contacted by them, I have provided a list of the known conspirators. It's in your folder on the table over by the main terminal. Also included in your folder is your shield indicating you have been deputized by the Coast Guard. The shield will get you inside both bases. I would like to have one of your men deployed to each base, one in the advance team in Anchorage and the other being a part of the inspection team at Fort Bragg."

"Which base do you predict will be hit first?" Eli inquired.

"Our intelligence suggests it will be Fort Richardson. Its next shipment of aviation kerosene is scheduled for Monday at 1105 hours. The next delivery at Bragg is set for the following Friday at 1620 hours."

"Vic, are you up to going to Alaska in the winter?" Eli asked.

"Better that way. There should be fewer personnel milling around outside the heated buildings. And that means a better opportunity to sneak around without being noticed."

"Mr. Majeski, your flight leaves Dulles at 0955 hours tomorrow morning. Your contact will be Secret Service agent Gil Stratford. I am handing you his contact information in this envelope. I will inform him this evening that you will be accompanying his advance team. He will provide you with further credentials at the airport. Place them in your folder immediately. Officer Darnell's photo and contact info are included in your folder as well. He will perform the communication patch at the control building. Part of your assignment will be to coordinate with our programmers here that the patch you have installed is working and that it allows us to control the fuel movements at the delivery facility there in Alaska. We will give him your contact info so the two of you can coordinate your activities at the base."

"Roger that, General."

"Good to see you are transitioning back into military lingo, Vic. It will serve you well on this mission."

"If the shipping schedule is not changed, the Fort Richardson event will occur first. However, if the Bragg shipments are moved ahead of the Fort Richardson deliveries, we prefer that your best man, Mr. Majeski here, travel to Fort Bragg and assume the same role there that he expected at Fort Richardson. Major Ray Fellows will be your contact at Fort Bragg. He's the IT electronics expert who will perform the tap into the Bragg control building."

"I'll be ready, sir," Vic replied.

"And last, once the taps and patches are operational, Mr. Majeski will need to confer with your man Dugan and our command center programmer here to make sure the devices we leave behind on site will allow us to operate each fort's controllers from here. After that is confirmed, we would like them to stand by at each location beyond the bases' gates as a local contact until the mission is concluded. Eli, you and I will remain here with Mr. Dugan and coordinate the mission."

It was running quite late in the evening, and General Detwiler had only a few things left on his list of orders. "In the equipment bag we gave you cell phones. You will need to charge the batteries. We will be using these phones exclusively to communicate on this mission. We've arranged rooms for you at a Holiday Inn one block from the Pollution Funds Center. Get some sleep and report here at 0700 hours tomorrow."

38. THE RETURN OF THE MEDIA

MATTHEW BERG'S ATTENTION TO THE ANTITERRORISM BILL WANED as he found that few supporting the bill were willing to discuss it, whereas those on the other side shook their heads in ignorance about what was fueling its fast track to passing. Three days ago it passed the House. Just a few minutes before, it had passed the Senate by a narrow but satisfactory margin.

Although it was a little late in the afternoon, he tried again to reach someone who was willing to go on the record about the impetus for the bill. That was when the managing editor of the newspaper appeared at his desk.

"How's it going with your antiterrorism story, Matthew?" he asked.

Matt was at a loss for words. He never got questions like that from the managing editor. That was a question he might get from the political editor for the White House. His mind was jumping, but he needed a cogent reply. Then he remembered that Congresswoman Shuster had recently told him the name of the snitch who had given her aide Eli's cell phone number.

"Yes, sir. I was about to call the contractor working on the Craney Island investigation and get an update."

"Why don't you do that? I'm anxious to see where he stands. When you get something, walk it into my office."

Isadore Andropolis had never asked Matt for anything resembling this invitation before. As Andropolis walked back to his office, everyone in earshot of Matt was staring at him. It was clear that something was up, but he didn't know what.

He looked up Eli's number and called. Eli didn't pick up, but he called him back on the satellite phone.

"How's it going, Mr. Taylor?" he asked.

"Another crazy day on the job. What can I do for you, Matthew?"

"I found out who gave the Congresswoman's aide your phone number. Do you know a Lieutenant Lemay?"

"I'm afraid so. That's good work, and I have no doubt that the information is accurate. So I guess that means that I owe you one. Are you ready to cash it in?"

"The timing couldn't be better, Mr. Taylor."

"Now that we are more than acquaintances, you may call me Eli."

"Thank you, I will. First off, the antiterrorism bill we discussed in the last conversation we had is on its way to the president for his signature. Do you care to comment on it?"

"Since our last discussion, I did read a synopsis of the bill. It appears to give the president broader powers to act militarily short of declaring war. Is that close to your take?"

"That pretty much sums it up. So, why do you think the timing seems to coincide with the Craney Island incident?"

"Before I comment on that one, I need to make a statement and then ask that you delay reporting my comments until your ultimate boss okays it."

"Are you talking about the editor of the paper?"

"Yes, I am."

"I don't get it. What does he have to with this?"

"It just so happens that I had to call him recently about a related matter. Where are you now?"

"I'm at my desk."

"Now would be a good time to visit with him and call me back."

Matthew Berg's brain was now in code-red danger mode. What the fuck is going on? he asked himself. He glanced at the windowed door to his editor's office, and Matt could plainly see his editor looking in his direction. In more or less a stupor, Matt picked up his notepad and pen and walked into Andropolis's office.

"Well, Matt. What did you find out?" asked his editor.

"My contact told me to visit with you."

"I was expecting that. I'll call Mr. Taylor and put him on speaker. Please close the door to my office." Isadore Andropolis dialed Eli on a secure line.

"Eli, I have Matthew in my office. I have full faith in him. As we discussed earlier, I've known Matt since he was a child back when I became friends with his father. We are both anxious to try to help you out. Please give Matthew a taste of what we can expect."

"OK, here it is. What I am willing to say about this matter is my own observation, and it's neither the position nor opinion of my client, the US Navy, the US military, or any other party. I am nothing more than an anonymous source who might be an unwitting accomplice to one of the most unbelievable stories of our time."

Andropolis looked at Matt and nodded, as if to say it was his turn to answer.

"I'm clear on that, but what is behind the timing of your statements, and why are you now more comfortable with providing answers to my questions?"

"Let's just say off the record that this is a fluid situation that is in the process of playing out. If the report of this conversation is released before I say so, it could do irreparable harm. And as for the other matter, there are things you can do with this information that I can't."

Eli continued, "I don't have any evidence that the legislation you've been tracking and the matters I need help with are connected, but from what we have been looking at, it makes sense that they are.

"My company's findings as to the cause of the Craney Island incident have ruled out human or mechanical error. You will have to deduce the gravity of that finding. But we have been following leads that point to a conspiracy aimed at ratcheting up the anger of the nation against the nations of Islam, creating false evidence of their complicity in the Craney Island event.

"The conspirators' goals are to goad the nation into declaring war on the nations of Islam as the false perpetrators, particularly Iran. Recently, my firm was asked by the attorney general to assist him and the opposition within the military to thwart those plans and eventually round up the conspirators. I am in Washington right now to begin that effort.

"Now, the reason I'm letting you in on all of this, and why the timing is right, is in what I'm about to tell you. It recently occurred to me that this elaborate conspiracy might include recruiting me and my employees as unwitting fall guys if something goes wrong. We need a safety net if that happens. Your editor told me the newspaper is willing to be that safety net. I will continue to feed you information, and if my employees and I end up as the accused bad guys, you can help set the record straight by what we've given to you, along with what investigations you've done on your own. All we would want is for the facts to come out—all the facts. For this, your paper will have the scoop on the biggest story of the century."

Eli provided them with more details, but before he concluded the call, he said, "For the next few days, I will be mostly unavailable for comment. If you try to reach me, I will try to respond. But don't try to reach any other Daneli employee. I need to be the point man. If it's urgent, text me a 911 message. I understand that what I have said is all very cryptic, but I am not comfortable saying anything more at this time. You will just have to take it from here."

When Eli hung up, Vic, who was approaching him, asked, "What was that all about?"

Eli replied, "That was our safety net. I'll tell you about it later."

Eli, however, could not help but wonder what his friend Isadore had up his sleeve. Eli had told him the entire story. But it was almost as if Eli was doing him a favor rather than making a desperate plea about the grim situation he was in. Eli had relaxed enough for his brain to consider the big picture of his dilemma. It was calculating the odds of a conspiracy so vast that it encompassed almost every branch of government. The computation was drawing a rational conclusion. In Washington, among the professional observers and reporters, something this big had to leave other signs that something was up. And an impending coup of the nation's foreign policy was big enough and complicated enough to leave clues and raise questions.

"Maybe," he thought, "there was already a lot of talk of what might be going on. Maybe they were simply missing the pieces we uncovered. Maybe that's why the editor of the New York

Times did not flinch even a little bit when I asked for his assistance."

Eli wasn't known as a deeply religious man, but he was now praying that his crisis had fallen into good hands.

39. THE OTHER TEAM

FORT RICHARDSON AND FORT BRAGG HAD NO CONTRACT IT EXpert like Craney Island's Eric Parma. Instead, they relied upon enlisted personnel to maintain their SCADA (Supervisory Control and Data Acquisition) schedule control system and programs. Their internal IT divisions simply trained enlisted personnel to perform the work. Back in March of 2006, when Witherspoon and his coconspirators devised their schemes for Operation Scalawag, they began a search for their own expert among the ranks of enlisted personnel who would be willing to intentionally overflow their tanks and cause a spill. General McEwen at Elmendorf and General Harvard at Bragg profiled the candidates from a list of precocious, mischievous enlistees who were repeat visitors to their forts' brigs. Those with a background in IT or the Internet were interviewed. Each fort commander found his own foil and readied him for their special mission.

THURSDAY, NOVEMBER 23, 0900

Private First Class Ray Baker was called for special duty to the officer's building at Fort Richardson. After checking in with the duty officer, he was told to see the fort commander, General Carl

McEwen. The general advised the private that his special mission was a "go" for the Monday morning deliveries. McEwen, however, would not be at the base. He would be in Washington, DC. Colonel Roy Hayworth, his second-in-command, would be presiding.

Private Baker had had the programming modifications in written form for a couple of weeks when Eric Parma was still alive to walk him through it over the telephone. Baker had practiced its implementation in a training program on his personal computer to the point of memorization. His next shift at the controller terminal was Saturday morning, and he prepared himself for that time.

At Fort Bragg, General Carver was advised by the Hero Club that the Fort Richardson event would occur first. His only duty at this time was to ensure that Corporal James Osborn, his chosen programmer for the mission, would not be on leave.

Outside of Vancouver, British Columbia, Canada, Eugene Kravitz, a.k.a. the Janitor, a.k.a. Mr. Straight, a.k.a. Emile Montag, was preparing for his trip to Anchorage, Alaska. He had been ordered to be the one to ignite the spilled fuel at the Elmendorf AFB/Fort Richardson fuel depot. He would also perform damage control from his sniper's position from outside the fort's fence. Although he wasn't fully back to normal, he hoped that by the time he had to perform, his medication would have done its job, returning him to his old, reliable self. His handlers chartered a small aircraft for him that would arrive Sunday afternoon in Anchorage.

***

Back at the Doss estate on the North Carolina Outer Banks, Congressman Findley sat with Wingate Doss and Purified's Dan Witherspoon and Art Daniels. Phase Two of Operation Scalawag had been initiated, and the chief schemers were assessing their posture.

Wingate Doss was in the middle of hearing Witherspoon's status report when he asked, "So where are the Daneli folks since your last report?"

Witherspoon replied, "We may have lost track of Taylor and Majeski since yesterday morning."

"What do you mean—lost track?"

"The FBI tail saw them enter their offices yesterday morning but never saw them leave. Their cars have remained in the office parking lot."

At this point, Doss went ballistic.

"That's fairly significant, wouldn't you say?" he barked back at Witherspoon.

"Apparently, that's not the way the FBI saw it. We just heard about it an hour ago."

"So you're telling me that at the identical time we launch Phase II of our mission, the only investigators who pose a threat to us disappear?"

Sheepishly, Witherspoon replied, "Not exactly, sir. Our surveillance has them still in their office. There is call activity on their cell phones. It's just that no one has visual confirmation that they are still inside."

"Well, that's just perfect!"

Witherspoon didn't know how to leave this subject well enough alone. He continued, "Greenwood has placed an all-out alert to all FBI branches."

"Are the two of you auditioning for a role in the remake of *Dumb and Dumber*? We might find them faster that way, but under what justification for the issuance of the alert?"

Art Daniels jumped in to deflect some of the criticism. "Greenwood is saying that they are characterized as material witnesses in a federal investigation."

Doss proclaimed, "That might satisfy John Q. Public, but I bet it will raise a lot of questions in Taylor's mind that he might not have otherwise."

Findley inquired, "Do we have suspicions that they are on to something?"

Daniels responded, "Greenwood assured me that there is nothing in their emails or phone calls on cells and office equipment suggesting they are on to anything. He's locked into their cell phones, landlines, e-mail, credit card activity, and the like. There is activity on all, but it's all coming from their office location. Once they make an appearance leaving the office, we will have visual confirmation again and be back on their tail.

"So let's not get paranoid about Daneli this close to the goal line. Even if they are on to the FBI's surveillance of them, the NAPCO irregularities, and the Janitor, what does that give them? I'll tell you what: a headache! And by that, what I mean is this: In what way are they going to act on it? Are they going to tell the FBI or the Craney Island Incident Command?"

"Maybe they'll call the local police. That's about the only level of government that's not represented in the club. It's simply a matter of time before they resurface. And if they are foolish enough to involve any level of political power, we will be so far ahead of them that by that time, they will be behind bars when the shit hits the fan."

Doss interjected, "That reminds me, where are we in the frame of Daneli?"

Daniels reported, "Greenwood told me the case against Daneli is pretty much locked up. He and Yarborough have now expanded their manufacturing of evidence indicating Daneli's complicity to being coconspirators with radical left-wing militant groups aimed at dismantling the US military complex. We understand that such a charge won't stick, but the evidence is enough that there will be just cause to take drastic precautionary measures. That will place them in the crosshairs of the newly amended antiterrorism law and in the custody of Homeland Security. That means that whichever way the intelligence investigation goes, Daneli will be the first folks to be detained and put on ice. If necessary, the president will have the power to send them to Gitmo and withhold legal representation."

Doss exhaled. "Well, that's more like it. I like that."

Findley interjected, "The vice president will love that. He just asked me the other day if they could be taken out of the mix. You all know how much he likes Gitmo as a place where problems evaporate into thin air."

Doss inquired, "OK, that only leaves loose ends. Where do we stand on loose ends, Dan?"

Witherspoon offered, "As you know, neither of the controllers at Richardson or Bragg knows that that the plan includes the fuel igniting. If they do not become toast when the depot ignites, then Mr. Straight will be just beyond the fence to finish them off. And as you know, once Mr. Straight will no longer be needed, he has promised to retire to his Serbian homeland. That is where he has essentially disappeared after his missions for other clients. There is nothing to suggest he will act differently this time."

"Well then," Doss commented. "I guess that only leaves you, Congressman."

Findley reported, "Between the vice president, Bobick, and me, we have stirred up a congressional majority to the point where they will vote for military action first and ask questions later. The campaign rhetoric has already been scripted and is ready to go. The cable news channels are already begging for some insight into the Craney Island event. We have the vice president, NSA Chief Yarborough, and me booked on the network TV shows for Sunday. By the time Fort Richardson catches fire on Monday, the public will be demanding retribution."

"Perfect!" Doss exclaimed. "I can't wait now that we are so close. Dan, please inform the others of our status."

"Will do," Witherspoon replied.

40. COUNTERTERRORISM

VIC MAJESKI ARRIVED IN ANCHORAGE AND MET UP WITH PETTY Officer First Class Kirk Darnell and Stratford. The three of them and a handful of Coast Guard enlisted men who would accompany their movements outside the fort would comprise the team to thwart the suspected sabotage at Fort Richardson/Elmendorf. Vic and Darnell headed toward the fort, and the Coast Guard attachment deployed outside the fort perimeter in case they were needed.

As the advance team for the visit by the former president, they were given a tour of the fort and Air Force base. After the tour and a briefing with the fort's presentation team, they were left on their own for a break before they set up for the visit.

***

At about the same time, Richard Dugan and Louis Milton walked into Eli's cubicle at the PFC. Dugan announced, "We've got the programming done. We've tested it in every way imaginable, and it performs. Both onsite Coast Guard intelligence officers have it packed on their laptops ready for installation at the base. Vic, the Secret Service officer, Stratford, and Darnell have already met in Anchorage and are due to begin their advance inspection at 1330 hours Eastern Standard Time this afternoon. They have two shots to tap into the controllers and get the minicomputer fully connected, online, and hidden before they leave Friday afternoon."

At 1515 hours, Dugan scrambled out of his chair and cubicle and sat next to Lieutenant Furman, operating the main screens in their command center. Vic had just called to say that their connection was complete and the minicomputer was transmitting the programming screen from the Fort Richardson controller. Within seconds and a few keystrokes, Furman had what amounted to a Fortran programming menu on the large overhead monitor.

"Eli!" Dugan shouted. "Get over here! We've got Fort Richardson's controller on our screen!"

Eli dropped what he was doing and walked over to the main console, where Dugan and Furman were seated. Dugan still had Vic standing by and was talking to him on one of the PFC telephones.

"OK, Vic, I'm putting you on speaker. That should do it. Can you hear me?"

"I've got you five-by-five," Vic responded. "Do you have the control panel on the big screen down there?"

"Roger that!"

"OK, now we are going to open up the screen showing the four tanks in the depot. Do you see it?"

"That's a roger, Vic."

"OK, now we will shut down the mini and fire it back up," Vic announced.

The screen went blue for a couple of minutes, with Vic talking throughout, saying that it was still warming up.

"OK, you should be viewing the control panel again."

Before Vic was through speaking, the Fort Richardson control panel appeared on the big screen. Vic ran through all of the various computer commands that controlled the fuel movement, and each played out forward and backward from Fort Richardson to the PFC, and then by Dugan from the PFC to the fort.

"OK, guys," Vic remarked. "We're fully operational. We picked out a nice cubbyhole in the back of the controller cabinet. We're going to hide the mini there—plugged into the wall outlet. Once we get out of here, I'll be back in touch."

With that Vic hung up, and Furman was on the telephone to General Detwiler. When Furman hung up, he said, "Colonel, General Detwiler is coming by. They should arrive by 1700 hours. Attorney General Goodman will be advised and invited to join us."

Vic was back on the telephone at 1650 hours Washington time. "Hey, guys, the advance team and I have left the base, and we are headed to Anchorage for a bite to eat. Man, these guys are real pros! They talked the fort's information officer into allowing us to split up. While Stratford occupied him, Darnell and I wandered out of the welcoming room, out the side door, and headed to the control building. We found the fuel depot control room right where the layout maps indicated. And, as expected, it was unmanned, and no one was milling around outside to notice us. We simply walked in, hooked up the mini, plugged it into the auxiliary port—and in a matter of a few minutes, it was viewing all of the programming screens. Hats off to Furman and Dugan for setting it up."

While Vic was on the phone, the general and Goodman walked in. Eli put Vic back on the speaker as an informal greeting was underway.

"Gentlemen, if you don't mind, I've got Mr. Majeski on the telephone speaker," Eli announced.

Goodman remarked, "That's great! How are you doing, Vic?"

"I'm living large up here by the Arctic Circle, sir."

"I understand that the first part of the mission has been completed," Goodman asserted.

"Yes, sir! I've got some great teammates up here. The fort command runs a tight ship, but we were too slick for them."

"We're going to discuss the rest of the mission with Eli for a little while, and he will be reporting back to you. Is that OK with you?"

"Roger that, sir."

Vic hung up, and the four of them—Colonel Milton, General Detwiler, Goodman, and Eli—sat down and closed the door to the office the general had claimed for his use.

General Detwiler looked at Eli and explained the rest of his operation plans.

"Eli, I want Vic and the rest of the advance team to head back to the fort this afternoon and complete their advance duties. Darnell will be mic'd up. The AG and I have arranged for the CIA to fly a drone under the base radar. It's a mission off the grid that will be viewed from this control center console on a Coast Guard cruiser parked in the bay. It's an exercise that will serve as a dry run for practice purposes. We want to make sure we can see everyone at the fuel depot area and outside the fence. We will be talking one-way only to Darnell as he and Vic walk around the base and at the depot. He will communicate back to us by tapping on the ear mike. I want them to hang around until we tell them to pack it in. It will be a little dangerous if the fort observes the drone."

"I don't think that will be a problem, General. They will be prepared if that occurs."

"OK, we'll stick around here and watch it unfold on the big screen."

It was the first time Eli and Dugan had ever seen a drone in use. They had heard of them and seen pictures on television news, but they had no idea that they were used on domestic missions. It was 1410 in Alaska when word arrived that the drone was over the target area. A few seconds later, an overhead camera shot of the base came into view. It was a partly cloudy day.

Detwiler commented, "That's decent weather for a low-altitude drone."

Before their eyes, the fort became closer and closer as the lens of the drone zoomed in to an ever-increasing close-up. When the zooming stopped and the picture stabilized and sharpened, they could see glowing objects moving inside the buildings.

Detwiler said, "The glowing objects are infrared depictions of the base personnel moving about. Three of the glowing objects are our men on this mission. They should be the ones at the fuel depot operations room at the left."

Lieutenant Furman was now talking into Darnell's earpiece. "Are you inside the base?"

One tap was heard.

Detwiler said, "That's a yes."

"Are you in the depot area?" Furman continued.

A single tap came back.

"Are you with Majeski and Stratford?"

A single tap was heard.

"Are the two other base personnel in the building occupying the corner room opposite the depot operations room?"

One tap was heard. Then Furman opened up a video toolbox and activated a curser on the screen. He moved the curser to where he believed the five men were located and created a visual tag that followed them as they moved around. Everyone looking at the big screen could now identify them and where they were at all times.

"Can you excuse yourself and ask to go outside for a smoke?"

At this point the aspect of the picture changed as it appeared the drone drew closer to the ground, but not so much overhead as off to the side. They could now see the glowing bodies in greater detail. As Darnell walked out of the building and into open view, they could now see his actual torso.

"Please raise your left hand as if you're hailing a cab."

All could clearly see the body that was outside the building was raising an arm.

"Incredible!" Dugan commented.

"Can you hear or see the drone? It is over your left shoulder."

You could see Darnell raise his hand slightly. Two taps came back. The answer was no.

"Thanks, Petty Officer Darnell. Our test is complete. Out."

The assembled group in front of the big screen at the PFC watched Darnell stomp out his cigarette and walk back into the building, to become a semiformless, glowing ball again.

"Pretty impressive," Eli commented.

"It's a tool just beginning to reach its strategic potential," Goodman said. "By the way, the cover story for your work here is our EPA coordinated drills. That's why the mission is named EPA. The Pollution Funds Center is coordinating with the EPA today and tomorrow. So if anyone asks, you were contracted to assist the PFC in the drill."

It was now past eight o'clock Eastern Standard Time, and everyone except the PFC nightshift personnel had left for the evening.

Eli called Harry Meeks from the satellite phone in his hotel room and updated him on events. He asked him to pass it on to

Hank and to ask Hank to pass it on to the rest of the Daneli team and Danielle in Atlanta. Harry complied, saying to everyone that Eli and Vic were enjoying their conference in Houston. He stated that everything was going as planned and that they would be back home Monday afternoon. All of which was obvious code in case someone was listening in, indicating that there was nothing for anyone to worry about.

After dinner, Eli retreated to his hotel room. He called home to tell Danielle that everything was well. In an effort to avoid their phones, Harry had visited with her and explained how the mission was proceeding so she wouldn't worry. Eli, however, was having a rough night. His anxieties about the mission and the risks were weighing heavily on his mind. He had never dealt with anything before that had anywhere near the importance of this matter. So much depended on Vic and him getting it right, and now that they were so close to the climax, he could feel his heart beating faster than normal, or so it seemed.

***

Saturday morning, Lieutenant Furman sounded an alert. Eli and Dugan gathered around the big screen. Someone at Fort Richardson was operating the controller.

Dugan shouted, "It's a drill. The operator is running training protocols. He must be the guy assigned to redirect the shipments."

Eli inquired, "Does he need to sign on?"

"Certainly," Dugan responded. "The static line at the bottom of the screen indicates the operator's name. We are watching the work of R. Baker."

"That's who's going to be the first witness to capture and protect once their plan falls apart," commented Eli.

Eli wrote down his name and called Louis Milton, who said he would pass on the information to General Detwiler. After about a half hour more of practicing his dry run, Baker ended his session and signed off.

Dugan remarked. "I was right. He was just practicing. No programming was altered, and the depot's vital statistics are identical to what they were before Baker's session started. This was a dry run and nothing more."

41. BLOODY SUNDAY

AS CONGRESSMAN FINDLEY HAD PREDICTED, THE SUNDAY MORN-
ing news programs had a red-letter day with their guests dis-
cussing the threat of terrorism. A feeding frenzy ensued, with
one network trying to outdo the other by interviewing as many
high-ranking politicians as possible. Meet The Press led off with
Vice President Calvin Harper predicting that enemies of America
were plotting "at this very moment" to capitalize on America's
failure to increase the pressure on al Qaeda.

When the vice president was questioned about what new evidence he had that had not been released, he waited until the
last possible moment before commenting. When pressed that
the interview was running out of time, he looked directly into
the camera lens with his best sober expression and calmly stated,
"The evidence will eventually point to the hit on the Navy Fuel
Supply Depot at Craney Island, Virginia, as a terrorist attack.
The investigation is still too incomplete for an official report, but
there are enough signs to draw that conclusion."

And as he had anticipated, there wasn't enough time left on
the live program for the newscasters to follow up. As the program

signed off, the smug expression on the vice president's face embodied the arrogant, self-righteous egoism of his seditious partners.

On Face the Nation, NSA Director Stuart Yarborough took over where Harper had left off. When he was asked about the status of the Craney Island investigation, he replied, "It's still unofficial, but Islamic jihad fingerprints are all over it." When pressed to elaborate, he commented, "There are countries out there that feel they have a score to settle with us. Rather than using diplomatic channels, they often choose to turn to terrorism, using untraceable mercenaries and suicide commandos."

Yarborough used the same tactic as Vice President Harper by delaying his best supposition to the very end of the interview time to avoid a cross-examination by the reporters. When the host newscaster finally inquired whether there was evidence connecting the Craney Island event with Iran, Yarborough remarked, "The attack on Craney Island demonstrates that our enemies are getting better intelligence about our military assets, and I don't believe this is a singular attempt. We are on full alert, but we should not remain in the position of defense if we want the Islamic nations to quit utilizing terrorism. We need to go on the offensive to prevent these religiously controlled regimes from carrying out jihad against America."

Congressman Findley's interview on the ABC Sunday World News Report was the pièce de résistance. When the Craney Island event came up during his interview, he stated, "If another attack on US soil occurs similar to that event, we should be prepared to declare war, not only on the responsible nation, but on all Islamic nations that harbor these terrorists or do not actively eradicate these cells that promote terrorism within their borders."

Attorney General Adam Goodman tried to get a meeting with the president to get a reading on his reaction to the interviews.

The president's secretary responded for him: "The president has a full calendar of appointments and meetings." She kept trying to put him off until Monday afternoon. He even tried going to the White House and taking a seat outside his door, hoping to catch his attention when he walked out of his office, but he never took a step outside. And when Vice President Harper had two visits with the president within an hour while Goodman sat there on his thumbs, he realized it was time to try another tactic.

Goodman called Detwiler. The general had a face-to-face with the secretary of defense, Frederick Greene, right after the interviews. The secretary said he was a little miffed that those interviews took place without his consultation beforehand. He told Detwiler that at 0725 hours this morning, he got an email from the president's chief of staff regarding the vice president's and the NSA director's expected remarks—way too late to complain. Detwiler told Goodman that he felt relatively confident that Secretary Greene was not a member of the conspiracy and that they should feel him out to see if he would be willing to join their effort.

By Sunday evening, and before Goodman and Detwiler could arrange a meeting with Secretary Greene, every US news broadcast was carrying portions of the earlier interviews as their lead story.

At 1830 hours on Sunday, Eli Taylor received a call from Louis Milton requesting he attend a meeting at the Pentagon, the only place that Secretary Greene would agree to meet. Although Goodman did not want to be noticed visiting with the secretary, he felt he had to take the chance no one would be paying attention on a late Sunday afternoon.

Eli Taylor sensed he was in deep water with these fellows. He had never been to the Pentagon, and this was not a social visit.

Eli had no fucking idea why he was included, except to connect some dots for the secretary. He rode there with Colonel Milton. Together they found their way to the secretary's office. Milton waited outside when Taylor, Goodman, and Detwiler were invited to enter the secretary's office. Secretary Green asked, "So what's this all about?"

General Detwiler responded, "I'm taking a chance, sir, a real risk to my career. I have been following an incredible story that has to be considered at your level of authority. I got the impression I could relate it to you when I spoke to you earlier about the morning news interviews on TV. I sensed that you were caught off guard by the accusations and insinuations that we are under attack by Islamic terrorism. I am betting that you are not a part of this campaign to incite the public with this false impression. You see, the reason I am here is that neither the attorney general nor I are a part of this campaign. In fact, sir, the men sitting beside me have aided me in uncovering a conspiracy among members of the military, politicians, and the president's cabinet who are trying to incite military retribution against the Islamic nations of the world. And this is no kind of conspiracy you might imagine. It includes the sabotage and destruction of our military assets to drum up irrational support. Do you wish for me to continue, sir?"

The secretary paused, looked at everyone eye-to-eye, and replied, "Please proceed, General."

For the first time, Eli heard how the general and the AG had gotten involved. Then he related to the secretary the entire account of Daneli's findings and what had been discovered since they had looked further into the potential of a high-level government conspiracy behind the events they were investigating. After Detwiler explained where they stood with regard to the scheduled deliveries to Elmendorf AFB/Fort Richardson, the secretary sat motionless and silent for what seemed to be an awkward amount of time. And then, without commenting, he picked up the phone on his desk, dialed a number, and spoke.

He inquired, "Are you in a position to meet me at my office right now?"

After a pause, he said, "I've got AG Goodman, General Forrest Detwiler, and the leader of the company that led the Craney Island investigation."

Secretary Greene then listened for a few seconds and hung up. Eli Taylor's brain was in a quiet panic. The dominant thought was that armed military men would be entering the office to seize him and haul him off to a dungeon in the bowels of the Pentagon, if there was such a place.

Staring at each one of his visitors for a moment, and after getting more comfortable in his chair, Greene told them something they all were surprised to hear.

"Forrest, you've got brass balls to take a chance like you did by telling me this story. That's a trait I wish I possessed. Gentlemen! We have a schism so deep and vitriolic in this administration that it's gotten to the extent that fear mongering has become the order of the day. It all started at the beginning of the year. I got a visit from two members of the Joint Chiefs of Staff. They were trying to convince me that I should join their effort to persuade the president to threaten military action against Iran. I was against it and told them so. They warned me that I was making a mistake that I would regret. Within the next few days, I got a call from VP Harper saying virtually the same thing.

"Next I got calls from two cabinet members saying they were strong-armed by the same guys trying to strong-arm me. The three of us started getting left off the invitation list to events we were accustomed to attending. We began to hear about meetings that should have included us. Just recently, rumors were being whispered that the president was interviewing replacements for our positions. The president stopped consulting me. Quite frankly, we merely thought this was just politics, and the president wanted his cabinet to think more the way he did. When the Craney Island event occurred amid rumors of terrorism and I was taken out of the loop, I began to worry that it was something more. Things just didn't add up."

As Secretary Greene was making that last comment, they heard someone walking toward the office. The door opened to reveal Cynthia Branch, the secretary of state. All stood, and Secretary Greene made the introductions.

"Madam Secretary, you know General Detwiler and the attorney general, and this gentleman is Eli Taylor. He is the CEO of Daneli Crisis Management. His company is the lead consultant in the Craney Island investigation."

Secretary Branch smiled and shook Eli's hand, then shook the hands of the other three men.

She sat down, cleared her throat, and turned to face Secretary Greene. "I am so glad that someone else has come forward."

Secretary Branch then focused her attention on Eli and Attorney General Goodman. And Eli was getting a full demonstration why she was so effective as the main US diplomat to the other nations of the world.

"After your call to Secretary Greene to make this meeting, he called me about the prospects of what he hoped it was about. I understand that our wishes have come true. Is that right, Secretary Greene?"

"Oh yes, Madam Secretary. And these men came armed with proof and evidence of a conspiracy so sinister, insidious, and revolting that we must take action immediately. However, I want you to hear all of it again from their mouths."

This time General Detwiler asked Eli to take the beginning, and he would wrap it up. Twenty minutes later, after they had told their story, Secretary Branch remarked, "My God, the inmates are running the asylum!"

Secretary Greene interjected, "You have our full support and influence. Do you have a plan, gentlemen?"

Detwiler and Green looked at each other, and Goodman stated, "That is where we come up a little short, sir. Mr. Taylor has some good ideas of what we will need to get started. Please proceed, Eli."

Eli took a deep breath and gathered himself. He dived into the Craney Island investigation and then into the murders of Calloway, French, Matusak, and Cohen. At this point, however, Eli planted a safety device that he had gotten permission to use before they entered the meeting. It was an alternate version of how they planned to thwart the plot to blow up Fort Richardson, just in case Greene was really on the other side.

"We have collected evidence of the operatives who performed all of these murders and terroristic acts, and we have uncovered a plot to destroy two more military fuel-supply facilities in the next few days in a similar fashion that they carried out at Craney Island. We are assisting the attorney general and General Detwiler to scuttle their plans by detaining the fort's fuel movements operator and substituting our man to take his place. We have the names of most of the implementers. Unless Attorney General Goodman and General Detwiler have more information that I am not privy to, what we don't have is hard evidence connecting the leaders with the actual crimes."

Secretary Greene inquired of Goodman and Detwiler, "Do

you have anybody involved who can connect the implementers with those who are giving the orders?"

Detwiler answered, "After tomorrow morning, we expect to have in custody the man expected to perform the next act of sabotage at Fort Elmendorf in Alaska. His name is PFC Raymond Baker, and if we are successful in having him detained, cloistered, and protected, you should have a live witness and a conspirator ready to squeal. Getting him away from his base and away from the conspirators is something I expect you can help us perform."

Greene next looked at Attorney General Goodman and asked, "Do you have any idea what will be necessary to bring the rest of the conspirators to justice before we are arrested by the conspirators and charged with treason? It appears to me to be a contest of whom the public and law enforcement believe."

"I believe," remarked Secretary Branch, "you have eloquently described our dilemma. The television interviews this morning were not only designed to gain more support for a military solution to the terrorist threat, it was to gain the support of the nation against detractors, naysayers, and whistleblowers."

Goodman commented, "We certainly don't have time to launch a public relations campaign before tomorrow when they attempt to blow up Fort Richardson's fuel depot."

Greene said, "What it will eventually come down to is a showdown of accusations, no matter how you try to play it. I think I can find enough men under me to detain and sequester some of the leaders and their supporters for at least a couple of days. General Detwiler, how confident are you that you can collect PFC Baker from Fort Richardson as soon as he attempts to overrun the fuel depot tanks?"

Detwiler replied, "I don't think that will be a problem. Keeping him is. And we will also have to hide him."

"And," added Goodman, "if we are all fired while all this is going on and nobody complains, that will be the least of our problems."

Eli then blurted out, "That's it! I think I've got it. Do you all remember when Nixon tried to fire the special prosecutor looking into his dirty tricks campaign? That was when his house of cards collapsed, and he resigned. It was called the Saturday Night Massacre. If you remember, the Watergate special prosecutor, Archibald Cox, demanded the president turn over evidence. Nixon refused. And when Nixon asked the attorney general to fire the special prosecutor and he wouldn't, Nixon threatened to fire him and the assistant AG, who also refused.

"When the facts were made public that Nixon's administration was trying to hide evidence and pressure cabinet members to do his bidding, the media came down on Nixon and his administration. Soon thereafter all the political polls indicated that the majority of Americans favored Nixon's impeachment. We have a similar situation here. If you want my opinion, you have to believe in the workings of our democratic republic. The media will shine so much light on the conspirators that the vice president will resign because the media will turn the country against him and his followers. Then everyone else will run for cover or turn themselves in. All we have to do is make our accusation first and be prepared to justify it."

The room went deadly silent. After a few moments, Secretary Branch spoke. "Fred, you know in your heart he's right."

Secretary Greene couldn't look at her or anyone else in the room. He just stared at the floor.

In a soft voice that was accompanied by tears, Secretary Branch uttered, "Gentlemen, we've been wrestling with this dilemma for some time. Until you came before us, we just couldn't find the evidence or allies needed to stand up to their mounting campaign. I'll work up a speech for a press conference for tomorrow after the attempt at Fort Richardson is squelched and the capture of PFC Baker is behind us. I think it's safest to set the event at the State Department. We can stay in the building without fear of compromise or arrest while word gets to the VP and his collaborators that the jig is up. Can you all make it here right after you get word that Baker is secure?"

Goodman spoke first. "No problem, Madam Secretary."

"I'll come with Mr. Taylor as soon as we get word," replied General Detwiler.

"And you, Secretary Greene?"

"Yes, Cynthia, I'll be the first one there."

Secretary Branch then asked, "Is everyone here in agreement?" They all voiced their agreement.

Secretary Branch continued, "Are you all prepared to stick this out and suffer the consequences if we are not successful?"

Again the group indicated their agreement.

She finally commented, "Let's pray that everything goes well tomorrow. We need luck to be on our side."

Secretary Branch, Attorney General Adam Goodman, General Detwiler, and Eli Taylor exchanged emergency contact information and left.

Their fates were now in the hands of each other's trust. In less than twenty-four hours, they would either be heroes or traitors.

That evening, Eli was on the satellite phone with Matthew Berg. He brought him up to date, and Berg and Andropolis called him back later.

"Eli, we're going to have the entire story ready to air just as soon as the Secretary of State's news conference is over. We've made arrangements with two cable news shows to be in their studio at that time. We'll have a copy of the next day's headlines in print with us to get it on camera.

"So that is your safety net, and I'll have an insurance policy of my own in case you get blindsided or double-crossed."

42. THE PROVERBIAL SHIT HITS THE FAN

LATE THE SAME EVENING, THE DOSS BROTHERS WERE HUDDLED with their generals, Greenwood and Art Daniels. Last-minute plans were being made.

Daniels was giving them the status of their preparations.

"Everyone is in place, ready to perform. From the tactical end, everything is a go."

Then it was Greenwood's turn. "We have not located Daneli's Taylor and Majeski, but we have gotten wind to what they are up to. Our sources say they have been recruited by the attorney general to try to fuck us over. They are somewhere in Washington, DC. The vice president's old nemesis, General Detwiler, has spent a lot of time with Goodman, and we can expect that they are plotting together."

Greenwood continued, "Ellingson and Yarborough figured as much when Detwiler got interested in the Craney Island incident after that Matusak guy had to be eliminated. We don't know what they are up to or how much they know, but we can expect they know about Fort Richardson and that they will try to prevent us from succeeding with our plans. That means we need to activate and deploy our fail-safe measures.

"Daneli's men have walked right into position to take a large portion of the blame when the tanks go up in smoke. We have camera footage of their Vic Majeski nosing around the base and fuel depot with the sham advance team that arrived on Friday to prepare for a visit by ex-president William Bailey. We can expect Majeski and his advance team are there to prevent our man Baker from overflowing the tanks. Majeski was a pipeline operator at one time, and we were told that he plans to substitute for Baker after they capture and detain him.

"We have alerted the base command that we have picked up terrorist plans to commandeer the fuel-delivery process and destroy the tanks. Majeski and his cohorts will be detained once they arrive in the morning to resume their advance team preparations. We'll be waiting for them and put them in the brig."

MONDAY MORNING, NOVEMBER 26, 0900 HOURS, ALASKA TIME

By the time the Monday morning news shows hit the air, the overnight polls were indicating an average of 70 percent of their audiences were favoring a military response to the Craney Island event. Eli Taylor sat watching the TV in the Pollution Fund Center along with General Detwiler, Colonel Milton, and Dugan.

The advance team that Vic was a part of notified the base that they would not be able to arrive until the afternoon. That call was made at 0830 hours Monday, one hour and thirty-five minutes before the fuel was to be delivered. It took a while for that information to reach the Doss brothers and their conspirators in their East Coast command center at the Doss estate. Apparently, the base personnel receiving the call about the rescheduling did not know the significance of that fact. Not until the acting base commander got a call from his superior, General McEwen, wondering why he hadn't been notified of the capture of the advance crew, did he realize this significance. General McEwen told the base commander, who was busy with other matters and recovering from a hangover, that he had better get on the stick unless he wanted to be transferred to the North Pole. That was when the base commander started asking about the advance team. It was a while before they connected all the dots. By that time, the delivery was about to commence.

1100 HOURS

Everyone on both sides of this drama were now in place, like two teams preparing for battle. In the PFC, the drone's camera showed that PFC Ray Baker was sitting in front of the controller's CRT screen in the Fort Richardson/Elmendorf AFB Fuel Supply Depot control room.

On the main screen at the PFC, the video also indicated someone was sitting in a deer blind just outside the fort's perimeter. It was positioned about fifteen feet above natural grade, two hundred yards from the base's perimeter fence. A high-powered rifle was cradled in a man's arms as he sat quietly in the blind.

Vic and the Coast Guard detail approached Fort Richardson in two vehicles, and they were positioned five hundred yards behind the man in the blind. Stratford's cell phone rang. It was General Detwiler advising him of an unidentified potential adversary in a tree blind just ahead of them. The detail moved forward, advancing quietly on the base entrance.

In the distance was a white Nissan Pathfinder parked off the road. They suspected the vehicle was being used by the man in the tree blind. They stopped to look for the man the drone had observed. They turned off the motors of their vehicles, and Vic got out of his Yukon SUV and climbed atop it with binoculars in his possession. As he was lying on his belly while scanning the territory between him and the base gate, his Coast Guard buddies did the same. Within seconds, Vic spotted the blind. There was a man inside it, holding a rifle, and as he watched, he saw him occasionally looking in a telescopic lens pointed in the direction of the fuel depot.

Vic whispered to his comrades, "I see him. In the deer blind at two o'clock, about fifteen feet up in a tree. I'll be damned! It's Kravitz. That's the guy who took out Craney Island."

In a matter of moments, they were all observing Eugene Kravitz in the tree blind.

Vic inquired, "Do we have a marksman here?"

From the detail came a response: "I'm qualified."

Vic asked him, "Do you think you can disable him without killing him?"

"Yes, sir," was the reply.

"OK, you keep your sights on him. That's what I want you to do on my order or if he prepares to fire his weapon."

"Roger that, sir."

The Coast Guard detail was armed with high-powered rifles and telescopic sights. They put away their binoculars and began to observe the scene through their scopes.

At the same time Elmendorf AFB was receiving a request from Air Force Flight 41, a C-141B Starlifter aircraft from Hickam AFB in Hawaii scheduled to land at 1110 hours.

Back on the mainland, two assembled groups were patiently waiting. One was at the Doss brothers' estate, where Admiral Ellingson, Art Daniels, and the Dosses were on the phone with the others. The other group was gathered around a speakerphone in a private office owned by the Bobick Law Firm. Present were Stuart Yarborough, Daniel Greenwood, General McEwen, and Congressman Findley. The desk speakerphone was on. The voice on the other end of the phone was Fort Richardson's acting commander, General Hayworth, explaining that the advance team called to say they would not arrive until the afternoon. They asked the general to hang up but stand by the phone. Wingate Doss, connected to the call from his East Coast estate, was irate again.

"What is the significance of this, Greenwood?"

Greenwood was the object of their disappointment once more. Only this time he had no slick reply. After stammering, he muttered, "I suppose they are not as far along as I was led to believe. Maybe their trip is merely a recon mission."

"You're pathetic," Wingate Doss shouted. "Well, gentlemen, do we proceed or abort?"

General McEwen chimed in. "It may be too late to abort. The delivery procedure is underway."

A quick look at their watches confirmed that it was 1106, Anchorage time. Daniels announced, "I'm calling Kravitz on my cell phone. General, get General Hayworth back on the speaker. Let's get some eyes on what's going on down there."

At the Pollution Funds Center were Eli Taylor, Colonel Milton, General Detwiler, and Adam Goodman, with Dugan and Furman operating the main console. The big screen had the feed from the drone hovering over the fort. The picture was decent but not ideal. Vic had relayed the confirmation of the Kravitz sighting, and on the PFC display screens, there was a cursor flashing at Kravitz's location in the deer blind on the screen. Another cursor indicated the presence of R. Baker in the control room. A third cursor indicated the position of Vic and the Coast Guard detail. On the secondary screen beside the main screen was the view of the CRT controller screen—duplicating what was visible on the fuel depot's CRT screen. Appearing on the bottom scroll was the session information indicating the operator, R. Baker, had logged on.

Dugan announced, "It's Baker again. This time it doesn't appear to be a drill. He is overriding the current orders of how the deliveries will be received. Now he is altering the automatic data stream from the sensoring equipment coming in from the tanks and resetting the tank volumes. And now he is revising the receiving orders to direct the flow into the tanks that are already full of product."

Eli took a photo of the big screen. Dugan asked, "Why take the photo?"

Eli replied, "I want evidence that Baker was at the controller."

Dugan advised him, "The controller will record the session and Baker's alterations."

"Not if something goes wrong at our end, and the fuel depot suffers the same fate as Craney Island."

"I see your point. That's one of the reasons you're the boss. Sorry about that."

Baker executed all of the commands to set the overflows in motion. The drone's overhead view indicated that Baker was still in the control room but that he had moved away from the control panel. Dugan waited a few minutes to make sure Baker wasn't going back to the controller to verify he had made the alterations properly. Upon being satisfied that Baker was finished, Dugan took over control of the controller. His actions and keystrokes were programmed into the mini, but they were hidden from the dialogue box at the bottom of the fort's CRT screen. In a matter of seconds, he reset the tank volumes by removing the programmed override Baker had entered. Once the override was gone, the tanks accurately indicated the volumes reported by the tank sensors. All was back to where it had been before Baker's latest session.

At 1110 hours, the computer screens of the controller at the fort and at the PFC were indicating an incoming delivery. The main valve opened, and a stream of aviation kerosene was pushed toward tank number three. PFC Raymond Baker was observing from a window in the control building. He glanced at the CRT screen indicating the operation of valves and the movement of the delivery. Suddenly, he was in a panic because the valve symbol to tank three was flashing, not the valve to tank number two. That meant the delivery was not going to the tank he had just programmed. Baker sat back down at the controls and called up the programming screen. He saw the original nomination and orders, not the ones he had programmed moments before.

Baker called the port operator and told him that there was an emergency at the fuel depot that would require a temporary suspension of the delivery. The port operator complied and shut down the pumps and closed the valve to the delivery line.

Both Baker and those assembled in the PFC watched the resequencing on the terminal screen as Baker punched the keystrokes.

Dugan said, "Baker is reprogramming the delivery into tank number two."

That done, Baker called the port controller and advised him to resume the delivery. As he was talking to the port operator, Baker noticed that his screen on the CRT was changing before his eyes. Dugan, back at the PFC, was overriding the commands Baker had just entered.

Baker was now in a stupor, watching his controller screen act as if it had a mind of its own. It took about three minutes for the port operator to reopen the valves and ramp up the pumps to resume delivery to the fort. Once this was done, the pipeline pressures aligned properly to allow the movement of fuel toward the fort again. By that time, Dugan had overwritten all of the commands Baker had entered just minutes before. Baker watched the tank volume indicator showing the level on number three was increasing. Tank number two remained idle. In a panic, Baker walked outside the control room and ran toward tanks two and three. Tank number two was not overflowing, the identical indication on the controller screen.

Baker ran back inside the control room and called General McEwen's cell phone.

"Something's gone wrong with the delivery! I can't figure it out. Nothing's working properly. The system's got a mind of its own."

"Get a hold of yourself, Private. Stay put while I figure this out," McEwen barked.

General McEwan announced he had the operator at Anchorage on his phone. "Gentlemen, we have a problem. The operator in Anchorage says the delivery system is not operating properly. He's in a panic."

McEwen explained what had happened at the base. After a short debate, McEwen related his advice to Baker. "Private, we'll have to allow the completion of the delivery at Richardson as is. After that, we can reconstruct what went wrong when I get there. Report to your barracks after the delivery is finished, but on the way back to the barracks I want you to drive close to tank number three to confirm it's full with fuel."

After McEwen hung up, the room erupted in agitated argument. McEwen was embarrassed by the failure of his operation to go as planned. Greenwood was red-faced and silent. Kravitz was ordered to head back to his hotel room and await new orders. The Doss brothers were livid. It was clear to them that the Daneli Company was behind what was transpiring in Alaska and that Greenwood had misled them.

Findley was going ballistic. "So, ex-division chief, Mr. Greenwood, you lose track of these guys, and four days later, our operation is scuttled. How's that for a coincidence! Are you still convinced they are so far behind they can't be a problem? Do you want to bet me they have nothing to do with this screw up? If you have any sense at all, you should be looking for a one-way ticket to a country without US reciprocity. Got any friends in Cuba or Russia?"

Art Daniels interrupted the shouting and said, "We have to initiate Operation Failsafe."

Wingate responded, "What for? We don't have that son of bitch Majeski and the advance team in custody as you predicted."

Daniels was now upset and shouted back. "Not all of Failsafe considers having the Daneli folks in custody. We've got one more ace up our sleeve. The vice president, the secretary of defense, and the secretary of state are standing by to announce a news conference at one thirty. They are going to say that they were part of a sting by the Defense Department to catch Daneli in the act of terrorism and treason. Daneli, Goodman, and Detwiler are under the impression that the news conference will implicate us, but it's they who will be accused. The only thing that's gone wrong is that the fuel depot in Anchorage didn't blow up exactly as we had planned. Instead of a tank overflow we can still blow it up. With Daneli in the bag and our frame of them working with Iran, everything will still work out. Have a little faith."

Findley suddenly realized a problem. "We can't let them capture Baker! Tell the Janitor to take him out."

"Don't worry, gentleman, I've got it all covered. Did you forget we have Baker's jeep ready to explode on our command? All we have to do is tell Kravitz to initiate the phone-activated trigger. If he's parked next to the full tank the explosion will damage the tank, ignite the tank's contents and kill Baker. That will be just as good as Baker overfilling the tank, Now, ask Kravitz if Baker followed our order to return to tank three.

Kravitz confirmed that Baker was standing next to tank three. An order was given and he placed the call. The jeep exploded. The sound of the explosion was audible on the other end of the phone connection. The conspirators at the Doss estate rejoiced

All eyes at the base were now focused on the drama. Kravitz reported to his accomplices that only Baker's jeep blew up, but he could not be heard over the celebration.

Vic was doing the same thing. "Holy shit!" Vic reported. "I think someone took out a vehicle on the base parking lot. All hell is breaking loose."

The drone's video was focused on the delivery facility, and everyone at the PFC could clearly see that Baker's jeep blew up, but Baker was nowhere near it. There was only one flaw in Daniels' revised plan. He forgot to confirm that Baker drove his jeep next to tank three. Baker did go to the tank, but did so on foot, leaving his jeep in the parking lot.

Baker was visible on the PFC video, starting to run toward the fort's barracks, but armed fort personnel were running out of the building, heading in his direction. He changed course and headed back to the control building as everyone else was heading for the burning jeep.

Kravitz was screaming into his cell phone, and Daniels finally heard him.

"What are you saying," Daniels shouted back.

"Only the jeep blew up. Baker and the tanks are unharmed."

Daniels was confused, but he had enough wits left to order Kravitz to take out Baker.

Vic was observing Kravitz observing Baker. When he saw Kravitz aim his rifle at the base he realized the drama wasn't over.

Through his binoculars, he saw Kravitz clearly. His rifle was equipped with a silencer. Vic saw it recoil from a shot. He looked back at the fuel depot through his binoculars and saw a bullet hole in the window to the control building. Vic realized that their star witness may have been shot.

Vic shouted, "Kravitz is shooting at the controller! We need to stop him before our star witness is killed! You have authority to fire at the man in the blind."

The marksman fired his weapon. But Kravitz was leaving the blind, and the shot missed him. The sound of the rifle shot and a bullet hitting the blind surprised Kravitz. His rifle fell to the ground as he climbed down the tree. He left the rifle there as he ran toward his vehicle.

Vic shouted at the Coast Guard marksman, "Quick now, let me borrow your pistol!"

The marksman took off his pistol and holster and handed it to Vic as Vic said, "Follow me, guys. I'm going to nail this asshole."

Vic jumped into his vehicle and tore after Kravitz. As Vic picked up the trail of tire tracks, the weather took a turn for the worse. A modest blizzard was growing around the base. The snowfall reduced the drone's visibility to zero. Now both sides were blind as to what was occurring at the base.

Due to the lack of visibility, the drone was ordered home. But before it departed, its cameras focused one last time on the control building as it flew in its direction. At the PFC, they were able to see Baker running out of the control building and toward the fort's barracks. He appeared to be uninjured. Apparently, Kravitz had missed his target.

Back at the PFC, there was eager anticipation that things were falling into place. Within a few minutes, Detwiler was on his phone calling Major Kip Brennan, who headed up a commando squad of Air Force personnel from Hawaii. They were the occupants of the Air Force C-141B Starlifter aircraft that had recently arrived at Elmendorf from Hickam AFB in Hawaii. During the drama at the fuel depot, Brennan and his squad had deplaned and were speaking with the base commander. Brennan advised General Hayworth of his mission: to take Private Baker into custody. Hayworth asked Brennan to stay outside his office while he made a call. Hayworth called his commander's cell phone, and General McEwen answered in a tone indicating he was agitated.

Hayworth asked, "Do you know anything about what's going on out here?"

McEwen had kept Hayworth in the dark and wasn't about to let him see the light now. McEwen had just been informed that only the jeep exploded, and he was in no mood to talk to Hayworth.

McEwen barked, "What the hell are you talking about, General?"

Hayworth was aware of McEwen's selection of Baker to be trained to conduct the fuel movements at the base, but he was ignorant of all the shenanigans going on. He sensed he was in the middle of something rotten. He told McEwen, "Go fuck yourself!" and hung up.

386

Before he would turn over Baker, Hayworth wanted to visit with him. He examined the orders again, noting they were signed by General Detwiler and Secretary Greene. He decided to fetch Baker himself. Hayworth had no dog in this fight, and he was in ass-saving mode. Detwiler outranked McEwen, and the secretary of defense's signature was enough authority to override whatever McEwen had in mind. He turned over Baker to the major.

While Baker was being detained, the weather in Anchorage remained at blizzard condition. Even with the head start Kravitz had and the weather, Vic was hot on his trail and the Coast Guard detail was not far behind. Meanwhile, Kravitz pulled off the road and into the woods, waiting to see if he was being followed. When he saw no pursuers, he called Art Daniels, who wanted to know if he had completed his mission.

"What about Baker, the fuel delivery operator?"

Kravitz replied, "I think I got him, but I wasn't able to confirm it. Someone was shooting at me, just missing me. It was the sound of a long-range rifle. I had to get out of there. I was barely able to make it to my vehicle without being shot. I think they either decided not to chase me or I lost them in the heavy snow that is falling."

"All right, that's all you can do for us right now. I think it's best that you get out of there. Call me when you are in a safe haven."

As Kravitz pulled back onto the roadway, Vic's larger and heavier Yukon SUV rammed his rear left bumper, sending Kravitz's Pathfinder in a spin and into a ditch.

"Take that, motherfucker!" Vic shouted as if reliving the episode he had had with Cota on the Dulles highway. Only this time, Vic was determined to finish off Kravitz there and then. He skidded to a halt. Looking into his rearview mirror, he watched the Pathfinder spinning its tires in the snowy ditch paralleling the road. He put the Yukon in reverse, and when he sensed his tires had full traction, he sped up and rammed the Pathfinder again.

Still peering in the rearview mirror, Vic eyed the groggy Kravitz crawl out the driver's side door and stumble to the ground. Vic, with pistol in hand, exited his vehicle and slowly walked toward the helpless Kravitz. Vic was all business. As Kravitz raised his hand, perhaps appealing to be spared, Vic stopped and put three bullets in him—the first in the forehead, the second in the chest, and the third in the pubic region as he shouted, "The last one was for Ann Calloway. Rot in hell, asshole!"

Kravitz lay there lifeless; however, Vic placed fingers on his carotid artery. There was no pulse. At that moment the Coast Guard detail approached. They carried the carcass of Kravitz over to Vic's Yukon and dumped him in the rear cargo area.

In the meantime, Brennan's squad, with PFC Baker in tow, departed for their awaiting aircraft. Moments later, he and his party were inside the Starlifter and took off, heading for Hickam AFB in Hawaii.

Vic called Eli on his cell phone and filled him in. He was so full of himself that Eli couldn't get him to settle down so he could understand all the details. At the end of his narration, Vic said, "Hey, boss, we caught a huge break. Luckily for us, Kravitz is not infallible. If he were a better marksman, Baker might be lying stiff in the fuel depot control room. Instead, Kravitz is lying stiff in the backseat."

Brennan called Detwiler and relayed the news that Baker was onboard, unharmed, and en route to Hickam. And when Detwiler announced the news, an instantaneous celebration ensued at the PFC. Eli found a quiet office, called Isadore Andropolis at the New York Times, and advised him of their victory.

***

Back in the Doss residence, the assembly was getting nervous about the status of Baker. McEwen called General Hayworth in Anchorage. Hayworth, however, had retreated to his quarters and was halfway through a bottle of Johnny Walker Red Label Scotch. He saw it was McEwen on his phone, but he ignored the call.

"Fuck you, McEwen!" he shouted in derision. He raised the bottle of liquor and said, "Here's to you for not telling me about your little scheme. I hope that whatever you had in mind backfired, you asshole."

Without knowing the fate of Baker, the Hero Club authorized Operation Failsafe, and they called the vice president and Secretary Branch.

MONDAY, 1222 HOURS

General Detwiler notified Goodman of the outcome in Anchorage. Goodman relayed the message to Secretary Branch and Greene, who were in their separate offices. Cynthia Branch was now in a quandary as to what to do. Both sides were claiming victory. Secretary Branch had prepared two opposing press releases: one for the success of Operation Scalawag and one for its defeat. It was her plan to maneuver to take the winning side, thereby double-crossing one of the sides.

Goodman told Colonel Milton and Eli Taylor to leave for the State Department. He expected that the drama was finally over—or was it?

In Washington, as Branch was mulling over what to do, her

secretary advised her that the New York Times editor, Isadore Andropolis, wanted to see her, and that he was standing in front of her desk.

She knew Andropolis well and couldn't imagine why he'd show up without calling. But she needed time to figure things out.

"Tell him I can't see him now."

After a pause, her secretary responded, "He says it's urgent. He says it's about Eli Taylor and Anchorage."

Cynthia Branch was a very sharp lady with a cool head. She was wondering if Andropolis was about to let her know which way she needed to go with her press conference.

"OK, show him in."

After a cordial greeting, Andropolis got down to business.

"I've got something you need to see."

Out of a folder he was carrying, he pulled out a page of newsprint. "It's the headline of tomorrow's paper."

It read, CONSPIRACY PLOT FOILED, VICE PRESIDENT, CONGRESSMAN FINDLEY, AND OTHERS ACCUSED.

"Cynthia, I'm on my way to CBS's studio. They want me on their broadcast to share my comments about your press conference. I just wanted to make sure that nobody has gotten to you, threatened you, or demanded that you change your mind. Our reporter, Matthew Berg, who's been in touch with Eli Taylor ever since he figured out what the conspiracy was all about, is on his way to CNN. We are both going to say that you and Secretary Greene are unsung heroes in thwarting the conspiracy. However, we will be prepared with a complete, blow-by-blow account of the conspiracy, implicating everyone, and I mean everyone, should your press conference go in the wrong direction. Since we are friends, I felt you needed to know what we are up to."

In her best acting persona, she calmly responded, "You are such a dear, Isadore. I didn't know that you had a role in this, but I have been quite impressed with Mr. Taylor. He chose the right guy to assist him. You needn't fret about what I have prepared for the press conference. However, if you'd like an advance copy, I can have my secretary make an extra copy."

"That would be wonderful. That way I can refer to it in my on-air remarks without having to remember every word. You are such a treasure."

Before Andropolis left with a copy of her statement, they hugged, and Cynthia asked, "Can you and Ruth come by later this week for a drink? I'd love to share all the gory details with you."

"We'd love that, Cynthia. Take care."

Andropolis departed, and Secretary Branch called Secretary Greene, explaining what Andropolis was ready to do. Branch and Greene were originally aligned with the conspirators, but they were never enthusiastic supporters, and they were too politically savvy not to protect themselves. They had made a pact to bail out if the scheme fell apart. That time had come. Greene agreed to support her against the coup attempt. After the call, she pulled an envelope out of her desk. She placed it in the hands of her secretary. "Please summon a diplomatic courier to take this to the president at the White House."

Concurrently, her aides were on the phones to all the major news outlets advising them of a press conference to be held at the State Department at 1:30 p.m. (EST).

MONDAY, 1255 HOURS

A State Department diplomatic courier arrived at the White House, carrying the resignation of Madam Secretary Cynthia Branch. Affixed to the envelope was a handwritten note reading, "To be opened before her 1:30 p.m. press conference." Four minutes later, Secretary Green's resignation arrived at the White House, also in a sealed envelope.

Ten minutes earlier, President Herbert Bennett had called Vice President Harper to visit him in the Oval Office. Harper was at the White House awaiting word from Anchorage on Operation Scalawag. Congressman Findley had already called and told him about the Hero Club's version of the outcome of the operation. Harper walked into the Oval Office, closed the door, and discussed the nonevent at the fuel supply depot at Fort Elmendorf with the president.

"Calvin, why don't you stick around and watch the news conference with me?" the president inquired.

"Certainly, Mr. President. I would be pleased to do so."

In complete silence, the president read what was inside the envelopes from Secretaries Branch and Greene. He kept the news to himself as they waited.

MONDAY, 1330 HOURS

Secretary of State Cynthia Branch entered the small press briefing room at the State Department. At her side was Secretary Greene. The room was jam-packed. An eerie air of anticipation and foreboding filled the room. Her aides were distributing her written statement as she took the podium.

Secretary Branch quietly cleared her throat and began reading from the printed statement.

"Today, November twenty-seventh, 2006, I, Secretary of State Cynthia Branch, have tendered my resignation to President Bennett. Secretary of Defense Frederick Greene, standing by my side, has done the same. These letters of resignation are now in his hands to do with as he sees fit."

Back at the White House, a stunned Vice President Harper stood up and gasped, "What? No, no, this can't be!"

Slowly Harper sat back down and watched the television in silence.

Breaking the silence, the president turned to Harper and said, "Apparently, your ship has sailed and left you at the dock. I will be separating myself from the rest of your comrades. If I were you, I'd try to reposition myself on the winning side of this fiasco."

The televised news conference continued as Secretary Branch was saying, "I have agonized over this decision over several months. The president and I hold differing opinions on matters of state, relationships with foreign governments, and general policy. These differences have grown wider and sharper in recent days.

"Over the same several months, other members of the cabinet and administration have become distant and difficult. These differences have come to a head in the past few days, beginning with the incident at the Navy's Craney Island Fuel Supply Depot on November sixth.

"The facts are clear and unequivocal, and they are well documented by an independent source charged with the responsibility to investigate the cause. Contrary to what you heard yesterday on several news outlets, no foreign power, country, or terrorist group was behind the Craney Island incident. The Navy, Coast

Guard, FBI, Homeland Security, and NSA have the same reports as I hold. The president and the vice president have been fully briefed on all aspects of the event and its investigation.

"In opposition to these facts, the vice president, NSA Director Yarborough, and Congressman Findley made statements on national news programs airing yesterday insinuating that the Craney Island incident was the result of al-Qaeda, Iran, or Islamic terrorists. Their statements were not only untrue, it is my opinion they were made to incite the American public against the nations of Islam and terroristic organizations led by Islamic factions."

In Bobick's office, there was an eerie silence. Findley, Greenwood, McEwen, and Yarborough were glued to the television picture, but Bobick had seen enough. He walked into his private anteroom and called his office manager to assemble some staff to escort his visitors to the parking garage. Then Bobick sat down in front of his computer and started deleting everything that might link him to the Hero Club.

Secretary Branch's statement continued, "I am not privy to their motives, but such extreme measures, misdeeds, murders, and treasonous acts do not escape my ability to draw the conclusion that they were not perpetrated merely to influence policy. We can only assume such extreme acts of sedition were meant for a more drastic and extreme retaliation.

"As of this morning, an event similar to what happened at Craney Island was attempted at another US military base by the same perpetrators. The attorney general and General Forrest Detwiler, however, were on to this potential before it occurred. The private investigators who worked the Craney Island event have been working with the attorney general and General Detwiler. Together they have incontrovertible evidence that this scheme, if successful, was planned to destroy the air force fuel depot at Elmendorf Air Force Base and Fort Richardson, much as we witnessed at Craney Island earlier this month. We assume the intention was to further ratchet up the rhetoric to hold the nations of Islam at fault. Only this time, it was prevented before any damage was done. The Air Force is holding a man in custody; he is the person accused of attempting to perform the sabotage for this group of conspirators. He is now willing to implicate General McEwen, the base commander, in the plot."

"Fuck you! Traitor whore!" McEwen shouted as he rose from his chair. "I can't watch anymore. I'm out of here."

Greenwood and the rest decided they would follow the general. Two associate attorneys were waiting just outside Bobick's door to accompany them to the garage, which they did.

Bobick couldn't keep his eyes off the TV screen. And there he sat shaking his head as Secretary Branch droned on.

"Because I cannot read minds, I cannot say why the government leaders who hatched this scheme felt that such action was necessary. I can say that I know that this administration knows the reasons and the names of those who are behind the attacks. I call upon the judiciary branch and Congress to appoint a special prosecutor to round up the conspirators and place them in line for trial for their treasonous crimes. I also call on the members of the administration not involved in this conspiracy to seek the resignations of any person holding office who was aware of the conspiracy and failed to take reasonable measures to prevent it.

"Standing at the back of the room are the true American patriots and heroes who have worked to bring this matter to light and collect the proof of what really was behind these incidents. That is all I have to say on this matter at this time. I ask you not to seek statements from me, my staff, or from the patriots I just mentioned who are at the back of the room. Instead, I suggest you direct your attention to the president and the vice president and ask them what they intend to do about my resignation and the matters I brought up to you this day.

"Thank you, and God Bless America."

President Bennett walked out of the Oval Office, saying nothing more and leaving Harper there to contemplate his future.

Attorney General Goodman could not resist the spotlight and the opportunity to revel in front of a nationwide feed. Outside the briefing room, he answered questions and provided some background to what had led up to this historic moment.

"There is someone you are going to want to write about who isn't here right now. He is in Anchorage, Alaska, soon to make his way back to Atlanta. His name is Victor Majeski. He works for Eli Taylor and Daneli Crisis Management. He's the person who figured this all out. You're going to love him. He's a peach of a guy. If you are watching this, Vic, I salute you."

Eli was standing just a few feet from the attorney general when he made his remarks. He turned to Colonel Milton and said, "That's all I needed to hear. How am I going to get Vic to shut up now? It's going to be miserable back in Atlanta hearing him talk about his exploits."

EPILOGUE

AS ELI TAYLOR PREDICTED, THE MEDIA COULD NOT GET ENOUGH of the intrigue behind the secretary of state's statement. Did they attempt to get further statements from Madam Secretary Branch and the gentlemen at the back of the room? You betcha! But only one was successful: Matthew Berg.

New York Times editor Isadore Andropolis called Secretaries Branch and Greene heroes as well as General Detwiler, Attorney General Goodman, Colonel Milton, Commander Brockington, Skip Blackmon, Richard Dugan, and Brian Matusak. He spoke of the exploits of Victor Majeski of Daneli Crisis Management as the unsung hero of the entire investigation, as if he were a mythical figure of larger-than-life proportions.

Media types from everywhere around the world descended upon the White House. When no immediate statement was released, a media vigil began like no other in the history of the republic. The vice president went into seclusion along with Congressman Findley and NSA Director Yarborough. Rumors suggested they were hiding out on some private island owned by a rich contributor. It wouldn't take too much of an imagination to figure out who owned the island.

However, the three of them collaborated on press releases. The gist of each release offered that no public statement would be made until they had had the chance to review the accusations. Not long after their press releases aired, a special military detail had them in custody.

President Bennett spoke to the American public on an all-network feed at 6:00 p.m. the day after the story broke. In an ass-saving attempt, he chose not to accept the resignations of the secretaries of state and defense. Rather, he stated that he hoped they would help him make the necessary adjustments and appointments to prevent fear-mongering from invading the administration and to repair relationships with the Islamic-led nations of the world. Bennett also stated that he wished to establish a more justifiable direction for foreign policy and military intervention. The media and political pundits were not giving the president decent odds that he would escape impeachment.

Admiral Ellingson, General McEwen, General Harvard, Deputy Attorney General Shearer, and FBI Divisional Chief Greenwood all resigned. The reasons they gave were varied, but they all revealed a similar message. There was no mention of any misdeeds or wrongdoing. Dan Witherspoon was eventually tracked down and incarcerated without bond. He is awaiting trial in the Patrick Henry Correctional Unit in Ridgeway, Virginia. His boss, Art Daniels, is a fugitive. Charles Bobick is an inmate with Witherspoon. He's been charged with conspiracy to commit treason. The Doss brothers and the rest of the conspirators could not be reached for comment. They are under house arrest at their palatial home on their private island. Eugene Kravitz is pushing up daisies in Washington State. PFC Baker confessed to the charges against him and is being held at Patrick Henry Correctional Unit, awaiting arraignment.

With the approval of Congress, Attorney General Adam Goodman appointed a special prosecutor to investigate the accusations made by Secretary of State Branch. General Detwiler earned a fourth star on his shoulder.

Eli Taylor and Victor Majeski sneaked back to Atlanta without incident. The picture of Eli included in the lineup of heroes at the back of the State Department press briefing room has gone viral in Atlanta, making him an instant celebrity. He's become as famous as his tennis-coach-to-the-stars wife, Danielle.

Daneli Crisis Management Consultants became a fixture as a preferred contractor by the US military complex.

Rumor has it that Victor Majeski was last seen leaving Atlanta on his Harley with enough clean clothes and provisions to last two people at least a week. An unidentified source said the passenger riding behind him looked very much like the alluring Angela Cramer. But that has not been confirmed. Since it could not be confirmed, it is assumed it never happened.

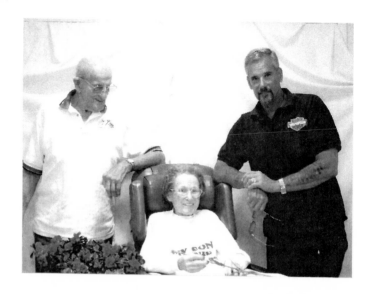

Vic with his parents; a sensitive, sentimental guy underneath.

The real Vic (alias) with one of his lady friends

CPSIA information can be obtained at www.ICGtesting.com
Printed in the USA
LVOW08s0056270216

476827LV00002B/2/P